Max

By Sarah Cohen-Scali

Translated by Penny Hueston

WALKER
BOOKS

This is a work of fiction. Names, characters, places and incidents are either the product of the author's imagination or, if real, used fictitiously. All statements, activities, stunts, descriptions, information and material of any other kind contained herein are included for entertainment purposes only and should not be relied on for accuracy or replicated as they may result in injury.

First published in Great Britain 2016 by Walker Books Ltd
87 Vauxhall Walk, London SE11 5HJ

2 4 6 8 10 9 7 5 3 1

This book has been typeset in Palatino

Printed and bound in Great Britain by Clays Ltd, St Ives Plc

British Library Cataloguing in Publication Data:
a catalogue record for this book is available from the British Library

ISBN 978-1-4063-6825-3

www.walker.co.uk

I hope that, as I did, you will be able to feel indulgent towards Max's flaws, and that you will love him, defend him, and adopt this orphan of evil.

Sarah Cohen-Scali

part one

1.

I don't know yet what my name will be. Outside, they can't decide between Max and Heinrich. Max, like Max Sollmann, the director of the Home where I'll soon be arriving. Or Heinrich, in honour of Heinrich Himmler, who first thought up the idea of my conception and those of my future buddies.

My personal preference would be Heinrich. I have a lot of respect for Herr Sollmann, but you should always aim for the top when it comes to hierarchy. Herr Himmler is more important than Herr Sollmann. He is no less than the Führer's right-hand man.

But who cares anyway; they're not going to ask my opinion.

It's the 19th of April 1936. Nearly midnight.

I should have been born yesterday, but that's not what I wanted. The date didn't suit me. So I've stayed put. Motionless. Rigid. Of course that means a lot of pain for my mother, but she's a brave woman, and she's putting up with the delay without complaint. Anyway, I'm sure she approves of my tactic.

My wish, the first of my future life, is to come into the world on the 20th of April. Because that's the Führer's birthday. If I'm born on the 20th of April, I will be blessed by the Germanic gods and seen as the firstborn of the master race. The Aryan race that will henceforth rule the world.

Right now, as I speak to you, I'm in my mother's womb and my birth is imminent. Only a few minutes to go. But you've no idea how nervous I am! My stomach is in knots. Even though I've got no cause for concern, I worry that the down on my little newborn head, and later when my hair grows, won't be blond enough. Because I *absolutely must* have blond hair. Platinum blond. The fairest possible, without the slightest tarnishing trace of brown. As for my eyes, I'm desperate for them to be blue. A clear blue, like pure clean water that you can't gaze into without the feeling of drowning. I want to be big and strong... Oh, I'm expressing myself badly. That sounds so flat and dull; I just can't find the right words. But that's normal. I'm not quite the finished product yet; I'm only a baby ... I'd be better off reciting the words of the Führer. I heard one of his speeches a few months ago, when I was still a tiny foetus, but his voice resonated so powerfully that it reached me here inside. I shivered with pleasure and that's precisely when I gave my first kick in my mother's womb – to communicate my joy.

Our beloved Führer proclaimed:

We must build a new world! The young German of the future must be lean and supple, as sharp as a greyhound, as tough as leather and as hard as Krupp steel!

So, that's exactly what I want to be: supple. Lean. Sharp. Hard. Tough. I'll bite rather than suck on the nipple. I'll yell rather than babble. I'll hate rather than love. I'll fight rather than pray. Oh, my Führer, I don't want to disappoint you! I won't let you down. Indeed, I'd better pull myself together. Why should I worry? It's ridiculous, unwarranted – it's obvious that I'm going to look like Mother.

Let me tell you about Mother. Tall. Blonde. She ties her beautiful golden hair either at the nape or in a crown of plaits. She never wears make-up. Make-up is only good for Oriental women, whose coal-black eyes are like cockroaches! Disgusting. Make-up is only good for whores. (I'm not frightened of saying words like that, even if I'm only a baby. It's pointless not to speak frankly to a baby, even if the words are crude; it only weakens the child by rendering it timid.) Let's get back to Mother and her hair: it's dead straight; she's never used dye or those products that make fake curls – they're for whores! She doesn't smoke, because that harms fertility, and she has broad hips. She's not one of those women who just pick at their food in order to stay thin. Anyway, on the eve of war that would be stupid, because supplies will be scarce one day and we have to make the most of abundance while it's here to enjoy.

Mother wears a brown skirt and a white blouse and she never wears heels. Thanks to her large pelvis, she's had no problems carrying me. She has to rest now but she used to love working here in the Steinhöring Home on the outskirts of Munich. She helped with setting up and decorating our nurseries. Because, as you are no doubt aware, I'm not the only baby who will be delivered here. There are hundreds and hundreds of us on the way; the programme for the arrival of the others was set up a long time ago. Hundreds will turn into thousands, thousands into millions. We'll make up an army!

Mother's expansive hips will make my task easier: I'll have no problem getting out, forging the way for my future half-brothers and sisters – because Mother promised our Führer that she would produce a child a year for him.

As for my father, it's a bit tricky to say much about him. I don't know who he is. I've never heard his voice. I don't know him and I'll never know him. That's what it's like for the children of the future. Our one and only spiritual father is the Führer. My biological father only met my mother once. One night. To conceive me. I know he's a *Sturmbannführer* of the Waffen-SS, meaning he's a major. Two ranks to go and he'll be a colonel. It'll be easy once the war gets started: he'll kill lots of enemies and be awarded a higher rank.

I hope I'll have a nice black uniform like him one day.

In the beginning, without knowing what to expect, my mother applied to be a *Schwester*, that's a Sister. She wrote a letter and they summoned her to the offices on Herzog-Max-Strasse, where she underwent a series of examinations. They weighed her. They measured her. Standing. Sitting. Squatting. Leaning forward. Leaning backward. They studied the shape of her skull and measured it, as well as the height of her forehead, the placement of her eyes and how wide apart they were set. They measured the length, width and line of her nose. The length of her arms, her legs, her torso. They measured the distance between her lips and her chin, between her cheekbones and her nose. They measured the back of her head, her neck. The doctors called out number after number and their secretaries recorded them. Then the secretaries did additions, subtractions, multiplications, and wrote down the results. They also recorded the colour of Mother's skin, hair and eyes: white, blonde, blue. Anyway, Mother wouldn't have been allowed into the offices if she had dark skin and brown hair and eyes. But the doctors also checked the colour of her pubic hair, which was as blonde as her hair, not overly lush, and sprouting in the right direction.

Next, Mother was sent to the *Doktoresses,* who took off her clothes. They studied her all over with a magnifying glass. Everywhere. Even inside her. Especially inside her. Right where her future partner's penis would go. To make me, yes, me. They pronounced, *Alles in ordnung!*

Mother was declared "perfectly suited for selection". That's top marks! Others were not so lucky; they only received "average suitability", and others, well, they got "not at all suitable". The latter were "relocated". Watch out, that's a code word! It doesn't mean they were relocated elsewhere. No, it means they were exterminated.

Garbage! Get out! Gone!

There are swear words and there are code words. You can use both with me as much as you like. The first lot don't shock me, and I know the hidden meaning of the second lot. Well, not all of them; I'll need to learn a whole lot more as I grow up. I'll also learn code names. Code names are extremely important. The programme for the years ahead, established by our Führer, is riddled with them. Here's an example: for the time being, my buddies and I have to be born in the utmost secrecy. Nobody knows yet the real meaning of *Lebensborn,* the code name of our programme. I'll tell you, but don't tell anyone else. It means "the fountain of life".

A programmed life, regulated according to precise parameters set up in advance. A life that feeds on death.

Getting back to Mother. She wasn't over the line yet. It's very difficult to become a talented Sister. It's not handed out on a plate. Even though Mother got through the first part of the test with flying colours, the second part was still to come: she had to assemble all the documentary proof that she belonged to the Nordic race, and present it to the fertility advisors in another office, the RuSHA (the SS Race and Settlement head office). She provided them with papers proving that her ancestors had been German since 1750, that they were in perfect health, and that not a single drop of Slavic blood flowed through their veins. And especially not Jewish blood… So here we are!

I'm a bit worried about the last point. Papers are all very well, but when you haven't got the guy in front of you, how can you be sure? What I mean is that if, for example, my great-great-great-great-grandfather had the unfortunate idea of sleeping with a Jewish woman, could a drop of this inferior creature's blood, given the mysteries of genetics, reappear in my blood to contaminate it? That would be a disaster! How would I know? How? Impossible.

The only thing I know for sure is that I'm a boy. Yes, at least there's no doubt about that – the little bump at the base of my belly is proof. My penis: I'm male. I'm so happy I'm not a girl. When girls become women they have to obey the rules of the three Ks: *Kinder, Küche, Kirche.** Whereas I prefer the K of Krupp: tanks, cannons, guns, war…

Enough of that! Let's banish depressing thoughts. It's impossible for me to have Jewish blood in my veins. I've got nothing to worry about.

Because of my father.

That brings me to the third part of Mother's examination. After being checked out by the fertility experts, and after passing the genealogy test, she had to send in a photo of

* Children, Cooking, Church

herself in a bathing suit. The doctors studied the photo (I think they took even more measurements) and put it alongside other photos – of SS officers, also in bathing suits – in order to work out who would make the best combinations, the best sexual partners. Imagine you had a stallion and you wanted to breed from it: aren't you going to choose the best performing mare to get the best result? How do Hitler's favourite Krupp factories make those cannons, which will soon turn on our enemies and annihilate them? With top quality steel, of course. And just as the best steel is made with the best materials, so I had to be the product of the union of the finest bodies. That's why the doctors studying the photos chose my father. Blond, blue eyes, tall, lean… You know the drill.

If even a microscopic drop of Jewish blood had tried to emerge, I'm sure my father would have dealt with it on the night he was set up with my mother, here, in Steinhöring, in a different building from the one where I will be born.

Right, now I must tell you about Steinhöring. I like telling you all this; it passes the time, and as I talk we're getting closer to midnight, to the 20th of April, to my birth.

The Home used to be an asylum. An asylum for mentally retarded people, imbeciles, idiots, in fact, all those useless people that society subsidizes. Parasites. They were "relocated". (No point in repeating myself, you remember what that means, don't you?) Then there was a huge redesign and the asylum was transformed. It had to be a radical renovation, a total change that reflected the difference between the old and the new residents. The old ones represented the country's shame, the new ones its pride.

First of all they disinfected the premises. Then they set up living rooms, dining rooms, birthing rooms, visiting rooms, treatment rooms, dormitories for the new mothers, nurseries for the babies, verandas. They had to knock down walls, erect partitions, construct a brick wall around the park and plant tall trees so spying eyes couldn't see us. It was a huge project that came together quickly, thanks to a large number of labourers who worked for nothing: prisoners from Dachau – a camp that imprisons Jehovah's Witnesses, homosexuals and political opponents of our Führer and his regime. (Unfortunately some of these people still exist. But soon they'll be gone, "relocated" like the others.) They worked night and day, without a break, and built our Home, as well as the building I mentioned earlier, the one where the couples go for their meetings, their sexual intercourse.

It's a smaller building. Inside there's a music room, a dining room – usually the selected couples have dinner together before doing what they have to do – and bedrooms. The bedrooms are not as inviting as the dormitories in the Home. That's intentional. No unnecessary furniture: only a bed and a table, that's all. A large window: it's very bright in there. Very cold too, so that the sexual act doesn't last too long. And so that if the individuals happen to like each other – which isn't necessarily the case – they don't get a taste for what they're doing. Apparently, some girls try to get out of there at the last minute, when they understand what is expected of a Sister. What on earth are they thinking? That they get to choose their partner and live happily ever after? How naïve. How cowardly. We have to make the most of these men, while they're alive. A lot of them are going to die fighting for their country. The birth rate will decrease. And we don't want a population of oldies in Germany. So we have to stay focused, take action. Hence our special programme.

From now on, the sexual act is *a patriotic duty*. So our country can be guided out of darkness into light. The sexual act (I remind you that I'm not frightened of words and I already know a lot) can no longer be about personal pleasure; even if it's difficult, even if it's painful, it's an obligation, a sacred task, destined for a higher purpose.

I think Mother had a hard time when she and my father did it.

I don't think she knew what the code word "Sister" really meant.

I think she was about to give up and try to get out of there, too. But my future father and I urged her on. My father made her drink a good slug of schnapps to warm her up, so she'd relax and do the right thing. I was still only a small inner voice, an abstract notion in my mother's mind, but I urged her on: "You have to do it, Mother! You have to! For National Socialism! For the Reich! For the thousand-year Reich! For the future!" So she kept her eyes glued to the portrait of the Führer hanging in the bright, cold room. She gritted her teeth and hung in there.

She did it.

I'm here.

And, now that it's after midnight, I'm off.

I'm getting out fast. As fast as possible! I want to be the first in our Home to be born on the 20th of April. I already have a few rivals in the birthing rooms. I have to get out before them, even if it's only a matter of seconds.

Cheer me on!

Wish for what I told you: I must be blond. I must have blue eyes. I must be sharp.

Lean.

Hard.

Tough.

Made of Krupp steel.

I am the child of the future. The child conceived outside the Law. Without love. Without God. With nothing but force and fury.

Heil Hitler!

2.

It was hard, extremely hard.

I can admit it to you, but it has to stay strictly between you and me, OK? Because the child of the future *never complains about hardship!*

Still.

Ahead of me was this narrow tunnel I had to go through. I couldn't see the end. Nothing. Not the slightest glimmer of light to guide me. It was like a long trench, mined with traps and all sorts of obstacles in which I could at any moment be snared. But with a headbutt here or a shoulder nudge there, I managed to widen my sphere of operation. Not by much, not enough. I realized that if I wanted to make headway properly, I had to alter my position. A quarter turn to the right and I was on my belly, which was much better. I managed to gain a bit of ground. Except I had to watch out that I didn't get tangled in my safety harness, the rappelling cord that keeps me alive – "the umbilical cord", if you prefer the scientific term. It was so tight that I wasn't getting much oxygen.

I hung in there. I edged forward as fast as I could. By manoeuvring my arms, I crawled over the hostile terrain, never hesitating to thrash out with kicks, headbutts, fist blows, like a little stallion, like the little warrior that I am… That's how I got most of the way, until I glimpsed in the distance, still too far away, a gleam of light that I followed through the darkness. It shone from behind the final barrier I had to cross: The Cervix. The notorious Cervix. The frontier to the world that was waiting for me.

I had to take it by storm.

There was a terrible uproar outside; I could hear it more and more clearly. Screaming, roaring, howling, an onslaught of noise. Wow! My arrival on the scene was causing chaos. My mother's cries were shocking. She showed no restraint. It was not very classy of her to let herself go like that. On the other hand, every scream was accompanied by a contraction that propelled me forward. I was grateful for that. I felt like a cannon ball catapulting towards the enemy.

Mother was in real pain. She was gritting her teeth, just like on the night she met my father, when they made me. Worried she'd run out of steam at the last minute, I took a few breaks so she could recuperate. When I felt she was on the point of exhaustion, I whispered to her, "Hang in there! Don't take your eyes off the portrait of our Führer!" (I know there's one in the birthing room. Actually, there's one in every room of the Home.) "Our Führer is looking at you. You promised to give him a beautiful child, your *first* child. Now it's time to keep your promise!"

So she pulled herself together, gritted her teeth again, took a few big breaths and began to push, push, push harder, urged on by the midwife, whose voice I could hear loud and clear (what a screamer she was, too).

Mother outdid herself from then on. She refused all medical assistance, including anaesthetic drugs. Bravo! It was all to her credit. And it worked in my favour: in the room next door, my rival was also making good time. Except that his mother, who was not as brave as mine, was given medical assistance; so the staff decided they could leave her for a while, and the whole medical team rushed to attend Mother and me. Josefa, the matron, along with three other nurses, joined the midwife. What a welcoming committee.

Josefa placed her hands on Mother's belly, right where I had positioned myself. Just as I was about to mount my attack again, she suddenly started screaming, "Oh my God! He's so big! Oh, yes, he's incredibly big!" And she decided to call Doctor Ebner.

SS-Oberführer Gregor Ebner.

The maternity and paediatrics chief of medicine, the one who decides everything. Power over life and death. The Führer's representative in the Home.

I felt incredibly honoured. Just imagine, newly enlisted privates rarely have the opportunity to be granted assistance from their colonel in person. I had to show that I was up to the task, and demonstrate all my strategic skills in this final showdown, without forgetting that the aim was to keep Doctor Ebner in the room with Mother and me. Under no circumstances could he go and see what was happening in the next room, in case he helped my rival! I had to make the most of the situation: my rival's mother's pain had eased and she was pushing less. He was sure to fall behind. All I had to do was widen the gap. Pluck up my courage and mount my attack on The Cervix.

As fast as I could.

I went for it. I charged, headfirst. But I hadn't calculated on the two bones that suddenly jutted into both sides of my skull. Huge spikes! There was I thinking my mother had wide hips. That was way too presumptuous of me… Nasty bones! My nose scraped against them, then my mouth, and my chin. But I ignored the pain and ended up with my head up against the wall of The Cervix. I charged even harder. *Come on! Come on! Full speed ahead!* I didn't care about the disfigurements I was inflicting on myself. So what if I ended up with a skull like a mortar shell? Warriors don't worry about their looks. Anyway, babies' bones are malleable, and I was sure that, even if I had a squashed head on arrival, it would soon find its proper shape.

The main thing was to be on the top of the list of births for the 20th of April. I mobilized all the troops I had for the attack and the wall began to give way. Oh yes, with every push, it yielded a little more, until… Wham! It opened up.

I made it!

I ejected myself into the world, just after midnight. Talk about precision.

Doctor Ebner's hands were the first things I saw. The white gloves made them look especially long, slender, pale and bony. Their appearance belied the strength with which they seized me. He slapped me around the head until I felt like I was in a vice; then he grabbed my shoulders and yanked, and yanked.

I yelled to show that I was alive, and breathing.

"Bravo, Frau Inge!" Josefa shrieked. "It's a boy! He is splendid. You should be proud of yourself."

Thanks for the compliment, but it wasn't news to me.

As I looked around more I spotted Doctor Ebner's tall black boots; which were partly hidden by his white gown. They were magnificent. I would have liked to slide inside one of them; I could have made it my bassinet. I also noticed bloodstains on the gown. Mother's blood. Or perhaps mine? I didn't gag; I didn't even hiccup. There's nothing more normal than blood after a battle. I had to get used to that from now on. I fixated on the gold badge of the Party insignia, pinned to the collar of *Herr Doktor's* gown. It was so beautiful, so shiny.

I screamed. I kept screaming, because I wanted to grab that golden badge. I really liked it. But I couldn't reach it, so I gave up and stared at Doctor Ebner's face instead. Obviously my eyesight wasn't yet functioning perfectly, but I could make out a bald head, smooth and shiny like the badge. I could see a big vein sticking out on the side of his temple, and I could see that his lips were as straight as the uppers of his boots. And tight, no sign of a smile. I saw that *Herr Doktor* was wearing round glasses, and that he was watching me with his bright, blue eyes. So bright they seemed transparent, a deep pool of water I seemed to be diving into, drowning. Icy water. Suddenly I felt cold, very cold.

I screamed even louder. But I could still hear Josefa worrying about the mother next door. There was a problem with her baby, who – what a dope – had managed to get knots in his rappelling cord! Josefa asked Doctor Ebner to go and check on her. He raised his left hand to tell her to be quiet – he was holding me tight against him in the crook of his right arm – and ordered her to sort it out herself with the midwife. Because he wanted to examine me first. Me.

Oh dear ... scary.

I knew what that meant. Even though I had won the contest against the clock, my victory wasn't yet confirmed. Just like Mother becoming a Sister, I had only passed the initial test before being anointed "Baby of the Third Reich, firstborn of the Aryan race".

The measurements test was still to come.

There was a chart hanging in the birthing room. (This chart, like the portrait of our Führer, is in every room in the Home.) It shows the hierarchy of the Aryan races. At the top is "the Nordic race"; in second position, "the Westphalian race']" living in harmony with the land; and in third place, those from around the Balkans, "the Dinaric race", with a deep sense of patriotism. The famous Bismarck and Hindenburg are two examples of pure Westphalians. But one man alone symbolizes the perfect union of these three superior races: the Führer.

Which category was I going to fit in?

With a sharp click of the scissors, Doctor Ebner cut my rappelling cord – I had no further use for it. *Snap*! – and took me into a nearby room. Away from Mother. She asked to hold me, but Doctor Ebner ignored her. As for me, a second ago I would have given anything to suck on a breast, any breast, and have a go at lying with Mother, who had what I wanted, but now I'd lost my appetite. Why? Because Ebner insisted that he not be disturbed under any circumstances.

Not a good sign.

He called in his secretary, who joined us in the room that looked like a laboratory, sat down at a desk and opened a big ledger. There were lots of columns drawn up on the blank page. My page.

When Doctor Ebner asks to be left alone with a newborn, it's a very bad sign. While I was still in Mother's belly, I heard rumours that spread through the Home. (Some women can't hold their tongue: magpies chattering non-stop and frightening the others.) It's said that when Doctor Ebner – he alone (and his secretary) – examines an infant and finds it lacking, he "relocates" it. He does it himself. Then his secretary writes "Stillborn" (= code word) in the ledger.

Believe me, I was worried stiff. I uttered a few requisite wails, but then, like Mother, I gritted my teeth – well, at least my gums. And, without so much as a whimper, I prepared myself for the worst. So what if my life was cut short? It belonged to my Führer.

After washing me, the doctor laid me on a little table next to various instruments that were lined up neatly. Among them, I recognized a set of scales, a ruler, a compass and a little container, like a jewellery box, with five or six pairs of eyes – glass ones, not real ones – in different shades of blue. There was also a hair chart in different colours ranging from dark brown to the lightest blond. Lying by itself, away from the other instruments, was … a syringe.

Ebner began the examination. "Height: 54 centimetres. Weight: 4 kilos and 300 grams."

They're the only statistics I retained. There were so many that followed and I was screaming so much that I couldn't hear Doctor Ebner's voice reciting them very fast.

Length of arms.

Length of extended arms in relation to pelvis.

Length of torso.

Contour of chest cavity.

Length of legs, penis, feet, hands.

Finger-span, toe-span.

Size of ears.

Distance between earlobes.

Distance between eyes.

Then he checked my reflexes. Sucking reflex: he held up his finger and I grabbed it and sucked hard, greedily.

His finger tasted like metal, like steel. Top quality Krupp. It tasted good. Rooting reflex: he stroked me in random places and I turned my head in the direction of the stimulus point. Then he held up his two index fingers and I grasped them, so tightly that he lifted me up. I went straight into the Automatic Walking reflex: one foot in front of the other, even if it was pretty lopsided. I felt like I was hooked onto a parachute. If Ebner let go of me, I'd crash for sure. I pushed down on the table when my legs reached it, but they felt as floppy as marshmallow. Next, Ebner started tapping me very hard. That startled me! Once again I extended my arms, fingers spread, then I held them against my chest, fists tight.

Everything was going well, I was confident, I trusted my instincts, and Doctor Ebner seemed pleased. The vein throbbing on the side of his bald head had almost disappeared.

He took the hair samples, placed them on my head and told his secretary to make a note that the down on my head was fair, very fair. (*Twice* fair, thank God!) He used the little box with the glass eyes to check my eyes. He chose an eye that was right at the top of the jewellery box and held it against mine. "2c!" he exclaimed. "Check in two months." Given that the eye in his hand was blue, I deduced that mine were, too. Did "2c" mean "twice blue", like my hair was twice blond? In my opinion, I didn't have anything to worry about on that account either – Ebner looked confident.

Next my head was examined. A rigorous, meticulous examination. It seemed to go on for hours. Ebner spent ages palpating with his metallic fingers. The top, the sides, the back, the temples. The forehead. That's when I started to lose the confidence I'd regained with the statistics, the reflexes, the colour of my hair and eyes. Oh dear, how I regretted struggling so ferociously in the trench before getting out, because – what an idiot – I'd given myself a misshapen head! It was oval, like a conical sugar loaf. Not round. Not round like Doctor Ebner's head, to be precise. As he was bald, you could see that his was in the shape of a soccer ball, whereas mine was only a pathetic rugby ball.

Stupid head.

Poor me. Fancy failing the very last test, the final criterion for selection. When Doctor Ebner grabbed the compass and brought it up to my head, I no longer had any doubts about the verdict. My fate was sealed. It was perfectly obvious that the span of the compass was too wide. If only I had known. It would have been better if I had been born after my rival. Hey, I wondered idly, despite my distress, had he made an appearance in the meantime? At least that way I wouldn't have damaged myself like this.

Come on, Oberführer Ebner! Let's get this over with. You might as well "relocate" me straightaway, that's what I deserve.

The tip of the compass point drew near, nearer and nearer ... I shut my eyes and clenched my little fists as it headed for my heart, which was beating like a drum. All my blood rushed to my head, I was bright red, my skull about to explode like a bomb.

But I didn't feel the compass tip stab me... What was going on? Did the doctor feel sorry for me? That wasn't like him. Anyway, I didn't want his pity. That would be dishonourable. So ... instead of the compass, it was going to be the syringe I'd seen on the table earlier. Obviously! The syringe was for the "relocation" injection.

Despite my panic and my screaming – I hadn't drawn breath the whole time – I saw Ebner scribbling a new set of figures on a scrap of paper. Then he did some sums out loud:

"The cephalic index being the transverse diameter over

the anterior-posterior diameter multiplied by one hundred, that gives us a result of … 86 centimetres. *Eighty-six centimetres!* Mark that down quickly," he ordered his secretary. "The occipital ridge is prominent and there's no frontal bulge. The cephalic index thus confirms what is visually apparent, namely the long and narrow head of the infant subject."

He paused for a minute, then, still to his secretary, he uttered a word I didn't understand. "Conclusion: the child is dolichocephalic," he said. "He fills all the criteria, without exception. He is perfectly suited for selection."

What? Was that a slip of the tongue? Did he say "perfectly" instead of "not at all"? I no longer had a clue. "Dolichocephalic", was that like "hydrocephalic", those babies who had a whole lot of water in their heads? Who were disabled, imbeciles, like the inmates here before the asylum became a Home?

Of course not. After writing Doctor Ebner's words in the record book, the secretary joined him and leaned over me. All smiles, she went into raptures and heaped praises on me. So I put two and two together inside my deformed head – well, not that deformed after all. I realized "dolichocephalic" was the trump card that classified me as having a long head and being of the Nordic Aryan race.

Hurray! Victory!

That was it; this time I could really claim victory. And I didn't hang back.

I yelled and yelled.

3.

I got lots of presents after my birth. Lots of them.

Firstly, traditional presents, the same ones all my buddies received: a candelabra, made by a prisoner from Dachau, and one mark (a symbolic amount). For each future birthday we will receive another mark and a candle for the candelabra.

And as I was born on the same day as the Führer, I was entitled to a savings passbook, to be topped up regularly.

Isn't this a great start to life?

Wait, that's not all. Apparently I'm going to get a fourth present. A surprise. Josefa spoke to Mother about it without telling her what it was. But, given her excitement – she stiffened, went bright red, stood to attention and put her hand to her chest as if she was out of breath – I knew it wouldn't be something trifling. It must be a special surprise, something important, impressive. Of course, I have an inkling, but I don't dare think about something so amazing. Well, maybe? After all, why not? I got here first, I passed all the selection tests hands down, so… Oh, just thinking about it gives me cramps in my stomach! OK let's see if my dream comes true.

On the other hand, there's one thing that annoys me: I still don't have a name, not even a first name. There's no hurry, according to the staff, since my friends and I don't have to be registered in the state records, and because we won't have our mothers' names. Besides, no one knows anyone's name here. The mothers are only called by their first names... No hurry. Easy for them to say! I want it to be decided, because in the meantime Mother is calling me "Max", as if she had the right to choose my name. Worse still, every time she takes me in her arms, three times a day, she carries on with "my little Maxie-pie", or showers me with all sorts of idiotic nonsense names: "my baby love, my darling, my little one".

I am not her love. I am not her darling. I am certainly not little! I am big, strong, tough. Has she forgotten how I was conceived? Thank goodness Josefa is keeping an eye on things. "Frau Inge, come now!" she often reprimands Mother. "Please speak correctly to this child. He is listening to you, he understands. Do not pollute his mind like that."

Mother must have made a terrible face, because Josefa added in a sympathetic whisper, "All right, if you are so keen to give him a nickname, I will let you have the one we thought of soon after his birth: *Klein Kaiser*. 'Little Emperor'."

Klein Kaiser. Two Ks. Not bad. Anyway, it's better than Max, for now.

Mother is worried. She is doing her utmost to find a resemblance between us. I can tell by the particular way she has of staring at me sometimes, frowning, with a questioning, preoccupied expression. Judging by her slightly sour expression, I'd say we don't look alike. What's more, the other mothers agree: "Oh, don't worry, this young man must take after his dad." And Mother has to wrack her brains, gather her recollections: the dad, the dad… What was he like, this dad? She can't remember. That's normal. It was at night, it was cold, the sex was quick and Mother was only looking at the portrait of the Führer. Perhaps she just recalls a trace of his scent, or the bitter smell of his sweat, of a wine-fuelled breath, the echo of a voice, of a groan, the glimpse of a tattoo under an armpit – SS officers have their blood group tattooed there. It's very useful when they need a transfusion.

I get the feeling Mother occasionally has bad thoughts. I can sense it, and I feel it when she does that thing of suddenly going stiff when she's holding me. Not much, you'd hardly notice it. Nevertheless, I can tell that a whole lot of thoughts are being tossed around in her head: questions, doubts. Regrets?

Doubts are not good. Questions even less so. Never question yourself. Always have blind faith in our Führer. As for regrets, sorry, it's too late.

When I feel Mother wavering like that, I start screaming. Her attitude has unpleasant consequences for me. She just stares into space, lets her breast slide backwards, so her nipple slips out of my mouth; I can no longer hit the right spot to latch on, so I can't feed any more. Furious, I cry as loudly as I can and without fail I manage to attract the attention of Doctor Ebner, who, up there in his office, on the top floor of the Home, picks up his spyglass to check on the terrace where we're sitting with the others. Mother is instantly aware of the spyglass on her, scrutinizing her every movement, and pulls herself together. She forces her trembling lips into a smile and starts feeding me again.

I suck and suck, hard; I'm hell-bent on sucking. Every

now and then I give a little bite.

I have to admit that, when it comes to feeding, I can't complain. Mother is a really good breastfeeder. Up until now, about three days after my birth, the nurses have recorded that Mother has produced 17,620 millilitres of milk – a lot more than the other mothers. She's got to keep up the momentum. If she continues to feed me this much, she'll earn a bonus and she'll be allowed to stay longer at the Home. And, as I am teamed up with her, I'll be able to break a record too, like when I was born.

Which reminds me, I haven't told you what happened to my challenger, my rival.

Kaput. Tot. Dead.

How about that – he was stillborn, not "purified". (I've learned a new code word: "purified", which means "to euthanize".) Actually, my rival purified himself by getting choked on his rappelling cord. The midwife couldn't undo all the knots he'd tangled himself in. She got the fright of her life when she had to report the loss to Doctor Ebner. She was really in danger of being "relocated". But Ebner didn't lose his temper at all. On the contrary. After glancing at the little corpse, he congratulated the midwife for having saved the injection that he would have had to administer if the baby had lived. An injection into the skull through the fontanelle. A little tremor, a little hiccup, and, there you go, it's over! Completely painless. (I was right: the syringe I'd been so frightened of, in the laboratory where I'd had my tests, was indeed used for "purification".)

Are you wondering why it was necessary to "purify" my rival? Because it's impossible to keep an *unharmonisch* recruit at the Home. Can you believe it, the baby was brown! I suppose, for lack of anything better, brown hair would be tolerated, but there are different shades of brown. My rival was brown-black, crow-black. And hairy as well, a real little monkey! And olive-skinned to top it off… Ebner did end up losing his temper: at the employees of RuSHA, from whom he demanded the complete records of the couple who had produced this defective product. There was definitely a flaw in the system somewhere. Either on the mother's or the father's side: one of them must have falsified their certificate of Aryan race. Or else it's what I told you before my birth: too little is known about the science of genetics. Fortunately we'll soon master it and avoid failures like this one. Those sorts of errors are especially useful for the future.

In this case, it wasn't genetics that was at fault. Frau Bertha, the mother of the little monkey, was the one who cheated. She had a Jew in her family tree! Straight after the birth she was transferred to a munitions factory. No more Führer's babies for her; she had to find another way to be useful.

This regrettable incident worked in my favour. My victory was all the more significant: my rival was my first enemy casualty! Nipped in the bud.

Right, let's not talk about unpleasant things any more. Let's enjoy a bit of sunshine and peace.

At the moment, the rays of a gentle spring sun are shining over the veranda where our bassinets are lined up. There are a good thirty of us. Perhaps more. And everything is calm, because I gave the signal. Earlier, when I burst into tears, all my buddies imitated me. The whole place was screaming! The nurses didn't know what had hit them. Then I stopped and the others followed suit. I'm a real troop leader.

A bit of quiet after a meal helps me sleep better. Our bassinets, lined up like toy soldiers in a perfectly straight line along the veranda, form a battalion ready to launch an attack. They're beautiful bassinets: big, comfortable, covered in a loose-fitting white fabric with flounces decorating the hems. We're protected both from the sun when it is too strong – don't forget how sensitive our bright eyes are – and from any nosy passers-by. We are in the country and it's best to be wary of the local farmers. Doctor Ebner himself designed our bassinets and insisted on sturdy construction materials in order to avoid any accidents. The fabric hides the bars. You see, Ebner attends to everything. He's the one who recruits the nurses and nannies, and works out which vitamins we should take. In the end he's father to us all. He's going to control our life, from our nappies now to the SS uniforms we'll one day have the honour of wearing.

Thanks to him, our whole environment is sparkling clean. The furniture in the Home is magnificent and apparently even more luxurious pieces will soon be delivered. Furniture requisitioned from enemies of our regime. When the war gets started, all the additional Homes being built throughout the country will be furnished thanks to the looting. In the years to come, there'll be so much more. We'll take back the riches stolen by the Jews all over Europe!

Ebner is also supervising the extension of the vegetable garden. The steward is growing carrots, spinach, all sorts of vegetables – great sources of vitamins for us when we start taking solids. The grounds surrounding the Home are constantly being extended and more labourers are called in from outside. I told you before how Ebner keeps a close eye on everyone with his spyglass: the behaviour of the mothers with their children, the nannies, the nurses, the delivery men; and he also makes sure no farmers come onto the property. Every now and then you see one trying to have a look around. *Out!* Ebner sets a dog-handler and his sniffer dog on them. So our peace is guaranteed.

But Ebner should set up another surveillance system as well: for listening. Because, believe me, I hear some crazy stuff. When the mothers all get together like now, boy, can they talk! I'll tell you about their gossip a bit later. That way I can introduce you to some of my buddies. It's impossible for the moment.

All hands on deck. The secretaries, the nurses and the steward stop work; Ebner leaves his lookout at the window. Even if they're still feeding us, the mothers gather – with us – around the radio set Josefa has just brought onto the veranda.

It's a direct broadcast of a speech by our Führer. Just imagine it! Germans everywhere, in offices, factories or schools, stop what they're doing to listen. If they're outside, they're lucky enough to have loudspeakers installed in town squares. Listening to the radio is a civic duty. Whoever doesn't will be denounced and punished. It's indispensible for developing a unified spirit, for creating solidarity in a victorious nation mobilized behind the Führer.

We're all gathered around the Führer's voice, transfixed. Well, some of my buddies can't help bawling, but Josefa raises the volume on the radio so the Führer comes through loud and clear. His voice is powerful, vibrant, exultant. It fills the air, drowning out the birdsong and the rustling of the wind in the trees that we could hear earlier.

So be quiet! I'm listening, too.

I take in my mother's milk.

I take in the words of our Führer.

This speech couldn't have come at a better time. Just before my nap. I am replete. I'll get back to you later, because I have to sleep now. Sleep helps me grow, especially my brain. It's crucial.

Josefa approaches Mother to take me back to the nursery. Mother protests; she wants to keep me with her a bit longer.

"Come on, Frau Inge," Josefa says. "You know the rules, don't you? I don't need to remind you."

Mother relents against her will. I know the smile she turns on is not sincere, I can feel it. Because, you see, even though the rappelling cord has been cut, it's like it's still working. There's magic in that cord. Yes, if I had the choice, I'd stay in her arms. She smells nice, her arms are warm, her breasts are soft; it's a cocoon. On the other hand, the gold badge of the Party, pinned on Josefa's smock, is so shiny, so tempting! I wonder when I'll be able to grab it.

4.

"Is it all right if I sit next to you, Frau Inge?"

"Of course, you're welcome to."

Heidi.

Just our luck.

Mother moves over to make room for her on the couch, which upsets my feed. It's so annoying to be interrupted during feeding times, again and again, for no good reason.

It's no accident that Heidi has chosen Mother. She's a whinger and she knows Mother will make her feel better. Crying is all very well, and apparently it's normal for some women after giving birth, but Heidi is weird, even when she's not crying. There's something not quite right about her. Passive, incapable of speech, withdrawn, she just stares into space for hours, without moving.

Consequently, her son, Helmut, is as spineless as she is. You hardly ever hear him. He is ridiculously calm. Oh well, it makes for a quiet evening feed, having him next to us.

We are in the big sitting room set aside for feeding. The room is lavishly furnished, very pleasant, with several couches and armchairs, and rugs strewn over the floor. In addition to the nice warmth from the central heating – the Home is allowed this luxury – a fire is blazing in the fireplace. There are flowers and bowls of fruit arranged here and there, and a piano takes pride of place in a corner. Sometimes, one of the secretaries plays a tune when she's finished her work; or sometimes, like now, the gramophone is turned on.

"Are you all right?" Mother asks, patting Heidi's hand once she has sat down next to us with Helmut.

Heidi nods to say yes, but it's a sort of code language between the mothers; in fact she means "no". And Mother knows, just like I do.

"If you want to … to talk to me, I'm happy to listen," she murmurs, after looking warily at Josefa, who is sitting on the other side of the room, signing papers.

Say no, Heidi! I want to have my feed in peace. I have a feeling that, once you start talking, it's not going to be much fun.

I call her Heidi and not "Frau Heidi", because she's very young, barely fifteen, as far as I know. She's the Home's youngest mother: tall, blonde (obviously) and very muscular. She must have done a lot of sport before her pregnancy because the muscles in her arms and legs are well defined, as if they've been sculpted. She looks like an athlete. The blonde hairs on her golden skin have a lustrous shine, proof that she's been breathing the good mountain air. She's pretty. Well, I think she is, except for her breasts, which are too small. (Perhaps the development of her muscles delayed that of her breasts?) It's bad luck for Helmut: it's not easy for him to get a feed. He has to struggle just to extract a few drops of milk. Poor thing, I feel sorry for him. Josefa claims that it's not a problem, that he has reserves of fat from birth, and that Heidi has to keep trying to breastfeed him. Easier said than done! Josefa knows three meals will appear on the table every day but how would she react if she was presented with a plate containing three measly little green beans and was told that, even if there was nothing more to eat, she could always draw on her reserves?

Mother breaks off feeding me again to help Heidi position her baby better on the breast. This time I don't scream; I have to show some solidarity with my buddies. Solidarity and friendship are important. All the more so given that it seems to have worked this time: Helmut has managed to latch on to the nipple. Heidi turns towards Mother, her big blue eyes glistening with tears of gratitude.

"Thank you, thank you," she splutters.

She waits a moment, then murmurs, on the verge of tears, "I miss my parents so much."

"Don't worry; you'll soon see them again."

"Oh, no, I don't think so."

"But why not?"

"Because I'll never have the courage to tell them what I've done, what's happened to me. I'm too ashamed."

She stops, stifling a sob. Mother puts her hand in her pocket and takes out a handkerchief that she offers to Heidi, telling her to try to pull herself together. (It's *my* handkerchief! The one she puts on her shoulder so I can burp and dribble if I need to. Too bad; after all, it's her white shirt that'll be the worse for wear.)

"Tell me all about it," Mother urges her. "It will make you feel better. Pretend I'm your big sister."

After hesitating briefly, she's off: Heidi tells her story.

She's from the Bund Deutscher Mädel*. She enrolled

* The League of German Girls, the girls' wing of the Hitler Youth.

voluntarily, with the support of her family. How lucky to be able to commit yourself to the Führer from the age of fourteen and be part of his mission!

The BDM had set up in Obersalzberg, in southern Germany – Hitler's favourite spot, where he loves to go hiking. The air is pure, with magnificent landscapes of snowy mountains, forests and fields of green. While enjoying the pleasures of a holiday camp, the girls were also serving their nation. Their activities were numerous and varied: singing, theatre, music, dance and also home decoration, hiking in the forest, building shelters – lots of physical activities that placed them on an equal footing with the boarders in the neighbouring camp, who were boys of the same age. The young people ran into each other from time to time, mostly when they were out hiking. The camp mistress made sure she instilled sound values in her flock: self-control, friendship, obedience, sacrifice and physical discipline.

The days were highly regimented. No breaks. No boredom. At 6.30, wake-up. At 6.35, a sports session: depending which week it was, athletics and an endurance run, or else gymnastics, gym-apparatus work and acrobatics. At 8 a.m., shower, tidy the bunkrooms, then all meet under the flag. From 8.10 to 8.30, breakfast. The morning was then devoted to political training. What is National Socialism? Why is it going to save the German nation? How can we be shielded from the decadent races? How can we dominate them, eliminate them? So many fascinating subjects. At 12.15 p.m., lunch. At 12.45, leisure activities of choice. As she was especially gifted and dreamed of being selected for national competitions, Heidi did more gymnastics. At 4.10 p.m., a session of self-criticism, self-criticism being indispensible for faithful followers of National Socialism.

At 7.15, dinner, and finally, from 7.45 to 8.45, the girls spent the evening together in the bunkrooms. They were supposed to discuss and exchange the magazines and books provided by the camp mistress, but, as Heidi points out, their main topic of conversation was ... the neighbours. The boys. How could they not be aware of them? Some of them were so good-looking! Some girls had already had a boyfriend before enrolling, but not Heidi. So, even though she was a bit embarrassed, even though her girlfriends' chatter sometimes made her blush, she listened to them keenly before falling asleep at 9.30 p.m. precisely, her head filled with sweet dreams of the future and of love.

Heidi enjoyed her life at camp, every minute of it, every second. She was enthusiastic, diligent, and volunteered for extra activities, including chores. She engaged unsparingly in the self-criticism sessions, and proved herself to be a good friend. She was soon rewarded: they singled her out and promoted her as an elite member of the camp.

One evening, the camp mistress gathered together the lucky elite group of girls, whose fervour, as in the case of Heidi, had distinguished them. The meeting was held in a room normally used for theatre and choir rehearsals. Standing on the dais that also served as a stage, the camp mistress announced two items of good news. The first was that the name of each girl had been included on a list sent to the Führer, and he had personally signed the list and added the word "Congratulations!". The young girls received this announcement with cries of joy, clapping their hands. They were allowed to file past one by one and admire the word written in the Führer's hand at the bottom of the list.

Then the camp mistress announced the second item of news. The girls were being put forward for a mission. An important mission in the service of the nation… What mission? When? What did they have to do? What an honour! Yes! Yes! Yes! Of course they would love to be part of this mission! Questions and exclamations were flying all over the room; the young girls forgot the most elementary rule of discipline: to raise your hand before speaking. The camp mistress had trouble calling for silence, but she forgave them, just this once. Besides, it wasn't up to her to explain exactly what this mission consisted of. That was up to an SS officer whom she called into the room.

Stand to attention. *Heil Hitler!*

After saluting the group, the officer issued the command "At ease!" and climbed onto the dais.

"Congratulations, young ladies!" he announced, as Hitler's spokesperson. "Here you are, fully fledged *Füherinnen*. But some of you can do even more."

The officer paused a moment. Twenty pairs of blue eyes were fixed on him, filled with awe, impatience and hope.

"If I told you that … you could give our Führer a wonderful, extraordinary present, would you say yes?"

In one movement, every hand was raised in consent, and all the blue eyes filled with tears.

"Even if this present meant a huge sacrifice?"

The hands remained raised.

"A woman's sacrifice? From future women like you."

The officer's words were becoming more enigmatic. Heidi would have liked to ask him to be more precise, but as none of her friends seemed curious she stayed silent. But the explanation wasn't long in coming.

"Well," the officer said, "that's all good."

He took out a bundle of papers from his briefcase and gave them to the camp mistress.

"Here are the contracts," he explained. "One for each of you. A contract binding you to the Führer, and stipulating that you agree to give him your first child. This is an act of bravery for which I congratulate you in advance and for which you will be respected for the rest of your lives."

With these words, he climbed down from the dais, saluted and left the room.

Heil!

Gradually the arms were lowered. There was murmuring in the ranks. The camp mistress let it go, then ordered her protégées to come up onto the stage, where they all sat cross-legged around her, as if they were outside, in a field or on a beach, around a campfire.

"We're going to talk openly now," she said to them. "You've worked hard and now it's only fair that you should enjoy yourselves. I was young once, too, and I know perfectly well that you're all only thinking about one thing ... meeting the boys at the camp next door."

Giggles, stifled laughter, blushing cheeks.

"Well, now you have the chance to do it, not only with my blessing, but with that of your families and of the Führer as well. There will be no restrictions, other than that of offloading the fruit of your visits to the neighbouring camp. Your children will not be recorded in the official civil registry. You will give birth to them in a *Lebensborn* Home, where they will be raised as good Germans, true National Socialists. They will be in good hands, I can assure you. They will constitute the generation of future leaders. The state will alleviate you of any concern you may have about them. You will have no moral or economic responsibility. As for your partners, you will have no further connection with them. And you will have only one further duty: to marry and to have more children.

With this, she stood up and handed out a contract to each of the girls. They all signed, including Heidi, despite all the questions she still had but hadn't dared to ask.

They returned to the bunkroom in a state of total euphoria. "Fantastic! We don't need to sneak out any more. Do you realize how lucky we are? We're going to combine duty and pleasure!"

Heidi had trouble falling asleep that night. She replayed the events of this remarkable evening over and over in her head. A pledge to the Führer. To serve the country. To give him her child. She had signed up for all this at once. She had no regrets. Not at all. She was just worried about the practical aspects. In order to give a child to the Führer, you first had to make one, and to make one, you had to… She suddenly blushed, all alone in the dark, terrified, the sheets drawn up under her chin. Then she was overcome by a rush of joy; she felt hot, cold. A picture of someone came into her mind. The camp mistress was right. Admittedly, she wasn't experienced like some of her friends, but, just like they did, she had feelings, a body, a heart; and recently she had noticed a particular boy. They had exchanged looks, smiles. One day, she had even made an effort to build a shelter by herself in record time, because she knew he was watching. So, if it was with him… She finally fell asleep, full of hope.

But it wasn't with him… It was with another, several others. In the neighbouring camp, the boys had been doing this kind of thing for a while. Sexual exercises were just another kind of sport for them.

"Frau Inge, they … they…" Her voice cracked with emotion. "They…"

Unable to finish her sentence, Heidi turned and stared

into space. As usual. Mother remained silent too, squeezing Heidi's hand as hard as she could. She was holding me against her, burping me, and I could feel her tears on my check. Tears are hot. And salty. One of them slid onto my lips and spoiled the taste of the milk. Yuck! It made me gag and, it was bound to happen, I vomited on Mother's beautiful white blouse – and she didn't have her handkerchief to protect it.

The word Heidi hadn't been able to say was "raped". (Don't forget: even though I'm only a baby, I know a lot.)

So what? What was the problem? Why didn't she just grit her teeth, like Mother? And keep her eyes on the portrait of the Führer, like Mother? Wasn't there one in the boys' camp? That's impossible! And wasn't Helmut the outcome anyway? Blond. Blue eyes. Perhaps not as tough and hardcore as I am, but with a mother like that, it's not surprising.

I'm screaming because I've vomited. Helmut's screaming because he's hungry. He hasn't had any breastmilk while his mother has been snivelling, telling her story. He'll end up with rickets. Herr Ebner gets very annoyed if he finds out a baby has rickets.

"Oh my goodness! What is going on here?" Josefa exclaims when she comes to check on us again.

Change of neighbour. About time.

After Helmut, it's Ella. A girl, a pleasant change, especially as she's cute. Her eyes! They're not just blue, they're turquoise. Real gemstones. I'm even a bit jealous, I have to admit, because I haven't forgotten what Doctor Ebner said in the laboratory where he did my postnatal examination: that he would have to check later whether my eyes were in fact *twice* blue. Ella's obviously won't need checking. Her eyes are at least *four times* blue. Her little bald head, perfectly smooth, not a strand of hair to be seen, suggests that her hair will be more golden than honey-coloured. And she has an adorable little mouth, well defined and pouty.

Ursula is her mother. She's very young, too, about seventeen. But nothing like Heidi. She'll burst out laughing at every opportunity. She's what you call a *bonne vivante*. And a chatterbox as well. You don't need to worm information out of her; she tells everything to everyone. When Josefa sent Heidi back to her room, Ursula came and sat next to Mother without asking. Once again the rappelling cord, the magic cord, is working at full capacity: I can tell Mother would have preferred to be alone. She's still thinking about what Heidi told her. She feels sorry for her. Just how sorry, I'm not sure. What a spoilsport Heidi is! In any case, during this last session we're granted in our mothers' arms before sleeptime, I'm happy to have Ella as my neighbour. The only thing annoying me is the tobacco smell; it really upsets my system. Ursula stinks of cigarettes because she went outside and smoked one secretly before feeding time. It's very bad for her milk. *Verboten!* Forbidden! Josefa must have a cold not to be able to smell it.

Mother is still quiet, preoccupied; she stares at me, caressing the end of my nose, my cheeks, kissing me. Every now and again, she cuddles me very close, as if she's frightened I'll be taken away from her. It's as if she's confused me with Heidi, who I think she would have liked to hug and comfort earlier. She was right to refrain from doing that. It would have been inappropriate. But it doesn't mean she has to suffocate me! Meanwhile, Ursula starts up straightaway.

She comes from the Rhineland. Her parents have disowned her and she couldn't care less. She never got on with them. At school she was a terrible student, always going out, especially with boys – she liked a bit of action, as they say. Whatever, she always had to lie, hide, skip school. Until the morning her life changed for ever. As the Rhineland had just been annexed, the principal of her school – a Jew! – was replaced by an Aryan. As soon as he arrived he gathered all the girls together outside, and Ursula expected him to launch into the same old speech: *I aim to improve the deplorable state of this establishment, you must study, get good marks, absentees will be punished severely,* blah blah blah… But he said no such thing.

"From now on I want you to be aware that you are truly German women," he announced, "and that the main duty of a German woman is to give as many children as possible to the Führer. There's no need to be married, as they insist in decadent countries. So don't reject the advances of young men, and, henceforth, be intimate with them as often as possible."

Ursula and the other girls couldn't believe their ears. Instead of poring over dusty boring books, they were being asked to … (She doesn't blush like Heidi at this point in her story; she bursts out laughing.) That same morning, during a German class, the students had to do a dictation entitled "Biological Marriage". For the first time, Ursula didn't make a single mistake, despite all the difficult words, agreements, double consonants, and she received an excellent mark. She even learned this dictation by heart and recited it to her mother, without noticing how uneasy her mother was becoming, fidgeting on the couch, trying to avoid eye contact with her daughter. "Now or in the future, we all have to abandon ourselves to the spiritually rich experience of procreating with a healthy young man, without worrying about the shackles of the outmoded institution of marriage."

Ursula didn't need to be asked twice to follow these instructions to the letter. All the more so because she was already pregnant – although she didn't know who the father was – and was indeed wondering how to break this catastrophic news to her parents. She didn't need to worry, the catastrophe was suddenly a blessing. She was transferred to the RAD (*Reichsarbeitsdienst*, the Reich Labour Service) and, given her situation, she was relieved of any duties like sweeping, emptying of buckets, peeling of potatoes or scrubbing the floor. Her only tasks were to dust the portraits of the Führer and do a few desk jobs. Then she landed here, at the Home. And, bingo, now little Ella is with us. And I'm pretty sure she'll soon have a bunch of half-brothers and sisters…

But Ursula really needs to be careful; she's so clumsy! She wanted to stand up – she can't sit still – and, forgetting that she was holding her baby, she almost dropped poor Ella. Thank goodness Mother was quick off the mark and saved the day.

Mother is extremely annoyed. All she wants is for Ursula to get lost. Her wish is granted soon enough: even though we are still allowed half an hour more with our mothers, Ursula takes it upon herself to deposit Ella with Josefa, as if she was getting rid of a large parcel or some other cumbersome object. I'm sure she'll head to the park for a smoke. Or else she's going to meet someone. She loves hanging around the building next door – you know, the one I told you about, where the intercourse happens, where there are always plenty of SS officers.

It looks like Mother is going to have some time by herself for a bit. No one comes and sits near us. She's so nervous! An undesirable effect of the magic cord is that all her nervousness gets transmitted to me. If she keeps on like this I'll get colic… Here she goes, off to pace the room, rocking me in her arms so I fall asleep. But she's not rocking me, she's shaking me. And anyway I don't want to go to sleep. Not yet. I like getting to know my buddies, finding out their stories.

I yell really loudly so she stops swinging me around. But she doesn't seem to get the message and keeps on striding across the room. I don't like this at all. I'm getting giddy. Finally, she comes to a halt in front of a wall of portraits: one of our Führer, nicely displayed in a magnificent frame, decorated with gold mouldings, and one of *Reichsführer* Himmler, of Speer, the Reich's architect, of Goebbels, the Minister for Propaganda, and of Ley, the head of the German Labour Front. That should calm her nerves… Well, it doesn't. What on earth is the matter with her? I can feel her heart beating furiously; she's breathing in spasms, sweating, gulping with difficulty, as if she had a big lump stuck in her throat. And then she's back on the move. She starts roaming the room again and stops in front of the mottos written in gold letters and framed above the piano, the list of principles all the mothers must adhere to in order to serve the country:

1) There is no nobler job for a girl than to be a wife or a mother.
2) A woman must be neither intellectual nor independent.
3) The social standing of a woman is determined by the number of children she has brought into the world.
4) A woman must not work outside the home.

Mother goes tense; she grabs my fingers and squeezes them so hard it hurts. Then she turns rapidly and glances at the door, terrified, as if she wants to escape.

Her fear is being transmitted to me. I feel awful, really awful.

So there, I've got colic. It's so painful. My intestines are in turmoil.

I scream at the top of my voice.

"What's the problem?" asks Josefa, alerted by my cries.

"Oh nothing, nothing at all," says Mother, trying to control her trembling voice. "Max had a bit of acid reflux earlier. He… He's feeling a little queasy."

"All the more reason not to shake him like that!" Josefa retorts.

Finally, someone sensible; she can see I'm fed up with being carted around. And she's not even aware of the bad vibes I'm getting from Mother.

"You look tired, Frau Inge. Would you like me to put our Little Emperor to bed now so you can get some sleep?"

Josefa stares at Mother without blinking, waiting for an answer. She can sense – perhaps not as subtly as I can, but enough anyway – that something is not right. Mother is not radiant. She is not displaying her regulation smile. She is not exhibiting correct behaviour.

"Give him to me," Josefa insists. "Clearly, a good night's sleep will do you a world of good."

Panic. Even though Mother is distressed, she wants to keep me with her as long as possible, as usual. She refuses Josefa's offer, on the pretext that her malaise has passed, and goes and sits opposite the fireplace. Next to Frau Gertrud and her son Rudi.

* * *

Frau Gertrud is an old woman. She must be at least thirty. She's already got four children, whom she had with her husband, a very respected *Obersturmführer.* His overseas missions were so frequent that Frau Gertrud ended up getting bored, so to amuse herself… (I keep using ellipses in the stories about the mothers, what sort of a fixation is that, I wonder?) To avoid a scandal, Frau Gertrud wrote to Max Sollmann and he let her give birth here, free of charge. In exchange, she's going to leave Rudi here. Debt squared, end of story.

Hey, what's happening? I can hear Josefa getting angry. She's got it in for Frau Gisela. Frau Gisela is a Sister like Mother. But she didn't have to grit her teeth in the sexual intercourse building. On the contrary… Do you get what I mean? She was silly enough to fall in love with the father of Léni, her daughter. So she's never without a photo of him, always staring at it, daydreaming. She's always sighing, wiping away tears, hanging out for the twice-daily mail, hoping to receive a love letter, which never comes. She's worse than Mother with all the nicknames for poor Léni, who, if you believe Gisela's nonsense, is the spitting image of her father… Josefa has just confiscated the photo and reminded her that it is *strictly forbidden* to have one, and even more so to show it around. (Just like it is *strictly forbidden* to take photos of us, the babies.) It is particularly poor form to speak about our fathers here.

In the end it would have been better if Frau Gisela had had to grit her teeth, like Mother did. At least the suffering would be over, whereas now it is never-ending.

Enough for tonight. It's Heidi and Frau Gisela's fault that Josefa is in a foul mood. And, even though it's not time yet, she announces that we have to leave.

Anyway, I can't tell you in detail about every single one of the women here. It would take too long. They all have such vastly different backgrounds and there are constantly more and more of them. Soon, when the war starts, French, Belgian, Dutch women will join our German women. They'll come from everywhere, and they'll all be inseminated by SS men!

Aryan seed. Despite the range of receptacles, they're all handpicked and the final result is a unique product: us, the army of the future.

The children's victory will follow an armed victory – that's *Reichsführer* Himmler's motto, hanging on the wall of our nursery.

Goodnight. I'm still too young to sleep through the night, but I've got plenty to think about over the next three hours.

5.

It was worth waiting a week, it really was.

I'm so excited, so emotional, that I don't know how to tell you what has just happened to me. I've got to take some time out to calm down. The shock has been so great that everything in my mind is muddled. Even though I have a dolichocephalic head, proof that I'm of the superior Aryan race, I feel like it's not big enough. Is there a spot in my brain that could receive and retain forever the marvellous experience I have just had? I would like to engrave the memory of it and keep it intact, indelible.

I have just been baptised.

But not in a church and not in a traditional way. I wasn't sprinkled with a few drops of so-called consecrated water by someone muttering incomprehensible Latin prayers. Not at all. I stayed here, at the Home, where baptism has been replaced by a new ceremony called *Namensgebung:* "name-giving". And who do you think presided over this? In person?

Yes, you guessed it.

That was the surprise, the extra present, and I hadn't deluded myself about harbouring this secret wish. It was my reward for being born on the 20th of April like our Führer, and Mother's reward as the champion milk supplier. Her record is 27.88 litres of milk in one week!

The three days of preparation were like a military offensive for the staff: Doctor Ebner, Josefa, the secretaries, the director. The nurseries, already very clean, were scoured from top to bottom until the walls and the floor shone like mirrors. The laboratory, the delivery rooms, the labour rooms, the offices, the kitchens and outhouses were not exempt from this massive clean-up. Outside, the gardens underwent a fair bit of landscaping. What's more, for the gardening team, the preparations began well before the big day. They mowed the lawns, clipped the hedges, put in new garden beds, hosed down the gravel on the paths so it would sparkle in the sunshine, and watered the flowers. The normal workforce, from Dachau, was doubled. The result is spectacular: the lawns are emerald-green, the beds of tulips and crocuses are in bloom, and the hedges and bushes are trimmed to within a millimetre.

Ebner was constantly on the prowl, ordering people around, keeping an eagle eye on everything: from the far reaches of the property right up to the little rooms on top of the building, which are used to store stocks of food and sundry supplies. He even allowed – and this is truly out of the ordinary – a few prisoners into the Home to back up the cleaning teams. (But it was only a "one-way" trip, if you see what I mean… Code word.)

All the Mothers were issued with new outfits: cream-coloured shirts with puffy sleeves and brown skirts decorated with a thin, red satin ribbon along the hem, to signal the red of our flag. As she was receiving a personal honour from the Führer, Mother wore a slightly different outfit: a white embroidered shirt with a swastika armband on the right sleeve and a black skirt cinched around the waist by a large, elegant belt. We babies were dressed in short one-piece romper suits, flared at thigh level, with puffy sleeves and a Peter Pan collar. A little red and black Reich flag was stuck on the end of each bassinet.

As the ceremony was to be filmed for a short documentary, a crew was setting up in the Home all morning. Mother and I, the stars of the film – after the Führer, of course – had to do lots of rehearsals. A technical adviser explained to Mother exactly how she had to hold me in her arms so that my face would be angled towards the camera lights. She was shown precisely how she had to walk, her torso held straight, and the way to smile and greet the Führer, curtsy, etc. And I was kept busy, too. The cameraman was all over me, watching my every gesture, every funny little expression. He was supposed to catch me smiling: you know that innate, angelic smile babies have. He explained to Mother that he had to stockpile lots of my smiles, so that, if there was a problem during the filming, the director could adjust some of the shots in the editing. It was awkward in the beginning: the blinding camera lights annoyed me, and it's not that easy to smile to order, especially in the middle of such commotion. But I think by the end he'd snapped a few pretty baby smiles.

They also filmed a whole lot of different sketches: Mother changing my nappies, or feeding me, me gurgling happily, or sleeping peacefully. Modesty got the better of us a couple of times: Mother objected to any part of her breast being filmed; and I wasn't that happy about having my penis, my bum and my dirty nappies on show. But through sheer determination and endurance we ended up doing it. Then they filmed in the main reception room: a close-up of the flowers, cakes, coffee, champagne, zooming in on Mother walking in a dignified manner towards the Führer so he could hold me. Except that, for now, an ugly technician was standing in for the Führer.

What an exhausting morning. After the midday feed, I slept deeply so I'd be in good shape for zero hour – which finally came.

The guards opened the large metal gate at the entrance to the property and ... gliding along the central driveway was the Führer's private car.

The Mercedes 770K. The only one in the world. Made to measure just for him. Let me describe to you in detail this jewel of modern technology. Length: 6 metres. Width: 2.20 metres. Motor: 8 cylinders, 400 horsepower with turbo-compressors. Dual ignition. Front and rear split hydraulic break systems. Armoured bodywork, special glass with ten layers of bulletproof bond on the windows, electromagnetic door-locking, puncture-proof tyres. A complete armoured fortress on wheels! In the back is a special raised seat, thirteen centimetres high, which can release a pedestal where the Führer stands during parades. It's a black convertible. The Reich's flag graces the bonnet of the car, to the left of the chauffeur. I hope that one day some toy manufacturer comes up with the idea to design a miniature model of this car. I can already see myself playing with it when I'm older, pushing it along the floor. *Vroom, vroom!*

The car behind is also a Mercedes, a more current model. Both vehicles park in front of the entrance. All the staff line up: Josefa at the head of the nursing team, Marina and the secretaries, the manager and his gardeners. Doctor Ebner, wearing his best SS uniform, opens the car door himself to greet the Führer. No sooner has our guest stepped onto the gravel than all the arms are raised: *Heil!* The Führer replies with a relaxed wave. Smiling, he gives Ebner a warm embrace, while the other guests get out of the second car and join them: *Reichsführer* SS Himmler, Max Sollmann (the director of the *Lebensborn* programme, the one I mentioned before I was born), as well as Doctor Karl Brandt and his wife. Herr Brandt is the Führer's personal doctor. His aim is to revamp modern medicine – and we represent such a very important part of the medicine of the future, so his presence today is indispensable. Apparently he'll soon be promoted to the Reich's High Commissioner of Health. His wife, Anni Rehborn, a champion swimmer for Germany, is a role model for German youth.

The little group gathers. While Ebner gives a quick run-down on our establishment, the Führer surveys the grounds, then admires the building's facade, lifting his gaze to the upper storeys. Our nursery is on the second floor, and it's as if the Führer's gaze travels through walls and settles on each of our bassinets. Obviously we can't greet him outside like the rest of the staff, and neither can our mothers. Josefa instructed them to stay with us. Every mother has to stand up, ramrod straight, next to her baby's bassinet. As for the missing mothers, the ones sent to munitions factories or "relocated" (Bertha, Heidi, Gisela and a few others), actresses have been substituted for them.

I don't need to tell you that I can't wait another second. I'm seething with impatience. And I can tell Mother is as nervous as hell, panic-stricken. She's shaking, perspiring, and keeps glancing anxiously at the actress standing in for Heidi, next to Helmut's bassinet. Something is wrong. Again. *Pull yourself together! Come on, pull yourself together!* The magic cord is still working at maximum capacity between us. But if Mother wavers, will I be able to save the day all by myself?

A nurse is stationed discreetly at the window, relaying the happenings below to the mothers so they don't miss a moment. The Führer is not in uniform, she tells them; he's wearing black trousers and a beige jacket with a swastika armband on the right sleeve. (The masculine version of Mother's outfit, so they match in the film! What a good idea. That's Herr Ebner's attention to detail for you.) The nurse announces that the Führer is shaking hands with the staff and addressing a few kind words to each of them. Apparently Josefa is turning crimson and is almost apoplectic. It's the first time she's met the Führer in the flesh. She already goes into a trance whenever she hears him on the radio, so how will she survive this? Not to mention that if today doesn't unfold exactly according to Doctor Ebner's instructions, off she goes to the munitions factory.

The guests enter the Home. They are touring each room, one by one. The living rooms, the birthing rooms, the kitchens, the laboratory, until they finally reach the nursery.

It takes a long time. Too long.

The wait is unbearable, the tension is rising. One woman has left her post and heads to the window to powder her nose in the daylight, another claims to have a pressing need and charges to the toilets, a third decides on the spot to redo her bun. Women! Actually the babies are scarcely better: one has an attack of colic and is writhing in his bassinet, bawling for all he's worth; another is hungry, his mother in a panic because she can't breastfeed him while standing to attention. There he goes… Oh no, one baby has diarrhoea! That bitter, acidic smell. What a stink. Quick! Quick! Change him!

Air the room! Let's pray he doesn't do it again in the next few minutes. Fortunately I did a perfectly shaped poo just after the midday feed, to be on the safe side…

Now what's up? The nurse who was providing the commentary on the Führer's arrival has just realized that she forgot Josefa's final instruction: to put the bassinets of the brown-skinned babies – Ebner keeps a few – in the third row, so that they aren't in the camera's field of vision. All hands on deck! She asks the mothers to help her redo the whole arrangement. In all the panic, they had better not end up putting me with the brown-skinned babies.

Here we go. Footsteps on the stairs to the nursery. The hammering of boots draws nearer. The wooden floor shudders. The door opens.

Heil! shout the mothers and the nurses all together.

The guests enter. The filming starts. The group examines the first row of bassinets. The Führer stops in front of one, then another. Handshake. Congratulations. *Smile, baby!* It's nearly my turn. My little heart is pounding in time to the rhythm of the boots, *thud thud thud.* Mother keeps her hand on my belly, as if she is afraid I will fly away. Her hand is cold. Heavy. Oppressive. She's stifling me. *Hey! Take your hand off. That hurts!* I can't even scream to let her know. The pain is stopping me from giving my best smile, like I did this morning with the cameraman. I must look horrible.

The boots have stopped. Phew! Mother has taken her hand off me to shake the Führer's hand. He's talking to her. Quietly, so quietly I can't hear what he's saying. His voice is not at all like it is on the radio. On the radio, he yells, his sentences are staccato, each word emphasized. Now it's nothing like that. I can feel Mother relaxing, and me along with her. Then Ebner hands my record book to the Führer, so he can see everything, from the genealogical tree of my parents to now, the details of my conception and birth. I feel like I've already lived a very long time because it takes him so long to read the pages. But suddenly a cluster of faces is leaning over me. Himmler, Ebner, Brandt, Frau Rehborn. *Move aside! Come on, move aside! I can't see my Führer!* Brandt undoes the top of my romper suit to study my torso, then extends my legs and arms, and palpates my skull. Hey, guys, you're not going to put me through a whole new selection process! I'm the star exhibit and you had better not forget it! Next thing Frau Rehborn is smiling at me and tickling my feet. It's unbearable. The faces all merge together in a sort of swaying motion and I feel dizzy.

Then someone lifts me up really high. I feel like I'm in an aeroplane, my insides churning. I feel sick. Then off we go, down again, as rough as the ascent. My heart is in my mouth. I can feel something moist on my cheek. The camera is rolling, rolling. They're not missing a second of what's going on.

What's going on is that ... I've finally worked it out: I'm in the arms of the Führer! The Führer just kissed me! I'm frightened that, with all this emotion, I'll "purify" myself: I'll have a cardiac arrest, sudden infant death syndrome, whatever. Why didn't Ebner think to give me some vitamins?

The ceremony downstairs in the main room proceeded without a hitch. There were so many people. Loads of them. The staff, the mothers, other mothers from Homes all over the country, the SS officers recruited for the special-meetings building next door, and all the stand-in actors and actresses so it looked like a real crowd. Because our Führer loves to address a crowd; he doesn't like to speak to small groups.

He needs a crowd in order to communicate his passion, to find the words that rouse people, make them spontaneously raise an arm in salute. The applause at the end of each sentence inspires him for the next sentence. The whole audience thrills to the sound of his voice, and men want to take up arms there and then to carry out the great future projects he is describing. Women, too, are eager to offer him everything: their bodies, their lives, their souls. Some of them even faint under the emotional impact of his speech. The Führer explained how we, the children of the future, purebred Aryans – of which I was the only representative in the room, the others were still in the nursery – are going to populate not only Germany, but all of Europe, once the Reich's expansion is underway and the war gets going and the Jewish Question has been sorted out. We are going to mount a holy war against foreigners, in order to safeguard the racial purity of the German people.

It was a momentous, awesome occasion. Hitler was so eloquent that we could envisage, right there in front of us, this new world stripped of degenerates.

At the end of the speech, at a sign from Doctor Ebner, Mother stepped forward to join the Führer on the dais. Well, what a transformation! No more nerves, no doubts, no remorse. She finally realized that it had all been worth it, gritting her teeth that night in the cold, overlit room in the meetings building. It had been worth a painful birth. It had been worth putting up with Doctor Ebner and Josefa's rules. Heidi was no longer in her thoughts. Mother was ecstatic. As if hypnotized, she seemed to glide through space, her feet no longer touching the ground. And I was like an angel from heaven in her embrace.

Except … there was one little incident all the same. When the Führer took me in his arms to christen me, out loud, with my official name, I … peed myself. His speech, although fascinating, exhilarating, was very long. I tried to hold on, but I couldn't. The vein on Ebner's bald head was raised and throbbing: I thought he was going to "purify" me on the spot, in front of everyone. Two nurses rushed over to sponge the Führer's sleeve, but he politely brushed them aside, laughing. The whole gathering imitated him, including Ebner, whose vein immediately receded.

Next there was a photo session. Mother and I had the privilege of posing with the Führer. Mother received a copy of the photo later, signed by the Führer himself. After that I was taken back to the nursery. With the music, champagne, coffee, cakes, I think they all had a great party. At least the guests did. The Führer retired to the laboratory with Herr Himmler and doctors Ebner and Brandt to speak about medical practices of the future, to organize the great scientific discoveries that will take place under the auspices of the Third Reich.

As for me, phew! Beddy-byes. I was exhausted.

Hang on! I forgot to tell you the most important thing: I have a name now.

My name is Konrad von Kebnersol. Two Ks, as in "Klein Kaiser". K, as in Krupp. As in the 770K, the Führer's Mercedes. They made up my surname from the syllables in Doctor Ebner's and Herr Sollmann's names, and they added the "von" to make it sound high-class.

Konrad von Kebnersol. The Führer wrote it in my record book. It sounds good, doesn't it?

So I dodged Max, the name Mother would have chosen.

6.

My nose is running. I've got diarrhoea. I've lost my appetite. I feel queasy.

What's wrong with me? They say the morning after a party is hard. Quite right. You'd think I was hung-over, like those nurses who drank too much champagne after the Führer's speech. But my christening was a long time ago. Two months already … I hate being like this. Sluggish, grumpy. Like Heidi's son, Helmut.

Deep down, I think I know why I feel lousy.

It happened two nights ago. I was fast asleep when I heard noises. Muffled footsteps, frightened whispers. What was going on now? The nursery really isn't a quiet place, you know, and the bawling of one or other of my buddies is not the only regular commotion. That's normal; I'm used to it, no problem. On the other hand, what's disturbing, for example, is when a mother, on a sudden whim, rushes down to see her baby. The night nurses spot her straight away and try to take her back to her room, which just ends in interminable discussions. Best-case scenario. Because sometimes ... there's no baby! The mother finds an empty bassinet.

"Don't worry, your child was unwell, nothing serious. He's in the infirmary," they tell her.

"I want to see him!"

"You can't right now. He's contagious. We've quarantined him."

"You're lying! You're lying!" screams the hysterical mother.

She's in a total frenzy; the nurse calls for assistance and she's given a shot to calm her down. How am I supposed to get back to sleep after a racket like that?

Especially when it stays in my head. I wonder if "infirmary" and "quarantine" are new code words I don't yet know the meaning of? Some nights, it's Josefa who prowls the nursery. She wears a big black cape as if she is going out, and there's a man with her. She inspects all the bassinets and stops in front of one or another and says, "This one! This one! And that one!" The man takes the babies she's picked out and puts them in a large sling and soon I hear the rumbling of a motor and a van takes off and disappears. Just like all the vans that deliver food early in the morning. Except there's only one van on those nights.

The next day, the bassinets are still empty, a dummy or a rattle the only signs of their former tenants. If the mothers are still living at the Home, there's sure to be a huge scene; if they've already left and been replaced by a wet nurse, it's not an issue. Anyway, within a few hours, the empty bassinets are home to new occupants.

So where do they go, those babies who vanish in the night? It bothers me. I wonder if there's some kind of trafficking going on? Could Josefa – honest Josefa, so devoted to the Home, Josefa, Doctor Ebner's right hand – be selling them? Our Führer assures us we're worth our weight in gold, so you'll understand why I panicked when, on this wretched night, Josefa's footsteps stopped at my bassinet.

Why mine?

I was sure I was headed for the delivery van.

"I'm doing you a favour, Frau Inge," Josefa murmured nervously. "I'm making an exception because you have an excellent track record here. But, for your own sake, keep this short."

Frau Inge? So it wasn't the man with the sling. That was a relief. Especially when I recognized Mother's smell as she took me in her arms. She hugged me and I immediately felt that tension she gives off when she's upset. She was shaking, weeping. Floods of tears. Some landed on my face and, since my nappy was soaking, I felt even colder.

"Come now, Frau Inge," protested Josefa. "You're making it harder for yourself. Here, this will cheer you up. You left it on your bedside table. Put it in your bag."

Mother said nothing. Her tears prevented her from uttering a word, other than Max, Max, Max. (She's stubborn: even though I was baptised Konrad, she insists on calling me Max.)

"Really, Frau Inge," Josefa continued, "this photo is wonderful. Signed by the Führer, how lucky you are!"

It was the photo from my christening. They could have shown it to me!

When Josefa realized that Mother wasn't going to respond, she stuffed the photo in Mother's bag and signalled to the two duty nurses. They rushed over to flank Mother, who still held me tight, not wanting to release me, kissing my hands, cheeks, nose, eyelids, smothering me in her embrace.

"Can I write?" she asked. "Will you send me another photo of him? Send me news about him?"

"You know very well that's against the rules," Josefa replied, tight-lipped. "Rules that I am already breaking right now, may I remind you, Frau Inge."

"Oh, please, I beg you!"

"Don't make me tell Doctor Ebner," Josefa threatened.

She tore me from Mother's arms so roughly that I came away with a few strands of her hair that my fingers had been tangled in. The nurses each took Mother by an arm and dragged her to the door. She kept crying, screaming, in the stairwell, outside. Until the growl of a motor drowned out her wails. A car started, drove off. Then there was nothing but silence, total silence. All the more noticeable after so much weeping. It was unbearable.

Mother's tears were still damp on my face, her hair hooked in my fingers. A gust of wind whipped the strands away. I would have liked to keep them to remember her by. I peed and no one came to change me. I couldn't go back to sleep. I started howling, so loud that the whole nursery followed suit.

It was a hell of a racket.

For my first feed the next day, I found myself in the arms of a stranger, my nose squashed into her breast, which, although ample, was nothing like a nice soft pillow. She tried to stuff her nipple in my mouth, but I kept twisting my head away. She didn't smell right. She wasn't tense. I felt nothing. There was obviously no magic cord between her and me. The magic cord could only work with Mother, who had left last night. Left for good, I realized.

I felt a strange sensation: as if the cord was still there, between my fingers, but no matter how I tugged on it, shook it, there was no one on the other end to answer any more.

I tried to reason with myself. If Helmut had got over Heidi leaving, if Léni had got used to Gisela's absence, if dozens of others had managed to do without their cord, why couldn't I? After all, I'd been baptised by the Führer himself; I was, in a way, the Chosen One. I should have set an example. I should have been the first to go through the experience of separation, since I was the veteran of the Home. But there you go, Mother had had the privilege of staying longer than the others, so the cord had attached a bit too strongly.

I tried to swallow the wet nurse's milk, but it made me want to vomit. Sour, thick, disgusting. Yuk! I couldn't stomach it.

During the next feeds, I scarcely managed a few drops before throwing up. My throat was burning; I was in agony. Over the following days, I kept up my cantankerous behaviour and yelled at every opportunity. I couldn't lie down without getting cramps. And they'd moved me: I no longer slept in the nursery with the newborns, but with the big kids in another room. Besides, the nursery was overflowing. The new arrivals were piling up, almost on top of each other, not in bassinets, but in large tank-like containers. Like battery-cage chickens. The construction noise only added to my anxiety. (Once again they had to renovate the premises to accommodate all the new arrivals.) Being held didn't calm me either. Overcome by hunger, I stopped being so fussy and resigned myself to drinking the disgusting milk. Result: diarrhoea, the runs!

On the wagon. Nothing but rice milk.

* * *

Then I realized I had to act, and fast. Two events opened my eyes.

First, the weekly visit to Doctor Ebner's laboratory.

Herr Ebner pursed his lips in disgust when he saw my nappies soiled with that foul, green, slimy, stinking stuff that was not at all in line with the nicely moulded stools of a child of the master race, evidence of excellent health and perfect bodily control. I was so ashamed! When Ebner put me on the scales, it seemed that, behind his round glasses, his steely eyes froze, like two beads of ice. The vein at his temple was bulging more than ever. He dictated my weight to his secretary, who recorded it in the "Adequate" column. I'd lost 700 grams since my last visit. Far too much. If this kept up ... Ebner didn't finish his sentence, but I knew that what he'd left unsaid was part of the code language.

I was getting scrawny. *Unharmonisch!*

Pull yourself together, Konrad! And fast!

The second event was Ursula.

She was still at the Home, even though she'd asked Josefa several times to get her an early release.

"I'm sick of being cooped up! I've had it with nappies, naps, feeds and the whole shebang! You never said I'd have to take a raincheck before giving another child to the Führer?"

"Of course," replied Josefa, "but you know perfectly well that you have to wait a decent amount of time."

Ursula also fed her baby well; that's why she was forced to stay longer at the Home. To stave off boredom, she indulged in her favourite activity: spreading gossip.

We were on the terrace. The wet nurse was trying to feed me a bottle of water, which I refused. After persisting for a bit, she gave up and made do with holding the teat near my mouth, to give Josefa the right impression, while she lounged in the sun. That's when Ursula came and sat next to us.

"Well, now I know!" she announced triumphantly.

"Know what?"

"I know where they took Edith, Klaus and Markus."

The other woman didn't seem to have a clue who Ursula was talking about, but I did. Edith, Klaus and Markus were the babies picked out by Josefa the other night, the ones who'd left in the delivery van.

"So where are they?" asked the wet nurse idly. (She had absolutely no interest and was just making conversation.)

"They were sent to the Steinhof Institute in Vienna. To Am Spiegelgrund, the children's clinic, Ward 15," whispered Ursula.

"Oh, good, they'll be well looked after there."

"You just don't get it!" snapped Ursula, playing her guessing game with a cheeky smile. Eager to reveal her big secret, she continued, "They are part of a new programme called 'Merciful Death'."

She rattled off the rest in a low voice, stopping often to look around and make sure there were no indiscreet eavesdroppers. Especially not the other mothers on the terrace. I hung on her every word, in particular the new code words.

"Merciful death" means that once the babies reach Ward 15, they're killed. "Merciful death" is not exactly synonymous with "purification" or "relocation"; it's different, subtler – it's inducing death following an incurable illness. Because, well, the doctors at the Homes realized that, even if we children of pure Aryan stock had been engineered with the greatest care and rigour, even if we were the fruit of an impeccable union, once we were born, we were prey to any sickness that we might be exposed to as we grew up. A sad truth and a huge disappointment. Klaus, for example, had been afflicted with a harelip, Edith was deaf, and Markus suffered from asthma. Other defects had been discovered in one baby or another in places outside Steinhöring. If we were meant to be the incarnation of a new generation of lords and masters, then these flaws were inadmissible.

Why did they occur? the doctors wondered. What could be the cause, the precise origin of these growth disorders? How could these congenital abnormalities be eradicated? In order to find a solution, they had to do research, experiments, tests.

On the sick babies brought to Ward 15.

First while they were still alive; then once they were dead. Their corpses were dissected, their heads, brains and organs preserved in formaldehyde and placed in jars on shelves – with labels.

Another code word: "weak heart" – the term used in the clinic's record books for cause of death.

Ursula waited for the wet nurse's reaction. The nurse remained silent for a while, opening and closing her mouth like a soundless hand puppet.

"I don't believe you. That's all nonsense!" she finally announced.

Annoyed that the nurse wouldn't take her word for it, Ursula ploughed on: "So what do you think our Führer, the *Reichsführer* Himmler, and the doctors Ebner and Brandt were discussing, here at this very Home, after the name-giving ceremony? Everyone knows the *Reichsführer* Himmler is passionate about scientific research, right? So why were certain bassinets empty after their visit to Doctor Ebner's laboratory?"

"Who told you all this? How did you find out?"

"I like being sociable, you know," said Ursula. "It's boring here with only women, so sometimes I have a chat with the delivery drivers in the morning. One of them told me. He's happy because it's more work for him. He delivers food in the morning, and in the evening he comes for the 'rabbits'."

Another code word. The "rabbits" are the babies taken to Ward 15 at the institute in Vienna to be used as guinea pigs.

The wet nurse stared at Ursula without saying a word, without even opening her mouth the way she had before. She looked anxiously round at all the mothers on the terrace, as if she wanted one of them to be her witness. Then, suddenly disenchanted, she shook her head. "Oh, you young people!" she exclaimed. "What will you come up with next?"

She leaned backwards, angling her face at the sun, while Ursula, still annoyed, walked off to put her baby back to bed and sneak away for another cigarette.

Markus, Edith, Klaus.

Markus the asthmatic. Edith the deaf one. Klaus the harelip.

I'd often hung out with them. In the nursery, our bassinets were next to each other. Were they contagious?

And my diarrhoea and loss of appetite, were they growth disorders? Defects? Intolerable flaws for a baby of the master race? I had just paid another visit to Doctor Ebner's lab. He hadn't finished his sentence… Now his silence resonated in my head, roaring, empty, terrifying. Now I knew what his silence meant: "Rabbit. Deliver to Ward 15."

No! No! I don't want to be a rabbit! I don't want to be chopped into pieces!

A nervous spasm went through me and I flung my arms back so violently that the bottle of water clattered to the floor. I threw myself onto the wet nurse's breast, latching on to the nipple as if I was going to swallow it.

I sucked and sucked until I was full, even if the milk didn't taste as good as Mother's. And I clenched my buttocks, praying that this food wouldn't end up in my nappy as soon as I'd gulped it.

The next evening, I had terrible nightmares. I dreamed I was a "rabbit" and they were injecting needles into my eyes to change their colour, make them bluer. I dreamed they gave me poison; that they drowned me in a bucket like a kitten; that they threw me into a furnace; that they strangled me. I dreamed of Klaus's twisted mouth: it became more and more warped and misshapen, opening like a gigantic oven that engulfed me. I dreamed of Edith's deaf ear and saw it swimming in the formaldehyde like a big fish in a bowl.

I admit I was afraid, terribly afraid.

So I battled to overcome my fear. And I succeeded.

Now I am doing much better. I never baulk at a feed any more, and I've gained weight. I came out of that ordeal a lot stronger.

I understand now that my buddies' sacrifice was essential in guaranteeing that the Reich's medical science is the finest in the world. Markus, Edith, Klaus and all the "rabbits" from the other Homes can be proud because they will be contributing to great discoveries: vaccines against tuberculosis and typhus (diseases spread by Jews and Gypsies), medications to heal the wounds of our soldiers at the front – once the war gets going, many of our men, alas, will be wounded. I now know that we make up a chain, every link of which, even the smallest, is vital. The weak die so the strong can become invincible.

Now I'm no longer distressed by the disappearance of the "rabbits" in the middle of the night. They're necessary. And lots of them are needed. I've heard that, in addition to the clinic in Vienna, other "scientific institutes" – a new code word – will be opened. Former prisons will be refitted as "children's hospitals", with ultramodern "operating theatres". (You've cottoned on, haven't you? I don't need to repeat myself? Let's agree that, from now on, words in quotation marks are code words.) *Reichsführer* Himmler intends to open another fifty "research institutes". Medical research will go ahead in leaps and bounds! Especially because, when they run out of "rabbits", the war will keep the supply going, in the form of prisoners.

There. I'm relieved to have confided in you about this moment of weakness and doubt, this bad patch I went through. I've undertaken my self-criticism, thus fulfilling one of the essential duties of any good National Socialist.

I'm fine now. I eat, sleep and grow. I'm in perfect health. *Harmonisch!*

And also ... no more magic cord! It no longer exists. I've cut the umbilical cord once and for all. My memory of Mother is fading. It's more and more blurred, like a reflection on the water's surface that ripples and then vanishes. I can't remember her smell any more, or the feeling of pressing against the soft pillow of her breasts. Soon I'll have forgotten she existed. Besides, I'm going to erase the word "Mother" from my vocabulary. It serves no purpose right now, so why would I bother myself with it, when I've got my work cut out learning all the new code words.

It's good to feel free, unencumbered. I let myself lounge in anyone's arms; I feed from any old set of breasts. Actually, soon I'm graduating to the bottle.

I'm growing. Tall. Strong. Tough.

Made of Krupp steel.

7.

They're completely obsessed with housework here. And everything connected with it: the delivery of new toys, new furniture, back-up cleaning staff (prisoners allowed to enter the Home for work).

Oh, boy! There's no time to get bored. It's all happening. Everything's running smoothly. All the mothers are new: the only ones here now are those who have just given birth.

Josefa is beside herself, running from room to room, racing upstairs and downstairs. Nothing escapes her eagle eye: a portrait of the Führer that hasn't been dusted, some wilted flowers on the piano, that crooked rug in the entrance, and that baby who's had a snotty nose all morning. She's shouting at the nurses, nagging the secretaries, scolding the mothers, hitting the prisoners. (She got stuck into one the other day and hit her so hard, the girl had blood all over her face, and then Josefa reprimanded her for getting blood on the clean floor and hit her even harder.) Josefa is a nervous wreck. Even the sound of crying babies – the sound one associates with the Home, like the whirring of machines in a factory – sets her nerves jangling. The secretaries have been on the job for at least a fortnight. They've received a deluge of mail and have to work overtime to deal with it.

In my opinion, all this carry-on – the housework, the new furniture, the high voltage tension in the Home – is also a code. It means we're about to receive visitors.

I've got a hunch: the secretaries are getting letters that are all applications for adoption.

In other words, after being conceived under the most rigorous scientific conditions, after passing the selection process at birth with flying colours and managing not to be disposed of as "bunnies", we babies of the master Aryan race are now going to be sent off all over Germany.

We're going to leave, get to know the outside world!

Our future adoptive parents, SS officers and their wives, have very specific requests: some want a brand-new baby just in, others want a three-or six-month-old who doesn't need to be breastfed, some want a girl, some a boy. (Lucky we're all tall, blond and blue-eyed: it narrows the criteria.) Before replying to the various requests, the secretaries have to check the rank of the prospective fathers. The higher the rank, the more attractive the assigned baby. For example, an *Oberscharführer*, a mere staff sergeant, can't expect as perfect a baby as an *Obersturmbannführer*, a lieutenant colonel, who would be less favoured than an *Obergruppenführer*, a lieutenant general. When it comes to a request from a private, the lowest rank, *Sturmmann*, the letter is not even opened; it goes either straight in the bin or on the stack of files pending. If there's ever a surplus of babies, which is not the case now, the private might receive an answer. So the secretaries have a difficult task: under no circumstances can they mix up the ranks, or else there would have to be a returns or exchange policy, which would be extremely difficult to manage. To handle each request properly, they have to study the racial history of the baby, estimate a suitable match, draw charts and graphs, and refer to scientific statistics. I'm pretty sure that's a lot of work.

Obviously we babies have been well and truly prepared for the occasion. Washed, changed, dressed in new outfits, sprayed with scent. The *newbies* (my name for the newborns) are in the nursery and the veterans, of whom I am the leader, being all of seven months, are in a separate dormitory. Those who can't yet hold up their heads are wrapped in pretty embroidered sheets and must be placed on their tummies because Doctor Ebner has observed that, given the malleability of the cranial bones, if there is pressure on the temple region of the baby's head this accentuates his dolichocephalic tendencies. Those able to sit on their backsides without too much wobbling are carefully placed in their cots, wedged between pretty little cushions to support them if they tip over. Finally, the babies who can move about more, like me, are strapped into specially fitted little chairs.

Girls on one side, boys on the other.

So here we are, all decked out for the visitors.

Our future parents' cars are heading up the main driveway. This time there's no nurse at the window to describe the scene outside, like there was when the Führer visited. Nurses only talk to the mothers, not to the babies, and now, given the circumstances, the mothers have been sequestered in their rooms under strict instructions not to come out. By and large, the nurses remain silent: they wash us, change us, dress us, without uttering a word. This gains time, maintains the rhythm, and thus keeps productivity at a maximum. But every now and again, when Josefa's back is turned, a few of them let rip and express their annoyance. "Oh no, come on! You've pissed yourself again, haven't you! What the hell are you screaming for? Shut it, will you!" Personally, I'm not overly bothered by this inappropriate language. I'm tough, as you know, and these sorts of comments, although pretty unpleasant, don't upset me. Especially as I always find a way of getting back at anyone who mistreats me: a well-aimed vertical squirt of urine onto a clean white blouse, a stool straight onto a nappy that has just been changed, a mighty burp right in the face, and, as a last resort, screams that could burst your eardrums and turn you into a bundle of nerves, the kind of howling that seems interminable, that makes you want to tie the culprit up in his nappy and chuck him out the window – a crime no nurse has yet committed.

I wish I'd been filled in on the cars of the prospective parents. If I have to be adopted, I'd prefer to leave in a Mercedes.

To tell you the truth, I have absolutely no desire to be adopted. If I'm chosen today, I'll obey orders and follow due process, since adoption is an essential component of the *Lebensborn* programme. We must populate Germany, ensure its families grow ever larger and, when the war begins and is successful, populate the annexed countries, give them a fresh start. That goes without saying. But I cherish the hope ... my secret wish... Anyway I've just managed to break loose from one mother, and erase the word "Mummy" from my vocabulary. You've witnessed how I suffered through this ordeal: I was sick, I lost weight, I lost faith, I was frightened, I almost got taken away in the delivery van, so I can't see much point in having an adoptive mother. I have no idea what will be expected of me: will I have to pretend I love this mother? How will I do that? That wasn't part of the plan.

My secret wish is to join the German Youth Movement as soon as possible. Unfortunately I can't jump the gun: I've got to wait five years – too long. When I'm six, I'll be one of the *Pimpfe*, the youngest members of the Hitler Youth, and I'll be able to begin my education: there'll be orientation classes in sport, combat techniques, and Nazi history. When I'm ten, after passing another physical selection test (I'm OK for now, pure Aryan, but it'll have to be checked again because you never know), I'll be one of the thousands of children who, every year on the 20th of April, are presented as birthday presents to our Führer and enter the *Napolas*, the National Political Institutes of Education, the Reich's elite schools. That will be such a hugely important moment in my life. I'll have to take an oath and, guess what? I know it by heart already:

Under the blood banner, which represents our Führer, I swear to devote all my energy and strength to our country's saviour, Adolf Hitler. I am ready to give my life for him.

I get goosebumps when I say these words in my dolichocephalic head.

At the *Napola* there's no more nonsense. I'll undergo intensive training until the age of eighteen, and I'll finally be able to join the army – to fight. That's the future of the new German youth as envisioned by our Führer. He announced – I heard his speech on the radio the other day, just before nap time – that henceforth every German child will be taken in hand at every stage of his or her youth. He said ... just wait till I remember his words exactly ... that's it:

The young people we raise will terrify the rest of the world. I want them to be a commanding, fearless and cruel generation. They will know how to endure pain, and will have no weakness or tenderness. I want them to incarnate the strength and beauty of young wild animals. I'll have them trained in all manner of physical exercise. Above all, they will be athletic: this is more important than anything. It's how I will return them to the innocence and nobility of nature. There will be no intellectual education. Knowledge only corrupts my young people.

Soon, he added, children aged zero to six will also be part of an organization. Unfortunately, due to lack of personnel, it's not yet set up. That's why I have to be adopted, to fill in this waiting period.

I have to gain some time. If I can delay my adoption, that'll be something. In the meantime, I'm in training by myself. I've already overcome my fear, and, with the business of my illness after I was separated from my mother, I've endured pain, just as our Führer requires. I'm also trying to do some physical training: when a nurse changes my nappy, I wait until she's not looking and, after she steps away to get some clean linen, I seize the moment and try to scoot forward and slide off the table she's propped me on. I've managed to fall once already and didn't even feel a thing! As often as I can, I haul myself up in my cot and hang on to the bars; in order to check out my fear of heights, I stand on my tiptoes, stick my bum in the air and my head between my legs. Anxious about my energetic behaviour, which they considered excessive and dangerous, the nurses told Josefa, who then alerted Doctor Ebner.

After serious consideration, the doctor announced, "Konrad is endowed with *Draufgängertum*. That's wonderful. Wonderful! A fundamental quality of our Hitler Youth."

Draufgängertum means "go-getter, daredevil", minimal self-preservation instinct. It's one of the first precepts taught in the *Napolas*. In other words, I am gifted.

Nevertheless, on Doctor Ebner's orders, Josefa asked the nurses to stay vigilant and not to let me out of their sight. So what! I'm pretending I'm a prisoner of war trying to escape my shackles.

I'll be patient and await my destiny. Let's see if I'm adopted today.

Here we go; the door's opening.

After anxious glances to check that everything is in order, Josefa is all smiles as she brings in the first group. She leaves the couples to potter around, before directing them towards the babies that have already been picked out as corresponding best to the couples' profiles. The women are perfectly at ease. The officers less so: they'd clearly prefer to be outside smoking a cigarette while their wives make their choices. They're only there to be polite, gallant even, but they don't really give a damn, do they? Any one of us would do the job for them. They've got other, more important things to think about. Preparation for war, no less.

The women in the room are animated, both excited and overwhelmed.

"I'm going for a girl," announces one woman. "I've already got three boys and, believe me, it's non-stop at my place. A quiet girl would be perfect."

"Well, it's the opposite for me. I've produced nothing but girls and now I'd really like a sturdy little boy."

The gender isn't an issue for others. They are out to adopt a new child in the hope of gaining the bronze, silver or gold cross. (Crosses are given out to the most worthy German mothers during an annual ceremony every 12th of August, the day Hitler's mother was born. Women with four children get the bronze cross, those with six, the silver cross, and the most heroic of all, those with eight or more, the gold cross. When you have a cross, you get discounts, allowances, and the right to a household maid, one of the prisoners from the camps.)

My neighbours, Baldur and Bruno, have attracted the attention of a couple of women.

Oh, sweetie, you've got your eyes on me, yes! Your little handy-pandies are reaching out! You want Mummy to hold you, don't you? Can you smile yet? Come on, give me a cute little smile. And what about a kiss?

Looks like it's a done deal for Baldur. That was quick. Whereas the woman keen on Bruno is requesting more information before she decides. How's his general health? His appetite? Does he sleep through the night? It's probably too soon to tell, but do you have an inkling about what his character traits will be? If there were a problem, what would the Home administration do to help? Josefa replies politely but firmly that, because Bruno is from the elite group of babies, he won't be a problem. An exchange might be possible, however, on a one-off basis.

Now it's on to Trudel and Erna, the girls opposite me...

I am so bored, just like the officers, most of whom have left the room, telling their wives to chose whichever baby they like. But there is one who has had enough patience to stay and who is following his wife as she comes over to me.

Josefa is on his heels and quick to sing my praises. "He is among the very best of our brood," she announces proudly. Then she reads out the details of my racial profile, emphasizing the characteristics that make me a magnificent specimen of the Aryan race.

The woman kneels down so she is level with me. She fondles my hands, pinches my cheek, tickles my feet and under my chin. Just like her husband, I try to be patient. There's no way round it. While I stare at her with my big blue eyes – you know that classic look babies have: you can't avert your gaze and you end up unsettled unless you smile back – the woman launches into a long speech. She tells me there'll be two big brothers for me at home, eight and ten years old, Friedrich and Rudolf, as well as two sisters, six and four years old, Katharina and Cora, who can't wait to see me and to look after me. They've already been in training with their dolls so they can change and dress me, and they've learned lullabies for the evening. I'll be sharing the boys' bedroom. I'll be able to have fun in the big garden where the dog, named Rex by the children, won't be allowed until I can walk. But later on I'll be able to play ball with him there. She carries on with a wealth of information about my future life ... which sounds *deadly boring!*

My ears are ringing, the woman's voice fades into an indistinct droning and I can no longer bear to listen. She lifts me up and my eyes are drawn to her mouth: she is wearing a lurid red-orange lipstick. I touch it. It feels sticky and I let my finger slide onto her cheek and draw some red marks there. She pretends to find my clumsy gestures amusing, while Josefa, with a strained saintly smile, hands her a handkerchief to wipe away the unsightly marks.

"They're so funny at this age, aren't they? I wonder what on earth goes on in their little heads!"

I'm already bored by the lipstick, so I try to find something else interesting about this woman's face. Nothing ... I have to turn away while she tries to kiss me. (Yuk! That's the last thing I need.) I'd rather be in the arms of her husband and listen to him, not her. Is he high up in the ranks of the *Waffen-SS*? Does he ever get to cross paths with our Führer? Does he get to hang out with him? Is he one of his advisors? Once our Führer has invaded the countries he set out to conquer, will this officer be sent to France, for example, with his whole family? He remains silent and only glances at me distractedly when his wife latches on to him, like he'd do in a shop if she were asking his advice about a new dress. I'll just have to find the answers to my queries myself. If I count the stars embroidered on his beautiful black uniform, I'll work out his rank. And it'll give me something to do...

So, if I'm not mistaken, if I've counted properly – which is not easy, given that this wretched woman hasn't stopped jiggling me around as she's continued to spout twaddle – he has three stars and two stripes, which means he's either *Obersturmführer* or *Haupsturmführer.* I'm not sure which. Unless he's *Obersturmbannführer*? No, that's rubbish, I'm getting confused. And I thought I knew by heart the lists of decorations and their corresponding ranks... All of a sudden I've drawn a blank. Oh well, I mustn't panic. It's just the incessant gabbling of this woman that's messing with my concentration. I'll do some quick revision and recite the list from the beginning to the middle, as if it were the first verse of a nursery rhyme. If I don't have to stop, I'll keep going with the second half. Here we go:

1 stripe for the *Sturmmann*, private.
2 stripes for the *Rottenführer*, lance corporal.
1 star for the *Unterscharführer*, corporal.
1 star and 1 stripe for the *Scharführer*, sergeant.
2 stars for the *Oberscharführer*, staff sergeant.
2 stars and 1 stripe for the *Hauptscharführer*, warrant officer.
3 stars for the *Untersturmführer*, second lieutenant.
3 stars and 1 stripe for the *Obersturmführer*, lieutenant.
3 stars and 2 stripes for the *Haupsturmführer*, captain.

Hurray! I made it to the middle of the list without stopping or making a mistake. Now for the rest. 4 stars for the…

What happened? The couple disappeared. I'm back strapped in my chair. Frau Josefa and a nurse are standing in front of me, looking at me anxiously.

"I really don't know what's wrong with him, Frau Josefa," says the nurse softly. "He does look strange right now. But this morning, I promise you, he was absolutely fine. Perhaps he's coming down with something?"

"And I thought he would be the first to go, that they'd be fighting over him." Josefa is clearly disappointed. Without another word, she heads off to join the couple at the other end of the room.

I think I know what happened. I was concentrating so hard on my mental recitation that it must have made me look like a real idiot. I won't be leaving the Home today. Great!

I hope Josefa isn't too cross and that this little incident doesn't reach Doctor Ebner's attention. My dumb look mustn't get me taken for a "rabbit". I took a big risk. But isn't that exactly the type of intrepid youth our Führer wants?

Anyway, I'm happy because I avoided getting adopted today, which is a win in terms of my secret wish. I might be a baby, but I'm certainly not made for family life.

I've got to be as shrewd as possible about finding a way to spend the next six years.

8.

Overcome my fear. Resist pain. Tolerate pain. Have the strength of a young wild animal. Just like our Führer wants.

I have to get my imagination working, to persuade myself that all this is ... whatever ... a simulation exercise, practical training to be one of the *Pimpfe* in the Hitler Youth.

Except that the reality is I'm not a *Pimpf* yet, only a baby!

It's dark. It's cold. I'm so frightened.

It's amazing to think that, during the recent weeks, using and abusing my *Draufgängertum*, I managed to rebuff the adoptive parents who were interested in me. I played a trick and it worked. I'm the only nine-month-old baby still at the Home.

And now I'm being punished.

I've just been "adopted" (a code word that doesn't exist, I've invented it for the occasion and you'll soon understand its hidden meaning).

It was last night, and everything happened so fast.

A strange noise in the corridor, a creaking, then silence. I prick up my ears. There it is again, for longer. Someone's there. Someone trying to walk as quietly as possible, someone who seems frightened by the noise of their own footsteps, because each step is followed by a sort of gasp. A hoarse panting, like an animal. A dog that escaped into the Home, away from one of the guards on duty outside? Impossible. Even if a dog pants like that, it gets around on four legs, not two. Is Josefa coming for another "rabbit"? No, Josefa walks with a firm, rhythmic step, even when she's trying to be quiet. And Josefa only chooses her "rabbits" from the newborns in the nursery. So who is it?

There it goes again, faster this time. Is the prowler barefoot? Then I can't hear it any more and I wonder if it's a ghost, or perhaps I'm just dreaming. Suddenly the blanket I'm lying on is folded over the top of me and I'm lifted up and carried away. I have no idea if I'm in the arms of a human creature – alive or a ghost – or in the claws of a bird of prey. I can't see a thing. The blanket envelops me in total darkness. From the bumping I can tell that the creature is running and then tearing downstairs at high speed. A gust of icy air rushes inside the blanket: we're outside. But not for long. More running, then I'm being pushed through a hole. It feels like an animal's burrow. The blanket unfolds but I still can't see anything. It smells like dirt, damp, mould. Dust gets into my mouth and I start to cough. I should be shouting instead – and why didn't I do precisely that in the dormitory? But before I can start the slightest bit of howling, I'm bundled up once more and we hurtle downwards again. A creature's left arm holds me tightly against its body. And that's when I realize it's not a ghost: ghosts can pass through walls and obstacles; and birds fly, they don't thrust deep into the earth. That's also when the creature's right arm – the free one – grabs on to a sort of ladder and we step down rung by rung. This descent into the underworld seems to last a lifetime.

The getaway finally stops. The creature drops to the ground and I hear irregular, fitful wheezing, as if it's about to drop dead. I hope it does. A few minutes go by like this, in stillness and silence. I'm in such a state of shock that I still can't find the strength to scream. Something tells me that it wouldn't be worth it anyway, as no one would hear me. The creature revives and places me on the ground, gently this time, even taking special care to cradle my head so I don't bang it on the ground. The creature steps away and I hear a match being lit. The flickering flame of a candle emits a feeble light.

I am in a cellar.

The creature returns quickly and holds me tight. I finally see its face. Thin, gaunt, pallid, its skin so stretched over the cheekbones that the skull is visible. A long scar runs down one cheek; it must be a recent wound, still red and swollen. A head of unevenly shaved hair, bits of scalp visible, tufts of stiff, coarse hairs growing back here and there. Huge eyes, staring, wide-open, almost bulging, like they're eating away at the face, to devour it. Blue eyes. Light blue. For an instant this reassures me. But these blue eyes have a desperate expression, filled with a wild, animal fear. Or are they a mirror of my own fear?

The creature is a woman.

She stinks.

Sweat and urine, mixed with other odours I don't yet recognize, and which make me want to retch.

I'm gagging.

I finally understand what's happened. This woman ... is one of the prisoners allowed into the Home to clean, in preparation for the visits by the prospective adoptive families. She managed, God knows how, to escape "relocation" and hide in the cellar. And she kidnapped me. (Damn Josefa and her obsession with housecleaning. She should have asked the mothers to scrub the floors, or got stuck into it herself. That way I wouldn't have ended up here!)

Me, a baby of the master race, in the arms of one of the dregs of humanity.

Who exactly is this woman? A Jew? A Gypsy? She's got blue eyes… Unless there are blue-eyed Jews and Gypsies? Can nature really give rise to such aberrations?

What's going to happen? Has she kidnapped me for food? Is she going to gobble me down raw? That must be my destiny. Jews and Gypsies are abject beings with filthy customs. Vile and lazy, they prey on children. They tempt them with sweets that are in fact poisonous. I've seen drawings of them in the newspapers Josefa reads.

I'll be brave. I'm a Baby *Pimpf*. I'll know how to die with dignity.

She didn't eat me. Quite the opposite: she tried to feed me.

She slept for a while. (She must have been holed up in this cellar for a few days: dashing up to the dormitory to kidnap me, combined with the terror she must have felt, has exhausted her.) Her head and chest are propped against the wall, while the rest of her body is spread-eagled on the ground. Her head is leaning to the side, her neck completely crooked, like a disjointed puppet. I've ended up perched precariously on her thighs. From time to time in her sleep she is overcome by a shudder, a violent convulsion that makes her flinch and contract her muscles – which makes me slide further down her thighs towards her knees. Then she relaxes again and sinks into unconsciousness. At every shudder, I progress a few centimetres. Soon I hope I'll reach the ground. Then I'll have to muster all my *Draufgängertum* and try to crawl along using my arms until I can find a way out. (I've never tried to crawl or walk on all fours before; it's time to launch into this new stage in my development.)

But I don't get a chance to try anything. She wakes up with a start, grabs me with surprising intensity, and holds me to her, hard. As if she's suddenly seen someone who wants to grab me away from her. Sadly there is no one. Then she unbuttons the jacket of her uniform (dirty, stinking rags) and squeezes me against her breasts. Her skin is clammy with sweat, even though it's cold in the cellar. She must have a fever from some sort of illness. Jews and Gypsies spread so many diseases; she's probably got scabies, or leprosy, or typhoid fever, or worse. I can feel her ribs jutting out under her skin. Her chest, like her face, is nothing but an assortment of bones. I realize that she wants me to latch on to her breast.

At first I'm disgusted. How revolting.

Then some sort of instinct awakens in me. Something deep in my brain is set off, a kind of signal. I remember the time when the fat wet nurse tried her best to get me to take her milk. But those memories are so distant. For a few weeks now, they've been giving me a bottle in the morning and at night, and at lunchtime I eat an excellent puree of carrots or spinach, cooked with produce from the Home's vegetable garden. So sticking a nipple in my mouth is a backward step: that sort of regression is beneath me. But the fact is, I'm hungry. I have no idea if it's still dark outside, or if the sun's come up. How would I have a clue in this pitch-black cellar? Especially as I still sometimes get day and night confused:

I've been known to wake a nurse up in the middle of the night so she can feed me. Right now, my aching stomach demands that I consume something. So, here goes, I'll try her breast… Except that she doesn't have any. Worse still, there are bones instead, bones all over, nothing but bones. What am I supposed to do, huh?

After a bit, she helps me; she pinches her skin hard and a bit of a nipple emerges that I can get between my lips. But no matter how hard I suck, pull, inhale and bite, nothing comes out. I must have hurt her – I'm getting my first tooth up top – because she cries out and pushes me away roughly. I really think she is going to hit me. Or throw me against the wall. But she pulls me gently back and starts laughing and crying at the same time, rocking from side to side, cuddling me to stop my tears. (Here we go: by now I'm so stressed that I yell my head off.)

She won't stop repeating the same word in her language. Her barbarian language. (Yiddish? Romany?) It starts with "Ma". Then there's a strange sound like she's clicking her tongue against her palate. It sounds like "tchetch" or "xetch". "Ma-tche-tche … Ma-xetch," she repeats, her lips grimacing in a weird smile.

I can't quite explain what happens next. The first syllable of this barbarian word, "Max", reverberates in my mind, over and over, producing a sort of echo that rekindles an even more distant memory than that of the fat wet nurse. I recall that before her there was another woman who held me in her arms. Who often rocked me, in exactly the same way the prisoner is doing now. And that woman called me "Max".

I stop yelling right then.

With all that thinking, my brain whirring, I feel wiped

out. No more *Draufgängertum.* I'm so exhausted I fall asleep.

We wake up at the same time. What time? No idea. An hour later, a day, two days, perhaps more. It's hunger that rouses us. I've got colic, cramps. And her belly is making all sorts of noises, like water trickling in a cave. I'm terrified again at the thought that she has her meal ready-made: she'll start eating me now. But she still doesn't. She takes a bottle of milk out of her jacket pocket. (She must have stolen it from the dormitory before kidnapping me.) She looks at it greedily for a second, then at me. Such a nasty, predatory expression! I can tell from her eyes what she's thinking: *Why should I give you this milk when I'm so hungry?* And right under my nose she starts drinking, like a glutton – what a nerve. But she only has three or four mouthfuls, no more, and then slides the teat into my mouth.

I drink and drink, *glug, glug, glug.*

It's so good. Cold, but good. And then it stops. She takes the bottle away even though there's at least a third left. I start yelling again straightaway. She cuddles me but, instead of calming me, it enrages me. Then, miraculously, she says two words in German. "For later!"

She doesn't want me to drink it all at once, or I won't have any left. I couldn't care less! I'm hungry now, NOW!

She rocks me again, chanting her "Max-whatever" word. I stop crying. This weird-sounding word is like magic. It calms me down... She starts talking, not in her barbarian language, but in German again. Perfect German, no trace of an accent.

She tells me the story of her life, beginning with the fact that she's German. (What a relief for me!) I relax and listen. One morning, some months ago, when she was pregnant, she and her husband were arrested by the Gestapo. They were charged with being "an insult to racial purity". (I counted my chickens before they hatched: this woman may be German, but she's among the people Hitler denounces. She has committed one of the worst crimes possible: she has slept with a Jew! How dreadful!) She says she doesn't know what happened to her husband, but she was taken to Dachau. When she arrived, she was beaten viciously by an SS soldier who kicked her and bashed her in the belly with a club. Her big baby belly. It made her go into labour on the spot. While she was on the ground in the snow, her face covered in blood, the SS guy screamed at her: "Go on, bitch! Get it out! Your Jewish bastard! So we can see what he looks like… Come on! Push! Push!" She howled. She sobbed. She pushed. And the baby emerged. There, in the bloodied snow. Then the SS guy shot the baby in the head.

The woman is sobbing, me too. But I don't know if it's because of the story or because I'm still hungry.

She squeezes me to her even tighter. Between hiccups, she says that she wanted to call her baby Maciej. A Polish name, because her husband was Polish.

Maciej. Maciej. She repeats the name. Over and over. She kisses me.

I'm not Maciej, I'm not your baby! My name is Konrad, or Max… I'm not sure which any more… My father is not Jewish! A German woman had intercourse with an SS officer to conceive me. The SS officer could be the one who killed your Maciej!

If only I could tell her. But I can't, so she keeps going.

"Maciej. Maciej…" Kisses all over me, on my forehead, mouth, hands and feet. At first it annoys me, disgusts me, and then I remember that the woman from ages ago, the one who rocked me like this woman is doing, she used to kiss me, too. And the good thing is that her moist lips warm me up and shield me a bit from the freezing cold in the cellar.

And the "Maciej" litany helps me to go back to sleep.

When I wake up I'm soaking. I mean sopping wet. Completely filthy. Wee, poo, the lot. The bad poo, the stuff that nearly got me sent off in the delivery van. What makes things worse is that Magda (that's her name) didn't wake up at the same time as me. In fact she dozes off for longer and longer periods. She doesn't flinch in her sleep any more either. Her body, still contorted in abnormal positions, stays as still as a corpse. She does manage to become aware of the disaster when she opens one eye… She thought of stealing milk, but not a change of nappies. She looks panic-stricken for a second – not at the stench, which is no worse than her own – but because she sees that my bum is as red as a monkey's. It's so itchy, I'm wriggling around like a worm. Even the blanket is drenched. So Magda takes her clothes off. Everything. Her trousers are already in shreds so she has no trouble tearing them a bit more to make a nappy that she slides between my legs and ties on the sides. Then she wraps me in her jacket.

Now I'm wearing a prisoner's uniform! Things are going from bad to worse. But, after all, no one can see me. No one can hear me either or they'd have come to find me. Has anyone noticed I'm gone? Apparently not. The Home has turned into a factory. One empty bed, so what? At least three others have been filled in the same time.

Even if I'm wearing a shameful outfit, at least I'm dry. Even if the arms around me are those of a woman who has had sex with a Jew, at least they're keeping me warm;

they're a comfort just like her voice. So soft, so gentle, so close … I can't hear Hitler's booming voice here in the cellar. No radio, obviously, and I feel, little by little, his voice getting fainter, a murmur in the distance, far off in my mind, heading towards the section of forgotten things.

Magda feeds me the rest of the bottle of milk. And after that, over the course of hours, days, nights, I don't know any more, she lets me nibble on a crust of stale bread – left over from one of her earlier pilferings, before she kidnapped me. She puts the crumbs in her mouth to moisten them, then into my mouth so I can swallow them without choking.

The crust of bread is soon finished. And an apple core, a few scraps of meat on some old chicken bones, and some potato and beetroot peelings.

Then there's nothing more. *Nothing.*

Hunger. Cold. Lethargy.

Magda starts talking again. She tells me about Maciej. How she loved him when he was in her belly. How she would have liked to see him grow up.

Maciej. Maciej. Maciej…

When I shut my eyes for too long, Magda shakes me gently until I open them again. She's frightened I'll die in my sleep. And I'm the same about her. I manage to squirm a bit and get my hand or foot into her face and wake her up. That's what the last of my *Draufgängertum* is good for. I know I'm bound to her. If she dies, that's the end of me, too.

And that's when the penny drops again. Because I'm sleeping in Magda's arms, and not lying on my stomach as instructed by that other fellow, the one who's above us somewhere, the *Herr Doktor* with the eyes like beads of ice – what's his name again? – I think my skull has changed shape. As it's no longer dolichocephalic, no longer as long and oval-shaped, distant memories have resurfaced. All of a sudden I remember "the magic cord" that worked with the woman who breastfed me so long ago. That woman was ... my mother... Yes, it was *Mutti*. "Mummy". The word I erased from my vocabulary.

Mutti. Magda says it to me every time she manages to wake up. *Mama ist da. Habe keine angst*. Mummy is here. Don't be scared.

But the magic cord doesn't work for long. After the hours, days, nights spent in the cellar, it stops functioning. When I pull on it, the response takes longer and longer to arrive. Until there's no response at all. Until I no longer have the strength to pull. This time it really is the end of my *Draufgängertum*.

I shut my eyes and let myself go. After hours, days, nights in this cellar, those arms close over me. Cold. Stiff as hooks.

9.

Apparently they had to break the bones in the hands and arms of the corpse holding me captive.

I spent five days in the cellar, two of them with the corpse. They thought I was dead when they found me. I no longer resembled a baby of the master race. Filthy, drenched in my own urine, poo and sick, emaciated, I was scarcely bigger than the rats, which had started to nibble on my meagre flesh.

As I had suspected, my disappearance went completely unnoticed. When she found my bed empty in the early hours of the morning, the nurse on duty didn't tell a soul. Unable to provide an explanation – how could a sleeping baby vanish like that? – and dreading a severe punishment if her unpardonable negligence were discovered, she bribed a secretary to fake an adoption dossier in my name. When Josefa returned from a tour of inspection of another Home, she learned that Konrad the daredevil, Konrad whom no one until then had wanted to adopt, had finally found a family.

She swallowed the story hook, line and sinker, thrilled by this wonderful news.

The gardener raised the alarm. One morning the chap noticed that one of the flowerbeds he was so proud of had been vandalized. At first they thought it was an act of sabotage committed by one of the prisoners on gardening duty. When they couldn't find the guilty party among them, they "relocated" the whole lot. The gardener started to repair the damage, digging over the mound of earth to plant new seeds, and discovered the opening to a dried-up well. Deep in the hole, on the wall, were some stairs. He reported his discovery immediately and they called in some back-up. Down in the well, they followed a long section of an underground passage leading to the entrance of a cellar that had not been marked on the plans of the building when it was an asylum.

A scandal erupted.

Sound the alarm. Action stations. An inquiry. Reprisals. Immediate "relocation" of the nurse and her accomplice. The architect who had renovated the Home was deported to a camp. As for the prisoner's corpse, it was hung on display at the tradesmen's entrance for several days, as an example, until the crows finished it off.

Then Doctor Ebner had to decide my fate. What should he do with the carcass I'd turned into? The delivery van? Given the pitiful state I'd been reduced to, I didn't even come close to a decent "rabbit". I'd die in transit before I got to a "scientific institute".

That left the incinerator.

What a waste! Reduced to ashes. Ebner couldn't bring himself to let that happen to the child he had personally brought into the world, the firstborn in the *Lebensborn* programme, who had had the honour of being baptised by the Führer himself. It would have been sacrilege. He decided to keep me in his laboratory as a study specimen for his own research. Due to the prolonged starvation I'd suffered, I had severe dehydration. I'd lost fifteen per cent of my body weight, so my blood pressure might drop at any moment and bring on "hypovolemic shock" (a medical term meaning that'd be the end of me).

Doctor Ebner was curious. As a young representative of the Aryan race, how exactly would I resist such an imminent prospect of death? How long could I endure such agony? The answers to these questions would provide precious data for the future of science. The *Herr Doktor* rallied himself and – in the record book that had been set up at my birth – he documented a meticulous account of my ordeal.

My eyes were sunken in their sockets; my skin was cold and mottled; I had "glossitis", another medical term, meaning my tongue was swollen, parched, red and covered in a yellow coating. I was tormented by a terrible, unquenchable thirst. When Doctor Ebner pinched the skin on my abdomen, it stayed shrivelled. To top it all off, I could no longer pee.

Doctor Ebner carried out emergency rehydration: an intravenous saline solution. It might have been good medical treatment, but it did nothing to stop my raging thirst. All I wanted was something to suck – for my mouth, which felt like cardboard, and my poor little chapped lips, which felt like sandpaper. I would have drunk anything. But no matter how much I screamed no one got the message.

I was also suffering from tachycardia and recurring episodes of altered consciousness, accompanied by delirium. What horrific, unremitting visions I had! First there was the vision of the breast I was so desperate for: it appeared as in a hallucination, full of the promise of milk I craved. I was overjoyed. But no sooner had I latched on to it than it began to swell up, and swell up into something monstrous – suffocating me until it had crushed me like a fly under a boot.

Then there were the times I could see myself inside my mother's belly, peaceful in my warm, watery sack, when all of a sudden there was a terrible jolting that became more and more violent and the sack tore open. No more shelter, no more protection. It was like a cataclysm, as if giants were stomping on the belly while I was inside it. I was pushed forward. Pushed. *Pushed.* I heard yelling, cursing: *Bastard! Jew!* I was so scared I tried to go backwards, but it was impossible. I could just see some light, white light, blinding, cold light, when … bang! A gunshot. And my skull exploded.

To compound my torment, Doctor Ebner needed to take blood samples every four hours and urine samples every six hours for his tests. He weighed me eight times a day and checked my temperature. He listened to my lungs, took X-rays to measure the size of my liver. He measured the perimeter of my skull and checked for signs of fitting.

My martyrdom lasted three days and three nights.

Until this morning, when my fever broke, my skin returned to normal, as well as my tongue. I had started to put on weight.

Ebner, who hadn't left my bedside, was studying me even more intently, filling in his notes, charts, statistics. I was in remission. Now they had to see if I could take being rehydrated orally. I drank from a bottle. Finally, water – lots of water. Then, bit by bit, some milk. I began to pee, to poo. Tiny little turds at first, like goat's poo, then nice big, firm ones.

Twenty-four hours passed. Forty-eight. My temperature remained stable. My weight continued to increase. Ebner listened, pinched, palpated. He kept me under observation: no more skin-fold calliper, no more diarrhoea, no more vomiting.

It wasn't remission; it was recovery, total recovery. A real miracle. No, it wasn't a miracle: the exultant Ebner had before him, in the shape of my little convalescing body, the tangible proof that the Aryan race could resist sicknesses that would destroy lesser races.

I was indeed a true member of the master race.

After recovery came convalescence, and re-education, in the literal sense of the word. This was left up to Josefa, who felt responsible for my misfortunes. Even though she wasn't one of the vast numbers of staff "relocated" after I was found half-dead, her sense of duty had nonetheless driven her to admit her share of guilt and to offer up her resignation. How had she let herself be duped by one of her underlings? It was unforgivable.

Her resignation was rejected and Josefa found a way of redeeming herself when Doctor Ebner, after reviving me, committed me to her care. She made it her business to return me to my former glory, which I had well and truly lost.

I didn't have an ounce of *Draufgängertum* left in me. Weeks passed. On the 20th of April 1937 I turned one, but I couldn't stand up, even with support. No coherent sound came out of my mouth. I refused to eat solid food of any kind. All I wanted was milk, only milk. What's more, only from the breast. I could sleep only if I was held, rocked for a long time, sweet nothings whispered in my ear. So many bad habits I had to get rid of … I gave no response at the sound of my name, Konrad – not even a tilt of my head. I was becoming an imbecile, autistic perhaps. Incapable of any communication, all I did was scream. There was nothing anyone could do. Josefa's patience was wearing thin: even a tour of the living room – after the mothers had left, so I didn't upset them – to peruse all the portraits of the Reich officials did not dispel my bad mood. On the contrary, it only deteriorated.

Josefa witnessed even worse: I was beside myself if I caught sight of a brown or black uniform. One day I was guilty of an act that ended up jeopardizing the poor woman's morale: she was leaning over to change me, when I grabbed the Party badge pinned on the lapel of her smock, tore the material, and hurled the badge onto the floor.

What the hell did that bitch of a dissident whore do to me, Josefa wondered, desperately upset by my behaviour. Not only did the creature starve me, but she polluted, corrupted my mind. Turned me into a half-breed Jew pig! It had only taken her a few days to destroy several months' work – several years', if you took into account the time preceding my conception.

The child of the future must be lean and supple, said the Führer. I was about to be fat and flabby from drinking only milk and turning my nose up at vegetables. *As tough as leather.* I was weak and floppy, from always lying on my back or sitting on my bottom, never doing any exercise standing up, let alone walking. *As hard as Krupp steel.* All I did was cry.

Josefa decided to use some strong-arm tactics.

She put me in quarantine. My body wasn't the problem; it was my brain, which had been infected in the worst possible way. To prevent me from contaminating the others,

I had to stay alone all day, locked in a room at the back of the building, so my crying wasn't heard.

Josefa visited several times a day, to wash me, dress me and feed me. When I refused to let her dress me, she just said, "Fine," and left me naked. When I wouldn't eat my mashed vegetables: "Fine." She put the plate on the floor and left. Hunger would knock some sense into me in the end. At night, nothing. Even when I yelled my head off – my arms outstretched so they'd open the door, so they'd come and hold me, cuddle me, comfort me – no one ever came. The door stayed shut and I finally fell asleep on the ground, exhausted. I screamed even louder when I woke up.

Josefa worked out a way of drowning out my screams: she left a portable radio in my room, the volume turned up high and tuned to a station that broadcast Hitler's speeches over and over. I couldn't compete for long with the vocal powers of our Führer. In the end I had to stop to listen and, eventually, enjoy the sound of him.

My brain slowly got back into gear.

I returned to my former self. One morning, Josefa was nearly in tears of joy when she found me up and dressed. Well, almost. I'd tried to pull on my trousers, but got tangled up, with two feet in one trouser leg; I hadn't managed to find the neck of my jumper and had my head stuck in the sleeve. But I wasn't holding on to anything: I was standing up tall, back on my own two feet.

My little right arm was extended in front of me, straight as a bow.

And I finally said my first words: *Sieg Heil!*

10.

Now I'm four years old.

Everyone says I'm very good-looking. I'm willing to believe it because people always turn around to stare at me when they pass by. I'm especially attractive to the mothers.

My racial assessment is looking good, even if it's not definitive yet. A lot of physical characteristics are not yet evident in a child as young as I am, but I'm hopeful.

I'm tall for my age, slim, skinny even, without it being an issue. Quite the reverse. (I'm not deficient in anything. We've got everything we want at the Home: semolina, rice, oatmeal, cocoa, fresh fruit, vegetables, even though the war began a year ago and they're handing out ration cards everywhere else.) Being thin means my little muscles – in my arms, thighs, calves – are well defined and guarantee an athletic body. My hair is not just blond, it's almost white, and contrasts strikingly with the blue of my eyes – two turquoise wells breaching a snowy expanse. When my gaze lands on a mother it's fatal: her heart melts. I was dolichocephalic at birth and I still am now. My complexion is pale, ever so slightly pink, as if someone has delicately powdered my cheeks. My ears don't stick out – thank God for that! – they're small, nicely shaped, like shells. I have a narrow face, delicate lips and a high forehead. My nose is thin and long, creating an uninterrupted line down to my chin.

I look like an angel. An Aryan angel.

You wouldn't guess from looking at me that I almost died. I don't remember a single thing about the horrific ordeal I endured, but Josefa never stops telling me, along with the new mothers in the Home, all the ghastly details about this shocking time. I was captured by a bitch of a dissident who tortured and starved me. She tried to kill me, but, despite my extreme youth, I was stronger than she was, and it was I who survived! I was the incarnation of one of our Führer's most important theories: *It is not by the principles of humanity that man lives or is able to preserve himself above the animal world, but solely by means of the most brutal struggle.*

Josefa maintains that I've been avenged, because a very important event occurred on the night of the 9th to the 10th of November, 1938 – that is, a year and a half after I was kidnapped by that bitch. That night became known as *Kristallnacht*, "Crystal Night". Throughout the whole country, several hundred synagogues were destroyed, as well as thousands of Jewish businesses. A hundred-odd Jews were killed, hundreds of others committed suicide or died from their wounds, and almost thirty thousand more were deported to concentration camps. So now, Josefa told me, no German woman would be tempted to have sex with a Jew. She assured me that henceforth I would be safe, that I'd never be exposed to danger like that again.

In any case, because this exploit of my young life has been told over and over, and spread around, it's become legendary in the Home. I've become some sort of mascot.

So they decided that I shouldn't be adopted. It's a bit like being in a shop window: I'm the perfect sample product, a piece of jewellery you can look at but not touch, and especially not wear. I'm the model that pregnant women and new mothers can study: here's the future of the foetus in your belly, or here's how your baby will turn out. It's good for morale, anyway, especially if they're having doubts. Same for the adoptive mothers visiting the Home. They swoon when they see my little angel's face and then burst into tears when Josefa tells them my story, how I overcame the trauma inflicted on me. They instantly want to take me in their arms, cuddle me, kiss me, but… No touching! Forbidden! And if they're sorry they can't take me away with them, they're more than happy to choose another baby, reassured that it will look like me in the future.

Good. That's great. I'm proud.

But the downside is that I'm bored. Having women worship me, fuss over me, cluck over me, none of that is ideal for my *Draufgängertum*. I haven't forgotten my secret wish. I'd like to have friends endowed with my toughness. What can I do, stuck here among all these wailing babies who only think about feeding and sleeping? The Home is like a cocoon that's become too cramped. I'm stifled. I need air. I need to move. *Get out, see the world!*

Especially because, outside the Home, all hell has broken loose. After the annexing of the Sudetenland, Czechoslovakia and Austria, last year's invasion of Poland really cranked up the conflict: the English and the French have declared war. Our allies are the Russians, who helped us crush Poland. But, even without their help, our army is clearly superior: France is about to capitulate. We've already invaded Belgium, Denmark and Norway. We're on the rampage! As for the English, they've tried a bit of strategic bombing in response to our air raids over London, but nothing to worry about. I've heard that the Berliners, far from being traumatized by the bombs, are getting together and having fun in the areas supposedly damaged by the enemy.

As a consequence of all these annexations, the Home is right now completely topsy-turvy: we're expecting an exceptionally good delivery of women from Norway and Denmark. There's no need for them to go through the selection process – we already know that women from these countries fit the criteria of the Nordic race perfectly. So our SS officers are under orders to carry out a "soft occupation" in those places, which means they're not allowed to make arrests or engage in mass executions (like in Smolensk, for example, where thousands of Jews were executed with a bullet to the head). Instead, their duty is to seduce the Norwegian women, invite them to the movies, out to dinner, to a museum or a concert, and bingo! Intercourse, then delivery of the baby, here in Germany, whether they like it or not. There's no doubt that the babies born from these encounters will be *harmonisch*. They'll be a wonderful gift for the Führer and for the German nation. (Whether they're a willing or unwilling gift will depend; even though they're beautiful, are the Norwegian women intelligent enough to understand how vital their sacrifice is?) Tall, blond, dolichocephalic, these Norwegian babies will be endowed with everything a child of the future requires and will include very few "rabbits", I imagine. In fact, now that I think about it, I'm a tiny bit jealous. What if one of them deposes me?

God forbid that should happen.

While they decide about my future, I keep busy, running around, climbing, jumping, yelling. Whenever I can, I charge into the nursery and create havoc. I pretend the cradles lined up are enemy soldiers I'm fighting. I bombard them with nappies and bottles, whatever I can lay my little hands on. If I'm told to leave my buddies alone, I'm stuck with my toys, which are pretty amazing – the war requisitioning means we've got a continuous supply. With my toy planes and tin soldiers, I pretend I'm a Luftwaffe pilot. *Nneeaooww! Nneeaooww!* I trace parabolas in the sky and then, *boom!* I drop a bomb on London! I also get to play with a magnificent toy castle and pretend I'm a medieval lord ruling over his subjects. But my favourite toy is a little wooden hammer. In my hands it transforms into Thor's hammer, the most powerful weapon of the ancient Nordic race, my ancestors. Either I'm one of the two dwarves who made this fabulous weapon, or, better still, I'm Thor himself, god of Thunder and Lightning. I'm wearing metal gauntlets when I launch my hammer at my enemy and, a few seconds later, the hammer is back in my hands (it's magic). I'm doing battle with the giants of the frozen north and I'm invincible!

They say there's a strong chance this myth might become reality, that Thor's hammer will be reconstituted. This is one of the tasks *Reichsführer* Himmler has set himself. He has sent research teams to Finland to analyse ancient sorcerer songs that hold the secret of the hammer's creation.

At other times, my wooden toy turns into the sacred

sword of King Arthur, who was a child king like me, a child warrior. I leap onto my steed and off I go to find the Holy Grail. And I find the goblet of immortality and I drink it and become immortal!

Woops! My Thor's-hammer-King-Arthur's-sacred-sword just landed on Josefa's head. She'll get angry and send me to my room. I know I annoy her, careering around the Home like this. Even though I'm the mascot, she'd probably like to belt me one. Just let her try, hey!

But Josefa doesn't lose her temper; on the contrary, she gives me a huge smile, the one she saves for special occasions and official visits. She tells me to gather up my toys so she can pack them in a suitcase with my other belongings. Because ... because...

"Guess what?" she asks me, her grimacing smile getting wider.

Because ... I'M LEAVING TOMORROW. I'm going away, far away.

"On a mission," she adds in a whisper.

Where on earth? Germany, or a foreign country? Who am I going with? With her? How am I getting there? By plane? In a Mercedes? What's my mission? To find Thor's hammer? The Holy Grail? I can't ask her all these questions properly and it's making me furious. I'm hopping up and down with impatience. But there's no point. The conspiratorial look on her face as she takes my hand, the way she's whispering and casting furtive glances to make sure no one has heard her talking about suitcases and trips, all makes me realize that my mission is a matter of secrecy.

Top secret!

Who cares if I'm not sure what's expected of me. I like

surprises. The main thing is that I'm finally leaving the Home to begin a new stage in my life.

So I'll catch up with you soon, in some new place, to tell you what happens next.

part two

11.

I travelled in a beautiful big black Mercedes, escorted by motorbikes – they cleared the road ahead so we could drive as fast as possible. The trip took two days, including a night spent in the home of a top Nazi Party dignitary, a friend of Doctor Ebner.

Munich, Ingolstadt, Nuremberg, Bayreuth, Leipzig, Dessau, Potsdam. Just imagine my amazement! I'd never ventured further than the row of poplars separating the Home from the Steinhöring countryside, and now I was passing through the most important cities in Germany. At last I was discovering my homeland. I was dizzy with excitement and kept my eyes wide open to take in the passing landscape. I would have liked to stop and walk around these cities, but I could tell there was no time for that in our schedule. This was a long way from being a tourist trip. Only a few toilet stops, that's all. (I had to hold on and not wet my pants, which was not always easy.) Anyway, I lost the urge to go for a wander, because the further east we headed, the more inhospitable the countryside became.

After we crossed the Polish border, there was nothing but devastation: ruins of bombed houses; smoke from fires; wounded bodies and corpses in the fields or on the roads; convoys crawling along, flanked by our soldiers. Every now and then, even if we sped past, I caught a glimpse of a haggard, ashen face, deformed by fear.

The Poles. Prisoners.

I was travelling with adults, important ones. I was quiet, well behaved: I sat up straight, made sure I did the raised-arm salute to the various important people who joined our group along the way, and I stopped myself from pestering with questions, even though I was dying of curiosity.

I didn't know anyone, apart from Doctor Ebner and Herr Sollmann, who had often visited the Home in his capacity as director of the *Lebensborn* programme. Josefa wasn't on board, which suited me just fine. I needed a change and it wouldn't have been much fun having that old bag on my back again. Josefa belonged to another time, and from now on I had to forget about her. When I was leaving, she cuddled me and even wiped away a tear. Hypocrite! The truth is, she was more than happy to get rid of me. The tear was probably for Doctor Ebner. She's got a crush on him. I made a quick escape from her embrace.

So long! Thanks for everything! See you around maybe!

Herr Tesch, a lawyer, was sitting next to Ebner and Sollmann. In Berlin, a second car, with four women, joined us. For the rest of the trip the men and women swapped cars, taking it in turns to talk with Doctor Ebner and Herr Sollmann. When I wasn't sleeping, I opened my little ears and listened – they were discussing extremely important matters.

In fact, they never stopped working: the Mercedes was an office and a meeting room. They pored over files, letters and pamphlets put together by *Reichsführer* Himmler. They wrote reports and provisional budgets concerning trains and convoys that had to head to such-and-such a town – Polish names, too complicated for me to memorize.

The woman in charge was Frau Inge Viermetz, first deputy to Herr Sollmann. Her job was to represent the "physiognomists", the specialists who could recognize at a glance if a person belonged to the Nordic race or not. Next in line was Frau Müller, of the NSV (National Socialist People's Welfare), an organization that looks after "the wellbeing of the German people". And then there was Frau Kruger, from the *Jugendamt*: "The Youth Office". I could tell what organization the women belonged to because they all wore badges on their uniforms – when it comes to recognizing badges and insignia I'm unbeatable. As for the fourth woman, she said she was part of the *Braune Schwestern*.

The Brown Sisters. I didn't have a clue, except that *Schwester* was a code word meaning neither "sister" nor "nurse". The Sisters are the women chosen for their reproductive capacity, the ones who get pregnant with children of the future like me. But those Sisters are blonde, not brown. They're also young and pretty. Whereas the one in the car with me was old and ugly, if not repulsive.

I'll have to wait a while before I can add Brown Sisters to my list of code words.

The main thing I did learn – when I pretended to be asleep, so the adults could be unguarded in their conversation – was that I, Konrad von Kebnersol, four years of age, have been chosen for a special mission with the code name "Operation Something-or-Other". Unfortunately, in the hubbub of the conversation, I couldn't catch the last word. What could this secret mission possibly be? Even racking my super-hyper-intelligent brain, I had no idea. You can't imagine how desperately curious I was.

Poznan, Poland. The end of our trip.

We're staying in one of the few houses that remains standing, next to the town hall, which has been requisitioned by Doctor Ebner and his team. They work tirelessly there all day, along with other important people who were already here before us. They're all constantly coming and going.

The house is large and beautifully furnished. The old owners must have been very rich. We're staying on the ground floor because the upper levels were damaged in the bombings. I'm in the children's room, where everything is still in place. The boy left without taking anything: his clothes are hanging on the back of a chair, the wardrobe is full and his toys are all over the floor. I reckon he is either kaput, or he's been taken prisoner.

I don't like staying in this room; I prefer exploring the upper floors, among the rubble and debris of collapsed floorboards. It's fun jumping around, over a gaping hole, or crouching under a broken window, like a sniper taking aim before shooting – so many great ways of keeping up my *Draufgängertum*. It's far better than doing colouring in, as advised by Frau Lotte, the Brown Sister looking after me. She's not the same one who was in the Mercedes during the trip, but she's just as ugly and just as old. And stupid to boot. Colouring-in! What does she take me for? I can already read and write: Josefa taught me. I can even do arithmetic. For example: a bag holds thirty sweets, a Jew steals twenty-five, how many sweets are left in the bag? Five – too easy!

Standing straight as a ramrod in her uniform, Frau Lotte looks a bit like Josefa. And she's always keeping an eye on me, lecturing me. I have to show respect, but inside I'm raging. I've had enough of being surrounded by women, especially when I thought this trip to Poland would change all that. I'm not a baby any more; I'm a *Pimpfe* now! So I'd like to have some *Pimpf* comrades.

I feel better about the fact that Lotte is not here simply to feed me, help me get washed and dressed – I'm going to do that myself from now on – but also to get me ready for my mission, to serve our Führer, to serve our homeland. The first stage of this preparation consists in learning a few Polish words and pronouncing them with as slight an accent as possible. At first I had trouble – it's a barbaric language – but I practise every day and I'm getting much better. I already know two whole sentences that I can recite fluently and without a mistake, just like a real little Polack: *Dzień dobry! Mam na imię Konrad. A ty? Chcesz się ze mną pobawić?* Which means: Hello, my name is Konrad. And yours? Do you want to play with me?

Over the next few days I have to learn: I'm four years old. And you? Do you have brothers and sisters? Where do you live? Do you live alone with your mother? And lots of other stuff as well. I've got my work cut out. But I like it and, anyway ... I'm not stupid.

Even if Frau Lotte didn't want to tell me any more about my mission, everything leads me to believe that it's going to involve meeting children.

I can't wait.

Here we go! It's starting!

Today's the day. Frau Lotte has given me some warm

clothes and heavy boots, because it's cold outside. It's snowing and there's enough wind to mess up my nice blond mop of hair. Lotte has put on her uniform again: a long dark-brown dress like a potato sack, with a white ruff and white cuffs. Over the top she's wearing a sort of grey apron with a large pocket in which she has stuffed a whole jumble of sweets, blocks of chocolate and bread rolls. (I've finally understood what Brown Sister means: it's the uniform. The Sisters want to be seen as religious sisters, which is not at all the case. But why? Another mystery.)

We don't use a Mercedes but a black Volkswagen, a more discreet car, more suited to our secret mission. Another Sister accompanies us, wearing the same uniform and carrying a huge wicker basket full of sweets, as well as a satchel full of index cards. Our chauffeur is an *Unterscharführer*.

After leaving Poznan, we pass through a series of small villages, most of them reduced to ashes. Nothing much is left of the farms, the barns are piles of charred ruins, just like the churches. Everything stinks of burnt flesh.

As we come into a village that looks more or less intact, the *Schwester* tells the driver to slow down, open the roof and slow to a crawl. Seems silly to open the roof in this weather, but it's fun and I like the cold on my face, and feeling the snowflakes melt on my platinum hair. Snow on snow…

We drive slowly, quietly, until we get to a school, where we stop and park a few metres from the entrance, hidden behind a stand of trees. There's silence in the car; no one gets out, no one moves. What are we waiting for? What's the point of stopping if we can't get out and walk? The Sister tells me to stay still and be patient. Soon some women turn up and wait outside the doors of the school.

OK, I understand I have to keep still, but I can't keep

holding my breath like this. We can see the women chattering but they don't know we're here. It's like we're spies, in a strange game of hide and seek.

A bell starts ringing, the doors open, and kids swarm out. Some of them run towards their mothers and they leave together, others gather in groups of two or three to walk home, and a few head off alone in different directions. They're the ones the Sisters focus on, staring after them, squinting – which just exacerbates the wrinkles on their faces. They're like vultures, or jackals checking out their prey. They're only interested in the blond children. And there are a lot of those, which surprises me. How come? So blondness is not unique to Germans and Norwegians?

"That one should be fine," announces Frau Lotte.

"No, his eyes are too Slavic."

"What about that one?"

"The forehead is not high enough… There, the one on the right!"

Frau Lotte gets out of the car and follows the child pointed out by her colleague, who stays still. Holding me by the arm, she indicates that I should keep still, too. I obey, as usual. I'm programmed to obey, but I'm impatient! Something tells me that I'm about to get in on the action.

Lotte approaches the child, taps him on the shoulder so he turns around, then runs her hand through his hair in a seemingly affectionate gesture. But it's not for real. Well, they don't do that to me. I'm pretty sure she's casually trying to find out if the little Polish boy's skull is dolichocephalic. From where I am, I can tell by the movement of her lips and by the way she's waving her arms around that she's asking him questions. She's trying to get him talking, but it doesn't seem to be working. Stock-still on the footpath, the little boy can't grasp a single word. Not even when she shows him the treasures in her big pocket and urges him to take his pick. The kid looks both terrified and tempted. Terrified by the Sister – and I'm with him on that. Her brown uniform makes her look like a scarecrow, and her smile is a leering grimace. Tempted by the contents of the big pocket he's staring at with eyes so wide (and blue, another surprise for me) they might pop out of their sockets. I wonder which will prevail: fear or hunger?

Fear is stronger. Without taking his eyes off the goodies, the kid starts to retreat slowly, walking like a crab. In a minute he'll take off.

That's when I come on to the scene.

"Remember what we've taught you! Off you go!" says the Sister who had stayed with me in the car.

I get out straightaway and, cool as a cucumber, skip over to the Polish boy. I say hello to Frau Lotte as if I had just met her and, after asking permission (in Polish), I stick my hand in the pocket of her apron, pull out a block of chocolate and take a big bite out of it. Then, while the Polish boy is looking at me enviously, I offer it to him, along with a big smile. (And my smile is not a grimace.) He responds with an even bigger smile.

The little Polack literally leaps on the block of chocolate and gobbles it up in a few seconds. Then he starts stuffing himself with sweets and biscuits. So, easy-peasy, I just recite my Polish phrases: "Hello, what's your name? Where do you live? How old are you?" He doesn't stop gorging himself and replies without batting an eyelid: he's five, lives alone with his mother, his father is dead, he has two brothers, eight and six, and he gives me his address.

Frau Lotte writes it all down scrupulously on one of

her index cards and then says goodbye, tapping us both on the head. I smile to pretend I like it – it's an effort because I hate being touched, and I particularly hate this gesture, just like petting a dog. I keep walking a bit with the kid who now won't stop talking. He's a real chatterbox. I have no idea what he's jabbering on about – I only know the few sentences I learned by heart – but I nod. After a while, I pretend my house is in the opposite direction and sneak back to the car where the Sister is waiting for me.

"Do widzenia!" Goodbye!

I wish I could have stayed with him, he's much nicer than the Sister. Unfortunately, duty calls.

The rest of the morning was the same: hanging around the school to pick out more blond children with blue eyes, approaching them, talking to them. All afternoon we prowled around the playgrounds, the local parks – what was left of them after the bombings.

I was wiped out when we got back. Too tired to play sniper games or even to play with Thor's hammer. I could barely manage dinner I was so full after having to eat all that chocolate.

The next day we set out again. And the days after that. And the same thing for weeks.

Of course, in the meantime, I found out what was going on, by eavesdropping behind Herr Ebner's office door in the evenings during his meetings. Now I know what I'm here for, and I know what happens to the children I've had to chat up.

Here's the lowdown: at the end of the day, the Sisters gather the index cards with the children's addresses and give them to a special squad of SS soldiers who then go and get the children. Not just the ones I've chatted up, but also their brothers and sisters, if they're under six years old and if they fit the criteria: blond, blue eyes. I'm pretty sure they have to take them by force.

It's the famous "Operation Something-or-Other", in which I'm a linchpin: the kidnapping of the elite Polish children, in order to Germanize them, to make them as perfect as the German children, like me, produced in the *Lebensborn* programme.

It's *Reichsführer* Himmler's idea: *By whatever means, we must Germanize the racially viable foreign children,* he announced, *even if we have to steal them. We have to take in whatever we can of the enemy's better quality progeny.*

It's a huge operation. The German youth army will be doubled, tripled, quadrupled; its numbers will be unsurpassable. We can't just rely on the mothers in the Homes any more, even with the addition of the recently requisitioned Norwegian and Danish women, unless each of them is to give birth to between twenty and forty children, which is impossible. Whereas, by stealing children who already exist, the sky's the limit. Such a brilliant idea! A bit like a blood transfusion. New blood for Germany, while weakening the enemy.

The prospect of having that many *Pimpfe* buddies really motivates me, so I try even harder. Doctor Ebner is very happy with what I'm doing and always congratulates me, so much so that my status as a mascot is even more enhanced. Thanks to me, "Operation Buddies" (I invented my own code word) has really got going after a slow beginning. They've already adjusted the procedures. In the beginning, SS soldiers were the only ones taking the children, from wherever, snatching them out of the arms of their mothers, which caused a huge panic. Then they added the Brown Sisters, to sweet-talk the children. Things were OK for a while but sooner or later, same deal, the Brown Sisters were seen as birds of ill omen. As soon as a kid saw one, he ran off.

Whereas my angelic looks not only stop them in their tracks, but actually attract them: they all want to be my friend.

Everything went well for a few months, then rumours started. People connected me with the Brown Sisters. It's so annoying. (They're not just ugly; they're real bitches.) More importantly, it means I became less useful.

But Doctor Ebner, my protector, always finds a way.

So long, Brown Sisters. From now on I'll be working with Bibiana.

12.

Bibiana.

In Polish it means "Lady of the Lake", from the Arthurian legend. I like it and I'm sure it's somehow connected to my destiny: I'm like King Arthur, the child warrior who would one day drink from the Holy Grail and attain immortality. I couldn't wish for a better companion than the Lady of the Lake.

So much for my personal take on her; the reality is much less poetic.

Bibiana is an informer.

Frau Lotte didn't use that term when she introduced me on the first day; she talked nonsense, full of flattery and lies: "Konrad, darling, come over here! Put your hammer down, please. You'll end up taking someone's eye out with that thing… Say hello to Bibiana! She's just joined our team and you two are going to play a new game together. You'll pretend she's your mother, you'll go out with her, and make lots of new buddies… Just look at the costume I've brought for you. Pop it on now, and no grumbling. Oh, I know it's dirty and full of holes, but that's so you look just right! You're getting dressed up like a real little Polish boy!"

Blah-blah-blah. What a load of rubbish. I knew exactly what the deal was.

Even though she speaks German well, Bibiana is Polish. She comes from the Ravensbrück concentration camp. The Sisters must have waited a few days before introducing her to me, so she could put on a bit of weight and look less like a walking corpse. She's still really thin: her dress hangs off her like a sack; her arms are scarcely bigger than mine; and her chest is completely flat, as if her breasts have been sucked inside her body. Her head has been shaved to get rid of lice and now she's hiding her bald head under a scarf. But nature has been kind to her: she's tall, blonde, with eyes as blue as mine and – it's a bit weird – she definitely looks like me. That was her salvation. They offered her a deal: she could leave the camp on the condition that she came here, to Poznan, and pretended to be my mother, going from village to village, making friends with single women with blonde hair and blue eyes, and getting their addresses to pass on to the Brown Sisters.

Between betrayal and death, she chose betrayal. It's understandable. Even if it is cowardly. I'd never betray. But, there you go, informers are useful. There are a lot of them working at the town hall with *Herr Doktor* Ebner and Herr Tesch.

The thing I picked up from Frau Lotte's spiel was that my mission has now become dangerous: I, Konrad, the prototype-child-typical-of-the-pure-Aryan-race, the child-elect, soon to be five years old – so defenceless – I am now going to be spending my days with a prisoner. It's a bit like the episode Josefa described to me countless times: the dissident-whore-who-had-sex-with-a-Jew, who kidnapped me when I was only a tiny baby, who tortured me, starved me, and almost killed me.

Of course, this time it's different: precautions have been taken to guarantee my safety, a car driven by an SS soldier will follow us wherever we go, and Bibiana has been warned that at the slightest false move the soldier will shoot her in the head. But I guess the car will be following us at a distance, so as not to arouse suspicion, which will leave me at Bibiana's mercy. What if, on a whim, she feels guilty and decides no longer to betray her compatriots? What if, just before dying, she directs her hate at me and strangles me? Or pushes me into a ravine? Or drops me down a well? It would only take a minute or two, if that. And then, it's all over!

Raus, Kaput, Konrad! Died in the service of his country.

The prospect of danger doesn't frighten me. On the contrary, it excites me, intensifies my boundless *Draufgängertum*. My superiors' trust in me has gone up a notch.

I'm no longer a spy, I'm an *infiltrator*!

So I'm happy to play the game and wear the stinking rags Lotte hands me. I slip off my navy blue Bermuda shorts, my brown shirt with the armband, my tie and my cap, and I swap them for a baggy sweater full of holes, a crumpled pair of trousers that has to be held up by a piece of string around my waist. Not very attractive, but very amusing. And from now on, not much washing: a quick top and tail on my face and bum, that's it. It doesn't matter if I have filthy nails, yellow teeth and foul breath.

Off we go, Bibiana and I, out along the Polish country roads. But it's quite awkward: the problem is that we're wary of each other. Bibiana more than me. She's scared to death and it's as plain as the nose on your face: a tantrum from me means she heads straight back to camp.

"Bibiana was horrible today! She was really mean to me! She said I was a dirty rotten son of a Kraut's prostitute!"

Lotte won't budge until we get home and that's the sort of thing I could report to her.

Oh yeah, I can make up whatever the hell I like! That Bibiana didn't give me anything to eat, that she didn't get someone's address because the woman was a friend of hers. And whatever else... Lots of kids my age lie, right?

So Bibiana is on her best behaviour. She addresses me formally, lowers her eyes as soon as I look at her, always walks a short distance behind me, or else on the road, leaving me the footpath, as the Poles have to do if they see a German. When it's lunchtime, she watches me eat and doesn't dare touch the provisions in the basket Lotte provides; she eats my leftovers, a bit of chewed bread, mashed vegetables I've stuck my dirty hands in, stewed fruit I've spat out. In the end, it's obvious we aren't the real thing and, even after a few days, no one's taken the bait.

We get back empty-handed. Not a single address.

Things are not going well at all. The Sisters have faces as long as a wet weekend. Things don't look good for Bibiana or for me: she could get sent back to camp and I could be demoted. Back to colouring-in with Frau Lotte in the bombed-out house.

So, one morning Bibiana decides to take action. She gets straight to the point. "Konrad," she says, uttering my name for the first time, "no one will believe I'm your mother if you don't let me hold your hand."

I'm grateful to her for speaking frankly, for articulating the problem we're up against. I'll ignore her disrespect in speaking to me so intimately, but really ... hold hands? That's a bit much, isn't it? I'm not going to sully myself like that, am I? I stare at her with my big blue eyes that make such an impression on people, and this time she doesn't look away like she usually does. (Which is normal, really, as I've noticed that my eyes only disconcert those with dark eyes, whereas Bibiana's are extraordinarily bright. Not the slightest fleck of anything around the irises. They'd get top marks from Doctor Ebner.) She's got a little smile at the corners of her mouth as she waits for my answer. I give a sidelong glance at the car, which is on the road some distance off, on the edge of the field we're standing in. I wonder ... I weigh up the pros and cons. It's true: when I hung around the school gates with the Sisters, I saw how the children reached for their mother's hands as soon as they got out of school. Her suggestion was worth considering.

OK. All right.

It's all part of the risk factor in my infiltration mission. I slide my hand into Bibiana's and walk in step with her instead of jogging ahead. My heart hammers in my chest – I absolutely hate physical contact! I'm just not used to it. In the Home, no one ever bothered to hold my hand. Or else it was so long ago that I've forgotten ... I'm expecting my skin to burn, or get itchy, or exhibit some other symptom of a contagious disease.

It seems not. It's OK.

The feel of Bibiana's hand is actually not too horrible. Less horrible than Frau Lotte's: sometimes, if I'm slow to obey her, she grabs me by the arm with her claw-like hands. That's when I feel her dry, wrinkled skin, as rough as cardboard, scratchy. No, Bibiana's is rather soft.

We walk a while in silence, then she says, "Every once in

a while, I should pick you up... All right?" She bends down to me.

What?

I stop in my tracks. I take my hand away as swiftly as if a bee has stung me. Bibiana is overstepping the mark now. Just thinking about her holding me fills me with panic. No one has ever held me. At least not for months, years. It must go back to when I was a newborn, so I have no memory at all of the feeling. I start to tremble, I'm hot all of a sudden. I was enjoying the sun – it's summer and a heatwave in this damned Polish countryside – but now it's beating on my dolichocephalic head, my ears are buzzing and I can't breathe. If Bibiana picks me up by force, I'll yell so loud, we'll rouse the whole town we're approaching. I'll kick her until she lets go of me, then I'll roll on the ground and bash my head until I bleed. And that'll be the end of her! The *Unterscharführer* in the car following us will notice something is wrong and she'll get that bullet in the head!

When she sees my reaction, Bibiana starts to panic, too. She takes three steps backwards. Her sunkissed cheeks turn pale, as if the blood has drained out of her face. "Don't worry! Don't worry!" she stammers. "Everything will be fine. I'm not going to force you to..."

She doesn't have time to finish her sentence because I also stumble backward, trip on a stone, and fall on my face.

"Oh my God!" she cries out, kneeling down next to me. "Have you hurt yourself?"

Our voices attract the attention, not of the *Unterscharführer* in the car, but of a Polish woman passing by. She hurries over to us and I can tell that she's asking Bibiana what happened. Bibiana makes out that I collapsed from the heat. Nothing serious. Everything's fine... Everything's fine. The woman looks at me while I get up and wipe the little trickle of blood from my hands. She doesn't have much to offer us, a bit of bread and some fresh water. That will calm me down, she says, and, as she has two children, a boy my age and a six-year-old girl, I could come and play with them to put a stop to my tears.

Off we go with her, and return that night with the address.

Pleased with this initial success, I decide to redouble my efforts.

The very next day, while Bibiana and I are walking hand in hand, I turn things over in my head. Do I give it a go? Is it worth it? It's not too dangerous. There's always the *Unterscharführer* who can shoot from behind, and I'm also perfectly capable of defending myself. I can be very violent when I want to be. Let's see. If I don't give it a try, I'll never know. I'm ready to go, but ... wait, three more steps and then I'm off.

One. Two. Two. Two and a half. Two and three quarters... Three.

I stop dead.

"What's the matter, Maciej?" asks Bibiana.

Oh yes, I forgot to tell you: yesterday, when we were with the Polish woman who gave us something to drink, we were talking – I didn't understand everything she said – but when she asked me what my name was, I was incredibly on the ball. If I'd said Konrad, as Frau Lotte insisted – she's such an idiot – it would have ruined everything; my cover would have been blown. My instincts told me to use a Polish name. I said, "My name is Maxètche!" It just popped out spontaneously, I have no idea why. Well, of course I do know: I love the sound of "Max".

The Polish woman started to giggle. "Maciej, that's how

you pronounce it! Not Max-è-tche! Say it after me," she said in a kind voice.

Mothers always go weak at the knees when children make pronunciation mistakes. And Bibiana looked surprised by my instinctive response – gobsmacked even.

So now Bibiana is asking me what's wrong, why I've stopped dead, and she starts to go pale again, like yesterday. She's scared I'm going to have another tantrum.

I hold my hands up to her.

"You… You want me—" she doesn't dare finish, she's scared stiff – "You want me to pick you up?"

Well, duh! You got it. Stop looking at me with those eyes like a dead fish. (Do fish even have blue eyes?)

She comes closer, gently, as if she's about to pick up an armful of freshly laid eggs. She leans over, puts her hands under my armpits and, upsy-daisy, she picks me up.

"Oh, you look so fragile, but you're heavy enough, my little chap!" she exclaims, still with an edge of anxiety in her voice.

Anxiety that I might suddenly start yelling. Because I'm frowning, my face is all scrunched up, my lips pursed, and my fists clenched. The thing is, I don't know myself whether I'm going to start yelling or not. I haven't decided yet. In the meantime, I'm staying rigid. She relaxes a bit and puts her right arm under my bottom and supports my back with her left arm. Then she starts walking again, as if, holding her armful of eggs, she is also stepping onto a carpet of eggs.

So…

It's not that bad, for the moment anyway. At least my feet get a rest. The soles on my stinking clodhopper Polish boots are worn thin and I've got splinters in my feet … I relax a bit and lean my head closer to Bibiana's. I've been holding myself away from her and now I've got a crick in my neck. I can smell her sweat, but it's not too pungent. At least she doesn't have stinky breath like Frau Lotte, who splutters over me when she's speaking – I always feel like I'm going to drop dead, her breath is so foul. I relax even more and let my cheek brush against Bibiana's. I can tell she's relaxing, too. She takes her left hand from behind my back, holds my right hand, and gives it a little squeeze. I know from yesterday that this is just fine. Out of the corner of my eye I notice she's smiling. A sloppy smile: as her smile widens, her eyes fill with tears.

I recognize this smile: it's the same one the mothers had when their hearts melted at the sight of my angelic little face.

That evening, we return with three addresses.

The more friendly Bibiana and I are, the more addresses we get.

The next day, she picks me up several times on our way to the village the Sisters showed us on the map. I even have a tantrum at one point when she tries to put me down and I don't want to walk.

Another Polish woman comes over to chat. "Aren't they naughty at that age? It's terrible."

Excellent result: the address of a house with four children.

Two days later, Bibiana says, "Let's see how fast you can run! Try and catch me!"

I catch up to her (because she cheated and let me win on purpose) and trip her up, and she falls over, taking me with her. So both of us end up rolling in the slimy mud, which is everywhere since the rain. When we get home that night, the Sister says, "Ach! You are disgusting! A real little Polack!"

What are you whingeing about, you old bag? You got your six addresses today, didn't you?

Another day, Bibiana tickles me and I start giggling like mad. Then she sticks her lips on my cheek... Weird. Sort of disgusting. I don't scream or cry, but I must look funny as I rub my cheek hard, because she bursts out laughing. When she asks me to do the same to her, I refuse. Not for now, at least.

One day after lunch we fall asleep together in the sunshine. I'm the first to open my eyes and I shake Bibiana, but she doesn't wake up. All of a sudden, I'm terrified. What's happening inside my head? I can't work it out. It's like I'm remembering that story Josefa told me, about when I was a baby and I was found in the arms of the corpse, the dissident whore who kidnapped me. So I think Bibiana is dead. Perhaps all the women who come from the camps are the same, and all die fast? It's as if Bibiana has the same face as the whore who tortured me. Oh dear, it's all so muddled in my mind. Sometimes, certain vague, shifting images haunt me. My brain is too immature to be able to file memories away, and the compartments get mixed up. Before they're banished forever, those memories invade my peace of mind.

Anyway, this day, a woman comes over to us when she sees me crying and shaking Bibiana. "What's the matter, you poor little boy? Is your mummy hurt? No, look, she's fine! She's just asleep. It's too much for our poor children, isn't it? The trauma they're suffering. It's no wonder," she says to Bibiana, who finally stirs.

We spend the afternoon at the woman's house, and she tell us about her friends in the neighbouring village.

That evening our pockets are full of addresses.

* * *

We continue like this for weeks, until one day, out of the blue, Bibiana asks me, "Maciej, where is your mummy?"

I don't reply; I'm eating. I can't do two things at once, eat my sausage and talk. I mean, I can't talk properly, can't articulate it like I'm telling you; my five-year-old way of talking is not up to putting it into words. So I just mumble a few sounds typical of a child my age. "Me, no mummy!"

Bibiana lowers her eyes and starts fiddling with a leaf – we're sitting on the ground in a forest; she'd decided we could have a little rest after working hard all morning. Now the leaf is in shreds.

After a minute of silence, she says, "I understand. Your mummy is dead, isn't she? In the bombing? After all, your people are getting a few bombs, too."

That's got nothing to do with it. Bibiana is on the wrong track completely. I don't have a mother. That's the word that I erased from my vocabulary. I don't even know any more what it means exactly, except for what I observe with the Polish children.

"And your father?"

I keep chewing my sausage, but I can't swallow. I'm sick of sausages! Frau Lotte always gives me the same thing to eat every day. Why doesn't she put sweets in the basket, like there were in the big pocket of her uniform when we were on the road together? I grimace to show how disgusting the sausage is.

"Your father's dead, too, is that right? Poor little Maciej, are you an orphan?"

Huge tears trickle down Bibiana's cheeks. It's ridiculous she's making herself sad like this, for nothing. She was talking to herself and answered her own questions.

Still, I don't like seeing her so upset, and I'm not an idiot – I can spout a few sentences when I want to. "My mother is Germany, and my father is the Führer!" And I raise my arm in a salute. Nice and straight, like a sword. Then I yell, *"Heil Hitler!"*

Bibiana recoils. There's a strange glint in her eyes. For a split second, I think she's going to smack me. Instead, she comes closer, grabs my arm, lowers it, pulls it towards her, and kisses my hand. I feel like doing the same thing to her, so I kiss her, too. On the cheek.

I thought we'd beat our record for addresses that day. In fact we didn't. Well, we did get heaps of them. But what the hell has got into Bibiana?

When we get back, instead of giving the papers with the addresses to the Sister and saying goodnight to me before going to sleep in the cellar of the town hall, like she does every other night, Bibiana stands in front of the Sister and, with an arrogant look I've never seen on her, which transforms her normally pretty face into a hideous mask, she proceeds to eat all the pieces of paper. She stuffs them into her mouth one after the other, so fast that the Sister, aghast, has no time to react.

Why did she do that? Why?

If she was so hungry, why didn't she tell me? I'd have given her my sausage. I forced myself to eat it and it's sitting like a stone in my stomach.

I've got a tummy-ache.

I want to vomit.

13.

The tummy-ache won't go away.

It feels like my intestines are refusing to obey the orders issued by my stomach. They're in revolt: twisting, cramping, making odd sounds, gurgles, as if there is a voice in my belly moaning and groaning. Frau Lotte says I've got diarrhoea from an illness I caught from Bibiana. But I don't have diarrhoea. I'm the one who sees what goes into the toilet bowl. Nice consistency, a bit hard sometimes. I can tell by the sound my turds make when I push them out. *Plop! Plop!* Mortar shells.

A stomach-ache at my age is a sign of *Psychological disturbance.* You don't even know that, useless Sister? Simply put, it means something's wrong in my head. As a result of stress, or a traumatic event.

I haven't done anything for days. I stay by myself most of the time. Lotte is with me in the house, but she's always got her nose in her dossiers, filing index cards on children for whom she now has addresses, sticking on code letters or colours. Anyway, she doesn't matter; she's too ugly, too old. She's not a real companion.

I don't want to learn nursery rhymes or do arithmetic like I used to.

All I do is daydream. I replay the recent days as if I'm watching a film: waking up early, getting dressed in my funny costume of rags, Bibiana arriving, and then us setting off into the countryside, hand in hand.

Hand in hand.

I go back over our long walks, the chasing games, the tickling, the laughs we had together. I picture Bibiana's face, her bright, blue eyes, her cheeks freckled by the sun, her blonde hair that had begun to grow back without lice. Sometimes, I can even hear her voice.

And I think about all the children we came across. When we went into the Polish women's homes, we would stay there an hour or two and I had time to play. Occasionally things wouldn't go well because I can be pretty nasty, I like to give orders, yell, be the boss. I even whacked a few little Polacks on the head with my Thor's-hammer-Excalibur-sword, or knocked them to the ground and stomped on them – to copy the SS soldiers in the streets when they decide, just like that, on a whim, to attack a Pole. That's when Bibiana pretended to reprimand me with a smack; the truth is she just tapped me on the bottom. I didn't mind.

I miss all that, and meeting all those mothers and children. I hate idleness. I've had enough of playing by myself upstairs in the bombed-out house.

I sit on the ground for ages, daydreaming, no longer aware of how my body works, but swaying backwards and forwards. When she sees me like this, Lotte grabs me by the shoulders and shakes me. "Heavens, Konrad, what's the matter? Would you please stand up straight? You look like an old Jew praying!"

Bitch. She knows how to touch a sore spot. I leap up straightaway and raise my arm in a salute to show that I am not an old Jew. I am the prototype-child-typical-of-the-pure-Aryan-race! The perfect specimen, conceived according to the wishes of *Reichsführer* Himmler. The protégé of Doctor Ebner. The mascot of the *Lebensborn* programme. *Sieg Heil!*

She's the one who must have Jewish blood, she's so old, so ugly. I don't know why Doctor Ebner doesn't put her through the selection process. They wouldn't have to measure her nose or her forehead or the position of her ears or the height of her cheekbones – it's perfectly obvious that nothing in her face corresponds to the standards of the Nordic race. As for her eyes, they're small and black like ball bearings. Like the eyes on the teddy bear that I found in the room of the boy who used to live in the house. He must have been very attached to it because it was snuggled up in his bed, under the blankets. I took out my anger on that bear and tore it to shreds. I yanked off its nose and eyes and ripped open its belly, until there was nothing left of it. That filthy disgusting Polack bear!

The older I get, the more I realize how weird and full of contradictions adults are. The Brown Sisters attended courses with "physiognomists" to be able to tell, at a single glance, whether a person can claim to belong to the Nordic race or not. Haven't they ever thought of standing in front of a mirror? Of requesting their own "relocation"?

As for the rocking – my mouth open like I'm swallowing flies, my gaze blank – somehow I manage to cut down on it; otherwise they'll think I'm mentally retarded and send me off to be "purified".

But I'm not retarded at all. In fact, I know exactly what

happened to Bibiana. It wasn't because she was hungry that she ate the addresses in front of the Sister. It was an act of rebellion. And rebellion gets punished. Very severely. After a few days, when no one came to get me in the morning, I asked, "When will Bibiana come?"

"She's not coming. Not today, not tomorrow. She is no longer a member of our team," Frau Lotte said stiffly, careful not to make eye contact with me.

A code sentence. The first possible meaning: Bibiana suffocated on the paper she swallowed. Not likely. Second possibility: she ended up getting shot in the head. Far more likely. Lotte pulled me aside when Bibiana started snacking on the paper; she took me to my room so I wouldn't see what happened next: the other Sister calling the soldier, and *bang!* The soldier firing. I've seen a lot of this, whenever I play sniper games in the house and look out the window. SS soldiers get a group of men or women guilty of sabotage and line them up against the wall, and *bang! bang!* they execute them. Or else they kill a bunch of innocent people to punish the guilty ones they haven't manage to arrest. Or else they lock them in a church and set fire to it.

Third possibility: Bibiana was sent back to Ravensbrück. And if she's not dead yet, it won't be long.

Or else…

Or else, there could be a fourth possibility; this one doesn't relate to the Sister's code language, but to my own one. Bibiana is the Lady of the Lake. She has returned to the magic waters where nothing can ever harm her again. All I have to do is drink from the goblet of immortality and I'll be able to join her there. But when? The *Reichsführer* Himmler's search parties had better hurry up and find that damn goblet.

* * *

Why did Bibiana decide to rebel? When she was gobbling the papers, did she think about me, even for an instant? Why did she introduce me to the feelings of *hand in hand, hugs, laughter, chasing games* and then abandon me?

I'm angry with her. Too bad if she's been killed after all!

I need my mental picture of her to join up with the others in the back of my dolichocephalic head, in the mixed-up compartments of my brain, the ones that are gradually heading for oblivion. I'm young, so it should be quick. But in the meantime…

I'm suffering.

Especially because Lotte has put me on dry rations – she's sticking to her theory that my stomach-ache is due to some kind of diarrhoea. Rice, steamed carrots and quince jam. Not only is it disgusting, but I feel even worse because I'm constipated. My belly is rock-hard from all the accumulated waste that can't get out. In the toilet just now, I let loose a series of farts so deafening it sounded like machine-gun fire. If there were living creatures in the toilet bowl under my bum, they'd never have survived such an asphyxiating attack of gas. Despite the pain, the idea makes me laugh. They should launch me from a plane over an enemy target: my exploding gut would cause as much damage as a bomb.

I'm still laughing as I leave the toilet, and then sadness overwhelms me. I get dressed in my Polish-child costume of rags and put myself to bed. I rub my nose in the stinky sweater full of holes and the filthy trousers; I breathe deeply and I feel better. I can pick up Bibiana's smell in a few spots.

Lotte tells me to do some drawing to distract myself. It's more so that I leave her in peace to file her index cards and write up her reports. "Oh, that's so pretty!" she says, glancing at the paper I've scribbled on. She has no idea what the picture means: the horizontal lines of black crayon are her. Dead. And the big blobs of red everywhere are her blood. Because she got shot in the head.

I can't sleep at night. It wasn't the same when I was driving around with the Sister, or out walking with Bibiana. I'd come home tired and be asleep as soon as my head hit the pillow. But there's a lot of disturbance in the house. Doctor Ebner comes back late with Herr Tesch and other important people, and they never stop talking, arguing. There's often shouting from the study.

And the SS officers get together in the dining room and put on loud music. Sometimes I sneak out of bed and have a look. They're all drunk, because of the schnapps, and surrounded by lots of women. At first I didn't understand what they were doing, but now I do.

Some evenings, the women arrive all dressed up, wearing lots of make-up. They eat masses of things you can't find anywhere in the country now (sweets and chocolate), they dance with the officers, laugh, drink plenty of schnapps themselves, or champagne if it's there, too. Afterwards, they take off their clothes, or stay just in their panties, or bra. Or just their stockings and high heels. They lie down on the rugs, or on the table, right in the middle of the dinner plates that haven't been cleared away, or on an armchair or couch. Or else they stay standing, leaning against the wall, and that's when the officers come and put their penises inside them. It seems like that makes them laugh more than the alcohol. When they push their mouths onto the officers' mouths, their lipstick get smeared all over their faces, as if they're bleeding. Those women are German. They're prostitutes, whores. They're paid to have sex with the officers.

On other evenings, the women are Polish. I can tell because they're dressed like peasants, they don't wear make-up, they don't dine with the officers, they don't say a word and they never laugh. Quite the opposite. They don't drink either, or sometimes the soldiers force them to swallow a big slug of schnapps and they nearly choke. And when the soldiers' penises go inside them, some cry, or scream; others grit their teeth until it's over.

The whores have sex with the higher ranked officers, and the Polish women with the ordinary soldiers. The whores shout, "Yes, yes!" And the Polish women, "No, no!" The soldiers rape the Polish women.

I watch all this very carefully. It's interesting to know how babies are made. Because some of this intercourse will produce babies for sure. Watching up close while people have intercourse will increase my knowledge quota and develop my thinking processes. No one will ever be able to spin me tales about babies arriving in baskets delivered by storks, or any other such nonsense.

Is that how I was conceived? With a blonde German whore who took off all her clothes to let the Aryan's penis enter her? Was she drinking schnapps and laughing, or was she crying and gritting her teeth?

I hang around the house for days on end, spying on the whores and the soldiers, which means I stay up late, so I'm tired enough to sleep most of the next day. Time passes faster this way.

But I'm soon bored again. Once you've seen one couple

having sex, seeing it over and over adds nothing. It's always the same. And, anyway, I never see Bibiana among the Polish women, even though I keep looking for her. She must really be dead. I'll have to get used to the idea.

I notice that, once they've finished their business with the women, some soldiers drive off in the middle of the night. I wonder where on earth they could be going at that time? I'm so curious that one night I stow away in one of their cars.

14.

It's not a car; it's more like a van. I haul myself up onto the tray covered by a tarpaulin at the back, and wait. It feels like for ever. Then I see two SS soldiers leaving the house. They can't walk straight; they're drunk and dishevelled. While they chat, they button up their flies clumsily and straighten their uniforms, before climbing into the front of the van. They both light cigarettes and I get a desperate urge to cough. But at least the smoke masks the horrible odour of the schnapps.

A few minutes later a Sister climbs in with them. I've seen her a few times before. She's the oldest and ugliest of them all: very tall, thin, with long, sinewy arms like tentacles. Her chin is square and covered with a fuzz of brown hair, like a man. Her deep black eyes are mean: the eyes of a shark.

The driver starts the van. The swaying doesn't help my nausea from the smell of the schnapps and the smoke. When my belly starts to gurgle I worry it will give me away. The bumps only make things worse. We must be on one of those potholed country roads. I try to hang on so I don't vomit, and so I don't end up rolling like a sack of potatoes from one end of the tray to the other.

I gradually get used to the discomfort of this impromptu trip, which, fortunately, doesn't last long.

After a few kilometres, the vehicle stops. The soldiers and the Sister get out. I deduce that they are trying to make as little noise as possible, because they extinguish the headlights, shut the car doors carefully, and walk on tiptoes, without speaking. As they didn't notice me hiding, as soon as they're far enough away, I lift up a corner of the tarpaulin.

We're in front of a house; I recognize it immediately. It's one of the last ones Bibiana and I visited. (Did they cut open her stomach to find the address?) Flanked by the two SS soldiers, the Sister approaches the door in silence. Then she raises her hand, and gives the signal with a nod of her head.

Off they go! One of the SS soldiers breaks the door down with a mighty kick, and that's the end of the silence and the tiptoeing around. I can hear doors banging, furniture overturned, things smashing, the SS soldiers' boots pounding around as they yell out orders, and soon the ear-splitting scream of a woman drowns out everything. It's the mother of the household. The cries of her children follow instantly. The house lights up: one window, then another and another, like fairy lights. And I watch as, behind the glass, shapes like Chinese shadows come and go, running, twisting and turning, fighting. I stay crouched in the van, motionless, wide-eyed, my mouth hanging open, fascinated by the spectacle.

Now I understand.

So I'm witnessing one of the kidnappings of Polish children that are orchestrated by the Gestapo and the Brown Sisters. I must have had a sixth sense when I chose this van.

I finally get to see the next stage in "Operation Buddies". And I deserve to, after being one of the main stars all these months.

The two SS soldiers rush outside, each holding a boy by the hand, while the Sister is carrying a little girl in her arms. She's got her wedged against her hip like a parcel so the little girl is lying horizontal, her head below her feet. The mother, who hasn't stopped howling, hurls herself outside and runs back and forth, trying to rescue one or other of her boys. She grabs the hand of one, the hair of the other, but no sooner has she touched them than they've slipped from her grasp – she can't fight the soldiers who shove her back. So she tries to rescue her little girl, who is reaching out her arms, sobbing. She manages to catch up to the Sister, who isn't running as fast as the soldiers, but the Sister slaps her, shoving her away violently, and the woman collapses to the ground.

When the soldiers make it to the van, they lift up the tarpaulin and drag the boys in next to me – I'm hidden at the back so they can't see me. The Sister hangs on to the little girl, and slaps her hand over the child's mouth to stifle the screams. It's a close call, but in the scramble no one notices me, thanks to the children's mother. She manages to stagger to her feet, dazed after the slap from the Sister, and drag herself over to grab on to the edge of the van. One of the soldiers is smashing her hand with his gun. She doesn't let go, even though her hand is pouring with blood. He keeps on hitting her, as if he wanted to break her bones. The other soldier is busy holding back the children, who are trying at the same time to help their mother climb in the van, and to avoid getting hit by the gun.

The mother collapses to the ground a second time.

The tarpaulin falls in on us and the van takes off.

The mother keeps on screaming and screaming. Once we're far enough away, we don't hear her any more.

That all takes scarcely a few minutes.

The two Polish boys recognize me; they even remember my name. The false one I used with Bibiana.

"Maciej! Maciej! You're here, too? Where are they taking us?"

I can just understand what they're saying. I'm proud they recognize me. That means they're my buddies. That also means they're not kids I had a fight with or beat to a pulp while we were playing. Or perhaps, given the urgency of the circumstances, they've chosen to forget and don't resent me any more... And I think I remember their names, too. The smallest one, the one trembling like a leaf – I can hear his teeth chattering – is Andrzej. Yes, that's it! And the other one, his older brother, who is panic-stricken and asking me all the questions, is Jacek.

"Yes, yes, they took me, too," I reply. Which is a lie, of course, but he won't know, especially as I remembered to put on my Polish-child costume before climbing into the van. "But I don't know where they're taking us," I add.

That's the truth.

"Mamo? Mamo?... Bibiana?"

Jacek has an amazing memory. I take a breath. *"Ona nie zyje,"* I reply.

She's dead. The truth again. I lower my head. I've got a stomach-ache thinking about Bibiana, about all the suffering she's caused me recently. Jacek pats me on the back to comfort me. He suddenly feels a whole lot better. His mother has just got a broken hand, she's not dead, he's counting on seeing her soon. I sulk a bit longer – I've made such an effort to forget that damned Bibiana, and here's Jacek making me think about her, here she is haunting me again. Finally, I raise my head and tell Jacek that I'm pleased he and his brother are with me, that they make me feel better. More of the truth. Tonight is by far the most excitement I've had since the beginning of my short life. It's much more fun being with buddies than endlessly watching soldiers having sex, or moping in my bed by myself.

Reassured for the moment, Jacek and his brother snuggle up with me and the three of us hug each other.

The Sister soon turns round to check, curious that it's so silent in the back. I hide behind Jacek, which proves to him how frightened I am, that I am in the same boat as them. As soon as the Sister has her back to us again, we continue our whispering.

I reassure my new buddies, jabbering away as best I can in Polish, that there's nothing to worry about. Even if I don't know where we're going, I'm sure everything will be fine. And it's true: they should be happy! They've been taken away from their miserable lives so they can become true German children. It's wonderful; they are so lucky. Unfortunately my vocabulary is too limited to explain all this in Polish, so I just keep a big smile on my face, which seems to keep them calm. They stare at me with their big – blue – eyes full of tears. Their little sister up the front seems to have calmed down too, as we can't hear crying any more, just her loud hiccups.

We drive a bit more, then the van stops again and the same thing happens. A house. A door broken in. Screaming. Smashing. And more children join us. And more. Until there's no room in the van.

With every new lot, there are tears and screaming, but

Jacek and I manage to reassure them. At the end of the trip, when we arrive with all the other vans, only the children in our van get out without crying and line up quietly on the orders of the Sister and the soldiers who've been waiting for us.

I'm proud my buddies know how to behave. I'm proud of their trust in me.

I've been in a Mercedes, and a van, and now I'm probably going in a train. So many new things in such a short time!

We're at the Poznan railway station.

There are people everywhere. Soldiers with dogs, officers, Sisters, women in uniform. And children, of course, lots of children. The soldiers line us up in single file along the platform. There are trains on both sides. The sign on one says "Kalish", on the other, "Auschwitz". I wonder which one Jacek, Andrzej and I will take. (We've done our best not to be separated.) While we're standing waiting, I sense that Jacek and his little brother are getting nervous again. That's normal: there are so many children and most of them are screaming and crying. Fear is contagious. And I must admit that, if I didn't know I was safe, I'd be frightened, too. The soldiers, the dogs, the barking, the steam from the roaring engines, the soldiers bellowing orders, children crying: you can't hear yourself think. And it's a cold night. I don't really feel the cold, and I've got on my sweater from my costume; even if it's holey, it's keeping me warm, whereas the others are in their pyjamas. (That's normal, too: they were asleep when they were kidnapped.)

The line is moving slowly, too slowly. I'm getting sick of waiting. Patience has never been my thing. I try to move out of the line but a soldier sees me and shoves me back into my spot, while a dog starts biting my ankles. What a nerve! I don't mind the dog, but how dare the soldier. And he's only got two stripes on his uniform: a lowly *Rottenführer*! When they find out that he's had a go at Doctor Ebner's protégé, he'll get into big trouble. But I don't want to come clean yet. It's much more fun pretending to be a Polack.

Stretching up on my tiptoes to see what's happening at the end of the platform, I sigh with relief and nearly shout for joy. Doctor Ebner is there, along with a few women I recognize from meetings in the bombed-out house. I'm so pleased that, when one of the Sisters gives us a push to straighten up the line, I kick her hard in the shins. I've been dying to do that for ages.

We inch forward. Each child stops in front of Doctor Ebner, who directs them to the right or to the left. Those to the right climb in the train marked Kalish, the others head for the one marked Auschwitz.

It's a selection process. A very quick one, because Doctor Ebner doesn't have his measuring instruments with him, or his case with the glass eyes and fake hair. As we move up the line, I can see that he is sending the blond, blue-eyed children to the Kalish train, and the brown-haired, scrawny kids to the other one. (In the scramble of the kidnappings, the soldiers and the Sisters just grabbed whatever kids they found. Brothers and sisters didn't always have the same coloured hair; but there wasn't time to work out which was which.)

I tell Jacek straightaway that I know the man with the bald head and round glasses, and that he won't separate us, so not to worry. Even though he looks strict, I say, he's really kind. I'd like to tell him that Doctor Ebner is my second father, after the Führer, that he brought me into the world and has never left me since, but it's too hard to say all that in Polish. The only thing I'm worried about is that, once it's my turn with Doctor Ebner, he'll recognize me and the game will be up.

But I've got a bit of time, the line is not moving fast and we're near the end. I like to keep active – unlike Jacek and his brother, who just stand there, waiting their turn – so I jump up and down a bit, look around, and that's when, over the general hubbub, I hear another noise.

"Psst! Psst!"

I turn to see a little boy waving in response to a call. Then he runs out of the line, quickly, quickly, over to one of the vans parked on the middle strip near the entrance to the station. Neither the soldiers nor the Sisters see him. Only I do. From where I am, I can see his legs and his bum, as he crouches behind the van. He waits a few seconds, then scampers off like a rabbit to the edge of the forest next to the station.

What's he up to? A few seconds later, I see a second child do the same thing, then a third, a fourth. "Don't move, I'll be back," I whisper to Jacek, and elbow my way to the back of the line. I take the hand of the little boy about to run off like the others, and I let him know that I want to leave with him. He hesitates, petrified, tells me to wait my turn, then nods and we're off.

We tear over to the van and wait. Terrified, the boy looks back at the soldiers, the dogs and the Sisters. Not that much is visible. We're crouching down, so all I can see are SS boots, the ends of their guns, dogs' paws, dogs' muzzles when they lower their heads to sniff the ground, and the hems of the brown potato-sack dresses worn by the Sisters. *"Raz! Dwa!*

Trzy!" the little boy hisses at me. "One! Two! Three!" We run over to the forest.

There, hidden behind a bush, is a group of about ten women. Polish women. Mothers. They must have known the vans were heading for the station, so they followed them to get their children back. Most of the kids who managed to leave the line are already in the arms of their mothers. The one I ran with has just found his and is snuggled in her embrace.

And what about me? Well, I just stand there, alone. Of course, since I don't have a mother. I feel stupid. Then all of a sudden a hand grabs me and pulls me away. Does one of these women want to pick me up and hug me? Why? Has she mistaken me for her son? I can't see a thing. It's dark; the streetlight illuminating the platform doesn't reach this far. While the hand pulls me feverishly and the arms encircle me, a crazy idea strikes me: is it Bibiana? Bibiana isn't dead, she's come back and is picking me up, crying for joy because she's found me again. She's escaped from Ravensbrück, she's met up with the other women and she's come here especially to get me. Yes, me.

But it's not Bibiana. It's Jacek's mother. I recognize her with her broken hand covered in a bloody bandage. She hugs me close and says two words over and over, right into my ear. "Jacek! Andrzej!" The names of her sons. She must have seen that I was next to them in the line, so she wants me to go and get them. She's sobbing, begging me, wringing her hands, and that must really hurt.

I stop and think. Then I say to her, "Yes, OK."

I go back the way I came and hide behind the van, waiting. Then I slip back into line and elbow my way to Jacek and his little brother.

"Where were you?" asks Jacek.

He's white as a sheet and shaking even more than his brother, who's crying again. I'm pleased they were anxious while I was away, that they missed me.

Jacek really is a cute kid. He has beautiful blue eyes, thick blond hair. I don't want him to go back to his mother. What's the use of a mother? Apart from giving you a shocking stomach-ache when she leaves? It would be so unfair if Jacek remained a common little Polack. He *must* become German. He deserves it. I can see it in his blue eyes.

So I leave the line again, brazenly this time. I run so fast that I manage to avoid the clutches of a soldier trying to grab me, and I head straight for Doctor Ebner.

He recognizes me. "Konrad! What on earth are you doing here?" he asks sternly.

The big vein is throbbing in his temple.

I point to where the women are hiding, where their children have fled to.

The siren goes off. The soldiers turn the dogs loose on them.

15.

Thanks to me, they managed to rescue a dozen children who would have gone off with their mothers, back to their hovels to die of hunger, running from bombs or SS gunfire. A dozen children who have found an adoptive mother. The same one as me: Germany. More young wild animals, just like the Führer wants, to swell the ranks of the all-powerful German youth. More future brothers for me.

You wouldn't believe how happy I am! My stomach-ache has disappeared and I feel as fit as a fiddle.

Doctor Ebner congratulated me. "Konrad! You're full of surprises!"

There was almost the trace of a smile on his thin, tight lips. The women representing the various organizations at the station also showered me with praise. Even the damn Sisters had to acknowledge what I'd done. The one who'd been in the van where I was hiding told Doctor Ebner that, thanks to me, the children had been much calmer and easier to handle in the selection process. Yes, the compliments flowed!

Except that Doctor Ebner did get a bit cross with me. Once we got back to the bombed-out house, he took me into his office. We were alone for the first time since the Home at Steinhöring.

"I have something to say to you, Konrad."

He double-locked the door, sat in a chair and signalled for me to come over. I stood to attention, shoulders back, feet together, arms by my side, chin up, looking straight ahead at the top of his bald head. To tell you the truth, I was scared stiff. I was convinced Doctor Ebner was going to make me endure another medical test, a new selection process, his speciality. Fortunately I'd got rid of my Polish costume. It stank of urine because the children in the van had been so terrified they hadn't been able to control themselves. I'd had a shower and put my *Pimpf* uniform back on: shorts, brown shirt with armband, tie and cap, which I had remembered to take off in front of Doctor Ebner.

"Konrad, do you realize what danger you were in?"

What danger? I gazed directly at him, questioning, with my big, blue, innocent eyes. Just in case he was planning on a little check-up of how my growth was affecting my ethnic connections to the Nordic race, I thought he could use this opportunity to confirm that my eyes were still bright blue. (I check them regularly myself, whenever I come across a mirror, to make sure they're not going dark.)

"We could have got you mixed up with a Polish child. With one lapse in concentration, and that can happen—" he clicked his fingers – "you would have been off to Auschwitz."

"What's Auschwitz?" I asked him, still gazing innocently, when in fact I knew the answer, I just wanted more detail.

"It's a place where Polish children work."

A code sentence if ever there was one. And easy to translate. "Place" = camp. "Where children work" = where they are exterminated.

"Do you understand?" Ebner added, holding my chin between his thumb and index finger, forcing me to look at him when I lowered my eyes. "Losing you would have made me very sad, you know."

Adults make such fools of themselves! "Losing you" = your death. Which just proves that I got the first sentence right. You don't work at Auschwitz, you die there. Or else you die working.

"You were told to stay here and not move," he continued in his stern voice. "You're not allowed to disobey orders, you know that."

"*Jawohl, Herr Doktor!* But our beloved Führer said that children must develop their *Draufgängertum*."

I fired off that long sentence without thinking. It just came out in one go. I didn't stumble on a single word. Earlier I'd pronounced "Auschwitz" wrongly, changing the "sch" sound into "se", because one of my teeth is loose and sometimes I lisp.

Ebner looked shaken. I had taken the wind out of his sails with my perfect sentence.

"Correct," he said, nodding.

From then on, he couldn't lecture me or threaten to punish me. To have criticized my risky behaviour at the station would have meant that he was questioning the principles of our Führer, which is *absolutely forbidden*. What's more, German children have been ordered to denounce their parents if they think they have doubts about the fundamental principles of National Socialism. So, I could denounce Ebner, seeing that he was sort of my father. After a moment of silence, I took advantage of my leading position. "What is Kalish?" I asked.

I remembered the sign on the other train at the station.

"It's a Home, like the one where you were born, except it's not for babies, but for foreign children who are racially viable. They're taught how to become true German children."

"Like in a school?"

"It's a type of school, yes."

I nodded so he would think that I understood. But I didn't understand properly. "A type." Code language again, and this time I didn't grasp the meaning. I didn't dare ask him to elaborate. Ebner stood up and was getting ready to start work at his desk, which meant that I had to clear out. But before saluting him and leaving, I thought I'd ask about Jacek and Andrzej. Did they go to Kalish or to Auschwitz?

Ebner gestured towards the files piled up on his desk. The answer to my question was somewhere among all those papers and he'd let me know soon.

I never got the answer, not then, or anytime later. Perhaps Jacek went to Kalish and Andrzej to Auschwitz. That would make sense, as Jacek was bigger and stronger than his brother. Or else, through a lapse in concentration, as Ebner had pointed out, they could both have been sent to Auschwitz. To death. That possibility upset me for a moment. I liked those two a lot, especially Jacek. We could have become buddies. We could have become brothers.

But I quickly forgot about them because Doctor Ebner gave orders for a big party in my honour, to reward me for my services to the nation. He said we would also celebrate my birthday, which had been completely forgotten. (All the other birthdays had been forgotten too, but Ebner had forgotten that they'd been forgotten.)

So the next day we would celebrate my five-and-a-half years.

It's been a good party, even if right now things are going downhill. But I couldn't give a damn. I'm having a great time. It's better than staying alone in my room, and I'm enjoying myself more now.

Earlier in the evening, everyone was seated formally around the big dining-room table, set for the occasion. I was at the head of the table. Doctor Ebner and Frau Lotte were on either side, of course. I wasn't about to make a fool of myself. The other guests included Herr Tesch, two or three SS officers, Frau Viermetz, Frau Müller, Frau Kruger – who'd witnessed my triumph at the station the day before – and several *Braune Schwesten.* If I'd been consulted, we'd never have invited Frau Lotte and her lookalike Sisters to my birthday party. Who better to ruin the atmosphere than that horde of old crows? I wouldn't have invited the others, either: all adults. No fun at all. Why couldn't I have invited Jacek, Andrzej and all the kids from the van? No one asked for my opinion.

The mood was deadly serious. Everyone was talking about business, statistics, the news from the front. I overheard that the Russians were no longer our allies and that we were invading their country. No easy task, it seems. At a standstill in Moscow and Leningrad, our troops were having a bad time in the freezing weather. I also overheard that the Japanese were now on our side. (But the Japanese are not Nordic people? So what! The Russians aren't either.) And that they didn't pull any punches: in a surprise attack, they had totally destroyed most of the American navy in the Pacific. Western Europe was still occupied by our armies, and the south as well. Of course, the super-pilots from the Royal

Air Force were inflicting serious damage on our Luftwaffe, but the guests didn't seem too worried about that.

I was bored, so I wasn't really paying much attention. We were going to win the war anyway. We'd known that from the beginning.

At the end of the meal, they gave me a beautiful cake covered in Chantilly cream. The real thing. Amazing in these times of rationing. I blew out my five and a half candles in one go. Doctor Ebner made a speech in which he said that my birthday present was the *astronomical* – he emphasized this word – sum of 100 Reichmarks deposited in my bank account, as well as an additional candle to decorate the candelabra presented to me on my birth at the Home. The guests all exclaimed, "Oh!", "Ah!", "Wonderful!" But I didn't give a damn about the *astronomical* sum. It wasn't real. It wasn't cold hard cash I could buy sweets with. So I made up for it with the cake and stuffed my face, right in front of Frau Lotte, to get my own back for all the boiled carrots, rice and quince jam she'd force-fed me recently.

"Slowly, Konrad! Slowly! You'll get indigestion," she hissed in a contemptuous tone, looking daggers at me with her shark eyes.

Oh, come off it, you stupid bitch! Tonight it's my party and I'll do what I like. I'm a hero. I can gorge myself!

I even ate the leftovers from the adults' plates. They didn't notice because, after clapping when I'd blown out the candles, they barely touched their cake before getting back to their discussions. No one was paying attention to me any more. I was supposed to go and play with the toys I'd received on top of the *astronomical* sum of money and the candle. The toys had been requisitioned from shops in Warsaw; I could tell from the labels. But I'd rather eat than play. Playing by myself is no fun at all.

Then Ebner called a summit meeting in his office, to get down on paper what had been discussed at dinner. (I've noticed how much the senior officers love all manner of paperwork and correspondence.)

So the guests had to vacate the dining room. Frau Lotte didn't see that I wasn't following her. She'd drunk too much champagne. She nearly tripped over the rug as she left. I'm pretty sure she won't have made it to Ebner's office and will be snoring in her bed by now.

The real party starts now. I can have fun with the soldiers who've just turned up in the dining room, like they do most other nights.

They're already drunk, because they began their evening in a cabaret, with German prostitutes. I like the prostitutes because they're not uptight like the Sisters or the officer women. They're relaxed, funny. They don't bother with stupid rules. Not one of them has said, "It's time to go to bed! Go and clean your teeth and put on your pyjamas!" That sort of twaddle. On the contrary, they insist that I stay with them. Perhaps prostitutes would really like to be mothers; whatever the case, they all fall for my angel face.

"Oh, he's so cute! Sweetie pie, little guy! Look at him!"

They pop me on their knees, pat my hair, pinch my nose, give me big sloppy kisses that leave red marks on my cheeks. Even though normally I don't like being touched, I let them do it. I don't know why, but with them it's different. A few of them drag me into the middle of the room and, holding my hands, pretend to dance with me. They let me taste champagne. I dip my finger in a glass and lick it: they burst out laughing at the grimace on my face. Champagne is bitter and it stings a bit, but it's not bad.

Prostitutes can really hold their drink. They get drunker and drunker. I keep being passed around, on their knees, in their arms. One even suddenly decides to show me her breasts.

"You're going to be one hell of a handsome kid, you are!" she says. "You'll have heaps of women. It's never too early to start learning. Here! Your first lesson in biology!"

She unbuttons her blouse, bares her breasts. It's nothing new for me, because, as you know, on the nights when I couldn't sleep, before my adventure at Poznan station, I spied on these parties. But nobody knows that. I don't want to upset the prostitute, so I pretend to be surprised. And I'm amazed to observe that breasts come in a range of shapes. Big ones, little ones, ones that look like apples, others like pears, some that sit up, others that hang down. I wonder if there are "Nordic breasts". I wonder if you can measure their position, the space between them, the space between them and the navel or the neck… Of course you can. The RuSHA must have standard measurements for breasts somewhere on their shelves.

Now that it's late and the bottles are empty, the prostitutes aren't bothering with me any more. They're just doing what they usually do with the soldiers. Intercourse. I stay out of the way and play with the dolls I was given as presents. I tear off their clothes and twist them into the same positions as the prostitutes. (Dolls aren't as flexible as prostitutes so it doesn't always work.) When I'm sick of that, I imagine that somewhere on the table groaning with glasses is the goblet of the Holy Grail, the one that contains the elixir of immortality. I have to find which one it is, so I drink the dregs from every glass, one by one.

And I black out.

Frau Lotte sounds the alarm next morning.

When she can't find me in my bed, she scours the whole house until she finds me on the ground, under the dining table, among the empty bottles. No matter how many times she calls out my name, slaps me, shakes me like a fruit tree, nothing happens, she can't wake me up. There's no sign of life: I'm completely floppy when she lifts me up, my arms and legs dangling, my head hanging down like a corpse. She calls Ebner in a state. *Hurry! Hurry!* I'm taken by ambulance to the hospital where they treat the wounded soldiers from the front. Doctor Ebner, assisted by other doctors, puts me through a barrage of tests and discovers that I have an alarmingly high blood-alcohol reading. I'm in an "ethylic coma" – the scientific term for "drunken stupor". It's serious.

I almost died. Just goes to show that Auschwitz is not the only place you can die.

Somehow I end up coming to, unharmed, like after the dehydration episode when I was a baby. Doctor Ebner is gobsmacked: he's now got yet another proof of my superior nature. I am truly *as tough as leather and as hard as Krupp steel.* I am truly *the prototype-child-typical-of-the-pure-Aryan-race.* But there's something Ebner doesn't know: the reason I survived was that the elixir of immortality was hidden in one of those glasses. And from now on it's flowing through my veins. Nothing will ever be able to harm me. I am *immortal, invincible*!

Over the following months I continue my mission as an infiltrator. Ebner has decided that my presence among the Polish children was so useful that, two or three times a week, I do the same thing as I did on my last escapade. I'm there to reassure the children straight after they've been taken from their mothers. I convince them that they have nothing to fear, that they'll be reunited with their parents as soon as they've moved into a better house. I make up any old story, I let my imagination run wild, especially as I'm getting better at speaking Polish. On the station platform I wander around wherever I like among the queues. The soldiers and Sisters are aware of the role I'm playing and pretend to hit me like they do the others, but they never really hurt me. I chat to this one or that one. Sometimes Doctor Ebner sends me over to the Auschwitz train if things are getting too panicky there. I climb into a carriage and tell the kids a quick story. "We're going to a really cool place, a huge park with cabins." Once the tears have stopped, I get off, just before the train leaves.

Sometimes it annoys me that I have to get off. After all, now that I'm immortal, why couldn't I go and check out Auschwitz? But Ebner is watching over me; he asked a soldier to keep an eye on me whenever I get onto a train.

Nevertheless, despite his vigilance, there's trouble now and again. One night, a dog bit me really hard on the leg. The soldier holding the leash lost control of it. The dog tore off a piece of my skin and I had to stay in bed for a few days. Now I've got a long scar like a war wound. Which makes me even *tougher.* Lucky the dog didn't bite me on the cheek, or I would have lost my angel-face good looks.

But most of the trouble comes from the mothers. They just don't seem to be able to resign themselves to handing over their children to us. Like the one from whichever village it was – I forget the names – who chose to hang her child rather than let it be kidnapped. Can you imagine that! Or the other one, who lay down on the train tracks as the train left.

Mothers have the strangest ideas sometimes. They're mad! I'm so pleased I don't have one.

One particular night, I was spotted by one of them. She'd managed to escape from under the soldiers' noses and had climbed into the Kalish train to rescue her child. Obviously I denounced her to Doctor Ebner, and when the soldiers grabbed her, she started shrieking at me like the devil.

"Damn you! You evil child!" she yelled.

I'm not even sure she was Polish. Gypsy, probably. Everyone knows that, like Jews, Gypsies perform black magic and take it out on children. But I'm not just any old child. Her curse will never harm me. *I am immortal.*

Soon enough, I get sick of my work at the station.

It's the same with toys. When they're new, you enjoy them, then you forget about them. The thing is that I've had enough of seeing children heading off together every night, while I'm left standing alone on the platform. I have to go back to the bombed-out house and spend the rest of the night in my room, still alone. And face Frau Lotte again in the morning. I can't stand her any longer, with her shark eyes and her stinky breath.

To hell with it. I'm out of here.

16.

It's a big step for me. A new chapter in my young life.

I'm six. I'm going to school.

I don't have a satchel or any school supplies. No new clothes either. I'm wearing my *Pimpf* uniform. In my suitcase is the candelabra the Führer gave me when I was born, with its six candles, along with a few toiletries and a couple of changes of clothes. Even though Doctor Ebner is taking me, we're not hand in hand like a father walking his son to school on the first day. I'm trying to keep up with the perfect rhythm of his step. Left. Right. Left. Right. The soldiers stand to attention and salute as we pass.

It's not your usual first day at school. That's normal. I'm an unusual child. And Kalish is not your usual sort of school. It's an old converted monastery, surrounded by a very high wall, covered in barbed wire – there's no way you could climb over it. No child has come willingly to this unusual school, nor have they been brought there by their mother or father. All of them think of only one thing: escaping. It's not surprising I suppose, when there's a guard with his submachine gun stationed near the main gate and soldiers with their dogs trekking back and forth in the courtyard.

Kalish is the school for the stolen children. The SS Gaukinder Home, or the central district home of the Polish *Lebensborn* in Poland.

It's about nine in the evening. It's dark and the courtyard is deserted. The children must already be in bed. But they're not all asleep yet, because I can hear muffled screaming from various spots: behind a locked door, a window, up there on the first floor, and the floor above. If I strain my ears, the sounds seem to be coming from everywhere, like background noise, a continual whirring that makes all the buildings seem to vibrate. And I can hear crying, from the chapel near the entrance.

I just keep going, pretending nothing's wrong, imitating Doctor Ebner, who remains unfazed as we cross the courtyard. Herr Ebner explained everything to me during the car ride here from Poznan. He said Polish children are learning how to become German at Kalish, that it's a rigorous and difficult apprenticeship. The severe punishments and beatings are only for their own good, so they'll be happy later.

Anyway, I'm so happy, so excited at the idea of being surrounded by kids my own age, of living with them, that I manage to distance myself from their screaming and crying. I'm used to it; the kids screamed and cried at Poznan.

But I don't cry, even if I am a bit scared to meet the director of Kalish.

Johanna Sander: tall, blonde, blue eyes. When we enter her office, all I can see of her at first is her tall outline and her brown uniform. When she raises her arm to salute us with a booming *"Heil Hitler!"* I glimpse a pistol stuck in her belt. A nine-millimetre Luger. She reminds me of Josefa. But she's the next model up. Stronger, stricter. Josefa didn't have a gun in her belt.

I try to make my *"Heil Hitler!"* response as forceful as I can, but my voice sounds feeble, pathetic.

The interview doesn't take long. After shaking hands with Frau Sander, Herr Ebner goes to his desk and starts in on his files. Frau Sander and I stay in the doorway of her office. She announces that she already knows everything about me, thanks to the correspondence Doctor Ebner sent her. Holding the letter in one hand, she slides on her glasses and reads, "Konrad von Kebnersol, born in the Steinhöring Home in 1936, on the 20th of April, our Führer's birthday ... (she skips the rest)... Baptised by the Führer himself!"

She takes off her glasses and looks me up and down. I do the same to her, trying not to seem arrogant. She's imposing, with a large face, high forehead and well-defined lips, the corners of which turn down, giving her a nasty, ferocious expression. To tell you the truth, if I wasn't one of our Führer's young wild men, I'd be scared to death of her. It's obvious she's not the type to go weak at the knees in front of my angel face, my platinum-blond hair and my blue, blue eyes. I hope the rest of Doctor Ebner's letter clearly specifies, with the statistical evidence, that I am a perfect specimen of the Nordic race. And that I also have to my credit some remarkable acts of bravery: my endurance as a baby in the face of kidnapping and illegal confinement by a dissident whore, my participation in "Operation Buddies", at first with the Brown Sisters, then with a Polish informer, and last but not least my incredibly useful performance at the Poznan railway station.

"Baptised by the Führer himself!" Frau Sander repeats, after a long silence. Her blue eyes fill with tears. "Baptised by the Führer himself!"

How long is she going to bang on about it? She's like a broken record.

She turns to Doctor Ebner, who glances up from his dossier to nod distractedly.

"The Führer in person!" A tear rolls down her left cheek and, miracle of miracles, the edges of her mouth lift into a twitch that could be a smile. But the smile is not for me. Frau Sander isn't looking at me any more; she's focused on a spot at the other end of the corridor outside her office. As if someone had just appeared there. But I can see out of the corner of my eye that no one's there. She must be seeing a vision of the Führer walking right up to her.

She turns back to me and pats my head. Gently, almost fearfully, as if my head was made out of porcelain and might break. But somehow I can tell that this large, strong hand, caressing my cheek and now my chin, is used to giving out smacks … I think Frau Sander is only caressing me like this in order to have the honour of touching something that the Führer himself touched, to have vicarious contact with him via a proxy – me, as it happens.

I'm feeling uncomfortable. My heart is beating too fast. I really don't like this hand touching me. But I force myself to put up with it.

Finally Frau Sander comes to her senses and removes her hand, brushes away her tears, and wipes the smile off her face. In a second, her face has regained its ferocious look.

"Do you know what we expect of you here, Konrad?" she snaps in an authoritarian voice that has nothing of the exalted tone she used earlier.

"Yes, I do know. Doctor Ebner told me. I'm here as a role model for Polish children my age. They have to think I'm Polish like them, but that I've taken in every aspect of the teaching at Kalish, and been transformed into a perfect little German boy. That's why I speak excellent German, and have forgotten my mother tongue, Polish. I have to be positive and encouraging to my buddies and tell them as often as I can how lucky they are to have been adopted by Germany."

"Perfect!" she exclaims. "Perfect! Now go and unpack." She clicks her fingers and a warden appears. "This is Konrad. Baptised by the Führer himself!"

Like it's my surname.

It must be a code language, because the warden's stern, icy expression changes instantly. Hearing "BBFH" ("baptised by…" you know the rest, I don't have to repeat it), she smiles and asks me kindly to follow her. She tells me that she's taking me to my dormitory, but if I'm at all hungry we could stop by the kitchen. I decline. She insists on offering me a bar of chocolate from her pocket. I bet she offers the Polish kids a taste of the whip I can see stuck in one of her boots.

"No, thank you."

I don't want any special treatment. Anyway, what if one of my future buddies sees us? My cover would be blown and that'd be the end of me playing my role here.

I can't sleep. I'm not used to going to bed so early. The dormitory noises don't bother me; it's just a whole lot of creaking, sighing, snoring, coughing, rustling of sheets – a rhythmic background sound. The SS and the German whores made much more of a racket in the bombed-out house in Poznan. The children stifle their crying so the warden standing at the door like a guard dog doesn't hear them. There's one recurring word, over and over, whispered, like a chant, a prayer: "*Mamo*" ("Mummy"). Then the whole sentence: "*Chce moja mame*" ("I want my mummy"). The Polish kids haven't yet erased the damn word from their vocabulary, like I did a while ago now. That's why they're sad. One of the first things I'll teach them over the next few days is how to get rid of that word from their memories. They'll feel so much better afterwards.

It's as dark as the inside of an oven, but when the warden took me to my bed she had a torch and I counted about forty beds. Twenty on each side. All I could see of my buddies were their shadowy outlines under the blankets. Of the ones who hadn't pulled the sheet over their heads – as if this thin material could somehow protect them – I glimpsed some hair, a hand, a foot.

The kid on my right isn't sleeping either. He just tosses and turns. From the creaking of the bedsprings, I can tell that he's leaning towards me. He wants to speak to me but is too frightened. The warden might hear him, or see him by the light of the torch she sweeps around the room every few minutes.

Eventually he falls asleep. His breathing is regular, with the occasional gentle snoring. There's a smell of urine coming from his bed, unless it's from the one on my left, or from all the beds. It stinks.

The whole dormitory stinks of pee. I've never wet my bed, or else it was so long ago I've forgotten.

As well as the stifled sobbing and the whispered "*Mamo*", there's also nightmarish screaming. "*Aj!*"

"*Nie! Nie, nie mnie!*"

"*Litosc!*" A body shoots up then collapses on the mattress

again. I know those screams. I heard them often enough in Poznan.

"Ow!"

"No! No, not me!"

"Please!" The warden isn't worried about the screaming, she must be used to it.

I'm still awake. It's hard for me to change my routine overnight. In the bombed-out house in Poznan, I wandered around freely all night long, listening at doors without Frau Lotte noticing a thing. Compared to the warden, Frau Lotte seems like an angel now.

I want to get out of bed. Too bad about the rules. The warden won't be able to punish me anyway. When her colleague brought me in here earlier, she repeated the magic phrase, "BBFH", with the same reverence Frau Sander used. (It must be a code name that was communicated to all the staff before I arrived.) So off I go, out of bed to tell her I want to go to the toilet. She's already removed the whip from her boot, and is about to lash me with it, when she sees I'm the BBFH, so she stops and lets me go. I pretend to head for the door she's pointing to, but as soon as her back is turned I head the other way.

I venture to the end of the corridor, where there's another dormitory. I can hear babies screaming behind the closed door. That's why there's no warden on guard duty. Obviously these prisoners aren't about to escape. I push open the door.

Chaos. Cradles everywhere. It reminds me of Steinhöring. Except, in my memory, the cradles were much more attractive, not half-broken, wobbly and dirty, like these. The walls were white and clean, and there were windows. Here the walls are grey and there's only one tiny skylight in the roof. The babies must range from about six months old to a year. The one-year-olds are longer but no larger. They're like rabbits.

Rabbits.

I suddenly remember that code word. One of the first I learned. Are all these babies going to be packed into vans and delivered to a hospital where they'll be chopped into pieces and stored in jars? No, I'm getting everything mixed up! Herr Ebner already told me that, as well as older children, there are babies at Kalish, and that the babies don't stay long: they're sent off first to Germany, where their adoptive families are waiting for them.

I hope they get a bath before they leave, because they really stink of crap. It is foul! In some of the cradles I can see liquid running out of the nappies and all over the sheets. The smell is absolutely atrocious! I have to block my nose so I don't faint.

There's screaming and crying everywhere. Obviously, with all that crap, the babies' bums must be chafed and infected. There are only two wardens for all these stinky, wailing babies. And they're lying down, asleep on two beds at either end of the room. When one of them wakes up, grumbling, she goes round handing out more smacks and swear words than bottles and clean nappies.

I'm getting out of here. The incessant noise is deafening and the stink is making me nauseous. I don't want to see what the other dormitories are like any more. And now I'm tired; I'd better sleep if I want to be in good shape tomorrow. Tomorrow is the start of my life as a schoolboy. I get back into bed and fall asleep straightaway.

* * *

I start having nightmares of sinking into a huge swamp of sewage. I dream of sitting alone in the dining room and being forced to drink wee and eat poo. I see the babies from the dormitory at the end of the corridor all rising together from their cradles, like an army of evil little creatures. They encircle me and bombard me with their filthy dripping nappies, which burn my skin and disfigure my little angel face.

I wake up with a start. My sheets are soaked and I'm scared I've wet the bed. But it's only sweat. BBFH doesn't wet the bed! I soon fall asleep again and this time I sleep peacefully, dreaming that my buddies are all neat and tidy, clean as a whistle, impeccable.

Germanized.

The next morning, at 6 a.m., the warden is striding along the dormitory aisle with her stick, hitting beds, and sometimes the legs of children, who bounce up instantly like springs.

17.

The days are full at Kalish. The timetable is scheduled to the last minute, with no down time and not a moment of respite.

It's designed that way so the children go from one activity to the next without stopping. If they stop, they'll think. If they think, they'll remember – their parents, their brothers and sisters, their home, their toys, their favourite food, everything about their lives before they were kidnapped. But they have to forget that life, *once and for all*.

I can personally attest that it's a very effective system. The longer I'm here, the more distant my stay in the bombed-out house in Poznan seems. It's like a dream now. Frau Lotte and the Brown Sisters are like faceless ghosts. If I didn't happen to run into Doctor Ebner regularly – his work here is to select the newcomers – I think I'd have forgotten him too.

6 a.m., gymnastics.

The German youth must be athletic! says our Führer. So we might as well start as early as we can to build up our muscles. Gymnastics is good for the body, and good for the mind. Physical activity is a great way to cleanse the brain of any harmful thoughts.

We jump out of bed in our singlets and underpants, half-naked, and run ten times round the courtyard, while the wardens set the pace with their whistles. If we slow down, we get hit. If we break formation in the perfect running circle, we get hit. If we don't lift up our knees in time – one, two, one, two! – we get hit. Breathe in, breathe out, breathe in, breathe out: that's all we think about. Otherwise, in this winter cold, we'll cough and choke. In the heat of summer, we'll suffocate and fall down faint.

In the winter, it's hard to see. Our eyelids are swollen with sleep and our legs are like jelly. We all shiver because it's a brutal contrast between bed and the icy air. In summer, it's also hard to see because of the blinding contrast between the dark dormitory and the bright courtyard, and because we're still damp from bed and it's already stifling.

In the beginning, we say, "I'll never be able to do it!" and then, somehow, we manage. Because there's no choice. There's no calling out "Mummy!" when you're running. Mummy won't come. Not any more. Never. While we're running, we forget the meaning of the word "Mummy". One! Two! One! Two! Faster! Faster! Those words are the only thing in our minds.

IT WAKES US UP.

Once gymnastics is over, we head back to the dormitory, still running. Then we each stand to attention next to our beds, while the warden inspects the sheets. Those who have wet their bed in the night have to go without breakfast and be punished: they carry the rubbish out, clean the toilets or unpack the deliveries. Everyone else makes their bed with hospital corners, a smooth bedspread, no wrinkles, and the top sheet folded straight, parallel with the wall.

Next, we wash ourselves – in cold water, summer and winter. Then breakfast at 7.30. All the children gather in a huge dining hall. The big kids, up to twelve years old, are in one half of the room, and the under tens, like me, are in the other half. From the number of empty spots in their rows, I'd say a lot more of the big kids are being punished. That's normal. The older kids find it harder to accept Germanization: they're confused by too many precise memories, and gymnastics is not enough to get rid of them. But, apart from wetting the bed, the young ones are well behaved for the most part. Of course, they don't cope very well with being tied up to a post in the middle of the courtyard and whipped if they misbehave. The older kids think they'll hold out, but most of the time they overestimate their strength and end up screaming out *"Mamo!"* too. But *Mamo* doesn't get them untied from the post or stop the whippings. Only the warden decides, depending on her mood, when to put an end to the torture.

Breakfast doesn't last long. We just have time to gobble a bowl of chicory and a slice of black bread before we assemble for roll call in the courtyard and then an hour of total silence, under pain of further punishment. Often this is when we see trucks arriving with newcomers, who have to go through the selection process in a room that's out of bounds to us.

The rest of the morning is devoted to schoolwork. When the teacher arrives, we have to salute her, *"Heil Hitler!"*, with a raised arm. It's become a reflex for me: I'm used to springing to attention and extending my arm as soon as I see a uniform, but my buddies haven't got it yet; their salutes are too limp. More punishment.

As soon as the teacher sits down at her desk, each child

in turn has to call out his first name and date of birth. It's not as easy as it sounds. Because it's got to be their *new German first name,* the one they were given when they arrived at Kalish. Same thing for their date of birth, the false one provided by Doctor Ebner. Immediate punishment for any boy stumbling over the pronunciation of his name. Some of them are lucky, going, for example, from "Jan" to "Johann". But it's harder to go from "Ryszard" to "Rutger", from "Tadeusz" to "Tomas", or from "Wojciech" to "Wolfgang". And if their dates of birth don't correspond to those on the teacher's roll, more punishment.

"You?" asks the teacher, pointing randomly to a boy. "What happened to your parents?"

"My father was killed by a Polish criminal."

Good answer.

"And you?"

"My mother had tuberculosis and died."

Not bad.

"And you?"

"My mother died because she was an alcoholic."

Much better.

This is the best answer: "My mother died because she was a whore." But no matter how many times the teacher repeats it, the kids hardly ever remember it. When I'm asked, I have no problem at all saying that my mother was a whore. The whores in Poznan were kind to me; I remember them well.

The main thing is never to answer, "My parents were shot." Or, "They died in a bombing raid." That could get you the worst punishment of all.

Die Kapelle. The chapel.

The children go pale and tremble in fear when they hear that word. If you're banished to the chapel at the entrance of the monastery, you have to stay kneeling all night long on the icy floor, arms spread-eagled, watched the whole time by the warden, who beats you if you so much as twitch.

The kids in my class hardly ever give the wrong answer, but the older kids often do. At the end of your answer, you have to repeat the following line, which the whole class chants with you, "I am grateful to Germany for rescuing me from my degenerate family."

When I'm interrogated, I reply straight up, in a loud voice and in perfect German, "My name is Konrad. I was born on the 20th of April, 1936. I have no parents, only my father and guide, the Führer, and my mother country, Germany!"

The teacher orders my buddies to clap in appreciation of my performance. And for the next hour they have to repeat after me all the new German words on the agenda for that day, making sure they don't use the broken German they usually speak – although I find it amusing – and trying to get rid of their Polish accents. You don't say "Me happy adopt by German family", but "I'm happy to have been adopted by a German family".

After a short break, during which it is forbidden to speak Polish, under pain of punishment at the post or in the chapel, class starts again. Depending on the day, we do History, Maths or Singing. In History, we have to colour in a map – pink for all the countries that make up the Reich, and green for those soon to be part of the Reich. Easy-peasy! Pink: Poland, Ukraine, Yugoslavia, France, Belgium, Luxembourg, Netherlands, Norway, Denmark, Sweden, Greece. Green: Russia, North Africa, Britain. So as not to make a mistake, the trick is to scribble green on all the countries that aren't pink. Bingo!

In Maths, we do calculations like this: *For his birthday, Helmut's mother ordered a cake. If the cake was attacked during the night by Jews who stole three quarters of it, how much of Helmut's cake is left?* The answer is obvious, at least to me, because I was already doing these sort of problems with Frau Lotte in Poznan. Poor Helmut only gets a quarter of his cake.

Some days, instead of classes, we have surprise tests. We're shown pictures and we have to identify the different ranks of SS uniforms. While my buddies panic at these tests, I give the answers in a flash. I've known the SS ranks by heart since I was a baby.

Late morning is a goosestep parade in front of Johanna Sander. In the afternoon, while the kids undergo their punishments, the others do gardening or woodwork.

And that's it for the day. After dinner, lights out. Off to beddy-byes.

The thing I like best about Kalish is the playground, with all my buddies.

I like my buddies a lot and I enjoy being with them. They soon understood that I'm the best, the leader, the role model. They see me smiling, well nourished – they have no idea that I get extra rations – and they realize that because I excel in my schoolwork I don't get punished, so naturally they think that if they imitate me they'll be able to have a better time. They just have to do their homework.

Nevertheless, some of them are curious about my behaviour and ask me questions when the teacher isn't looking. "Konrad? True, you never think Mother? You never more speak Polish? You never want cry, die?"

By way of response, I launch into a long, half-invented story. One thing I've learned is that, for a lie to sound credible, you have to add some elements of the truth. So I embroider the story that Josefa told me dozens of times when I was in the Home, about being stolen by the dissident whore, being hidden in a cellar…

I tell my buddies that sometimes I do think about *Mamo* – I scatter a few Polish words throughout my story to make it sound more authentic – but this *Mamo* doesn't have a face any more. I tell them that we were both in a cellar so we'd be protected from the bombings in Warsaw, that *Mamo* was wounded, that she died and I was left for three days in her arms, which were as stiff as hooks, with nothing to eat or drink. I'd be dead too, if a German nurse, Josefa, hadn't found me and taken me to Doctor Ebner. As soon as I mention his name, my buddies flinch and their eyes widen in terror. So I hasten to add: Doctor Ebner looks mean with his bald head, his big pulsing vein and his icy eyes, but in fact he's really kind. And he's a great doctor, because he cured my dehydration when I was a baby. I end the story by saying that it's not hard to forget your *Mamo*. Look, I'm the proof!

When I've finished, my buddies look at me in awe and admiration, and call out, "Poor baby Konrad! You much suffer! Some kind Germans, possible, this?"

The result: the students in my class make huge progress and head off quickly for adoption. A new lot arrives and I'm back helping again.

I like some of the subjects and compulsory activities, and I hate others. (I guess it's the same in all schools, not just Kalish.)

My favourite activities in ascending order:

Morning gymnastics. I'd like the sessions to be longer, more difficult, and to include obstacle courses like the ones the big kids have. I can run fast and I'm strong.

Goosestepping. I love it. Except it's stupid to goosestep

when you're wearing shorts and ankle socks. You need a uniform and a weapon in your belt.

What I don't like:

Making my bed. In Poznan, Frau Lotte never forced me to make my bed. A Polish prisoner did it, as well as the rest of the housekeeping. Most of the time I manage to get my dormitory neighbour, Wolfgang (ex-Wojciech) to make mine. In exchange, I let him copy off me during the surprise tests and I pass him my breakfast under the table. (Because I'm BBFH, I can go to the kitchen whenever I like and get more food.)

History and Maths. My class is just too weak. I can do it all with my eyes shut, so I'm bored off my face, yawning the whole time. And I hate being locked up in a classroom all morning.

What I hate the most: going to bed early at night. I just can't get used to it.

Sometimes I get sick of being the model child. It's not enough stimulation for my *Draufgängertum*. I'll end up a sissy if I'm not careful. So I do something stupid: I start loudly talking in Polish, or I answer the questions wrongly in class, or I colour in green the areas that should be pink, or, worse still, I leave blank the countries that should be invaded by Germany. I speak in broken German, I sing out of tune, I change the words of "The Horst Wessel Song". Instead of singing "An empty road for the brown battalions", I sing "for the *red* battalions".

It really annoys the wardens and the teachers. They'd like to use their whips on me. They're dying to: they go bright red in the face, and start mumbling that I must be tired. That way they resist the temptation of beating me to a pulp – or else they take it out on another kid. Ha! It won't be long before I get one of them to crack!

The person I hate the most is Frau Sander, the director. She's the reason I had a stomach-ache for several days. Not the stomach-ache you get from the revolting food in the dining hall. (BBFH gets better food than the others.) It's the gutache from *psychological disturbance.* The illness I thought I was immune to now.

It happened one morning just before roll call in the courtyard. I was walking with Wolfgang, my dormitory neighbour who is now my friend. An SS guy was crossing the courtyard in front of us. All of a sudden, I heard *bang!* Wolfgang collapsed. A sticky, hot liquid spattered my cheeks. Then I saw red stuff all over my shirt, on my shorts, on the ground, coming out of Wolfgang's head. A dribble that became a puddle. I realized it was blood, that the *bang* was a gunshot, that Wolfgang was *dead.*

Tot. Kaput.

At first I thought the SS guy had killed him. But he hadn't stopped when we walked past. And he couldn't have used a gun because he was carrying a big pile of dossiers. From the sound, I could tell the shot had come from above. I looked up and saw Frau Sander at the window of her office. She was putting her Luger back in the holster, leaning on the ledge, smoking a cigarette.

She shot Wolfgang in the head. She had been observing the courtyard, as she did every morning, and saw that Wolfgang didn't salute the SS guy correctly. From her window she saw that he didn't raise his arm. She *saw* Wolfgang, but she didn't *hear* him.

"Konrad," he had asked me, just before the shot, "me

forget if salute officer with one star and a stripe or two stars?"

I didn't have time to tell him: you salute them when they have one star and a stripe – that is, exactly what was on the uniform of the *Scharführer* before us. Wolfgang drew a blank right at that moment, whereas the day before, during the surprise test, he knew it all, without even copying off me.

That blank earned him a bullet in the head that was definitely not a blank.

That night in the dormitory I found it even harder to go to sleep. Usually, after lights-out, I got Wolfgang to recite the list of stars and stripes and their corresponding ranks. It helped him to feel confident for next day's class, in case there was a test, and the murmur of his recitation helped me to fall asleep. It was more effective than counting sheep.

The empty bed next to me gave me a stomach-ache. And the stomach-ache reminded me of what I'd been through in the Poznan house after Bibiana disappeared. I thought I'd forgotten Bibiana and there I was remembering her. Her face suddenly popped up in one of the compartments of my brain. Her face is associated with my stomach-aches. And, because memories come in a domino effect, I remembered the terrible stomach-ache I'd had in the Home at Steinhöring. But there was no face attached to that memory. It was too long ago.

When I was playing in the bombed-out house in Poznan, I saw SS soldiers shoot Polish people, but it was from the window of the attic on the top floor. From that distance, the Polish people and the soldiers looked tiny, like figurines, toys. The blood on the walls looked like paint.

The blood didn't splash onto me.

In Poznan, Frau Lotte took me into my room so I wouldn't see the bullet go into the back of Bibiana's neck. But I definitely saw the one that went into Wolfgang's forehead.

I had nightmares for two nights running. I dreamed that Bibiana's head with the hole in her neck was lying on top of Wolfgang's body. I dreamed that Wolgang's head with the hole in his forehead was lying on top of Bibiana's body. I dreamed that my head had a hole in the neck and the forehead.

I wet my bed. Twice. I wasn't punished by the warden, because BBFH can't be punished, but if she'd so much as tried, I would have killed her. I would have riddled her head with a thousand holes!

Over those two nights, while the bed next to me was empty, I learned that memories are not that easy to eradicate. Even with a full schedule like at Kalish. Even when you've got a dolichocephalic head.

18.

The bed next to me is occupied now. Wolfgang was replaced quickly.

I recovered from my stomach-ache. But not from my inclination to stay up late after bedtime. My new neighbour, exhausted by the Kalish routine, sleeps like a log as soon as his head hits the pillow.

So I'm bored. But I've got an idea, one I've been harbouring for a while.

Girls.

We're separated from them. You get a glimpse of them when they arrive and climb out of the trucks, and then *poof!* They disappear. But I know they go through the selection process before leaving. Here, at night. I know they're completely naked for the selection process.

I get out of bed and find the warden. Of course, rather than telling her I'm going to spy on naked girls, I tell her that I have to speak to Doctor Ebner. It's late and the warden is grumpy; she frowns, hesitates, and then lets me go. She doesn't have a choice; she's obliged to agree to requests from

BBFH, especially when he asks for his protector, Doctor Ebner. Especially since Wolfgang's death. Because, since that day, BBFH has treated the wardens like shit. He tells on them when he sees them smoking in secret. He tells on them when he sees them going to rendezvous with soldiers outside the monastery wall. Or when they sneak some of the supplies. Or when they're on their break and they turn off the radio during a broadcast of one of our Führer's speeches. BBFH denounces them at every opportunity, even when they're not breaking a rule. BBFH is not afraid to lie. BBFH knows that the Führer encourages people to inform on others.

The selection of newcomers takes place in two basement rooms: one for boys, and one for girls. When I ask Doctor Ebner's permission to stay with him in the boys' room, he seems surprised, but doesn't say no. Johanna Sander has told him how well behaved I am, and what a good influence I am on my buddies. Sometimes, of course, I do misbehave, but hardly ever and, besides, my occasional slip-ups make me seem more like a real little Polish kid in the eyes of my buddies. My nightly wanderings annoy the staff but, after all, isn't insomnia a sign of a strong character? My presence during the selection process could be useful. Dirty and exhausted after their long train trip in overcrowded carriages, the new arrivals can see a flesh-and-blood example of what Kalish will make of them in a few weeks: an attractive, lively child with pink cheeks, clean hair and smart clothes. (BBFH's cheeks and clothes no longer sport traces of Wolfgang's blood, and now he's got a smile on his beautiful angel face.) I will calm their fears.

Doctor Ebner agrees on the condition that I stay in the corner and don't interrupt. I promise to be as good as gold.

I sit on a stool and I'm so quiet that after a while no one notices when I slip into the next room.

It was a good move; there are lots of girls! Blonde, blue-eyed (maybe I won't bother mentioning those particular details any more), aged between two and twelve. And, just as I'd imagined, they're all naked. I'm only interested in the older ones, not the little girls, who snivel when a warden takes away their teddy bear or a favourite toy they've managed to hold on to during their kidnapping.

The older ones are snivelling too, because a warden with a club is hitting them – to make them drop their arms and stop trying to cover their breasts. It's just a gentle tap; they can't be damaged before the selection process. I don't see why the girls are carrying on like that. They've got nothing to hide. Just two little budding breasts, some more prominent than others. Most are mere bulges, nothing resembling decent breasts.

It's funny how they obediently drop their arms, only to put their hands straightaway over their lower belly to hide what's down below. So, hey presto, another hit from the club to keep their arms at their sides. And they've got nothing to hide down there either, in my opinion. No pubic hair at all. Nothing, just the outline of the slit between two bits of pink flesh. I know exactly what that is. I saw it in Poznan when the whores took off their clothes to have sex with the SS soldiers. A big tuft of pubic hair and, underneath, a slit that stretches open, like an elastic band, to let the SS penises in.

The girls line up in front of a Sister in a white lab coat. She measures them with a ruler: head, hips, pelvis. For some it's over quickly. "Bad impression," says the Sister, before moving on to the next girl. I can tell that's a code expression.

"Bad impression" means "Discard". Translation: "Kill," or, better: "Transfer to a camp."

On the other hand, those who make a "Good impression" ("Keep") line up in front of a second sister in a white lab coat who takes photos of them. A photo of their body, especially their breasts, pelvis and buttocks, and a photo of their face, front-on and profile. At this point – it's really quite complicated – the girls who made a "Good impression" are separated into two groups. One group leaves immediately for the Homeschool in Illenau, a school like Kalish for girls only, where they'll be Germanized, like my buddies, and then adopted by German families.

The girls in the other group line up in front of a third Sister in a white lab coat. She starts feeling their breasts. She squeezes them, pinches them, pulls and pushes them, and measures them. Is she trying to guess what they'll look like later: large, small, round, pear-shaped, eggs sunny-side up? Will they produce a lot of milk, or not very much?

Next, she makes them lie on a table while she measures their pelvis again, to check her colleague's earlier calculation, and then she spreads their legs.

To look at their slit.

Now the girls are in a total panic. They start crying again, shouting, their legs shaking so much that a warden is called in to hold them down. They are terrified that the Sister will stick the examination torch right inside their slit. But she doesn't, obviously. You don't stick a torch in a slit. That's where a penis goes. An SS penis. It's the only thing that can get inside there. I saw it in Poznan.

Once they're off the examining table, the Sister calls out another code expression: "Good for the Führer's fertility programme." (That code language is just too obvious; at least for me it is.) To finish off, the girls line up in front of a fourth Sister in a white lab coat, who gives them a tattoo, using an instrument like a long pencil that emits smoke. She draws a sort of lozenge shape on their forearm and on the nape of their neck. It doesn't look that painful. The girls scream and fight to get out of the clutches of the warden, but once the pencil starts tattooing they stop screaming and don't even flinch.

I need to stop and think. There's something I don't get. What's the difference between the tattooed girls and the others? Tattooed or not, they're all heading for Illenau; they're all registered for adoption. But that damned tattoo must have a meaning, some particular purpose? They've been branded, so they'll be recognized.

One girl is making a huge fuss, yelling and throwing herself around so much that all the Sisters have rushed over to help the warden. While they're distracted, I sneak a look at the adoption register, where I see that the tattooed girls are being marked in a special column headed with the number sixteen.

What on earth does that mean? I've only learned code words, not code numbers. OK, let me work it out like a maths problem. I go over the wording of the problem: the girls get a tattoo after their slit is examined, when the sister says that their slit is "good for the Führer's fertility programme".

I've got it!

Sixteen means sixteen-year-old. The tattooed girls are adopted up until the age of sixteen, to give them time to grow, for their slit to get big enough for an SS penis to enter it. That's it! At sixteen they're made to have sex with the SS and produce babies. Beautiful blond babies with blue eyes. Presents for the Führer. Just like I was!

So, if I pursue this line of reasoning, the tattooed girls are the whores of the future, who will make babies like *me*. Does that mean my mother – my biological mother, the one I have no memory of, apart from the stomach-ache when she left me – was also a whore? Is that why, when the teacher asks me in class, I'm the only one who can say that my mother was a whore? I guess so. That could also explain why I got on so well with the whores in Poznan, who liked to pop me on their knees and give me champagne... Yes, that all seems highly likely.

So, in the meantime, the tattooed girls are only *future* whores. No breasts, no pubic hair. They're not having much fun. And they're not fun to look at. The whole show is repetitive: measurements, table, photos, tattoo.

I'm tired. I'm not used to doing maths problems this late at night. It's bedtime for me.

Back in the other room, I'm about to say goodnight to Doctor Ebner, when I stop in my tracks. Suddenly I'm not tired at all. There's no way I'm off to bed now. I hop back on my stool again and stare, wide-eyed.

My beautiful, bright, blue eyes fix on a pair of eyes just as beautiful, just as bright, just as blue. Those eyes are mesmerizing, with a fierce, arrogant expression, and not the slightest trace of fear. It's the real thing: the look of one of the Führer's young wild animals, ready to bare his teeth and pounce. That expression alone says loud and clear, "Fuck you, whoever you are."

Above that pair of eyes, the blond hair has never been stained by dirt or sweat. Those eyes and that hair belong to a boy. He's tall. You can tell he's only recently got skinny. Even though his rib cage is visible, his shoulders are broad, and his thigh and calf muscles are prominent. If he were given the same food rations as BBFH, after a few days he'd be back to his normal strength. He's much older than I am, perhaps twelve, or older? But it's crazy how much he looks like me. I feel like I'm looking in a mirror at myself in a few years' time.

This boy is me at his age. This boy could be my older brother.

I even wonder if the mother-whore who gave birth to him is the same as mine? It must be an error. Either the boy is not Polish, or I'm not German. In that case, perhaps the story I like telling my buddies, while we work in the garden in the afternoon, might actually be true? I don't know. I'm not sure of anything any more. The only thing I'm certain of is that *I want to be with this boy. He has to make it through the selection process* so that we won't be separated. It's the first time I've understood why, at Poznan station, the children screamed so much when they were torn from their brothers and sisters, and why here, too, brothers are desperate to see each other, to exchange a few words, even if it means they'll be whipped, or end up in the chapel.

It's almost the same selection process as for the girls. The boys are naked, but they don't have to lie on a table for the examination torch (that's the advantage of having a penis hanging on the outside and nothing inside). But that doesn't stop the older ones from having the same reflex as the girls, as soon as they're naked. They cover their penises with their hands. All except the fierce-looking boy, who couldn't care less about displaying his penis. And he's right, because that means he avoids being beaten.

The first doctor (there are two officers in white lab coats, as well as Doctor Ebner) measures the boys. Head, neck, torso, legs, arms. And out come the code words, different ones from those used with the girls. This time they're saying that the children represent "a desirable increase in the population", "a tolerable increase", or that they're "undesirable". Too easy. No need to translate that.

The fierce-looking boy is put into the "desirable" group. Phew! He made it through the first stage. As soon as I saw him, I was sure that would be the case, but you never know, and you can't always trust the measurements, as they have to correspond to a precise grid. He has his photo taken, then he's sent on to the second doctor. I would have preferred him to be examined by Ebner himself, but he's supervising the process from his desk, providing a new name and date of birth for the chosen children, without getting directly involved in the selection. I'd really like to ask him to go and oversee his colleague – or, even better, for him to examine the fierce-looking boy himself. Doctor Ebner is infallible, there's no one better at recognizing the specimens of the Nordic race. I'd also like to go and give this advice to the boy: *Don't be frightened, you'll get through. It was the same deal for me – examination, measurements – at birth, and afterwards. You'll be fine.*

But the boy doesn't look a bit frightened. He's not moving at all, not the slightest twitch on his face. It's like he's wearing a mask.

A doctor examines his penis. He pulls on it and measures how long it is; he ties a ribbon around it to measure its width; and he pushes up the foreskin and squeezes the head of the penis for a long time, pressing and crushing it, as if he was testing its elasticity. Next he palpates the two balls on either side. (They're called "testicles".) He weighs them in his hand to make sure they've descended into their sacks; perhaps also to calculate, like with the girls' breasts, whether they'll end up decent-sized or small and shrivelled. The other boys are terrified, shaking, backing away from those fingers manhandling them so crudely.

But not the fierce-looking boy. On the contrary. For the first time, his face relaxes, his jaw muscles are no longer clenched, his mouth falls open slightly, and there's a trace of a smile on his lips. His eyes – his beautiful, blue, bright, mesmerizing eyes – light up as he stares at the doctor bent over his penis. No child, boy or girl, ever smiles during the selection process. And especially not at this point! What's up with him? Is it does it, really ... feel ... like in Poznan, when the whores held the SS penises in their hands? The SS guys looked like they really liked it; they begged the whores not to stop... But, hang on, something's wrong. The doctor is a man, not a whore... Oh, I get it. The boy I thought was like our Führer's young wild animals ... like my big brother ... he's just ... a homosexual. A homo. A dirty little homo. Oh no. That's terrible. The Führer hates homos. Homos have to wear a pink triangle and they get sent to camps. That damn boy, HE'S HAD IT!

No. I'm wrong. The boy is not smiling like that because it feels ... whatever ... while his penis and testicles are being fondled. He's smiling because right now he is urinating in the doctor's hands. And we're not talking about a little accidental dribble. This is one huge intentional powerful spurt of urine that traces a perfect arc and, given the doctor's position, sprays not just his hands, but his entire face, too.

I'm about to burst out laughing, but I stop myself, terrified.

They're going to tear him to pieces, smash his beautiful

angel face. He'll be completely disfigured. The doctor who got urine all over his face is furious; he gives the boy a violent punch that knocks him to the ground. So now the boy is spurting blood: his nose is broken and blood is pouring from it. His lip is split. But his little mocking smile is still there, so one of the officers swings his boot and lands him a huge kick in the face, smack in his eyes, his beautiful, bright, blue, mesmerizing eyes. They won't stay like that for long. His right eye is already swollen, his eyelids puffy, and his cheekbones are sunken.

"Filthy dog! Piece of shit! Polish vermin!" bawls the officer, as he signals the guard on duty at the door.

I know what that means, "Take him away! Kill him!"

No! I don't want this boy killed!

Just as I'm about to leap from my stool and get Doctor Ebner to intervene, he himself gestures to the soldier who has the boy by the hair. He gives the order for silence and asks the doctor to bring him the sheet of paper with the measurements of the penis that urinated on him.

Let's hope it measures up well. I'm quite convinced there's nothing to worry there – his penis is beautiful! And his testicles too! Well descended. And they're big! What's more, I can't believe Doctor Ebner hasn't noticed the physical resemblance between this boy and me. He's a "desirable" of the highest quality. They can't kill him just because he urinated on an officer. (I try to erase the memory of Wolfgang, killed for a much more minor misdemeanour.)

The boy lies sprawled on the ground, dazed after the blows he's just received. A few minutes pass while Ebner stares at him. My heart is racing. Ebner should have looked at him earlier, when his nose wasn't bleeding and his eyelids weren't swollen. Now he looks like nothing on earth, and no longer like me, that's for sure.

I'm waiting for Ebner's verdict. I've got pins and needles in my arms and legs, I'm struggling to breathe, my chest is heaving faster and faster, and my fingernails are digging into my hands because my fists are clenched so tightly. I just want to go and punch that officer's face in. And Ebner's too, if his verdict is negative. Or better still: have I got time to run over and grab the gun in the soldier's belt? For sure. I'm a fast runner. This place has taught me that. As soon as I've got the gun, I'll shoot anyone who moves.

Silence. Three seconds more and I'm off. Then, finally, Doctor Ebner orders the soldier to take the boy to the warden in charge of handing out clean clothes, so that he can then get in line outside Ebner's office.

End of incident. Everyone gets back to work, and I can breathe again.

He's through. He just has to wait his turn. Once he receives his new name and date of birth, he'll be sent to the big kids' dormitory, where I'll go and find him. I can't wait to see what name he'll be given.

When his turn comes round, Ebner consults his notes for the boy's Polish name and date of birth, then dictates to his secretary, "Lukas. Born 18th March, 1932."

Lukas. Lukas, with a K, like Konrad, like Krupp steel. Excellent choice. I love that name. But, the date of birth … I do the maths in my head: 1942–1932 = 10. Lukas isn't ten, he's at least two years older. Doctor Ebner knows that, but he also knows that German families don't adopt children older than ten. The false birthdate shows that Doctor Ebner is convinced Lukas will make a perfect German adolescent, a magnificent *Jungmann*.

But…

"Mam na imię Lucjan! A nie Lukas! Jestem Polakiem! A nie Niemcem!"

Oh, what an idiot! What's the matter with you? Have you got rocks in your head?

"My name is Lucjan! Not Lukas! I'm Polish, not German."

That's what he just shouted at Doctor Ebner, staring straight at him.

The warden immediately raises her whip and belts him. The boy ignores it and shouts the same thing again.

A second lash of the whip, which knocks him to the ground like before. But he lifts his head and shouts, *"Lucjan! Mam na imię Lucjan!"*

A third lash of the whip. His new clothes are all torn, and his skin underneath, too, striped with three long red welts from which blood is pouring.

A fourth lash of the whip.

That's the one I took. When I leaped off my stool and threw myself on top of Lukas.

19.

Not a word of gratitude from Lukas when we were both transferred to the infirmary. Even though I copped most of the lashes that were aimed at him. That warden was out of control. In her furious ecstasy of hitting, again and again, she didn't notice that she was hitting the BBFH, that she was ripping and slashing mercilessly at the very skin the Führer had once caressed with his own hand – my own perfect, white skin, a control sample of the superior race. Even Doctor Ebner had trouble recognizing me. (As I'd slipped off discreetly to look at the girls, he thought I'd left ages ago.)

Whipping the BBFH was sacrilege. BBFH was in shocking pain. BBFH thought he was going to die. BBFH lost consciousness.

And Lukas didn't utter a word to the nurse after he and I had regained consciousness: we were both lying on our bellies, unable to move without feeling that our backs would shatter into a thousand pieces. The only sounds we could make were long, pitiful groans. Like two half-paralysed old men.

And still not a word from him when we left the infirmary after our wounds had healed. Lukas went to the older kids' group and I returned to mine. At least my buddies welcomed me like a hero.

"Bravo, Konrad! You very brave! Little Konrad very strong! So tough not break with bloody warden whip!"

Normally, their words would have filled me with pride. But I don't want their praise, I want Lukas's. It's OK that he hasn't said thank you. (The Poles are real pigs if that's how they raise their kids.) But at least he could say a few words to me. Anything! Even *Gowno!* ("Shit!")

Try as I might to approach him over the following days, it's a waste of time, he doesn't even notice me. He just looks through me, as if I were nothing more than a pebble, a stone, an obstacle to avoid. It's the same with everyone, so at least I have the consolation of knowing that he hasn't got it in for me personally. Not a single boy, from his dormitory or his classroom, manages to engage with him. It's like his mouth is sealed.

But he does find ways of opening his big mouth when he wants to.

During History lessons one morning, for example, he suddenly stares straight at the teacher and announces that everything is about to change: when the Americans enter the war, allied with the other European countries, he decrees, they'll bring Germany to her knees. He proclaims that Germany will never be capable of invading Russia. (The teacher can't respond to him; she's on the verge of a nervous breakdown.) Another time, instead of reciting words of German vocabulary, he shouts out their Polish translation. He insists on calling himself by his Polish name, Lucjan. And he refuses to goosestep. In fact, at every opportunity, he systematically and intentionally contravenes all the toughest regulations.

He gets landed with all sorts of punishments, beatings, chores. He scarcely goes to classes in the mornings any more: he has to clean the toilets and rubbish bins, when he's not staggering under the weight of boxes of supplies that he unloads by himself, a rifle aimed at him as he labours. He's tied to the post in the courtyard so often it's as if it's reserved for him alone. Same for the chapel, where he spends more nights than in the dormitory.

At first, I think he's brave, and I admire him. You have to admit, he's got amazing *Draufgängertum*! But in the end it's no longer bravery, it's madness. And it's making me go mad. At night, when I'm lying in bed and he's still tied to the pole after a whole day there – no food, like a neglected dog – I try to say to myself, *Forget about him! Let him die! Go and get your extra rations from the kitchen and gorge yourself to pass the time, then go back to bed, and tomorrow his corpse will be gone…*

But I can't help myself. I get up, leave the dormitory and untie him. I help him out of the courtyard, up the stairs and into his bed. I bring him something to eat – my extra rations. I tuck him in like a baby and stay with him until, exhausted, he falls asleep.

He never says a word.

I can't help myself because I know that, if I let him die, I'll end up with that damn stomach-ache-psychological-disturbance thing. It'll be a shocker of a stomach-ache and, this time, it will knock me out.

A few days go by. Lukas regains his strength and does the same thing again. So I'm back on task. At dawn, I rush into the chapel, where the warden whipped him and left him for dead all night long. He is unconscious on the icy floor.

He doesn't look so great now. Feverish, shivering with cold, sobbing in pain, he is too weak to extricate himself from my arms. So I do my best: I feed him sips of hot broth, and push bits of bread I've chewed and softened into his mouth. The roles are reversed now: I'm the big brother and he's the helpless, weeping little brother. Of course he's blubbering, what do you expect? You can't just keep on getting beaten and abused and not break down and cry your guts out. When he's moaning and sobbing, choking on his snot, or when his fever makes him delirious and he mumbles a few incoherent, almost inaudible words at me, I encourage him. "Don't worry. I'm here. It'll be all right. It'll be all right. Just do what they say and they'll leave you in peace."

I tell him that in the beginning I missed my mother too (just kidding), but that I ended up accepting my fate. I wheel out my story of hiding in a cellar to escape the Warsaw bombings, of spending days in the arms of my mother's corpse. He listens to me, and squeezes my hand, his big blue eyes fixed on mine and filled with a look of dismay. Right then, I'm convinced I've got it made: our friendship, as brothers, is guaranteed… But when he gets the better of the fever, he reverts to his snide, mocking smile. And I'm filled with rage. I feel like grabbing the warden's whip off the ground and lashing him on the mouth to wipe away that wretched smile.

"They're going to kill you, don't you realize?" I yelled at him one day. "They will end up killing you! They've already killed kids for far more minor things."

And it's true. He's got it coming to him. And so have I.

Obviously, when I untie him from the pole, rescue him from the chapel, bring him food when he's supposed to starve, it's not simply because I'm BBFH. It's because Doctor

Ebner has ordered everyone to let me do it. He wants to know just how far Lukas is capable of going. It's a type of test, an experiment to measure the physical resistance of an adolescent. In case, later, our youngest soldiers have to go into battle.

Once I'd left the infirmary, after the incident when Lukas and I were whipped on the evening of the selection process, Ebner called me into his office. He demanded that I explain my behaviour, the consequences of which could have been *catastrophic*. (He emphasized this word.) The Kalish model child rebels? That's just too much.

I poured my heart out to him, without batting an eyelid, without any shame. Kalish has made me stronger, more arrogant. Unless it's simply because I've grown up.

I told Ebner that I had no mother other than Germany, no father other than the Führer – the same old story – but I added a personal note: now I wanted a brother. *It was my right to have a flesh and blood brother. Lukas.*

Ebner thought for a while, massaging the big vein throbbing at his temple. "All right, Konrad, all right," he said. "I'm happy to give you a brother. Especially as Lukas is a magnificent specimen. A seed of the highest quality, which has not been planted in the right spot and which we have to salvage. You'll be finishing your time at Kalish in three weeks. Then you'll be going somewhere I'll tell you about when it's necessary. Lukas can go with you. On condition that, between now and then, you turn him into a true German. You have three weeks, and not a day more!"

I manage it in three weeks. I'm about to win my side of the bargain. After ten sessions on the pole and five nights in the chapel – a huge record – Lukas seems to have calmed down.

He still doesn't talk, to me or the others, but he doesn't make any more scenes, or break any more rules. One morning, he even consents to goosestep. And because he cuts such a figure – despite being thin, he incarnates natural elegance and strength – he attracts the attention of Johanna Sander, the director. Although it's highly unusual, she addresses a few words of praise to him.

But it was all a trick. He was just pretending. For me, that night was the last straw in his betrayal: he ran away.

No one knows how he managed to escape the soldiers and dogs on guard duty, how he managed to climb the high monastery wall without getting impaled on the barbed wire. Anyway, I'm the only one to wonder about it, because everyone else is urgently trying to capture him. They've instigated a real manhunt, a search of all the surrounding area that lasts three days and three nights. In vain. The soldiers and dogs come back empty-handed.

Three sleepless nights for me. Nightmares of Lukas being tracked down by the dogs and torn to shreds, devoured like some old scrap of meat. I see myself reduced to a zombie. Once Lukas is dead, I will no longer exist, an amputee without legs or arms, nothing more than a tortured belly: a giant gut in appalling pain.

The fourth day comes round. While we're all lined up in the courtyard for morning roll call, a dark lump crashes down out of a tree and smashes on the cobblestones. What on earth is it? A crow? A dead cat? A bomb about to explode and tear us all to pieces? Neither crow nor dead cat, but a version of a bomb, yes. It's him, Lukas. After racing round and round the periphery of Kalish without finding an exit that would allow him to run away, he hid in a tree and fell asleep, exhausted and drained from lack of food and drink.

Johhanna Sander is at roll call, and fate would have it that Lukas falls right at her feet. (I even wonder if he didn't do it on purpose: plan to jump on her at some point and try to knock her out.) Shocked, she steps back quickly to gather her wits. She casts a disgusted glance at the object on the ground, the way she'd look at a large rotten tomato that could splash her beautiful uniform as it's being crushed. The piece of filth no longer bears any resemblance to the adolescent whose elegant good looks she admired when he goosestepped in front of her a few days ago. He's just rubbish she has to get rid of. She's not listening to Ebner's orders any more; she's the director of Kalish and she's going to prove it. She's had enough of this filthy Polish dog who causes nothing but trouble in her institution.

She puts her hand on her belt to draw her Luger.

"No!"

The cry that comes out of my mouth is so loud it echoes in the silence. Nothing like the reedy little voice I greeted Frau Sander with when I first arrived. I'm surprised myself. Frau Sander is totally shocked. Her arm is frozen in midair, as I march towards her, my steps strong and rhythmic, the way she likes them. I stand to attention. "*I* want to kill him!"

Unaware of who had uttered the scream that dared to contradict her, Frau Sander was full of fury seconds ago. Now her expression softens. Not only does she recognize BBFH, but she realizes that BBFH's request means he has decided to drop his mask in front of all his pseudo-buddies, and to show his true colours, to show that he is the toughest of all.

Whatever their age, the Führer's children are not frightened of killing.

She's not wrong. I'm prepared to go the whole way: I'm ready to kill Lukas. I *must* do it. If he's going to die, since that's what he wants, I might as well be the one to do it. If I'm the one who kills Lukas, I won't suffer, I won't be anxious, and I won't end up with a stomach-ache. I'll never have another stomach-ache again. I will have made myself, once and for all, a proper set of armour forged from Krupp steel.

The time has come for BBFH to be consecrated by another baptism – blood.

Beaming from ear to ear, Frau Sander hands me the Luger. I turn to Lukas and take aim. Head. Forehead. Like Wolfgang. Right where, in a lot of his filthy fellow countrymen, the eyebrows join together – not in his case, because, go figure, he exhibits all the characteristics of the pure Nordic race. Just a tiny hole and it will all be over, for him, and for me. I've never used a real pistol before, I've only ever played sniper games, but I know I won't miss the mark – the target is so close. It's child's play.

Regaining consciousness after his fall, Lukas stares at me with those extraordinarily bright, blue eyes, which still have a glint of provocation in them.

"You're not up to it!" is what those eyes are saying.

Of course I am. Just like him, I can't go on like this. I can't put up with the baiting and insults that Lukas has made me endure since he arrived. It's time to put a stop to it.

He can sense my determination, sees that my fingers are in position, that I'm about to pull the trigger. In an instant, he crouches, twists around, and grabs my feet to unbalance me. Just before I fall to the ground, the shot fires. Into thin air? At a child? A soldier? Frau Sander herself? No time to check. We're rolling on the ground together, fighting like dogs. Kicks, knee jabs, punches, biting, anything goes.

Normally, Lukas would have had the better of me, but he's been weakened by starvation, by all the tortures inflicted on him, and by his three days away. And, from the screams of pain he utters every time his right arm touches the ground, I suspect he broke it when he fell out of the tree. So I go for it: at every opportunity, I hammer away at his broken arm. If the bones are broken, I'll smash them to smithereens. What's more, I turn my disadvantage – being much shorter than him – to an advantage. I manage to roll into a ball to protect myself from his blows, and to headbutt him in the belly. I jump up faster than him and leap on top of him. He's so underfed that our body weights must be almost the same. When I'm straddling him, I lean on his chest and stop him from breathing; I grip my legs around his abdomen to trap him in a vice. I lacerate his face with my nails and try to poke out his eyes. I pull on his blond mop of hair; I feel like I could rip it off like a scalp. I get one hell of a thrill smashing up his face. The mirror effect I experienced the first evening I saw him is now multiplied: by destroying his beautiful angel face, I'm destroying *my* beautiful angel face – the very one the *Lebensborn* programme put so much effort into producing, with its selection processes, its measuring sessions, its calculations, photos… As for Lukas, he tries to get his hands around my neck to strangle me. Every now and then he manages to get his fingers in the right spot, but his broken arm prevents him from exerting enough pressure to asphyxiate me. Guess what? I finally manage to loosen his tongue! He speaks to me. And it's in German.

"Dirty little Kraut shit!" he whispers in my ear. (My face is stuck against his, my cheek crushed under his, and I'm trying to bite him.) "You're not Polish! You're being protected by these Nazi bastards! They killed my family!

You and your people, you killed my family!"

"Yeah, of course I'm German!" I answer. (And I spit on him, right into his eyes to blind him, to dirty those eyes that are not worthy of being blue.) "I'm the Führer's favourite child! Too bad if your family is dead! You should thank me, because I'm going to help you join them!"

After that, I can't hear what he's saying. There's too much of an uproar. The courtyard is echoing with screams and shouts. Everyone is there, surrounding us, staring at us. Our fury spreads to them. All the rules are forgotten. The children break rank to form a circle around us, some taking Lukas's side, some mine. Some of the younger ones are crying, begging us to stop. The dogs are kept firmly on their leashes. The soldiers don't intervene to separate us. Quite the opposite: they choose sides, too, and barrack in the fight to the death. If I can't succeed in killing Lukas, they'll do the job for me.

Only one person remains motionless. Silent. This person is, however, in the front row. The blood dripping from my skull is clouding my vision in red, so I only catch a glimpse when I collapse, exhausted, on Lukas's body, which is no longer moving. It's *Herr Doktor* Ebner. He's been there, right from the start.

He was there at my birth. He brought me into the world. He was the first person I ever laid eyes on. He'll be the last person I'll ever see. We've come full circle.

I've killed Lukas and I'm going to die.

20.

I'm not dead.

I'm in the infirmary.

Doctor Ebner is at my bedside. Again! What time is it? An hour after the fight? A day? A month? A year? I haven't the faintest idea.

My whole body hurts; it's in shreds. I want to cry, howl, so I can breathe, so I can get some air inside me. Like a newborn baby. Like when Ebner pulled me out of the belly of the mother-whore who gave birth to me.

I try to get up. It's not easy standing to attention when you're lying down, when you feel like you've lost your limbs. I'm going to cop another lecture... This time I really overstepped the mark. I'll be sent away from Kalish and I'll never be assigned another mission. And so on and so forth... But I don't give a damn about what Ebner's going to say to me. I don't give a damn about anything, including him. And anyway, I've had enough of being stuck with him, ever since the beginning of my wretched life.

His speech is not at all what I expected. *"Jungmann!*

Hand-to-hand combat is one of the most important disciplines taught in the Führer's elite schools. Hand-to-hand confrontation allows future young leaders to get rid of the fear of killing. Your fight today has shown that you are eligible to enter a *Napola*. This is a huge honour for you. The Potsdam *Napola*, near Berlin, will welcome you as soon as you have recovered from your wounds. That is, in four days' time."

He raised his arm in a salute, clicked his heels, and left.

My brain is set on slow motion. I can't quite grasp the meaning of what I've just heard. When I put my hand to my head, I feel bandages. They must be blocking the circulation of messages to my brain. Or all those blows to the head mean that I'm no longer dolichocephalic: I've turned into an idiot.

I try to recall exactly what Ebner said, as well as the tone he used. He didn't give me hell after all; he praised me. He told me I was going to where I've always dreamed of going: a *Napola*. And not just any old *Napola*, one of the best, near Berlin, when I could have ended up in one that was in the occupied territories in the east. So, that's good. Very good. But why did he address me so formally? Is he already treating me like a fully fledged *Jungmann*?

My heart is pounding. Even though it hurts to move, I roll over onto my side.

There's Lukas, lying in the next bed.

His head is bandaged too, his face is swollen, and his right arm is in plaster. He looks like a mummy. Sitting up in bed, his back wedged comfortably against a pillow, he looks over at me, lifts up his left arm and waves.

"They thought they'd got the better of me," he says, pointing at the door Ebner has just shut behind him. "All because

I garbled a bit of German in front of them. I didn't need them to teach me German; my mother spoke it fluently."

He stops, grabs a plate from his bedside table and stuffs a big piece of bread and bacon into his mouth. Completely uninhibited, he chews and smacks his lips.

"Didn't you ever wonder why I came back and hid in the tree, when I could have got clear of that piece-of-shit monastery?" he continues.

I shake my head. Just hearing his voice, I am lost for words.

He finishes munching, swallows, gulps, then burps loudly. "I came back to get you, you little jerk!"

Little jerk, yourself.

But I don't care about him calling me names. I'm used to insults; I hear them all day long, even if they're not aimed at me. Anyway, Lukas's insults are better than the silence he's inflicted on me for so many months. What he said before the "little jerk" bit is what's important.

To get me. Came back. Me. He came back to get me.

I can't believe my ears, and my voice has still not come good.

"I owe you," continues Lukas. "That's all. But don't get any ideas. Once we're even, that's it – we'll never see each other again."

After the bacon, he gobbles a big bowl of soup, then hoes into an apple. I can tell from the empty plate and bowl on my bedside table that he's already downed my rations while I was asleep. I get the impression he could devour the furniture; although, you have to admit, he's got some catching up to do. I've got a terrible migraine and the sound of his chewing is like a drill inside my eardrums.

"What's up? Swallowed your tongue? You used to be a

chatterbox." He finishes the apple, gulping down the core and pips, and spits the stalk onto the floor. "That tall bald guy who was here before, he said we were going to a *Napola*. What is that exactly?"

"It's ... a school. A really good school." (Phew! My voice came back.) "That's where the best members of the German youth are trained to become soldiers and then future leaders of the Third Reich." I'm proud of my description.

"The best members of the German youth?" he repeats, picking his teeth with his fingernails.

"Yes. The sons of senior officers. It's really a great opportunity for us. Well ... for you," I add condescendingly. "For me, it's normal."

"The sons of SS officers, you mean?"

"Yes!"

He doesn't say anything for a while, just stares at the ceiling. "Well then, we're off to a bad start," he says finally. "A very bad start."

"Why?"

"Because I'm a Jew."

I've lost my voice again.

Worse. Total paralysis.

I can't think at all.

I don't know what to say. What to think. My head is spinning, I feel sick. It feels like the ground is shaking, the whole world crashing down around me.

A Jew. He's a Jew. Lukas.

The one I thought of as a brother. The one I bent over backwards to protect. The one for whom I flouted all the most basic rules dictated by our Führer. The one I risked my life for. In the end, I would have done better to let him die.

He's staring at me, relishing the look of shock on my face. He's not even ashamed of the admission he's just made. In fact he looks pleased with himself. He's smiling. He's taunting me again with that little snide smile; that wretched, goddamned smile he used on me when I was caring for him after he was tortured by the wardens. And that ghastly grin is even more odious today, on his swollen, bruised lips, still streaked with dried blood.

"So? What are you going to do?" he asks arrogantly. "Will you denounce me?"

I'm silent.

"Yes? No?"

I still don't speak.

"OK, while you're deciding, I'll have a little nap. I'm knackered!"

He lies down on his side, his back to me, and within a minute I can hear him snoring.

21.

Bastard! Low life! Scumbag! Filthy pig!

It's one thing that he's Polish. We got over that. As Ebner said, "A seed of the highest quality that has not been planted in the right spot." But Jewish, JEWISH! A YID! A KIKE!

It's just too much. A Jew is beyond help.

What does the bastard think I'll do? Chicken out? Of course I'll denounce him! Right now! I leap out of bed, ignoring my pain, and head for the door to call the warden who is standing in as a nurse. She's there in a flash. (She must have received her new instructions: her charges are no longer just BBFH and a Germanized Pole, but two future *Jungmänner*. Yeah, sure! Wait till she finds out!)

"You have to warn *Herr Doctor* Ebner immediately!" I point in the direction of Lukas. "He is…"

I choke back the last word just before it comes out, so abruptly that I start coughing. I've just had a brilliant idea. At last all my powers of reasoning have returned. Lukas lied to me! To think that I nearly fell for it. At a pinch, I could have believed in an aberration of nature – that is, a Jew with blond hair and blue eyes. But Lukas forgot one very important thing. The first time I laid eyes on him was the night of the selection process. He didn't know I was there. He was too busy being defiant to notice me. But I saw ... his *penis*! All of it! Not a cut-down penis like Jews have! He lied to me because he's a lunatic; he's missing a compartment or two in his brain. He's developed some kind of compulsion to put himself in danger. It's an obsession.

I let out a huge sigh of relief, as the warden stands to attention in front of me, waiting for me to finish my sentence.

"He is what?" she asks finally.

"He is... He is ... asleep." That's all I can think to say.

She glances over at Lukas. "Yes, so?"

"So, nothing! Nothing! It's just that ... before, I thought he was dead. But I made a mistake. Everything's fine."

Lukas's snoring starts up again, as if to reinforce my explanation. But it's not enough to get rid of the warden, who is looking at me warily.

Piss off, you old bag! Piss off! I said everything was fine!

She comes closer and puts her hand on my forehead. "You have a fever," she declares.

Of course I've got a fever! How could I not, after such an emotional roller-coaster? She jams a soup spoon of disgusting syrup in my mouth. It's sticky and bitter and I clench my buttocks as I swallow it so I don't spit it back out in her face. She better get lost right now. It's urgent.

Once she's gone, I leap on Lukas and shake him roughly to wake him. "Liar! Filthy liar! You're no Jew!"

To prove my point, before he has time to move – he's still groggy from the deep sleep I've woken him from – I pull down his pants.

He rubs his eyes, growls a few insults (I think he calls

me a faggot), pulls up his underpants, and rolls over. "My mother didn't want me to have it," he mumbles, ready to fall asleep again.

I don't get it. I shake him again.

He sighs, exasperated, and sits up. "On the day of the circumcision," he explains, "my mother fainted when the rabbi turned up with his scalpel. She wasn't a practising Jew and hated all the mumbo-jumbo of religion. And that's why I wasn't circumcised: because my father loved her, he respected her wishes. Got it now?"

Yes, I sure do. My hopes are dashed. Lukas is a Jew. Even his uncircumcised penis doesn't prove anything. I run over and shut the door. On the other side of it, a few metres from us, is the warden. I still haven't decided whether, in a few minutes' time, I'm going to denounce Lukas or not. All the same, I have a feeling he wants to keep talking, and I'd rather no one heard for the moment.

I sit on the edge of my bed, facing him, arms crossed, waiting.

After an interminable silence, Lukas decides to continue. "My mother was..." He pretends to clear his throat, but really he's choking back sobs. "She was really special. She wasn't just any old Polack with a scarf on her head and wrinkled stockings around her ankles. She was beautiful, intelligent, independent. She smoked, wore make-up, had been to university and spoke French and German fluently. She often went to Germany because she could stay with various family members there. That's how she got to understand very quickly that your piece-of-shit Hitler was going to ruin everything. And that's why she taught me your fucking language when I was young, barely four years old. She told my father, "People have to believe he's German." And, because I wasn't circumcised, it worked out well. As for my father, he'd been a professional soldier in the Polish cavalry. When he married my mother, he stopped everything to help her manage the shop she'd inherited. A bookshop…"

As he talks, he's gazing at the ceiling. Now he glares back at me. "Huh! Skullface! Do you even know what a bookshop is? Do you know what books are for? Books are for reading, not for burning like your mates do, yelling like barbarians."

I don't react to his insults; they're water off a duck's back. It's an effort, but I can do it. I've decided not to respond to his provocations. I'm much cleverer than he is and he'll end up getting sick of it. Anyway, the door isn't far away. As soon as I've had enough, I'll call the warden.

"When the first German soldiers entered Lodz, my mother said to my father: 'It's all over for us, but he might have a chance to get out.' Him, that's me, not my little brother. He was… How old are you? Six? Seven?"

I separate the fingers on my right hand, raise my left thumb, then place my left index finger on my right index finger to show that I'm six and a half. I don't want to stoop to talking to him. It's already enough that I'm listening.

"Six and a half? Yeah, he must be about… He would have been about that age now. But back then he was only three. Too little to escape by himself. I was ten, that's why my mother chose me. So, anyway, my parents gathered together everything they owned – silver, chandeliers, jewels – and they gave it all to a customer at the bookshop, a Polish goy, so she'd hide me at her place, pretending that I was her son. After a week, I ran away and came home. My mother locked herself in the bedroom with my little brother, so they wouldn't see me, while my father gave me the worst thrashing of my life. 'You will never ever do that again, understood?' he said after three whacks with the leather belt. 'You do not know us any more, you are no longer our son! Get lost!' The next day, all the Jews in the town were locked up in the ghetto."

Lukas stops talking. I have no idea if that's the end of his tale or not. Nor can I tell if he just happens to be staring at the door, or if he intends to go over and open it and denounce himself. He's perfectly capable of that. Maybe he's waiting for me to say something. But … I don't know what to say.

"At the entrance to the ghetto, there was a big yellow sign: 'Jewish residential area. Entry forbidden. Danger of epidemics.' The whole area was surrounded by a high fence and barbed wire. The doors were two huge blocks of wood. It was impossible to get in. But I knew my family was behind the fence and the barbed wire. So one day I tried to sneak into a hole I'd spied in the fence. Sofia, the Polish goy who had taken me in, grabbed me by the trousers and gave me a smack, screaming, 'Don't be crazy, Lucjan! You'll catch typhus if you go in there with those Jewish vermin! Do you want to bring lice back home?' She winked at me so I'd know that her words were meant for the ears of the passers-by, to prove that I wasn't Jewish, to prove that I was really her son. Back home, she gave me another smack and said, 'Lucjan, never ever do that again! It's too dangerous. I promise we'll try to see your parents, but first you have to promise you'll do as I say.' I promised and she explained that she was going to find a way to get a message to my parents. They would work out some sort of meeting.

"A week later, Sofia announced, 'Listen carefully, Lucjan: tomorrow we're going to take the tram that goes through the Jewish neighbourhood. You'll see your parents, but you're not allowed to move, or say a word, or make the slightest gesture at all. Otherwise, you'll die, I'll die, and so will your family. Got it?'

"The next day, we took the tram. We sat in the carriage reserved for the 'lower-class' people (that is, the Poles); the Germans had their own carriage reserved up front. The ghetto doors opened, but as soon as the tram had entered, it stopped. A Jewish policeman climbed on board. He went into every carriage and locked all the doors with a special key, so they could only be opened from the inside. So no Jews could try to escape from the ghetto. As he went through the carriage reserved for Germans, the passengers put handkerchiefs over their mouths – they were so terrified of catching a disease. If only that had been the case. If only the three SS bastards who were there had caught a deadly disease."

Lukas is clenching his fists – even the one sticking out of the plaster cast – and grimacing in pain. He gives me a black look. (Yes, you can have a black look with blue eyes, and it's pretty terrifying.)

I withstand the black look and I keep staring at him, even though my eyes are smarting. I don't know what the matter is; dust must have got under my eyelids.

"The tram started up. Sofia had told me that my parents would be at the crossroads of the fourth street. I had to look at them as discreetly as possible, without moving or showing any emotion at all. A wink, that was all, as the tram crossed the street. My heartbeats counted the streets. *Boom*, the first. *Boom*, the second. *Boom*, the third. The fourth street was further away, only by a few metres, but it felt like kilometres. Then I saw my parents. Standing on the corner, my little brother between them. They stayed motionless when they saw me. I met my mother's gaze just as the tram passed in front of her, but that was it. I glimpsed her lips trembling. Was she trying not to cry, or trying not to smile at me? I could see how my mother, who had been so beautiful, was now thin and shrivelled. She had been so elegant, too, and now she was wearing dirty rags. My father didn't look at me: just as the tram passed, he leaned down to my little brother. Afterwards, I worked out that it was so Czeslaw wouldn't see me, but so that I could still see him, and that's all. He was too young, he might have screamed, or called out to me. It was too dangerous ... I didn't move. I didn't leap at the tram window like I wanted to, I didn't knock on it, I didn't scream out. Sofia held my hand. She squeezed it hard, very hard; she was hurting me, but I didn't realize until I got back that night and saw the red mark on my wrist. When the tram kept going, I didn't turn around. I didn't run to the back of the carriage. I kept it together, even when I saw the rest of the ghetto. All those people who were so horribly thin, dying of hunger, filthy, in rags, riddled with illnesses from lack of hygiene and food. They were dying a slow death, killed by those bastard Germans who had locked them away in that foul neighbourhood. And not one person on the tram showed any sign of caring. For them, what was going on outside was normal."

Another break. My eyes are hurting even more. If only the dust hadn't got into them, but I've got a feeling that if I rub them they'll get worse. I'll end up crying and Lukas will get the wrong idea.

"Sofia arranged that we'd see each other like that once a month. Each time, my parents had got much thinner. My father, who was once a big guy, was half his former size and barely able to stand up. The same went for my mother. As for Czeslaw, there was no longer any need to stop him from crying: he was nothing more than a little parcel in my mother's arms, weighing hardly anything, I imagine. There were people sprawled in the gutter, rats swarming all over them. They were so weak they could no longer move. Or they were dead and no one had removed their bodies. There were men roaming the streets, piling corpses into carts, but more often than not there wasn't room in the carts... We saw my family like that five times. The last time, at the crossroads of the fourth street, I only saw my mother and father. Czeslaw wasn't there. Do you know what that means?"

I stare at Lukas.

"That means he died, of hunger, or of cold, or of a fever. That day I stood up, I didn't obey Sofia's orders. I couldn't leave my parents alone, without their children. Here I am, me! I was alive and I belonged with them. But Sofia tripped me up, she made me fall over, to stop me from throwing myself at the tram door. By the time I got up, the tram had moved forwards and my chance had gone. That evening, Sofia punished me. No more meetings: it was too dangerous, she no longer trusted me. Three months went by. I begged Sofia. I swore that, whatever happened, I wouldn't move. She said no, no, and then she said yes, and she organized another meeting. Off we went. At the crossroads of the fourth street, only my mother was there. My father, the soldier, the ex-cavalry lieutenant, the big guy, the tough guy, was dead. It was too much for him. I kept my promise, I didn't move. I didn't cry. There were no more meetings. There was no point any more. A week later, all the Jews from the ghetto left for Treblinka."

Lukas stops to look at me. I'm expecting one of his really black looks; but no, this time I don't feel like I'm under fire.

"Do you know what Treblinka is?"

Of course I know. Treblinka's the same as Ravensbrück or Auschwitz. It's a prison camp.

"It's a concentration camp," explains Lukas, echoing my thoughts, "and hardly anyone ever comes back from there. When I found that out, I ran away from Sofia. I just ran, down whatever road it was, straight into one of those Sister bitches, who carted me off."

There's a long silence. This time I think Lukas has come to the end of his story. He's not crying. Nothing. His eyes are dry, whereas mine are wet because of this dust that makes them so horribly itchy. He's smiling: he seems to find it funny, idiot that he is. Then he lies down again, rolls on his side like before, ready to go back to sleep.

"You'd better decide this time, Skullface!" he hurls at me. "After everything I've told you, you shouldn't hesitate. You can raise the alarm!"

I fell asleep too. *Thump*. I landed on my pillow as if someone had knocked me out. Except I had a bad dream. The warden came hurtling into the room.

"Get out, Jew! Get out!" she yelled, furious, whacking as hard as she could with her club, until the body under the sheet turned red, soaked in blood. "Do you want to see your fucking Jewish mother in Treblinka? That's where you're headed, believe me! If I don't kill you beforehand!"

But…

She'd made a mistake, and was hitting the sheet covering me. She was pounding me to a pulp. I tried calling out, "No, not me! I'm not Jewish! It's him! I'm the BBFH!" But she only roared louder, "I don't give a damn! How do you expect me to work it out, now there are Jews with blond hair and blue eyes? Jews with uncircumcised penises! The Führer probably made a mistake when he baptised you!"

I woke up with a start. I think I was screaming, or sobbing. I must have smothered the sound with my sheet; fortunately the warden didn't hear – the real one, not the one in my nightmare – and Lukas didn't wake up either. The good thing is that I must have cried a lot in my sleep; my tears washed away the dust that was hurting my eyes before.

I have to gather my thoughts. I get out of bed, otherwise I might have another nightmare. I'd rather walk round the room; when I get to the door, I'll decide: to open the door and call the warden.

Or not.

First I go over everything Lukas told me, in order. He's Jewish. No doubt about it. He's a Jew.

I glance at the door. Perhaps I have blurred vision from the tears still in my eyes, because it looks like the handle is moving, that some invisible hand is turning it.

The next thing Lukas said was about his mother. "She wasn't just any old Polack." She had a job, she was independent, she smoked, she wore make-up… So, she must have been a whore! She spoke German, she went to Germany regularly. On one of her trips she probably slept with a German guy, and never told her husband about it when she found out she was pregnant… Which means that Lukas is half-German. Which means that the German blood he inherited from his father – his mother's lover, not the Polish cavalryman – was more dominant than the Jewish blood!

I'm heading towards the door now and my vision has cleared; the door handle isn't moving any more.

So, Lukas then told me about what happened to his family when our troops entered Poland. I know from History classes that we invaded Poland in September 1939. Lukas said he was ten then. It's 1942 now. A little bit of elementary arithmetic: from 39–42 makes 3. And 10 + 3 = 13. Lukas is thirteen. (Ebner was completely wrong to make his date of birth the 18th of March, 1932.) But I don't care if he's thirteen, more than twice my age; he still doesn't mean a thing to me. A thirteen-year-old Jew – or a half-Jew, or a three-quarter Jew – is still inferior to a six-and-a-half-year-old pure Aryan.

Then there was the whole story of the ghetto, of the dead little brother, the dead father, the mother deported to Treblinka. The death of the little brother reminds me of Wolfgang's death. That was tough. I had a very sore stomach, and nightmares for several days… Perhaps Lukas's family didn't deserve it? Perhaps they should have made an exception for them? Perhaps there are good Jews? How do you know? At this point in my thinking, I admit that I'm lost, even though I've gone a few steps further towards the door.

I reckon the main problem, for Lukas and the other children, whether they're Polish or Jewish or neither, is that damn connection with their parents. They'd cope much better if, like me, they didn't have a family.

All right. The door. Now I'm here. Do I open it or not?

No.

My recapping thoughts haven't helped me to come to a decision, but – I should have thought of it earlier – I'm not going to denounce Lukas, if only to infuriate him. He really wants me to, and I'm not going to give him that pleasure.

I run over and wake him up. "I'm not going to denounce you," I declare, "but only on one condition!"

"What?"

"Stop calling me Skullface!"

He raises an eyebrow in surprise. "OK, but I want to know who you are. Your turn to tell. Fair's fair... Are you the son of that prick, Ebner?"

I shake my head.

"Of one of the SS officers around here? Of that director bitch?"

Another shake.

"Of who then?"

"Of ... nobody." I wait a moment. "Do you know what *Lebensborn* means?"

"Yes, it means ... 'the ... fountain ... of life'."

"No, that's the literal translation. The real meaning, the code meaning, do you know that?"

I'm only asking for form's sake. He hasn't a clue what I mean, and he'll never guess. It's my turn to enjoy the surprise element before revealing my secret.

"So, fire away."

All right, OK. Here I go. I tell him my story from the beginning.

The selection process for the woman who was to have intercourse with an SS officer and carry me in her belly; my birth in the Steinhöring Home; the replacement of the mother by a nurse; the selection process I went through, too; how Doctor Ebner weighed me, measured me, examined me. The selecting of the other babies, some of whom became "rabbits" and ended up chopped into pieces inside jars stored on shelves in "scientific institutes". How the best specimens from the Home were adopted out to German families, and how other Homes were started up in Europe and throughout the occupied countries. I described assembly-line programming and the production of the future German youth of which I am the perfect sample product. The perfect prototype. Flawless.

I'm pleased with myself when I've finished and eagerly await Lukas's reaction.

But guess what?

He doesn't say anything at all for a very long time. No comment. He just stares at one spot on the floor. He seems stunned, bewildered, which makes him look like a total imbecile. Then he looks up at me and I see that ... he's crying. For real. Crying his eyes out. His cheeks are all wet.

I don't get it. He didn't cry when he told me his story, and yet he's crying now, after hearing my story, which is absolutely ASTONISHING, EXTRAORDINARY! Is he crying because he's jealous?

After what seems like an interminable time, he stammers a few words. "So... So ... they do that, as well... They kill Jewish children and replace them with ... with—" he gives up trying to find the word he's looking for – "like you."

I nod vigorously in agreement. He's got the message now.

He falls back onto his bed, as if he's been knocked out. Surely he's not going back to sleep?

"Listen," he says, sitting up abruptly and grabbing my shoulders. "I'll go with you to this fucking *Napola* place. From now on, we're in this together. We'll be brothers. But on one condition."

"What?" I'm only asking for the sake of it. He can make any demands he likes. Whatever it is, it's yes! Yes!

"When the war's over, and if we manage to survive it, we both have to bear witness. Me, for what the Nazis are doing to the Poles and to the Jews; you, for what they have done to you."

"OK!" I reply, even though I don't have a clue what "bear witness" means.

Bear witness before whom? Why? When the war's over, the Reich will begin its thousand-year reign. There'll be no more secrecy about the *Lebensborn*… All right, too bad, there's no point arguing with him. You never quite know how he'll react.

"OK!" I repeat, to confirm our mutual pledge.

We shake hands vigorously. Vigorous like the *Jungmänner* we'll become in the near future.

part three

22.

Let's be clear before we go any further. I'm telling you: don't just go and feel sorry for him. Lukas's tears, all that emotion after he'd heard my story, it was all rubbish. In fact, as you'll find out in the rest of my story, he's the one who reduces people to tears.

He didn't keep his promise. He kept on calling me Skullface, even though I'd asked him to stop. I hate that nickname, especially when I look like an angel. The other morning – a few days before we left Kalish – I went to find him, to have it out with him. I lashed out at him, ready to tear him to pieces, punch his lights out again. But he just laughed. All he did to parry was give me a few smacks, as if he couldn't be bothered tackling me. It was humiliating. I could easily have got under his skin, forced him to fight, at the risk of being torn to shreds – he's got his strength back and would have had the better of me – but I didn't force the issue. Not because I was frightened. I'm not frightened of anything. But so I wouldn't get to Potsdam with a smashed-up face. That would not have been a good look.

Just to get back at him for insulting me, I called him a dirty Jew. This time I hit home. He was not at all amused. His expression suddenly changed to one of belligerence, and he called me a son-of-a-bitch-whore. That didn't bother me, because it's true.

The Potsdam *Napola.*

It's magnificent, mind-bogglingly spectacular. Words fail me. Kalish was a dump in comparison.

The school is outside the city, so the students can't have contact with the outside world – our activities have to remain secret. The buildings are surrounded by a huge park, which is enclosed by a wall. Inside, there are lawns, landscaped gardens, flower beds. Before its creation in 1933, the *Napola* was a psychiatric hospital with two thousand beds. *Raus!* – move out patients! In came young people of sound mind and body, to live in the fifty-odd buildings. As well as the living quarters, there are sporting facilities (for team sports, as well as an Olympic swimming pool, a horseriding school and stables, a gymnasium, running tracks, athletics ovals), a carpentry workshop, a horticulture workshop, greenhouses, a shooting range, and even a farm. All of which means the *Napola* can be self-sufficient. The old barn has been turned into a garage for cars and motorbikes, and the chapel has been transformed into a function room. Good move. Herr Rosenberg, one of the creators of the Reich, is opposed to Christianity because it's an Eastern religion. So, no more *Kapelle*! I'm happy about that because I still have very bad memories of the Kalish chapel and those warden bitches. Lukas will be pleased, too; first because the wardens put him through the ringer; second, he won't have to pretend to pray in Latin.

The whole place is so enormous that I don't know where to look. I can't wait to see inside. Right now, we new kids are assembled in one of the courtyards in front of the central building that houses the dormitories and classrooms. On either side, two towers add to the aura of invincible power about the whole place – it's like a Prussian castle, or better still, a fortress. I can tell we're going to have a marvellous time here: when we leave we'll be big and strong. True members of the master race!

Lukas hasn't said a word since we got here. He seems impressed, too. We're both standing to attention, next to each other.

Doctor Ebner enrolled us as brothers and *Volksdeutscher*, "pupils of the German nation". He's done exactly what I asked him at Kalish, when Lukas wasn't yet Germanized. He's reverted to the true date of birth of "my big brother" and chosen Potsdam so we won't be separated, as it's the only *Napola* that combines primary and secondary classes. In order to endorse our enrolment, he provided the director, *Obersturmbannführer* Schmidt, with two green racial-fitness certificates, so that we wouldn't have to go through the selection process like the other new arrivals. No trial period for us. Doctor Ebner has gone out of his way for us: he made a point of listing Lukas as a Germanized Pole, otherwise he wouldn't have been allowed in here; he would have been sent to the *Napola* in Alsace.

I can't believe the things I've told you. A Jew with a racial-fitness certificate! At one of the most prestigious *Napolas* in the Reich! Needless to say, from now on Lukas will be like a tightrope-walker, balanced high above the void: the slightest false step and it'll all be over for him.

Right now I'd rather not think about it.

But I hope he understands how lucky he is. While the director is giving us a welcome speech and explaining the rules and organization of the school, I elbow him. "What do you reckon?" I whisper. "Isn't Germany amazing to have built something like this? Were there schools as good as this in your country?"

"In my country, we didn't kill off the sick to make a clean sweep of the place."

His voice is cold, dispassionate, and he keeps his eyes on the director. Lukas is referring to the "relocation" of the previous residents. How does he know about that?

Noticing my quizzical expression, he smirks and bends down to mutter in my ear. "Don't you know what happened to the patients who were here before?"

"Of course I do! They were 'relocated'." I quickly explain the meaning of the code word. "Relocate", meaning to kill.

Lukas turns to me and gives me one of his hostile looks. His smile gone, he chews on his lips and frowns, a deep furrow on his forehead. I can tell he wants to give it to me, to get back at me. But he holds off, regains his composure. "So, Skullface, do you know exactly how they were killed?"

No. I don't know precisely. And do not call me Skullface any longer!

"They were put into trucks. Then the trucks were locked up. A big hose was attached to the exhaust pipe and lethal gas was pumped into the truck. The poor bastards were asphyxiated. It took a while, quite a long time. They tried to fight their way out, banging on the doors. In vain. From the outside, the trucks looked like huge cooking pots, shuddering, vibrating as if they were full of boiling water. It was a slow, horrendous death." He enunciates each word:

drops of poison trickling into my ear.

He speaks deliberately slowly, to give me time to properly imagine what he's describing. Then, as if nothing has happened, he stands to attention, perfectly straight, proudly staring ahead, whereas my shoulders are slumped and my legs have turned to jelly.

Bastard! Just like him to ruin my arrival here, my special moment. I don't respond at all, even though I really want to put him in his place. Anyway, they soon separate us: Lukas goes off with the students from the secondary school, and I leave with those from the primary school.

My dagger of honour.

I've got it, at last.

I was so excited, so proud, when the officer presented me with it. And it feels so good to have it on me, right here, slipped into my belt. From now on it will be a part of me, not just my uniform but my body, as inseparable as my arms and legs. It's gorgeous. Twenty-five centimetres long. The hilt is nickel-plated. The haft is decorated with Nazi insignia, an enamelled diamond shape. The upper and lower sections are red, the cross-sections white, while the central swastika is black. The flat of the blade is engraved with a motto: *Mehr sein als scheinen.* (It is better to be than to seem).

As one, my new buddies and I raise our right arms enthusiastically and recite the oath: *The future of Germany and of our beloved Führer is henceforth the focus of all our energy. We belong to him today, tomorrow and for ever.*

Our voices are high-pitched, shrill, which is normal given our youth – some of my buddies are only five – but we're so loud the walls around us seem to shake. It's giving me goosebumps.

When silence falls again, however, I'm gripped by fear. The silence will be shattered by screaming, won't it? Or by gun shots? Some sort of panic as a result of an incident in the secondary school? I can picture Lukas refusing to take the oath and screaming out loud and strong, *The destruction of your fucking Germany and its fucking Führer is now my sole purpose in life. He can go and get fucked, today, tomorrow and for ever!* I can just see him spitting in the face of the officer who presents him with his sword. In a nutshell: I can see him slipping from his tightrope and falling into empty space.

I listen, keep my eyes peeled, and look around furtively.

Nothing. Everything seems normal. Lukas hasn't made a scene.

The timetable at the *Napola* is almost the same as at Kalish; nothing has changed in the slightest for me.

6 a.m. Wake up, exercises in our underwear, whatever the weather.

6.45 a.m. Shower. Every day. (At Kalish the shower was weekly. At least here the dormitories don't stink. Well, not too much.)

7 a.m. Everyone in uniform. Roll call and *Flaggenparade* ("raising the colours").

8 a.m. Disciplinary action for those being punished.

8.30 a.m. Classes begin.

12.30 p.m. Lunchbreak. We eat during a reading; that is, the section leaders read aloud extracts from the writings of important people in the Reich.

1 p.m. Politics class. The teacher gives a commentary on the same extracts and we learn some of them by heart.

2 p.m. Physical activities for the *Jungvolk*, paramilitary activities for the *Jungmänner*. (It's so great – we have about

fourteen hours of sport a week!)

4 p.m. Maintenance of the school and of our own personal property. One group has to clean the dormitory, another the showers, while a third group has to sweep the classrooms. Of course, there are official cleaners, but these chores teach us to respect the premises and keep them completely hygienic. Household and farm duties, as well as manual labour, are all part of our education.

5 p.m. Supervized homework.

6.30 p.m. "Lowering the colours" and roll call.

7 p.m. Dinner.

7.30–8.30 p.m. for the young ones, 9.30 p.m. for the older ones: free time. Evening gatherings. A teacher reads out loud – again! – from more texts. Or else we do collective criticism or self-criticism. Twice a week another teacher gives us a commentary on the military situation.

Before bed there's an inspection of the dormitory and of our gear. Once we're in bed, there's an inspection by the unit chiefs. We have to be lying properly on our backs, our hands clearly outside the sheets.

Let's be clear about this topic: why hands outside the sheets? At first I had no idea, and just did what I was told. But it's so we don't "masturbate". As I had no idea what this was, I asked. It means "to caress your penis". Apparently it feels really good. Maybe I'll try it one day, but not right now. Because the punishments are terrible. The teachers tell us that if we caress our penises we'll have shocking mental problems later: we'll become homosexual, have a pink triangle stuck on our chests, and we'll be interned in a concentration camp. If we caress our penises we will also end up with "deviant sexual behaviour": that is, we won't be able to have sex with a woman and have children and make a family home like every good self-respecting German. So that's why it's forbidden to put your hands under the blankets, even when it's cold. Otherwise you spend the night standing up. (And it's very cold in the dorms: the central heating is only turned on in a few rooms, and hardly ever now, given the lack of coal.) For the same reason, it's forbidden to put your hands in your pockets. If, during morning inspection, a student is found to have holes in his pockets, he is punished. (Holes are proof that you've got to your penis through your pockets.)

Still, I'd like to try it, at the risk of getting punished. But that means I have to try not to fall into a sleep so deep it's like death. All the more so because the day doesn't necessarily end at lights out. Twice a week, at 10 p.m., there are "night-time exercises".

I'm surprised how, Polish or German, Aryan or not, we're not that different. For the most part, my buddies are just like the ones I had in Kalish. They have the same faults, especially the five-year-olds. It's hard for them to get up at 6 a.m. on the dot to go running for forty-five minutes when it's raining cats and dogs or snowing. And hard to get dressed in a rush for roll call and *Flaggenparade*. Hard not to fall asleep in class. Hard during afternoon exercises to jump into a net from the second floor or to throw themselves off a diving board without knowing how to swim. Hard to clean toilets that the big kids have purposely soiled beforehand. Hard to endure corporal punishment, being quarantined, the night marches, solitary confinement... So there are a few escape attempts. All failed, of course. At night in the dorms there's a lot of snivelling and sobbing.

But, as our section leader says – a *Jungmann* aged

twelve, because here the ruling principle is that *youth educates youth and youth is educated by adults* – says, once these little brats have forgotten Mummy and Daddy, everything will be fine.

Of course. It always comes back to the same issue. Parents. Such a pain in the arse. At least it is for the little ones. Because when you grow up inside the *Napola*, you end up separating yourself from your parents. Most of the *Jungmänner* don't go home any more for holidays, or, if they do, they come back denouncing their parents to *Obersturmbannführer* Schmidt for defeatism or pessimism.

I have a lot of advantages over the students in my class. First of all, I don't have parents. Because I've never been cuddled or cosseted by a *mutti*, I don't miss that pampering. Also, because of my time at Kalish, I've had a taste of corporal punishment and still have the marks on my back from the whipping I copped when I wanted to protect Lukas. When it comes to my *Draufgängertum*, the quality all the teachers try to detect in the new recruits, I've been putting it into practice for a long time. So, walking over an abyss on a ladder? I'm up for it! Hand-to-hand combat with my buddies? I'm always the winner.

Very soon I'm considered a sort of gifted child and the teachers decide to change my placement. I go from level two to level four. Now I'm hanging out with children aged from nine to ten. I'm proud of this promotion.

But I'm not the only one in this position. One day, to my surprise, I find out that Lukas has been promoted too. He went from level eight to level nine. Him! The Pole, the … (Sometimes I don't dare utter the word, even in my head, in case someone hears me.) Despite his … what shall I say? …

handicap, he too is considered a gifted child. He's coping. He's coping perfectly well.

But how? I'd like to know, but to find out I'd have to see him, speak with him. And that can't happen. Although other older brothers visit their younger brothers in the afternoon, often during the hour set aside for looking after our personal effects, or during the free time before bed, not him. Nothing. *Nichts*. He never visits me. He never even sends me a note. So ungrateful! Sometimes I glimpse him at the end of the dining hall or when he's leaving for drills with his group. He's changed a lot. He's got bigger and more muscly. His blond hair, in a crew cut, is now golden. He has a glowing complexion and his eyes – no more dark circles or the wild stare that gave him wrinkles around his eyelids – are a mesmerizing blue. He carries himself even more proudly and is handsome in his uniform. Handsome when he salutes, his arm as straight as a truncheon. Handsome when he clicks his heels. Handsome when he calls out loudly, *Heil Hitler!* And he knows it. And he plays on it. You'd think, through his promotion, he was out to make a whole generation of homos!

He's made himself some friends, two in particular, with whom he trains all the time. They're the sons of officers holding important jobs in the government. The tough guys. Lukas, Gunter and Herman are as thick as thieves, and are now nicknamed the Three Musketeers. They strut around, laughing, making fun of the others. Or worse. The other day they had a go at a guy in the study hall: they ripped up his notebooks, beat the hell out of him, yelling insults that he was an intellectual. Incidents like this are dreaded in the *Napola*. They're feared far more than the teachers' punishments. Precisely because the teachers approve of them, claiming they contribute to "self-selection", "self-purification". That way the weakest are eliminated.

I know about the incident because Herman has a brother in my class – whom he looks after. He comes to see him at least twice a week. He even dared to call me Skullface in front of my buddies. No need to ask where he got that from. I had a fight with him and ended up in quarantine: I was forbidden from talking; I had to eat by myself in the dining hall; and the rest of the time I had to stay in the dorm. All because of Lukas.

I don't get it. He seems to be in his element at the *Napola*. And yet…

23.

How? I'm obsessed by the question. How does Lukas cope, when…

In class this morning, we were a bit worried about meeting our new German teacher, just back from the front after nine months. (The previous one, with whom we started the year, took his turn to head off there.) He made a solemn entrance and saluted the class. There was no indication of his being exhausted from combat, except that he was thinner – you could see around the neck and waist. Relieved to be back in the cocoon of the *Napola*, he didn't want to start off with a grammar class, or a text commentary, so he announced that, as he was happy with our progress as reported by his predecessor, he wanted to reward our efforts by starting the day with something relaxing. We could close our exercise books. We were going to sing. He handed out song sheets and wrote the chorus on the blackboard in his beautiful Gothic script:

The Jews cross the wide dry sea,
They sink beneath the waves,
The world is at peace and raises a prayer.

How does Lukas cope, when…

We do the knife-throwing exercise. Instead of a disc with concentric circles painted on it, our teacher produces a special target, so we can be motivated and have fun at the same time. It's the silhouette of a life-sized man. A Jew. An old Jew with a hooked nose, wearing filthy black rags and with fingers like claws. His belly is deformed and, instead of a heart, there's a big gold coin. Obviously, we have to hit the coin to be successful.

The teacher places the target ten metres away and the exercise begins. We take it in turns to throw our knives. Once we've all had a go, we gather round to assess our accuracy. The Jew has a knife in each eye, one in an ear, his upper lip is split and his hat is shredded. Not bad. But some knives, thrown by the less able, only reached his belly, legs and fingers. Not one knife hit the gold coin. So the teacher tells us we're all hopeless and threatens us with a collective punishment if our second try is not better. In order to get us going, he makes us all chant one of the many *Napola* slogans:

It's only once Jewish blood is splashing off our swords that we'll be truly happy! We'll keep up our progress, we'll turn everything upside down. Today Germany belongs to us, tomorrow we'll own the whole world!

We scream it once, twice, three, ten, one hundred times. Louder and louder, until our throats are sore. And then, swiftly, while we're in the swing of it, while the echo of our screams is floating in the air, we aim and let our knives fly.

Bravo. Most of the blades land right on the gold coin. When we take the knives out of the target, right where the heart is, there's a big hole.

How does Lukas cope, when…

The whole school is gathered in the dining hall, standing to attention. The meal has been served, but we aren't allowed to sit down and eat yet. Today, for the reading of texts, the section leaders are off the hook: the *Heimführer* himself does it once a fortnight.

The dining hall is one of the most beautiful rooms in the school. The decor is particularly attractive: the walls are covered in pictures of the Viking heroes and scenes from Germanic mythology. The high ceiling is decorated with hundreds of swastikas, scattered like flaming stars in the sky. Halfway up the wall, the *Heimführer* takes his place on a little wooden balcony, which he reaches via a staircase, like a priest who climbs into the pulpit to give his sermon. In this case, it's not a sermon but a reading, with a microphone, of extracts from *Mein Kampf*, our Führer's book, done in total, religious silence. We have to keep our eyes glued on the *Heimführer* and must under no circumstances lower our eyes or let them wander. No throat-clearing, no coughing, and definitely no yawning – all seen as disrespectful and punishable offences.

The Jew … was never a nomad, but only and always a parasite in the body of other peoples. That he sometimes left his previous living space has nothing to do with his own purpose, but results from the fact that from time to time he was thrown out by the host nations he had abused.

The *Heimführer* raises his head and surveys the audience. This is the signal for us to applaud.

His spreading is a typical phenomenon for all parasites; he always seeks a new feeding ground for his race.

*This, however, has nothing to do with nomadism, for the reason that a Jew never thinks of leaving a territory that he has occupied, but remains where he is, and he sits so fast that even by force it is very hard to drive him out... He is and remains the typical parasite, a sponger who like a noxious bacillus keeps spreading as soon as a favourable medium invites him. And the effect of his existence is also like that of spongers; wherever he appears, the host people dies out after a shorter or longer period.**

A salvo of applause erupts, not triggered by the *Heimführer* this time, but by the *Jungmänner*, the oldest students. Some of the younger students didn't understand everything. What does "sponger" mean? And "bacillus"? But they copy the others and clap like crazy anyway. The *Heimführer* smiles at such enthusiasm, then, before continuing, commands silence with a gesture of his hand.

Consequently, this people has always formed a state within states. It is one of the most ingenious tricks ever devised, to make this state sail under the flag of "religion", thus assuring it of the tolerance which the Aryan is always ready to accord a religious creed.

* *Mein Kampf*, Adolf Hitler, translated by Ralph Mannheim, Houghton Mifflin, Mariner Books, New York, 1999, pp.304–5

*For actually the Mosaic religion is nothing other than a doctrine for the preservation of the Jewish race.**

A new salvo of clapping. With these acoustics the rat-a-tat-tat of the applause sounds like a machine gun.

"Bon appétit!" says the *Heimführer*.

At ease. We can sit down and eat.

On the menu today: vegetable soup, bread, cheese topped with artificial honey, tea. I dip my spoon in the soup, but it's cold now. I can't tell what the vegetables are, because everything is mashed up and diluted in a huge amount of water. But, as I stir, I can make out a few beans that have escaped the crush and rise to the surface.

I'm not hungry any more. Before the *Heimführer*'s lecture, I was ravenous. I could have eaten everything on the table. My belly was growling so loudly I was frightened it could be heard, which would not have gone down well.

Now the soup is cold. Cold soup is disgusting.

And the *Heimführer*'s words are swimming in my head, like the beans in the soup. *Parasite. Bacillus.*

I'm more intelligent than my buddies, I know what that means. Parasites are germs, filthy microscopic bugs that creep into your body and make you sick. "Bacillus" is what you call a synonym, and, guess what, I've got another one: "bacterium". As for "sponger", that's the person who steals food off your plate, deprives you of nourishment, starves you and makes you sick. What I'm not sure of is the shape of the bacillus-parasite-bacterium. Perhaps it looks like the beans floating in my soup?

I'm starting to get a stomach-ache. (It's been a while.) As

* *Mein Kampf*, Adolf Hitler, translated by Ralph Mannheim, Houghton Mifflin, Mariner Books, New York, 1999, p.150

if I can feel a bacillus-parasite-bacterium beginning to gnaw at my intestines.

The *Heimführer*'s words are on a loop in my head. The Jews are parasites-bacilli. They contaminate everything, they make you sick.

I keep stirring my soup mechanically. Now that I think about it, parasites have a similar shape to beans. Jews are like beans. The beans have contaminated my soup. There are Jews in my soup! So many miniature Jews scowling and sneering. And Lukas is among them. Lukas, the bean – both literally and figuratively – hiding the fact that he's Jewish, and performing with such zeal in front of his superiors, along with his two idiot mates. There, I can see him, like a tiny evil being, diving into the liquid when the back of my spoon touches him, then resurfacing immediately.

It's impossible to eat soup with Lukases in it. I give my serving to my neighbour.

I raise my head and try to catch Lukas's eye. The real, life-size Lukas, not the bean splashing around in my soup. Is he managing to eat? Did he clap earlier? After the *Heimführer*'s reading, did he have his say about "Jewish contamination"?

I can't make him out among the mass of blond heads bent over their plates. The dining room is too huge; I'd go over there, but it's forbidden.

How does Lukas cope, when…

In my History class the teacher outlines our Führer's denouncement of the iniquities of the Treaty of Versailles and explains to us how the Polish people, with the help of the Jews, attacked socialist Germany in September 1939. (I was only three then, still at Steinhöring, but I remember the event. In the Home, didn't we celebrate the *German attack*? Same deal at Poznan.) The teacher continues with an analysis of the lightning victory of our troops and the necessity of defeating the inferior Polish race.

So what happens in Lukas's class? Does Lukas take notes? Does he manage to write down the teacher's words? When he has to do his homework sitting at the table, a crude, brainless thug on either side, copying his work, does he elaborate the teacher's theory in eloquent prose?

And how does he cope during the politics class, when it's drummed into us that we are the elite, that tomorrow we will rule the country and occupy the top positions?

I don't know how Lukas manages. I still haven't spoken to him alone. But, when I think about it, my mind races. Just like with the leech things in the soup. Lukas seems so much at home at the *Napola* that, once he's finished his education, after all the months and years, he could become a government minister, couldn't he? Then why not the successor to the Führer? What will he do then? Will he still hide the fact that he's Jewish? Will someone end up finding out and denouncing me, because I didn't denounce him? Or what about the other scenario for Lukas, with his full powers, wreaking vengeance by throwing the whole German population into concentration camps?

My head is spinning. I ask special permission to leave during the politics class and, because I'm an excellent member of the class, the teacher grants it, with a warning that it mustn't happen again; but as I leave the room, running as if I was going to wet my pants, my buddies are making fun of me.

How does Lukas cope, when…

Here the calendar revolves around festivals celebrating National Socialism. We don't respect Christian festivals, apart from Christmas.

Today is the 29th of January. Tomorrow, the 30th, is a holiday, celebrating the Führer's assumption of power in 1933. As we don't have classes tomorrow, we're allowed more free time before bed and, to make the evening a bit more fun, the teachers have planned a book burning. In other words, it's party time!

During the day, it's all my buddies can talk about. They can't wait for tonight. For some, it won't be the first time; they've already attended book burnings in their home towns. Others, like me, are novices. Instead of the regular afternoon physical training, we unload truckloads of books, which have come from all over the place, private libraries in Germany or the occupied countries. We form an assembly line to ferry the boxes from the trucks to the middle of the courtyard. They're heavy! Our muscles are getting a workout. We're all bare-chested, but our exertions soon make us forget the glacial temperature. The mood is relaxed and we're allowed to talk and laugh among ourselves.

"Filthy books produced by Jewish vermin!"

"Bertolt Brecht, Sigmund Freud, Heinrich Mann, Karl Marx, Stefan Zweig. So many typical German names. And yet!"

"The Führer is right, the Jewish parasite knows how to hide behind a veil!"

To brighten up the festive afternoon, once the unloading is finished, they serve us tea and slices of bread – normally our physical activity is never rewarded with snacks. After the break, we tackle the boxes, tipping their contents out unceremoniously, as if it is all rubbish. It *is* rubbish and that's exactly why we have to burn it. It's fun seeing the books falling to pieces as they land. It's fun jumping in the big pile, trampling on them, breaking the spines, ripping off covers, tearing out pages and scrunching them into balls and throwing them at each other, yelling out, just like a snowball fight. Some of the boys even crouch down and pretend to wipe their bums with the pages: "It's so soft! Like a kiss!" Everyone roars with laughter at their performance. It's a wonderful afternoon; everyone is in a good mood.

At zero hour, we're all gathered, teachers and students, showered and scrubbed, clean as a whistle, dressed in full uniform. The section leaders, two steps ahead of the others, carry the flags of the Reich. With our right arms raised straight, we encircle the pyramid of books piled on top of each other. Four *Jungmänner* are given the task of pouring petrol from large cans, before they take it in turns to strike a match and throw it on the pile. The flames begin at the base of the pyramid, cheered on by the songs we're chanting. Songs to the glory of our Führer, of the Reich and its thousand-year reign, freed from Judaism and Bolshevism. The fire is slow at first, just a few timid flames running around the base of the paper pyramid, far from the summit, which seems to call down mockingly, "I'm far too high! You'll never reach me! I represent centuries of knowledge and erudition! You can't reduce that to nothing in a few moments!"

But we sing louder and louder, pounding out the rhythm on the ground with our boots. We stagger into a sort of dance around the blaze. As if we have invoked it through our incantations, the wind rises, blowing strong gusts that fan the fire. And the fire gets bigger and bigger, and the covers of the books blacken, shrivel, twist; the paper burns, the flames crackle and soon reach as high as the first floor of the building next to us. The flames are reflected in every window, creating as many sources of light. It's night, but we can see as clearly as in broad daylight. The weather is cold, but the fire is keeping us warm.

I'm singing along, too. And dancing around the inferno. And, once again, I try to glimpse Lukas, through the flames. To see how he's singing, dancing... I'd like to know if he remembers the words he said to me, in the Kalish infirmary, when he told me the story of his parents. When he told me about his mother who ran a bookshop. "Hey, Skullface!" he said. "Do you know what books are for? Books are for reading, not for burning like your mates do, yelling like barbarians."

I sing and hurl books, just like my mates, the barbarians. But that doesn't stop me thinking, or stop my imagination from running riot. After the Jewish beans in the soup, after the vision of Lukas as Führer, my imagination reveals not a simple pyramid of burning books, but a whole bookshop, the bookshop run by Lukas's mother. And his mother is inside, being burned alive. The air is filled with smoke and the smell of charred paper, charred leather, charred flesh.

I want to be sick.

Where is Lukas? I can only see flashes of him, behind the flames, swept up in the surging *Jungmänner* group. Of course, he's flanked by Gunter and Herman, those two idiots, who are shouting louder – and charging round the fire faster – than anyone else. It looks like they're drunk; they must have been drinking schnapps – some *Jungmänner* get hold of it on the sly. What with the heat and my nausea, I can just imagine them throwing themselves into the fire to turn the whole scene into something even more spectacular, and to prove their *Draufgängertum*. And they've dragged Lukas along with them.

How does Lukas cope, when…

Biology class, one of our favourite subjects. Why? Because the classroom is decorated with funny pictures – our drawings, as well as those of the art teacher, who often works with the biology teacher. Our artworks are practical assignments to illustrate the theme of the lessons: "Characteristic and distinguishing signs of the Jew."

Our work wasn't on the walls at the beginning of the year; there were only photographs of Jews (real ones) taken full-face and side-on. We had to study them, and discuss them freely, without thinking about whether our comments were respectable or our speech refined enough.

"It's totally intolerable to look so gross!"

"That's a scarecrow!"

"Yeah! He should be stuck in a field, scaring away crows!"

"Lucky photos don't smell!"

"Otherwise it'd stink of shit!"

It was fun just to say whatever came into our heads. But it didn't last long. The teacher told us to give it a break because we were making such a racket. We moved from the fun stage to the scientific stage. We had to study the photos with precision, measuring the length of the nose, the eyes, the ears, the height of the forehead, the thickness of the lips, the width of the eyes. And find appropriate terms to designate the colour of the eyes and hair. We had to enter our results in a chart and compare it to a chart of Aryan measurement statistics. Too easy. The figures were diametrically opposite. And we didn't need to rack our brains about the colour of the eyes and hair: black. The whole class passed that test with flying colours.

Then the teacher stuck a sketch on the wall, entitled: *The Wandering Jew*. An old man, hunched over and shrivelled up, with a thin, scowling face, as wizened as a rotten apple, leaning on a stick, and dressed in rags, carrying a filthy bundle on his bag. At the bottom of the drawing the caption read: *They arrived from the Orient like this…* The teacher emphasized the ellipsis. We had to find out the meaning of that particular punctuation. Our homework was to imagine the Jew's transformation once he'd settled in Germany or another European country. Our presentation could be either a drawing or an essay.

I don't like writing essays.

I don't like drawing either.

Chewing on my pencil in front of a blank page is not my thing. Nor is daydreaming about a landscape – or, in this case, a silhouette of a face – in order to make a drawing. Writers and artists are highbrow wimps. But I had to produce something, or else I'd be punished. I'm no idiot, so I worked out that the other section of the sketch must be in the reading room, where they leave piles of newspapers with news from the front for us to read. There are caricatures of Jews in almost all the papers. I just had to dig up the one from which the first part of the sketch had been cut out. But I drew a blank. Obviously. The teacher had predicted that smart-arses like me would try something sneaky, so he'd already removed the newspaper from the shelves.

If only we'd been set this task after the *Heimführer*'s reading in the dining hall, I could have drawn a parasite shaped like a bean. It's easy to draw a bean: you just add hair and eyes to a sort of concave semicircle, and that's it.

But I'm telling you about a class that happened before the reading... So, what was to be done? Copy off a classmate? It was tempting, but dangerous. Copying is dishonourable (the opposite of denunciation and spying, both considered fundamental values). The punishment could be as severe as confiscation of your dagger of honour, in public, in front of the whole student assembly. That was out of the question. I intended to keep my sword.

I finally worked out a deal with Manfred. He's hopeless at sport and has about as little *Draufgängertum* as a parish priest, but he's an artist and loves drawing. To whip up an extra sketch for me was no trouble at all for him. In exchange, when we had to take each other on in a boxing match, I let him win. The instructor was surprised, but didn't tear strips off me. "There are some days when we're not up to scratch," he said, "but be careful all the same, Konrad. Pull yourself together. Next time I won't let you off the hook."

He winked at me. I think he understood that I was forced to "go down", as they say in boxing. Our boxing instructor is not a nobody, far from it; he's Herr Rohloff, European boxing champion. I guess that if he's not world champion, it's precisely because he too had to "go down" at some point. (We're lucky at the *Napola*. As sport is the most important subject, our teachers are famous individuals; our javelin instructor, for example, is the Olympic champion, Herr Stöck.)

Getting back to the topic in hand, Manfred did a wonderful drawing for me. A fat, pot-bellied Jew, sitting with his legs splayed on a huge sack in the shape of a globe of the world, with the word MONEY written in capitals across the front of the globe. He's sweating, his cheeks are scarlet, as if he's been drinking, and studded with black dots because he's unshaven. He looks like he's well dressed but his suit is ugly and crumpled. Manfred used colours that clash: purple shoes, green socks and a red tie. The sweaty, fat Jew's black hat has slid off his head and is lying on the ground.

The teacher praised me and I got ten out of ten. My drawing was framed and hung on the wall. Manfred got 9.5 for his drawing, *The Poisonous Mushroom*, which was also inspired. The top of the mushroom was a Jew's hat, the stem a Jew's face, with a big nose, sticking-out ears, and a red flared beard. The root of the mushroom, emerging from the ground, was a five-pointed star. I mean, why didn't someone think of that before? The teacher explained that the only reason he didn't get full marks was that, although his drawing was a perfectly accurate representation of reality, it did not follow the instructions, which asked for a portrayal of the transformation of the Jew, once settled in Europe. Likewise, my mates were off topic with their drawings of Jews with pig ears or hairy ears.

The teacher finally showed us the second part of the original sketch from the newspaper. It was the same Jew, but instead of being scrawny and in rags he'd become fat, wore a suit in bad taste, covered in gold and sparkling diamonds, and he was smoking a cigar. With his foot, he was crushing a German peasant, whose face wore an expression of agony. You could almost hear his cries of suffering, and he was so thin you knew he was dying of starvation. The caption read: *And turned into this in our country.*

My classmates clapped. The mood was relaxed, happy, which is rare during lesson time.

I started daydreaming about the photos and sketches on the wall. I compared that old Jew arriving from the Orient with a young Jew arriving, if not from the Orient, then from the East. From Poland. Lukas. Yes, him, obviously. Could he be the old Jew's grandson? When Lukas arrived at Kalish, he was already blond – the *Napola* didn't change his hair colour, nor his blue eyes. But he was thin, dirty, dressed in rags, with lice in his mop of hair, and a wild stare. And now… If you did a drawing of him now, he'd be sporting the handsome *Jungmann* uniform, pink skin, and a clear, pure gaze. You could draw Walter's face under his boot, the kid he beat up in the study hall with Gunter and Herman. Under the sketch you could have the same caption as in the paper: *He arrived from Poznan like this … and turned into this in our country, at the Napola.*

But, on the other hand, something wasn't quite right. If you wrote Lukas's statistics into the chart the teacher had given us at the beginning of the classes, his would be identical to the Aryan measurements. Moreover, Lukas had the green racial-fitness certificate.

I wanted to tell the teacher everything, that Lukas was Jewish *and* Aryan – so he could explain the contradiction to me, once and for all.

But I said nothing.

And now I'm sick of biology lessons. I'm bored to death. There's no more drawing, no more writing. All we do is learn by rote. The theme of the lessons has changed to, "How to recognize a Jew?" This was our written dictation:

The Jew's nose is curved at the end. It looks like the number 6. If some non-Jews also have a curved nose, we must bear in mind that this curve is angled upwards. The Jew has thick lips and thick eyebrows. He is small in stature, with short, bandy legs and shrunken arms. He has a short, receding forehead, black curly hair like Negros, and jug ears. He has a foul odour, a beard infested with lice and grimy clothes.

I hate dictation. I can never get my participle agreements right. I get confused with double consonants. I don't like learning by rote, and even less reciting in front of the class.

What's more, for homework, we have to find other descriptions to add to this text, which is also framed and hanging on the wall.

I can't find any damn descriptive adjectives. Unlike my classmates.

I don't take part in the oral.

My marks take a dive.

It's a relief, a few weeks later, when the biology classes seem to change tack. The teacher starts to talk about animals. What does an animal lack, compared to a human? Easy, a brain! The faculty of thinking. I'm the first one to raise my hand and give the correct answer. Then the teacher outlines how very small animals behave, like ticks and fleas, which feed off blood and transmit diseases to humans. Using information about medical and scientific progress, he explains how it is necessary to fight such creatures in order to preserve human health.

I'm fascinated by the lesson and, for the first time ever, I get a surprise when the bell goes.

Before he dismisses us, the teacher gives out some homework for next lesson. Good news: that should lift my marks.

He writes on the blackboard, "Explain the necessity of exterminating the Jewish people."

How does Lukas cope, when…

The shower.

I've already told you we have daily showers at the *Napola*, which is nice, as well as necessary given our fourteen hours of sport a week. Flawless, sparkling clean and tidy, they're located next to the dormitories and fitted with separate basins, another element of comfort aimed at instilling a keen awareness of hygiene, something particularly indispensable to us Aryans.

The only hitch is the damned soap we're supposed to wash ourselves with. It's really bad quality, but, for several months now, there's been no other soap to be found in all of Germany. It just doesn't lather. Even if you hold it under the water and rub it hard between your hands, all it does is scrape your skin, without even the slightest bubble of lather appearing. And, on top of that, it stinks, a nauseating odour, a bit like a piece of rotten meat left to dry. If you add to that the water restrictions we're forced to adhere to, the shower is really not enjoyable any more. My classmates and I are forever whingeing about it, even if it's become a standing joke.

"Damned Jewish soap!"

"It stinks like shit!"

"Come on! Give me some, even if it's useless!"

Ever since I'd arrived at the *Napola*, I'd heard the soap referred to as *RIF*. I had no idea what this meant. Not wanting to look stupid, I hadn't dared ask. I tried to guess. R as in … *Reich*? I as in … *Immer*? F as in *False*? Which makes: "Reich always false". Meaningless. Or R as in … *Reisen*? I as in … *Im*? F as in *Führer*? "Journey in the Führer", completely incoherent. I had another go: *Richtig Ideal Farbe* ("exact ideal colour"), but what did that have to do with soap? The soap's colour is, incidentally, as disgusting as the smell. I kept racking my brains doing endless combinations of letters – in vain.

I gave up and asked Manfred the wimp. As he's hopeless at sport and spends all his time drawing, it was not in his interest to make fun of me. He replied politely, in his reedy voice, "*RIF*? They're the initials of the industrial company *Reichsstelle Industrielle* ... something or other, I forget the last word. But, at the *Napola*, they've turned it into *Rein Juden Fett*. And changed the I to a J." *Rein Juden Fett*, he repeated as, gobsmacked, stock-still under the water, which had gone from tepid to freezing, I turned into a statue.

"That's why the soap stinks and doesn't lather," concluded Manfred. "But it's better than no soap at all."

Rein Juden Fett.

Rein Juden Fett.

Oh right, of course, you'll need the translation, won't you, to understand why I remained motionless under the freezing water. Here it is: "Pure Jewish fat."

Soap made out of the body fat of Jews. The Jews in the camps... Like, for instance, Lukas's mother, in Treblinka.

I can't wash myself any more. I am dirty and I stink.

But Lukas takes a shower every single day! He's clean, impeccable. He's even starting to shave.

He's becoming Aryan, and as for me ... it's as if I'm becoming Jewish.

24.

I discovered how Lukas coped. Despite my superior intelligence, I couldn't work it out by myself. He had to explain it to me. I could never have imagined anything like it.

Study hall. I'm racing to finish an essay I have to hand in tomorrow. The title is: "Imagine the transformation of an animal by a magic potion". Just think how much children my age love that sort of homework. Ordinary children, that is. Not students from the *Napola*. The point is not to waffle on about inanities, describing the transformation of some sweet little puppy playing with a ball into a huge scary dragon breathing fire and terrifying a beautiful princess. This essay, like all our assignments, has to be written from a Nazi perspective.

I've got a few ideas... The animal could be Lukas, and the magic potion could be the *Napola*, which has made him a hardcore Aryan. Or, the animal could be me, and the magic potion, with poisonous properties this time, could be Lukas. Because, and I'm fully aware of it, he has really messed with my head since the day I met him. And it's not getting any better. Contact with Lukas is transforming me. He is "de-Aryanizing" me, and "Jewifying" me. (I'm making up new words for this situation.) Well! Whether the animal is Lukas or me, I'll know how to structure my homework and I'll be able to describe a very precise transformation. But how can I work on either of these two ideas without getting myself into deep shit?

Impossible.

I'm stuck. I don't have any other options. Here I am, facing my blank page, chewing on the shaft of my pen, biting my nails, staring gloomily out the window. It's dusk outside and it's barely 5 p.m. I feel like chucking it in. I'm fed up.

Just to top off my annoyance, Manfred is sitting next to me, bent over his exercise book, scribbling away without stopping. At the rate he's going, he'll use up our ration of paper for the evening. The scratching of his pen echoes in the silence of the room. It's giving me the creeps. What can this moron possibly be writing? Reading over his elbow, I can see that his chosen animal is Germany after World War I and his magic potion is the Führer. He's gone for the simplest, the most obvious idea, and he'll get the best mark. Idiot!

I'm abandoning the bloody essay for now and I'm going to do something else. Once a month, each of us has to send a letter of support to a soldier at the front. My correspondent is a certain Harald Schwarz, *Rottenführer* by profession. OK, at least this is easy: I'll just write the same things as for the last one, rephrased. He has to stand firm, even if the fighting is tough; his mother country cares for him, believes in him, is proud of him, and has no doubt about the final victory, which is approaching rapidly and to which he will have contributed through his sacrifices. He will be rewarded for his devotion to the Führer, he will return from the front covered in glory, and so on and so forth… So now, I'm off and running, my pen racing faster than Manfred's. I write ten lines non-stop, and only stop for a second when I get a slight cramp in my hand. (I can run or swim for two hours in a row without getting a cramp, but it hurts to hold a pen for so long!) When I look up, I realize that it's dark. The days are getting shorter and shorter; soon it will be the winter solstice. It's as if the night will last for ever, and that's an awful feeling.

Why do I feel so melancholy all of a sudden? Is it yet another weird side effect of the "magic potion" gnawing at me from inside? Despite the shadows, I decide to get back to work and, as I pull myself together, I recognize the silhouette crossing the courtyard. It's heading towards the primary-school building. *My* building… What is *he* doing around here? After all this time, is he finally condescending to recognize that I exist?

I wait, motionless, on the alert. Soon I hear footsteps on the staircase, then on the other side of the study hall door, which opens soon enough.

"Hi there, Skullface."

The main thing is not to move, not to turn in his direction. Not to exhibit any emotion – excitement, annoyance – none whatsoever. Especially not joy.

Anyway, I have no reason at all to rejoice. If Lukas has deigned to appear, it's not out of friendship for me, but because he's suffered a real blow lately. Has he come to be comforted by me? He can get lost. Perhaps I'll get my own back…

* * *

The real blow was the death of Gunter last week. I'm not aware of the exact circumstances; all I know is that it happened during a paramilitary exercise. It could have been Herman. It could have been Lukas, since the three of them were inseparable. And Lukas was wounded; he's swathed in a big bandage below the waist, which doesn't in any way diminish his elegant demeanour – on the contrary, it looks like a bullfighter's belt. His posture is even more upright and his bearing even prouder.

Anyway, Gunter's gone; there are only two musketeers left. And he continues to make our lives hell: because of his death, the Christmas and winter solstice festivities have been cancelled. The school is in mourning. The ceremony we did end up attending was a funeral wake. The *Heimführer*, the head of teaching, the bursar, the service staff (admin, kitchen, laundry, medical) and students, of course – we were all gathered around Gunter's coffin, which was draped in the Reich's flag. We were all in full uniform, decorated with a black armband. The speeches and ceremonial rites went on for ever. And it was cold in the snow. And we were tired. Gunter's parents were the guests of honour and left with the body as soon as it was all over. I have no idea how significant it was that *Obergruppenführer* Lübeln was present, or how appropriate it is to sing the praises of the dead. But the fact is that Gunter the idiot, Gunter the thug, as thick as two planks, Gunter who had a pea (or make it a bean, because I'm so funny!) for a brain, has become Gunter the brave, Gunter of the elite intellectuals, Gunter the model *Jungmann*. He died in a remarkable demonstration of his courage and incomparable *Draufgängertum*. He magnificently embodied the major slogan of the Hitler Youth movements: *We are here to serve the Führer and to die for him.* I swear he wouldn't have received more honours if he had single-handedly destroyed twenty Russian tanks at Stalingrad.

Yeah, well ... I'd like to see that.

Serious accidents – never fatal – are frequent at the *Napola*. A month ago, a guy tried to escape and they organized a manhunt. Every student in his class joined in wholeheartedly. When they found him, they threw him naked into the river behind the school, then they thrashed him with their leather belts. A few weeks earlier, a guy was denounced for stealing money. His punishment was to jump into the courtyard from the fourth floor, without a net. He broke his pelvis. He's still in hospital.

Gunter did well. He didn't just settle for being seriously wounded, he checked out in the process. He excelled himself there, at least.

"You've grown, Skullface."

Obviously I've grown, I'm nearly eight. And same to you. You look a lot older than fourteen. You look like a man.

Lukas sits down next to me, after giving Manfred the order to clear off and wait somewhere else. Manfred was quick to obey, Lukas being one of those *Jungmänner* respected and feared by the younger kids. Despite the circumstances, I can't help feeling proud.

Lukas lays his broad, strong hand, the nails impeccable, on top of my letter. I can smell some kind of perfume on him, like eau de cologne. Where could he have got hold of that? Is that how he masks the stink of the *RIF* he soaps himself with every day?

I give a quick "Hi". Cool, detached, as if I just saw him last night, when it's been ten months since we arrived at the *Napola*. I push his hand away to grab my letter, which I intend to keep writing. But he takes it from me and reads it.

His smile stretches from ear to ear, that interminable mocking smile that has the knack of making my blood boil. "Rubbish!" he shouts, throwing the letter on the table.

I give him a furious look. He snatches my pen and turns over the sheet of paper. "I'm going to help you write this letter," he tells me.

"No way! I'm not letting a dirty Jew like you dictate what I have to say to our soldiers."

Manfred and another student in my class, also sitting in the study hall, turn around and burst out laughing. They find it funny because calling someone a "dirty Jew" is either the latest joke, or an insult as trivial as "bastard" or "stupid idiot". They don't know, they *can't* know, that, coming from me, it is not a joke.

Lukas laughs too – it's a bit forced all the same; I recognize that characteristic twitching of his lips – then, after making sure that Manfred and Kaspar have settled back to work, he puts his index finger on my mouth to stop me from replying and then beckons with it for me to come closer. He writes on the paper, one word.

Gunter.

There you go, just what I thought. Saddened by the death of his alter ego, he's come to talk about it with me. I manage to refrain from telling him that he can go and cry on Herman's shoulder. His smile, that glimmer of jubilation in his shining eyes… It's odd. Lukas does not seem at all sad. But, during the wake, his eyes filled with tears, he received the condolences of his classmates as if he were Gunter's brother. Something is not quite right.

Do you know how he died? Lukas writes.

"Of course I do, everyone knows, he…"

Again he silences me with his index finger, and glances suspiciously at Manfred and Kaspar.

How he actually died?

I shake my head. Lukas stares at me for a long time, no longer smiling. He's tense. He picks up the pen again and starts writing, quickly, without stopping.

The night before the exercise, Gunter got hold of some schnapps. He asked me to drink with him, like we often did. Not such a great idea, given what we had to do the next morning. But he didn't have the slightest idea what we had to do the next morning. He didn't know that a very dangerous exercise was scheduled for dawn. But I did… It's always possible to bribe an instructor … I pretended to drink, to get drunk with him. It was just the two of us; Herman played it safe and went to sleep. Gunter passed out at 2 a.m. and, at 5.30, when the wake-up bell dragged us out of bed, he was in a shocking state. He had a raging hangover. I had to help him get dressed, put on his underpants, trousers, button his shirt, like a baby. Then, so he wouldn't topple over, I had to support him while we stood to attention during roll call. In the truck, on the way to the parade ground, he spewed up his guts. If he hadn't been the son of Obergruppenführer *Lübeln, I'm sure the guys in the section would have lynched him. When we got down from the truck, the* Scharführer *on duty threw us some spades and lined us up opposite three tanks, stationary in the fog, their motors firing. Three Panzers. Metal mastodons: each one seven metres long and fifty-five tonnes.*

"You'd better dig fast, you bunch of shits! And deep! Now we separate the smart-arses and degenerates from the real soldiers, the ones with balls!"

We got started. In these situations, it's each to his own. There's no time to look out for your neighbour. We all knew that the sadistic Scharführer, *who was swearing and shouting at us as we dug, could decide at any moment to give the signal for the Panzers to start moving. Like the others, I just kept digging, without worrying about Gunter. I caught a glimpse of him out of the corner of my eye, his hands clamped by the cold onto his spade handle; he hadn't even managed to make a dent in the layer of ice covering the ground. The tanks started up. I jumped in my hole. Gunter was still standing, motionless, terrified. I screamed at him to get in next to me. I told him there was enough room for two, that I had dug deep. He believed me. He jumped. He almost broke my back when he fell on top of me. The moment he realized that the hole wasn't deep enough, that the top of his head stuck out, the tank was only a metre away; he didn't have time to climb out. He started hammering me, kicking me, stomping on me, to crush me into the ground. He was yelling, sobbing. At one point, I felt a warm liquid running over me. He had pissed himself. But it was so cold in that fucking frozen hole that the piss was almost welcome. In any case it gave me the necessary strength not only to resist his blows, but to push him up from the hole, at the very instant the tank rolled over us, so that it took off his head.*

Lukas stops briefly. I'm reading as he writes. He's writing fast, his hand trembling. It's hard to decipher his scribble. And it's hard to believe what I'm reading, so I re-read a sentence here and there. When I put my hand over his to make him slow down, I can feel the tremor.

In the Scharführer*'s report on the "accident", he pointed out that Gunter had not dug a hole and had jumped in mine, thus endangering both our lives. (He didn't know that I had got Gunter drunk the night before. And the noise of the tanks prevented him from hearing me tell Gunter to jump in with me.) Schmidt summoned* *me and asked me, for the school's reputation, and for Gunter's parents, if I would corroborate another version of events, an "official" version. An unfortunate set of circumstances, the caterpillar tracks of the tank had jammed ... a whole pile of rubbish. I agreed and Schmidt was extremely grateful.*

I raise my head. I open my mouth as if I'm going to scream, but nothing happens. There's definitely a scream inside me, but it's stuck in my throat. It won't come out, it's choking me. I turn to Manfred and Kaspar. Still busy with their homework, they don't notice me. *Help!*

"What? What's the matter?" says Lukas out loud. "Do you think my letter is too tough? You're wrong, Konrad. You have to see things as they are: your correspondent, our brave soldier Harald, knows very well that he could die at any moment at the front. Your duty is to explain to him that his death is necessary, perfectly justified. That will give him courage. Here you go, I'll add this:

When Gunter carked it, squealing like a pig, I thought about my father's death. My little brother's death. And I thought about my mother, too, who has probably died at Treblinka... That's one against three. Not a fair deal. But it's just the beginning. Do you know that old Jewish saying, "Eye for an eye, tooth for a tooth." I intend to avenge the death of my family. I strike right where I am. From the inside. That causes more pain. When Gunter's mother held me in her arms, sobbing, I said to myself, "You dirty bitch, now can you imagine what thousands of mothers have gone through?" When her bastard of a husband shook my hand, I said to myself, "That's for every one of them shot under your orders."

I still can't react. I'm dumbstruck.

You haven't denounced me as Jewish. Thank you. One day I'll repay you. But you could still denounce me as a murderer. Up to you.

Lukas looks at me, smiling. He's no longer trembling. He's pulled himself together in no time at all. He picks up the piece of paper he's been writing on, waves it under my nose for a second, then gets up and throws it on the coals of the wood stove.

Once the paper has been reduced to ashes, he comes back over to me. "What did you think, Skullface? That I was going to write your letter for you? Too easy! I gave you some ideas to inspire you, but there's no way you can content yourself by copying out mine; you have to find your own words. See you soon!"

Lukas left the hall. After he'd gone, Manfred came back to sit next to me.

"You are so lucky to have a big brother like Lukas," he said. "He's such a great role model for you."

I punched him in the face.

25.

Number two on Lukas's list: Herman.

Obviously.

Should I warn him? How? By slipping an anonymous note under his pillow? By confiding in his brother, Ludwig, who is in my class? To warn Herman would reveal Lukas as Gunter's murderer. To warn Herman, I would reveal myself as an accomplice. The events are all connected now; they're snowballing. I didn't denounce Lukas the Jew, the Jew who disguised himself and who, under the veil of the perfect *Jungmann*, intends to stir up conflict in the *Napola* by killing some of its students. (How many, exactly?)

I hated Herman before; now I feel sorry for him. Every time I see him, laughing, eating, drinking, running or bullying a classmate, I want to say, "Enjoy yourself! Pretty soon, you'll be *kaput*." If only I had an idea of how Lukas was going to commit this second murder. I haven't the faintest idea when he's going to strike. Not immediately, in any case.

Several weeks go by without an incident. And if the

threat of losing his big brother hangs over Ludwig, it seems as if, on the contrary, my big brother has been restored to me.

Things are changing. Lukas visits me whenever he can. Often in the afternoon, when we sort out our personal belongings. The first time was two days after his confession. Just when I thought he was giving me the cold shoulder, he turned up in my dorm. I was at the sink, washing my singlets.

"Hi, Skullface! So we're doing our handwashing? How sweet. Hey, while you're at it, wash this!"

He threw his bag of dirty laundry at my feet, lay down on my bed and, completely at ease, started to flip through a magazine.

I saw red. I threw the sopping wet singlet at his face. Straightaway he took off one of his muddy boots and threw it at me. In turn, I chucked the whole pile of soaking clothes from the sink at him. Then he threw his other boot at me, then his belt, and his trousers. Now I went for the heavy artillery: from the bottom of the wardrobe I grabbed my dirtiest underpants, the ones from the time when I couldn't get used to the *RIF* and I couldn't work out how to wash them with the school's ersatz washing powder. I bombarded Lukas with these impressive weapons.

It was like a starting signal. All the other students, who had been on the sidelines until this point, now joined in a mighty dirty-clothes battle. Stuff was flying everywhere. (And I noticed that I was not the only one to hide items of my dirty washing. I saw underpants as stiff as cardboard, so impregnated were they with dried urine. Others displayed evidence of more significant deposits. When they hit the bull's eye, it must have been a tasty mouthful. The victims rushed, screaming, to the sinks to douse themselves with water.) When we ran out of dirty laundry, we pounced on the sheets and pillows. What a hoot! It was great to unwind, to flout the basic rules of discipline by ransacking this damn dorm, turning it into a pigsty, making one hell of a mess.

Alerted by the uproar, the section leader soon turned up. He almost had an apoplectic fit when he walked into the chaos. The floor drenched in water, soiled with mud, the beds torn apart, the pillows ripped open, feathers everywhere, underpants full of dry crap strewn all over the floor. He immediately threatened us with a collective punishment for defacing the premises. But Lukas – who in the meantime had taken off all his clothes – stood in front of him and, with every centimetre of his 1.7 metres, stared him down, full of scorn. The other wimp, who barely reached Lukas's chest, understood immediately that it would be in his interest to keep the incident a secret and to forget his threats of punishment. Defeated, he lowered his gaze. And clapped eyes on Lukas's penis – do I need to remind you that it is uncircumcised? – and the two huge testicles framing it. Red as a beetroot, he turned on his heels and disappeared without further ado.

Lukas also comes to visit me in the dining hall after lunch and we head off for a walk before the afternoon activities, far enough away for him to smoke a cigarette. (*Jungmänner* smoke on the sly and tobacco is one of the items most frequently traded on the black market.) Sometimes he offers me a drag. The first time I thought a grenade had exploded in my chest. Little by little, I'm getting used to it. I like it, it makes me seem like a *Jungmann*. But I prefer the jam Lukas gives me once in a while. Real jam, not the disgusting beetroot puree they serve up to us these days. Sometimes Lukas even gets me chocolate. He manages to get his hands on a whole lot of food that's not available. I'm glad because the meals are getting worse at the *Napola* and my stomach is often rumbling when I leave the dining hall.

We also see each other at the farm, when we engage in "experience in agricultural labour". More and more, students have to muck in to make sure we still get provisions from the farm, and to look after the few remaining animals. Lukas is by far the best at catching chickens. Even when he demonstrates his technique to me, I can't do it. Filthy creatures, they're so fast when they smell danger. They slip through my fingers and I end up flat on my face, my nose in their bird poo.

"Just think of them as Jews," Lukas said to me one day with a forced smile. "The only difference," he added under his breath, "is that at least the chickens don't allow themselves to be led to the abattoir without putting up a fight."

Lukas let the last surviving chicken on the farm go free. I didn't stop him because I knew it would never end up on our plates but on those of a few teachers and the *Heimführer*.

"I anoint you head of the Jewish resistance," pronounced Lukas ceremoniously, as he let the chicken go behind the outer wall of the school. Earlier, he had filled a little bag with grain that he tied around the chicken's neck, so it would have something to live off for a while.

We also have to milk the cows, which is getting really difficult. They are so thin and underfed that they only piss out a trickle of milk.

"You know what? I've had enough! I'd rather pull on

something else than the udders of these fucking cows."

Without a second thought, Lukas headed to the other end of the stable and pulled his pants down. He had his back to me but I could see the movement of his right hand going up and down without stopping, really fast, as he groaned "Oh!, Ah!, Aahh!" I knew he was fondling his penis. He was *masturbating*.

"But you're not allowed to!" I called out, furious. "Isn't it enough that you're Jewish and a murderer? As well as the yellow star and the green triangle, do you want them to stick a pink triangle on you? Are you trying for the full collection of geometric shapes?"

"Shut up, Skullface. Watch and learn."

He showed me how to do it, but it's not easy – my penis is too small. Sometimes, it sort of works; I manage to rub it against my pants and it feels funny, like heat spreading through my lower belly. It's kind of nice, but it doesn't work often. I reckon smoking is easier.

Lukas also sometimes takes me to the carpentry workshop. We don't talk a lot, not freely in any case, because we're hardly ever alone, carpentry being more popular than farm work. Lukas is working hard at making a wooden object, a sort of statuette. He's told me it is a toy, for me, that he'll give me when it's finished. I can't wait.

All that doesn't stop the two of us from fighting a lot. It's in Lukas's temperament to blow hot and cold.

"You son-of-a-bitch-whore Kraut!"

It comes over him all of a sudden, like he want to piss from his mouth.

"Filthy Jew!"

"Nazi!"

"Polack dog!"

"Reich's sprog!"

"Subhuman!"

"Bastard!"

"Parasite!"

"Your parents screwed in Nazi fornication factories!"

"Yours will never screw again!"

I don't mind it when we argue and insult each other. That's supposed to be normal between brothers: we love each other and at the same time we hate each other to the point of sometimes wanting to kill each other. What I can't stand is when, just when I least expect it, in a really creepy way, Lukas's poisonous magic potion infiltrates me, drop by drop.

Movies are important teaching tools at the *Napola*. They show us a lot of films, at least one a week. In the beginning it was mostly films of the huge mass demonstrations organized by the Reich: the singing, the crowds, the public speeches by our Führer – it was all wonderful. Now, we watch films about the war, which is also wonderful: we're kept up-to-date with the new weapons developed by the Reich. We had seen, for example, demonstrations of the Panzer V and the Tiger. The commentator explained – in his deep, warm melodious voice and with perfect diction – that the Panzer is the tank most feared by the Allies, who can only put up their inferior Sherman against it. The Allies themselves acknowledge that three of their armoured vehicles will be destroyed before a panzer can be overtaken.

The commentator also talks about the Goliaths. They're brilliant! Tiny little armoured cars stuffed with dynamite, operated by remote control to infiltrate a bunker and explode inside.

We bring the house down with our applause. And that's the opportunity Lukas takes to kick my neighbour out of his seat and sit down next to me. He's clapping, just like everyone else. He's smiling, just like everyone else. But at the same time, imitating the commentator's tone, he turns on a strong Polish accent and whispers crazy things in my ear: "The Panzer V was only in response to the formidable Russian tank, the T-434, which is a total destroyer." He describes twin-engine Russian ground-attack aircraft that fly silently at low altitude in the Leningrad night skies and destroy German convoys. "They're nicknamed the 'Flying Tanks'."

"Shut up! You're talking shit."

I shove him away with my elbow and try to concentrate on the screen where they're showing scenes from the sieges of Moscow and Leningrad. Even though our soldiers are suffering from the cold, and they're thin and exhausted, they are smiling at the camera, looking confident. The commentator moves on to the campaign in North Africa, where Rommel's Afrika Korps is well entrenched. North Africa seems so far away, and yet this region now belongs to the Reich. Occupied Europe is ancient history now. As for the attack on Pearl Harbour by the Japanese, although the teacher in charge of the screening doesn't have any images of it, he describes it in minute detail several times a week. You've got to hand it to them, those Japanese were amazingly courageous with their kamikaze planes. Everyone in the room is enthusiastic – the older *Jungmänner* leap up, as if they're about to climb into one of the suicide planes. In the end the teacher stops his commentary and tries in vain to restore order.

Once the room is silent again, Lukas goes back into attack, too.

"It's all just a montage," he whispers in my ear. "Nothing but dumb propaganda. These films have been tampered with, and they're not at all up-to-date. I'll tell you the truth: there's a pincer attack on the Afrika Korps, by the British from the west, and the Franco-Americans from the east. Since the Americans have entered the war, there's a whole lot of new military technology: decoding of enemy communication, radar, sonar, and the German submarines have all been destroyed. The Krauts surrendered at Stalingrad. There were 91,000 prisoners. You and your little buddies can start shitting yourselves because the Red Army is on its way fast. It entered Kiev, liberated Leningrad, and is on the outskirts of Warsaw now. Ivan's* army is on its way, Skullface! They'll march on Berlin any day. I'm telling you, there'll be trouble!"

It's all lies, rubbish. Where could he find out all that? From the chickens he plucked at the farm? Did he listen to a radio in a cow's udder?

Nothing proves what Lukas said. Not a thing. Well, hardly anything. So, there is a lot more food rationing. So, quite a few teachers have left for the front and haven't been replaced. So, the sixteen-year-old *Jungmänner* are undergoing intensive training in case they need to be mobilized under exceptional circumstances. But apart from those few hitches, it's business as usual inside the *Napola*. So surely things must be the same outside … surely?

The Reich is invincible. *Invincible.*

I can't bear listening to any more of Lukas's nonsense, so I leap out of my seat like a spring and disturb everyone as I try to find another spot. The teacher is furious; he storms

* The name used by the Germans for Russian soldiers.

over, grabs me by the ear and frogmarches me out of the room, all the while yelling out my misdemeanours: inability to concentrate, insubordination (because I'm trying in vain to object), causing a disruption during an important training session.

I'm grounded for ten days.

No more chats at the farm or at the carpentry workshop. That's the end of cigarettes, jam, chocolate and penis-rubbing. I'm banned from all official ceremonies. (I don't give a damn! And anyway, there haven't been any ceremonies for a while.) I eat by myself, I exercise by myself, my bed has been moved to the other end of the dorm.

But one evening I find something under my pillow. The statuette. The toy Lukas was making for me. He finished it and somehow found a way to get it to me. That cheers me up a bit, especially as it's really well made – it's a miniature Führer. The wood is incredibly well carved. It has the moustache, the hair combed to the side, the inscribed belt buckle. There's a piece of string, with a metal bead on the end, hanging from the right hand. The statuette works like a puppet when I pull on the string: the right arm rises, the Führer leans forward, which makes his buttocks stick out and…

The noise echoes in the silent dorm and everyone bursts out laughing. I pull the sheet over my head in shame.

The noise was a fart.

I quickly hide the statuette under my mattress before the section leader turns up.

Lukas is a bastard.

Once I'm no longer grounded, I run into the secondary-school building to return his so-called present. But they turn me back at the entrance. Official ban on entering the premises.

There's been a shocking incident, they tell me.

Herman is dead.

26.

Number two.

The third victim – who will it be? – should start worrying.

Herman died during "hand-grenade training".

The routine exercise goes like this: each *Jungmann* has to place a hand grenade on his helmet, and time it for detonation in three seconds. The exercise is successful if the *Jungmann* manages to stay completely still, without shaking, perhaps even without thinking – an idea could make him flinch. The grenade stays balanced on his helmet and explodes there. No damage to anything. The apprentice soldier comes out of it unharmed. Sure, he's a bit shaken, stunned by the noise of the explosion and by the terror he experienced during those three seconds that felt like an eternity. But he's in one piece.

The exercise is a failure when the grenade falls – either it wasn't placed in the right spot on the helmet or the *Jungmann* moved slightly, a sudden urge to sneeze, or cough, or there was a gust of wind – and it explodes at his feet. Half the student's leg is torn off, or the whole leg, or both, but he's alive and quickly rushed to hospital. The *Napola* pays for his treatment and provides him with a compensatory pension for the rest of his life.

In Herman's case it wasn't just a failure, it was a bloodbath. Butchery. The grenade fell on his shoulder, so the explosion reduced his head to a pulp.

Just like Gunter.

The mastermind behind this second murder is obvious. At least it is for me, as I know there was a first murder. By Lukas. This time I don't need him to explain what happened. Herman didn't flinch, Herman didn't sneeze, or he would have only had his legs blown off. *Lukas wanted him gone. Lukas wanted to decapitate him.* So he made sure the grenade fell in just the right spot: on his shoulder. It was just a matter of a small dent in the helmet. Lukas must have tampered with it while Herman was asleep. Or else, on some pretext or another, he exchanged helmets at the last minute.

I'm sure my hypothesis is correct, but I'll never know.

Lukas was absent from the dining hall that day. He wasn't at the farm or at the carpentry workshop in the afternoon. Had he already been unmasked before the news of his arrest had been announced? I could already see him being interrogated by the *Heimführer*, declared guilty, hanged on a butcher's hook and, by way of example, put on display, bleeding, in front of everyone gathered in the courtyard. He didn't turn up at dinner either. I couldn't stand it any longer so I asked one of his classmates and was told that Lukas, along with a few other students, had left on a training exercise.

Phew!

During their training at the *Napola*, the *Jungmänner* often undertake training outside the school: study exchanges overseas, at a *Napola* in an occupied country, for example. Or time spent in German families, in cities or in the countryside, to lend a hand while the men are away, and to prevent any defeatist attitudes developing. Or work with the potato harvest. Lukas's training is in "Special Missions". He has to supervize prisoners of war in factories (it used to be in Volkswagen assembly factories; now it is armaments and munitions factories). The workers are from France, Belgium, Holland, and there are Russians, who have the worst reputation. He has to check their production times and make sure they don't steal.

I'm doubly relieved. Lukas hasn't been unmasked and, over the coming months, no more students will lose their heads – literally.

But in the meantime, I'm losing the plot. There's something wrong. The mood at the *Napola* has changed. There are fewer and fewer of us every day, both students and teachers. The final-year students go straight into the army, without even sitting an exam. So many others graduate, in waves, to the next level, as if, all of a sudden, they have all been deemed gifted. The morning classes are down to a strict minimum: no more German, History or Maths classes, only Biology now and again. But the physical training is more intense: we do it mid-morning, all afternoon, and in the evening instead of supervized homework. It's exhausting; we're allowed no mistakes and any sign of weakness is severely reprimanded by instructors, who are on the edge of hysteria.

Same deal with the *Heimführer*, who bombards us, at every meal, with a double ration of speeches instead of his normal readings. His voice, usually so modulated, often rises to a screech. His face is swollen, sweating; he makes big theatrical gestures, scanning the rows anxiously to find any looks of incredulity among us. The *Volkssturm*!* That's all we hear about. The *Volkssturm* is rising. A new army is on the march. Nothing will stop it, it will guarantee the Reich's victory, just like the finale of a fireworks display. We, the *Jungvolk*, will be the main members. We are going to take up arms. We have to be ready to undergo the final sacrifice for the Führer.

Double ration of speeches. Half rations on our plates. Even though the physical training leaves us ravenous. I'm really missing the extras that Lukas used to sneak me.

He's still not here.

But it's as if I can hear his voice contradicting that of the *Heimführer*'s. The "magic potion" flushes out of my system a lot more slowly than food does. A voice inside me – Lukas's? Mine? I don't know any more – is telling me that our missing teachers are at the front. If we're mobilizing younger and younger soldiers, it's because the adults have called it quits. They're prisoners, or they're dead.

There are rumours that, every now and again, instructors form commando units with students who haven't been called up. One of the units that recently left on a mission was made up of five young boys, the youngest of whom was thirteen. Only two out of the five made it back. Severely wounded. The boy of thirteen had half his face blown off. There are rumours about schools all through the country having to retreat to other schools as the enemy advances – the Russians, for the most part. But we don't have anywhere

* The name given to the people's militia launched in Germany in 1944 and composed mainly of very young, or very old, soldiers.

to retreat to: Potsdam is too close to Berlin.

It's hard to untangle the truth from the lies. It's hard to know if we should be frightened of dying or thrilled to fight. Or be frightened to fight while being thrilled to die.

The good thing about the changes is that security is less strict, especially at night in the dormitories. The section leader isn't always on our back. And, even if he were still here, there's not much to supervize. Most of my buddies are so exhausted they fall asleep even before their heads hit the pillow. They go to bed early and are scarcely awake during the free time before lights-out. I wonder sometimes, in the mornings, if the wake-up bell will ring in a completely silent room, unable to wake corpses.

Fatigue makes me nervy and I can't sleep. Without having to worry about my fellow dormmates, I can "play" as much as I like. I've still got Lukas's present under my pillow. The farting Führer. (I didn't throw him away, and I won't until I've extracted from Lukas exactly how he made the farting mechanism.) In the end, I like the toy. I play with him every night. I talk to him.

"Do you think somehow you might have tricked us?" I ask him. "Lied to us? Were all your fancy speeches just hot air? Like your farts? Go on, answer me! Answer me, you idiot!"

He says nothing and that really annoys me, so I slap him. I yank on his arm to pay him back for his silence. And he farts, and farts. And that makes me laugh. I laugh so much I end up crying. Afterwards, I'm ashamed, full of remorse. I insulted our Führer. What sacrilege. I doubted his word. *Verboten!* In order to redeem myself, I undertake a self-criticism: I was under a negative influence, but I have removed myself from it and I still believe in victory and in the invincibility of the Reich. I deserve a punishment. As there is no one here to punish me, I'll do it myself. I take my dagger of honour and, with the tip, I make cuts on my hands and on my arms. It hurts. It feels good. And I end up falling asleep with my face on the Führer's bum.

Every night I do the same thing. I put up with it better than the toy does. Even if I have more and more cuts, they're not deep and scar over well. But the Führer can't cope with being handled so much; not only does he not fart any more, he falls to pieces. I chuck him in the bin.

27.

I thought he'd come back fighting fit. That, as soon as he arrived, he'd rush to confirm the bad news from outside – bad for me, good for him – the Allies' advance, the looming defeat of the Reich. I'd already prepared my response, in which I'd argue for the strength of the new *Volkssturm* army.

I was certain he'd immediately start exploding the heads of all the students in his class. That he wouldn't even bother about premeditating the perfect crimes, like the other two, but would take advantage of the relaxed atmosphere of the *Napola* to hit out randomly.

Not at all.

He's come back completely changed. I hardly recognize this new Lukas. Skinny, pale, hunched shoulders, a haggard, lost look about him, he resembles the Lucjan of Kalish. No, not at all. The Lucjan of Kalish was arrogant. The Lucjan of Kalish had the look of a warrior.

I go up to him as often as possible, but without managing to connect at all. "Hi, Lukas, how's it going?"

Silence.

"How were the Russian workers? What did you do at the factory?"

Silence.

"Did you bring back some chocolate? Jam? Sausage? I'd kill for some sausage!"

Silence.

"Hey, is it true that the shit's hitting the fan out there? It's pretty shit here."

Silence.

"For God's sake, what's the matter with you?"

Fed up, I plant myself in front of him. Right up against him, nose-to-nose. His gaze goes over my head, like a blind man. I pull on his sleeve, I shake him, slap him, but he's like a puppet. I swear at him, call him every name under the sun, but he doesn't even bat an eyelid. He just stands motionless, lifeless, fixed on a point in the distance, some ghost only he can see and which he might be trying to contact.

In the dining hall, during the *Heimführer*'s speech about the *Volkssturm*, I notice he has trouble standing up and that a classmate has to support him, help him stand to attention, otherwise he'd collapse on his chair. Then he doesn't eat a thing and someone else gobbles his food without him protesting at all.

As we leave the hall, I rush out to join him while he has a cigarette. At least that hasn't changed. Well, actually he smokes a whole lot more than before. He lights one cigarette after the other, with a weird ritual: he takes a big drag to extract as much smoke as possible, and watches the swirls of smoke as they disperse in the air. Then he takes a few awkward steps, as if following the path of smoke. He makes crazy gestures, stretching out his hand, closing his fist to trap the smoke, opening it and looking at his empty palm. And that's not all. Instead of tipping his ash on the ground, he scrupulously collects it in a little wooden box. (He must have made it himself. Oblong-shaped, with a sliding, air-tight lid, it's like a miniature coffin.) Once he's smoked a good dozen or so cigarettes and the box is full of ash, Lukas shuts it, kneels down and scratches a hole in the ground. Then he buries the box. After that, he puts a handkerchief on his head and recites a strange litany in an incomprehensible, barbaric language. I suspect it's Hebrew, and I suspect it's a prayer.

Something must have happened during his stupid training. Perhaps it wasn't really training, but a commando mission instead? Perhaps Lukas ended up in the middle of some violent exchange, and a grenade, or a bomb, exploded next to him? Even if he was lucky enough to avoid being blown up, the shock would have traumatized him, made him deranged.

He's a nut case, an imbecile.

When I check it out with his mates, who do not exhibit the slightest sign of trauma, they disprove my hypothesis: they actually did undergo training in a factory. Sure, it was cut short because of the bombings, but the factory wasn't touched. In fact, in the beginning, everything seemed to have gone very well for Lukas, who made friends with the SS guy supervizing the prisoners. They were often together, laughing, joking, then suddenly, yes, Lukas did change. His mates thought it must have been because of Herman's death. Often you don't fully comprehend the death of a friend until a while later. Herman died just before they left for their training, so Lukas must have been in a daze. It was only later that it hit him, poor thing. His two best friends dying within a few months, it must have been really tough.

I don't believe their explanations for one moment. Who do they think they're kidding?

Something happened.

Finally, one night, I find out what it was.

The smell of smoke wakes me up. I'm tired, exhausted, my eyes are shut tight. Once I manage to open them, I see a thick cloud of smoke around me. What's going on? A fire? And I didn't hear the siren?

I'm not dreaming. The smell is real, it gets in my nose and makes me cough. With a gigantic effort I get my eyes wide open and my head off the pillow. And there's Lukas sitting on my bed, bending over me. Armed with his little ash box, he's smoking away, and must have been at it for a while, judging by the three butts I can make out on the ground when I sit up. A ray of moonlight from the dormitory window illuminates his face, accentuating his pallor, so that his head seems to be floating by itself, detached from his body. Once my eyes get used to the darkness, I see that his head is well and truly attached to his body, a body wearing striped pyjamas that are nothing like the mandatory shorts and singlet worn at night in the *Napola* dormitories. He's wearing … the uniform of a concentration-camp prisoner.

I glance around to make sure no one else is awake.

"Are you completely crazy, smoking in here? And what the hell is this outfit? Are you out of your mind?"

I quickly grab the cigarette out of his mouth and stub it out. He doesn't protest but just as I'm about to demand an explanation, he places a finger on my mouth to shut me up, while also checking that no one is watching.

So is he going to speak, or write his secret on a piece of

paper for me, just like he did in the study hall after Gunter's murder? (If he's come here, in the middle of the night, it must mean he has something of vital importance to tell me.) But he still hasn't made a move. I wait without pushing him away because, despite not moving, he hasn't got the same empty look about him that he's had recently. I'm guessing that he's just finding it hard to speak, as if the words are too difficult, too much, to pass his lips. Is he about to tell me that he's killed the *Heimführer* himself?

After a few moments that seem like an eternity, he brandishes in front of my face the wooden box filled with cigarette ash.

"That's how they end up."

"What do you mean? What's *that*? Who ends up? You're making no sense at all!" I'm trying to whisper but it feels like I'm shouting loud enough to wake the whole dormitory.

"The Jews. That's how they end up. They go up in smoke, reduced to ash."

My turn to be speechless. Lukas's answer makes no sense at all, and yet he is his usual confident, articulate self. "It's a programme called 'The Final Solution'," he continues. "It started in 1942, when we were in Kalish. It's been very successful, and is functioning more and more effectively. In every single concentration camp, Jews from all over Europe are piled into gas chambers, then their bodies are burned in crematorium furnaces. Tens of thousands die at a time."

"No! No! That's impossible. We would have known. Our biology teachers would have told us about that, they…"

I don't finish my sentence because in biology we did study the issue of "the necessity to exterminate the Jewish people", without ever finding out exactly how this extermination might be carried out. The events of the last few months have shown me that they don't tell us everything at the *Napola*. Information is filtered, altered. The things Lukas told me before he left for his training, things I refused to believe, have proved to be true. The reason I chucked the farting Führer in the bin was that I realized the puppet was nothing but a pale reflection of the real thing.

While I'm trying to work all this out in my head, I feel a weird sensation. A physical reaction. Like flashes in my brain. Like auditory memories, voices, overheard conversations at Kalish, and earlier, in Poznan, when I was in the bombed-out house and I heard snatches of conversation at night, from behind Doctor Ebner's door. Those voices start to come back to me, little by little, then stronger, confirming what Lukas has just said. Doctor Ebner and his colleagues were listing figures, so many for this camp, so many for that camp, and they talked about "increased efficiency levels".

Lukas explains that he got this information about the Final Solution from the SS guy he pretended to be friendly with at the factory. The SS guy had worked at Treblinka. He saw everything. He himself herded hundreds of Jews into the gas chambers. On the last day of training, he gave Lukas the horrible pyjamas as a present, a memento.

A memento. Flashes start in my brain again. Those pyjamas are atrocious, disgusting, and yet I'm attracted to them. I delve back into my earliest memories … and there it is: the dissident-whore-who-kidnapped-me-when-I-was-a-baby. The story Josefa told me over and over has stayed there, filed away in one of the compartments of my brain. The whore wore those pyjamas, I was in her arms, my face buried in that rough, filthy material, my source of warmth and reassurance.

I look up at Lukas.

He's lighting another cigarette. I can't think of a thing to say in protest. And there's no point anyway. He stands up and walks out of the dormitory, leaving in his wake a cloud of smoke and the taste of ash in my mouth.

28.

Everything has turned to shit.

Black shit that lasts for weeks. The sky is more and more threatening. I don't mean rain or storms, but bombs. Enemy planes crisscrossing the sky above the *Napola.*

It's new, disturbing, traumatic. Planes circling above our heads like birds of prey. No one ever led us to believe this would happen one day.

The first time the siren went off, it was the middle of the night. We didn't take any notice, thinking it was one of the night drills, like "the gas siren", when the instructors release tear gas through the buildings. In total darkness, and plunged in toxic gas, we have to put on our uniforms and gather in the courtyard for inspection. If a student is not dressed properly he has to charge back to the dormitory, then come out again for inspection. Everyone hates these drills. So many of my young friends end up almost choking, as they are made to dash back again and again for a forgotten cap, belt, or because their boots aren't properly polished. And if the drill isn't stressful enough, it is often followed by a night march or a river crossing.

This particular night, when the siren went off, hardly any of us got up. Those who did manage to stir got dressed in a rush. Who cared? Most of the instructors were away, so no one would check uniforms. But, as soon as we were outside, we could tell that the orders were being shouted differently. Panic was in the air. This wasn't a drill; it was an "air-raid warning 15", which meant enemy aeroplanes were fifteen minutes away. We rushed back to get the lazy boys who might have ended up asleep for ever after the bombing. Then we all hurtled down to the air-raid shelters.

Lukas didn't come down with us that night.

And he doesn't come down any other night. In fact, he doesn't get out of bed at all. He just lies there, refusing to speak, smoking, smoking all day long. He doesn't respond to the sirens, and refuses to turn up for training. Because of his excellent student track record, the directors turn a blind eye and ascribe his "depression" to the distress caused by the deaths of Gunter and Herman. But not for long: depression is a shameful, intolerable condition for a *Jungmann*. Especially for a *Jungmann* who is expected to excel in order to soon join the ranks of the *Volkssturm*.

I'm chosen – they still all think we're brothers – to get Lukas back on track. I'm given a month to do it, an ultimatum that seems almost identical to the one Ebner gave me in Kalish. But I really don't want to relive that experience. And I'm fed up with this role reversal. Lukas is the big brother; I'm the little brother. And it's about time he woke up to that.

Still, I do as I'm told. I don't have a choice: the directors might not be aware of it, but I have a much stronger connection to Lukas than our so-called status as siblings.

* * *

My only real success is to get him to hand over his striped prisoner pyjamas and let me dispose of them. Otherwise, all I can do is rescue his meal rations from a greedy student at his table, and take them up to him in the dormitory. I spoon-feed him, like a baby. He only eats a third at most. But he keeps on smoking like a chimney, as if he wants to incinerate himself, disappear in smoke like those others. And I'm the one who provides him with cigarettes. The *Heimführer* told me that, given the present circumstances, my bank account, funded by Doctor Ebner over the years, had been closed, but I could have the money in cash instead. I said yes. So I have plenty of money, but I can't buy chocolate, or butter, or jam, because there's no longer any available on the black market. The quartermaster at the *Napola* – the nerve centre of the black market – is only selling cigarettes. I give most of mine to Lukas and smoke the rest, which makes me lose my appetite a bit.

The trouble is, with all that smoking, Lukas coughs and spits and stinks. It's disgusting. What's he on about? Dying a slow and horrible death so he can share the same fate as those Jews?

I try to keep him occupied as best I can. While he's slumped on the bed, I ask him, "What about we masturbate? Like we used to before you left for training?"

No response.

At the end of my tether, I even incite him to murder. "Why don't you kill some more students? It's easy now with the sirens. When the air-raid 15 siren goes off, you quickly knock off one or two and then head down to the shelter, you can't go wrong."

"Nie dośi!" Not enough.

At least that gets a response. So he hasn't turned completely stupid, his hearing and speech faculties are still functioning. Of course, his latest thing is to start speaking Polish again. He doesn't utter a word of German.

I think for a moment. "Why don't you go for the teachers? They should be your main targets, and then there'd be fewer at the front!"

"Nie dośi!"

Whatever I say, he comes out with the same thing, as well as a few Hebrew prayers. He looks so ridiculous when he mumbles in that barbaric language, with his handkerchief on his head and the cigarette stuck in his mouth.

"Why do you pray? You said you weren't religious."

"Musze uczcic pamiec mojego ojca." I have to honour the memory of my father.

"Well, your mother wasn't religious. What would she say if she saw you risking your life because of a prayer?"

"Moja matka zginela." My mother went up in smoke.

"You don't know that! She might still be alive."

There's a glimmer of hope in his eyes. For a second, he stops sucking on his cigarette butt, then shakes his head. *"Nie. Nie ma zadnej szansy."* No, not a chance.

End of dialogue.

Fortunately his mates don't bother speaking to him any more. They're determined to fight the Russians no matter what, so for them Lukas is now just a loser.

"You really want to help him?" one of them says to me. "Tell him to commit suicide. It's the only way he'll get out of this and save face."

Thanks for the advice.

By staying in bed during the air raids, he seems hell-bent on suicide anyway. One of these mornings, I'll find him reduced to a little pile of ashes, incinerated in a fire started by one of his damned cigarettes. Or reduced to a pulp on his mattress after a bombing raid.

It stinks. It really stinks.

29.

Things never go according to plan in life. It's so annoying. When you're taken by surprise it makes you flustered. I hate that. I hate it when events don't follow a predetermined, logical order. I hate things being subject to a series of unexpected accidents.

Here are the three most serious accidents in my life to date:

Lukas being Jewish.

The affection I have for him *despite that*.

The imminent defeat of the Reich.

The last of these being by far the most aberrant, the most unimaginable, the most unpredictable of all possible events. I still can't get my head around it.

And yet...

There are rumours that the British landed in Normandy last month, that soon France and Belgium will be liberated. Others say the Soviets are already in Germany. The directors of the *Napola* haven't confirmed the rumours, at least not in words, but recent decisions speak for themselves.

Once again the *Napola* is undergoing changes, little by little losing its primary identity. There's an air of desertion about the school.

For the younger children, it's an authorized desertion. Most of them have been sent home. For good. A mass exodus was already organized a few weeks ago, when no one knew for sure that elsewhere the shit was hitting the fan. Parents – those still alive, with a house somewhere in the country, outside the cities under siege from the enemy, and with means of transport – came to collect their sons. Up to now, the children who didn't hear from their families were gathered in groups from the same region and had to find their own way home, one of them designated as platoon leader and issued with a regulatory travel order.

This return-to-sender system seems to have worked well in the case of the most resourceful children. (Although no one actually knows if they made it home. Perhaps they stepped on a mine, or perished in a bombing raid, or were shot by enemy guns.) In any case, they didn't come back here, unlike some, the really dumb ones. Just like those dogs, abandoned in the middle of nowhere by their owners, who somehow find their way home, kids arrived back at the school two or three days after leaving. They were in a dreadful state, wretched and starving. Sobbing, they told us how, when they produced their travel order to use as a train pass, the stationmaster sent them packing, telling them they could "wipe their bum with it". They were allowed a few days' rest at the *Napola*, before being sent off again.

Manfred is one of a group that is leaving today. Carrying his little case, he heads over to say goodbye to me. I'm quick to put my hand out and avoid him kissing me, which is clearly his intention. (Oh my God, he's such a homo!)

"Why don't you want to leave with us?" he asks tearfully.

I am a ward of the state. I have neither parents nor home. Nowhere to go. That's why I'm the only one of the younger children allowed to stay at the school. But I'm free to leave if I want to. Manfred knows this and launches into an emotional appeal that he hopes will touch me. (He is seriously kidding himself.)

"What will you do, all alone here with the adults? What's so great about that?"

"I'm not alone, I've got my brother."

"Your brother's sick, he won't be able to protect you from the Russians when they arrive."

"Who says I need protecting, you piece of shit? Who says my brother's sick? Who says the Russians are coming? Why are you so full of bullshit?"

Manfred lowers his head at my outburst. "I need to be protected," he mutters after a moment. He looks at me with eyes filled with tears, and flutters his eyelashes like a girl. "I'd feel safer with you than with Erwin. I bet he pisses off as soon as we get to the station."

He's on the money there. Erwin is the platoon leader assigned to Manfred's group. He is a total idiot, not the slightest bit reliable. "Oh, come on, don't worry, everything will be all right."

I have to encourage poor Manfred. I feel sorry for him now. He looks like he's about to piss his pants, he's so petrified. He's never felt at ease at the *Napola*. I often heard him calling out, "Mummy!" at night in the dormitory, and now... Now, how do I tell him that it's highly likely his mummy, and his daddy, are dead. It's obvious, otherwise they would have come to collect him while there was still time. But I'm not trying to break his spirit, so I give him a friendly pat on the back.

"Don't worry, you'll be fine." I force myself to smile, try as hard as I can to reassure him, so that we part on good terms. I do it all in good faith. And then the stupid numbskull goes and puts his foot in it and says exactly what he shouldn't have said.

"You know, my parents are really nice. I'm an only child and you're an orphan. I'm sure Mummy and Daddy would love to adopt you, and then we'd be brothers and we could live together once the war is over."

Orphan. Adoption.

Those words give me goosebumps. Especially the second one. It's bloodcurdling. It makes my hackles rise. It makes me crazy. I do not want to be adopted. *I have never wanted it, even when I was a baby.*

So I smack my fist into Manfred's face, and finish him off with a kick up the arse in case the message didn't get through. "Your parents are dead. Get out of here!"

Now I'm alone in my dormitory. They said I could join another one but I don't want to. I'd feel like a deserter. At least here, as I go to sleep at night, I'm free to imagine things: I'm a hero! I'm the last soldier left on the battlefield. I'm as tough as the *Jungmänner* who have stayed at the *Napola*. They're the fierce ones, the fanatics, those most devoted to the Reich. Those who renounced their parents a long time ago. The *Heimführer* and the instructors are counting on them to defend the school when the Soviets arrive at our gates. Well, despite my youth, they can count on me, too!

But, try as I might, I just can't motivate myself. It's like there's a broken spring inside me. It's sinister in the dormitory. The silence is sinister. I've almost got to the point where

I'm hoping for an air-raid siren at night, to smash the lead weight that's suffocating me. On top of that, the weather is exceptionally stifling this July.

I'm stewing in my own sweat, and in a torpor.

20th of July, 1944.

I know the date because I make myself say it out loud every morning when I wake up, so I can keep my bearings a little. (Gone are the days when a student wrote the date on the blackboard in class. No more students, no more class, no more anything.)

It's 6.30 p.m. and the heat is still extreme. I'm hanging around in the dormitory. Late afternoon used to be the time we'd do supervized homework, and I always hated it; now I can't bear not having it. I wander among the empty beds, talking to myself like an old man, trying to fill the silence, when another voice talks over mine. It takes me a few seconds to realize that it's a radio announcement broadcast over the school's loudspeaker system.

Joseph Goebbels, the Minister for Propaganda, is speaking to the German people. It seems he's about to say something quite extraordinary.

I freeze. The whole school freezes. Even though I'm alone, I can sense it, as if we were all together in one body. Mine. My blood freezes in my veins. Each slow heartbeat is like a death knell in my chest. I can hear the minister's voice. I can hear his words, but those words don't make sense. Or if they do, I refuse to admit it.

What has happened is impossible, inconceivable.

What has happened, says the minister, is that today, 20th of July, 1944, at 12.30 p.m., there was an assassination attempt against the Führer. There was a bomb planted in the room where he was meeting with his generals.

Then, nothing. Amplified crackling of the microphone.

The attempt failed. Only just. It was a miracle, the minister concluded.

The *Heimführer* takes over, to announce that nothing further is known about this tragic event, and that we will be told as soon as news comes through.

It feels like the ground has been torn from under my feet. I collapse onto my bed and stare at my pillow as if it could fill in the gaps for me. But the damned pillow doesn't say a thing, apart from reminding me that, a few weeks earlier, it had been my hiding place for the toy Lukas gave me, the farting Führer – that I had broken and chucked in the bin. I can still see it, smashed, in pieces, the strings and springs that held the limbs together all broken. Like a body after a bomb explosion. With that evil toy, did I predict what happened to the Führer? The minister said Hitler survived the attack, but not what state he was in. In pieces? Pieces that somewhere in a hospital doctors are trying to stick together again? And, even if he's in one piece, wouldn't he have lost his marbles? Are they going to announce in a few hours that Germany no longer has a Führer? Which would mean that, this time, I really wouldn't have a father. That I am, once and for all, an orphan and I would have been better off leaving with Manfred?

Assembly in the dining hall at 1 p.m. Everyone is here, but the room seems somehow empty. There's barely a hundred of us now. This room that I used to think was so dazzling is now a shadow of its former glory: the ceiling has been bombed, the paintwork is cracked, some of the swastikas have lost their colour as well as their arms, and look like cripples. Just like the faces of the *Jungmänner*: hollow, starving, exhausted.

I notice in passing that Lukas is here, and that he's clean, dressed and without that moronic look on his face. But I couldn't care less. I'm not worried about him in the slightest any more.

Perched on his chair, the *Heimführer* begins by reassuring us that the Führer is safe and sound. He only sustained a few scratches, nothing more, and didn't need to be hospitalised. He even honoured his appointment with Mussolini, and went to pick him up from the station, as arranged.

A sigh of relief passes through the rows. Faces relax. The *Heimführer* explains how the assassination attempt occurred in Rastenburg, in Eastern Prussia. It was more than an assassination attempt, it was an attempted *coup d'état*, incited by a group of opponents of the regime, who wanted to take power, hasten the end of the war, and hand over Germany to the British. The Führer and his generals were studying maps, when the chief conspirator, the vile traitor, Count Claus von Stauffenberg, Chief of Staff of the Reserve Army, planted a booby-trapped suitcase next to Hitler, under the table, and left the room on the pretext of an important phone call. Fortunately, one of the generals pushed the suitcase out of his way slightly, so that the Führer ended up being protected by the leg of the table when the bomb went off.

There's chatter among the assembly now; everyone is hugely relieved. The *de rigueur* cheerfulness emerges again. Everyone has a theory about what happened. No, the Führer wasn't protected by a common or garden chair leg, he was protected by the Germanic gods! In fact the Führer doesn't even need protection, nothing can touch him, this is the proof: he's immortal!

The voices get louder, the sound punctuated by a rallying cry, *Heil Hitler!* They roar is repeated several times and the *Heimführer* joins in his students' chorus. He doesn't silence them, because he knows that his young boarders have just had a terrible fright and need some relief from their tension.

The *Jungmänner* shake hands, pat each other on the back, and break rank without receiving the order, some even taking the liberty of going to sit down, their heads between their hands, sobbing for joy.

The *Heimführer* suddenly raises his hand. Silence! He's just heard that the Führer himself is on the radio.

We all stand to attention. An edgy voice echoes through the hall. I only remember one sentence of the long speech, *There will be severe reprisals.*

Another assembly a few days later. This time in the projection room, where we watch pictures of the traitors' trial. One is particularly memorable: a general, whose name I've forgotten, standing before the judges, has to hold his trousers up with both hands, because he doesn't have his belt any longer. When the judge orders him to stand to attention to hear his sentencing, his trousers fall down and we see his underpants.

Everyone in the courtroom laughs, echoed by the *Jungmänner* in our room.

The *Heimführer* informs us that the traitors were executed straight after the trial, in the courtyard of the Benderblock. The conspirators were executed one after the other and their bodies hung on butcher's hooks.

And that's exactly when the thing I wasn't thinking about any more happens.

Even though the images of the trial, and of the executions, which I can easily imagine, are playing in a loop in my mind; even though I can still hear the Führer's voice announcing the *severe reprisals;* even though I'm desperately hoping one of the *Jungmänner* next to me doesn't suddenly take out of his pocket my smashed farting Führer and hold it up, pointing an accusing finger at me and shouting, "Him, he's another conspirator! Look what he did!" – it turns out that what happens is none of those things.

One of the *Jungmänner* does stand up, but not just any old *Jungmann.* It's Lukas. He stands in the middle of the room and, in front of us all – students, teachers, and the *Heimführer* – he unthreads the belt on his trousers, which fall round his ankles, just like the general in the film. As if that isn't enough, Lukas then takes off his underpants and leans forward to stick his bum out at the whole assembly. "Long live the conspirators!" he starts shouting. "Your Führer has just about had it! He'll be dead soon! It's all over! Listen up! I'm not German, I'm Polish. Polish and a Jew! A Jew! A Jew!"

There's panic in the room. A speechless panic. Nobody says a word as Lukas, out of his mind, keeps on and on, repeating his last sentence, in Polish. *"Jestem Polakiem! Polakiem i Zydem! Zydem! Zydem!"*

Everyone is staring at him, agape, incredulous.

Finally, under orders from the *Heimführer,* the first one to react, two *Jungmänner* grab Lukas and drag him off to an isolation cell.

This time he's really done it. He'll be executed too. He'll hang on a butcher's hook in the courtyard.

So the scandal broke, but not how I'd imagined it would. Just like I said before, things never happen as expected. This is unbearable.

And that wasn't it for surprises.

I'm asleep, overwhelmed by nightmares. All the images I saw during the day are jumbled into some kind of diabolical dance. There's Hitler with his trousers down, showing his bum to the German nation. There's Lukas being shot, slumped, bleeding, his body riddled with bullets. As for me: I'm hanging off a butcher's hook like a giant ham, while starving *Jungmänner* with knives circle me, chopping off bits of my flesh, tearing them into strips and eating them. Just as I'm about to scream, I'm woken up by someone shaking me violently.

What's the matter? An earthquake? An air raid?

No, it's Lukas, completely together, alert, in a hurry, and carrying a suitcase. He puts it on the ground, opens it and rummages in my drawers, tipping everything into the case, higgledy-piggledy. "Got any money?"

I point under the mattress where my stash is hidden.

He yanks me out of bed and grabs the notes. "Hurry up! Get a move on!" he shouts as he throws me my clothes. "Get dressed, we're getting out of here."

"What do you mean, we're getting out of here? Where to? How did you get out of the cell?"

"I never went," he says, showing me his dagger of honour covered in blood. "I bumped off those two guys. And, five minutes ago, I set fire to the school. So, if you don't want to end up barbecued, Skullface, follow me!

part four

30.

Make your present something useful, give a coffin!

The slogan for Christmas 1944. It's written everywhere on the walls all over Berlin, as well as in the U-Bahn where we're holed up like rats.

For five months now, we've only seen underground Berlin. Only occasionally do we sneak out above ground, where there are fires, mountains of rubble, buildings that have been destroyed or are in ruins. The air is clogged with plaster dust that sticks to your skin, sifts into your mouth and gets encrusted on your teeth. It's impossible to get rid of and makes you cough and spit. Endless columns of smoke climb into the blazing sky to form dense black clouds that clump together and never dissipate. It's as if the light itself is dirty, or there's no more light at all.

The Third Reich was supposed to take us out of darkness. Instead it seems to have thrown us right inside.

When Lukas dragged me out of bed to flee the *Napola*, and told me we were heading for Berlin, I was thrilled. At last I'd see my country's capital city. But I couldn't work out why we were walking in the opposite direction from everyone else; why the Germans were deserting the city, marching night and day, with their suitcases, exhausted, their faces blank, like crazed sleepwalkers; why we'd come across ditches filled with a mess of weapons, kitchenware and horse carcasses. I realized soon enough that it was a massive rout, every man for himself in a terrible debacle.

So it ended up being nothing like the tourist trip I had imagined.

And we had to keep clear of the *Volkssturm*. Somewhere along the way we came across a group of *Jungmänner* who were organizing their own resistance at the edge of a village. They were piling up tree trunks, hoping it would serve as a blockade against a tank. Their leader, who looked about fifteen (the same age as Lukas), saw we were wearing the *Napola* uniform and wanted to enlist our help. I would happily have joined his unit. Why not? I still wanted to fight to defend my country, to try to save it.

Lukas stopped me. "Come off it, Skullface, forget all the bullshit they've indoctrinated you with. Save yourself, that's all there is left. And cut the crap."

Then he knocked out the leader of the group and when the others, scarcely older than me, tried to protest – even though they had no weapons – I went up to them. "That was a close shave for you lot. He could have decapitated him or stabbed him to death. He's already killed four *Jungmänner*, you know. He's a serial killer!"

I left them standing there, half-hidden under their oversized helmets, their eyes as round as saucers, and ran off to catch up with Lukas.

Since our departure he's taken his role as big brother

very seriously. He decides everything. I prefer him like this to the zombie he was at the *Napola* for the last few weeks, but I'm pretty sick of him ordering me around.

I should never have followed him to Berlin. Lukas wants to be there when the Russians arrive. He says they're his friends, which means they're my enemies, doesn't it?

He's started to call me Skullface again, so I'm getting him back by calling him Lukas, when he's now insisting on his Polish name, Lucjan.

In the subway. We're surrounded by women, children and old people, all squashed up together like sardines in a tin. There are mattresses and pillows between the train tracks and coathangers with clothes – suits, dresses, coats – hanging from the train signal cables. It's giving Lukas the creeps.

"What the hell are they on about, the Krauts? As for their obsession with hygiene and appearance… What do they think is on the cards – a dinner dance at 8 p.m. tonight?"

He's right: the coathangers are just taking up precious space. What's the use of ironed clothes if they're covered in ash? What's the use of a change of clothes when you can't even wash yourself? During the blackouts all those coathangers on the cables look like ghosts, or hanged people swinging above our heads. But, when you think about it, the nicely ironed clothes on hangers help to maintain a bit of dignity around here. Lukas doesn't get it, of course. And I hate the way he criticizes my compatriots.

"At least the Krauts are clean," I snap. "Not like the Polish pigs."

And the proof is that the filth and lack of sanitation doesn't upset Lukas as much as me. He doesn't give a damn about having torn, dirty, stinking clothes. He does his business in any old place, even in the disgusting toilets, which are blocked, covered in all manner of matter, liquid and solid, the composition and provenance of which I do not want to know. I still manage to pee okay, but taking a crap is difficult. I'm constipated most of the time. And, if I do manage to push out a tiny turd, I hop around stark naked because there's no toilet paper and my bum gets so itchy when it's dirty. In the end it's probably better we have so little to eat – we don't have to go through the toilet business if there's not much to get rid of.

Anyway, so much for Christmas spirit. I couldn't care less about Christmas. At the *Napola*, that was when we celebrated the winter solstice and I don't miss those all-night candle vigils in the snow.

"Do Jews celebrate Christmas?" I ask Lukas.

"They celebrate Hanukkah. They have a lit candle in a candelabra for eight days and at the end of the week the children receive presents."

Right, so it's almost the same deal. Candles in a candelabra, or tinsel on a pine tree, plus the presents – it's six of one, half-a-dozen of the other.

A little girl sitting next to us must have been listening and asks her mother, "Will we have roast turkey for dinner? And will Father Christmas come down into the subway?"

With a forced smile, her mother ruffles the girl's hair. "We won't be having roast turkey, my darling."

She looks furtively at her suitcase where, under a pile of linen, she's hidden a loaf of bread and a thermos of tea that she managed to grab as she rushed out of her apartment. "But Father Christmas will come, I'm sure. Look at all the messages on the walls to show him the way."

What a lie. Just like outside on the walls of buildings, all the scribblings here in the subway are messages left by families to a brother, a son or a husband returning from the front, so he'll know where to find them.

Why doesn't she tell the truth? That this year Father Christmas will look redder than usual, Bolshevik-red, blood-red. That he'll turn up on a tank, not a sled, that he'll have weapons in his sack and that he'll shoot anything that moves?

The little girl has got my mouth watering with all her talk of roast turkey. It's torture: I'm salivating, I've got cramps in my stomach, I can picture that turkey before my eyes, steam coming off it, making my nostrils twitch. I could take revenge on her by spilling the beans about the truth of our situation. I could.

We can speak freely now. There's no longer any danger of being denounced for your opinions, or your nationality, religion or whatever. Lukas could stand on the tracks and yell through a megaphone that he was Jewish and I don't think anyone would react. I'm not a hundred per cent sure, but I don't feel as paranoid about it as before.

On the other hand, I'm having trouble with a few new habits. For example, no one raises their arm to salute any more. It's all over. No one says *Heil Hitler!* That's actually bad form. Instead, they say *Bleib übrig!* "Endure!" I still sometimes instinctively go to raise my arm. Lukas, who anticipates my reflex even before I move, grabs my wrist and forces me to stay still.

"Stop acting like a fucking robot!" he says, glaring at me.

The Berliners don't have any respect. Their graffiti is making a joke out of everything. They've turned the initials *LSR*, for example, which mean *Luftschutzraum* (air-raid shelter), into *Lernt schnell Russisch*, "Learn Russian fast".

I'm scared to death.

Before we ended up in the subway, we stayed for a few weeks in the zoo's bunker. It's one of the biggest air-raid shelters, a fortress of reinforced concrete with a battery of anti-aircraft defences on the roof. It's a huge safe haven for countless Berliners.

One day I wanted to get out. After all, we were at the zoo and I'd never visited a zoo. At first Lukas said no, then, as I kept asking, he seemed tempted, too, so up we went. It was a quick visit. Not because of the bombing raids – it was calm for the time being – but because all that was left of the animals were corpses. The cages were broken, smashed, and the monkeys, bears, gorillas were all dead, as if they'd taken part in some violent battle. The corpses of the monkeys were totally butchered. Lukas and I realized that we'd already had our visit to the zoo without knowing it. In our stomachs. The evening before, a woman had shared a big piece of meat with us. We'd feasted on it without wondering where it had come from.

We had to leave the zoo's bunker because of the toilets. The hygiene was disgusting, but, worse than that, people would go there to commit suicide. That's where my constipation started. It's pretty hard to do your business when swinging right in front of your eyes are the feet of someone who has just hanged himself.

Before that we were in the bunker at the Anhalter train station. Made of reinforced concrete, it has three storeys above ground and two underground. The walls are four and a half metres thick. In the beginning it was quite comfortable. There were big benches so people could sit down, like in a dining hall, and a good supply of tinned sardines. But the sardines didn't last long and the benches were turned into firewood to keep us warm. Then the water supply was cut off and we were all unbearably thirsty.

The zoo's bunker and the station's bunker are connected to the U-Bahn by five kilometres of tunnels, so you can walk through without danger.

Guess what we found on one of the steps of the station bunker? Sitting there like a Christmas present, or rather a Christmas reject … Manfred. Shrivelled up, wizened, even smaller and frailer than he was at the *Napola*, his limbs no thicker than a spider's legs. He was like an old man, his hair, eyebrows and eyelashes covered in white dust, and his skin gouged with wrinkles from the ingrained plaster particles.

Their platoon leader had, of course, abandoned them. While the rest of the kids had managed as best they could, Manfred had just sat down on his step and hadn't moved. For five months! He didn't try to go home, find his parents, nothing. He stayed there, immobile, waiting. He had only survived thanks to passing women who gave him food.

He didn't recognize me. When I went up to him and tapped him on the shoulder, his arms shot up in defence, as if I was going to hit him. Unbelievable, he thought I was a Russian soldier. Once he recognized me, he jumped up and hugged me. "Konrad! My Konrad!" he shouted. "Is it really you? I'm saved! I'm saved!"

"I knew you had a girlfriend, Skullface!" said Lukas, when he saw the little dickhead clinging to me.

So now we're stuck with him. Manfred, our ball and chain. As soon as one of us goes anywhere, he starts panicking, shaking all over. But things are also on a more even keel: Lukas orders me around, and I order Manfred around.

* * *

What strikes me the most in this devastated Berlin is not the bombing, or the ruins, or the filth, and not even the defeatist attitude, which I find very disappointing.

It's the women. There are so many of them, everywhere. They've taken charge of the city. They're running it. I'm not used to being surrounded by women. At the *Napola*, apart from the cooks, whom we scarcely glimpsed, there were only men. I have vague memories of the nurses in Steinhöring, much stronger ones of the Brown Sisters – those bitches – and of the prostitutes of Poznan. The women I have been around more recently, and whom I remember the best, are the warden bitches from hell at Kalish.

But the Berlin women are neither prostitutes nor bitches.

No more three Ks. Now the women have taken over from the men – with confidence, determination, energy and efficiency. They're not tall and blonde, like we were taught in Biology at the *Napola*. With few exceptions, they are dark, petite, strong – muscular from carrying sacks of coal and heavy suitcases in which they pack all their belongings before descending into the shelters. And they're brave. When there's no more water, they're the ones who risk their lives outside at the water pumps. They're not afraid of the bombs. They queue for hours in front of shops for a few grams of margarine.

There's still a little bit of the three Ks about them: some just can't help cleaning. Their nickname is the *Trümmerfrauen*, "the women of the rubble". In between the bombings they form a human chain to clear the rocks and paving stones, which they load into buckets. And they're always sweeping, sweeping – debris, dust, shit. They're creating order in a city that is falling to pieces.

The other day one of them caught Manfred and me. She'd got it into her head to wash us. She was suddenly obsessed with the idea. "It's simply unacceptable to be this grubby!" she exclaimed, nabbing us by the collar, like a lioness grabbing her cubs by the skin of their necks.

With a scrap of cloth that she dipped in a jar of boiling water, she rubbed our faces, hands and armpits. She even tried to take our pants off to wash our bums. Manfred let her, but I gave her a kick and ran off.

Another woman had a go at Lukas in a shelter. Not about washing him; she couldn't have grabbed a big guy like him. But she'd heard him swearing. Without hesitation, she slapped him across the face. "There are children here," she snapped. "You watch your language, my boy!"

"I'm sorry, madam," Lukas said, his eyes lowered.

The other day, I saw a woman cutting up a horse killed by a mortar shell; she was putting the pieces in jars filled with vinegar. She gave me one. We cooked some of the meat and had three meals in a row from it. Horse is easier to chew and digest than monkey. But less tasty.

I'm sick of the subway. Sick of shelters. Sick of being underground. Sick of all these people we don't know. Sick of following their rules. For once, I'm with Lukas: after Kalish and the *Napola*, we've had enough of communal living. We want to be by ourselves and make our own rules, that is, no rules.

So we decide to leave and set ourselves up in an abandoned house. There are plenty of them. Outside, Berlin is deserted. Who cares if we have to watch out for bombs and mortar shells, as well as the crime squads of the SS and the Military Field Police, who arrest individuals and forcibly enlist them in improvized military units. Nothing like the

Hitler Youth groups we passed when we fled the *Napola*. These guys here are hardcore. They string up anyone who is reluctant from the trees along the road, or from lampposts, and they hang a sign round their necks: *I was a coward*.

31.

"Here's to the arrival of the Russians and the Americans!" yells Lukas. After gulping a swig of schnapps, he passes me the bottle.

"To the victory of the Reich!" I yell, raising my arm to kill two birds with one stone: to annoy Lukas and pass the bottle to Manfred.

"To the arrival of the Russians and to the victory of the Reich!" yells Manfred.

I choke on my schnapps. "You're such an idiot! That's impossible," I spit, and the mouthful of alcohol that went down the wrong way lands on him.

"What's impossible?"

"To toast the arrival of the Russians *and* the victory of the Reich. It's one or the other, you have to choose sides!"

"But … but why do I have to choose? You're brothers, and if Lukas is for the Russians and you're for the Reich, that means both are possible at the same time, doesn't it? You … you're not on the same side?" Manfred whines, with that hangdog expression he gets whenever he says or does anything stupid.

He really is thick. Hell, he clearly didn't understand a word in our History and Politics classes at the *Napola*. And he has no idea about the present situation. (He still thinks we're brothers because we're too lazy to tell him the truth. It would take too long to tell him the whole story and he wouldn't get it anyway.)

"Shut up!" interrupts Lukas. "You're both as stupid as each other. And you more that anything," he adds, pointing to me. "You're talking shit. When is it finally going to sink into your head, your puny Skullface head, that the victory of the Reich is impossible?"

I'm about to respond but he stops me. He suddenly breaks into a huge smile and proclaims, "Come on, we're not fighting today, it's a celebration! Happy 1945!"

He's right. We can have a truce for the 31st of December.

"Happy 1945!" I grab the bottle back from Manfred and take another swig of schnapps, which goes down fine this time.

"Happy 1945!" repeats Manfred.

Yes, it's New Year's Eve, and we're doing fine. Even if the noise of the bombings is getting louder and louder and we have to shout to be heard over the din. The sky is blazing red. It's almost as if the explosions have been arranged especially to create a festive atmosphere.

It's midday, not midnight. We're having the toast now, because there's no guarantee we'll be alive at midnight to see in the new year. We've got schnapps, cigarettes and a piece of bacon, a sausage and boiled potatoes. We're lucky; it's a good meal, even if the potatoes taste like soap. The schnapps warms us up, the cigarettes stop us from feeling hungry, and we're comfortable in an apartment.

Yes, we did find one. When we left the U-Bahn, Lukas

asked Manfred, "Do you know how to get to your place? Do you remember your address?"

"Yes! Yes, of course! Number 1, Reichstrasse. It's this way."

Manfred's eyes lit up, as if they were lit by those little Christmas tree candles you see in normal times. As if suddenly the word "Mummy" was twinkling in his left eye, and "Daddy" in his right. For him, going back to his home was like finding his parents. He hadn't dared do it alone, but with us he felt up to facing the danger. He was imagining that, once we got there, he would see his mummy in the kitchen preparing him a delicious snack, and his daddy in the living room, welcoming him. "So, son, how was your last term at school?"

Lukas and I made sure we didn't tell him there was absolutely no chance that he'd see his parents again. And probably not his apartment, given how few buildings were still standing. We had to make sure first that he would take us there. And that's what he did.

Of course, the apartment had been bombed, gutted. The glass in the windows was broken and a thick grey layer of plaster dust covered everything, as if a nearby volcano had erupted. But the roof and floors were still intact, only slightly damaged, just a few holes here and there that were easy to mend. There was no more central heating or electricity, but it was good enough for us. At least it was for Lukas and me. Manfred, however, was in shock.

"I can't believe it! I can't believe it!" he kept saying as he took in the damage.

All his special belongings had disappeared – his toys, his drawings, most of his clothes, the furniture in his room – as well as the crockery, knick-knacks, sheets. There was almost nothing left. The fact that his parents weren't there didn't dawn on him until later, which meant we didn't have to put up with the floods of tears we were dreading. He started looking for a letter, a note that his mummy and daddy might have left somewhere to tell him where they were. But there was nothing at all. Zilch. To cheer him up, Lukas assured him that the letter must have blown out of one of the broken windows.

Lukas and I checked out the apartment. A kitchen. The cupboards were empty, of course, the hotplates on the stove didn't work, but the room had potential. After all, the kitchen is where you prepare *food*. (We just had to find some.) A living room. Two big armchairs, which the looters must have decided were too heavy to carry, still had pride of place. The upholstery had been ripped apart – they probably thought money or jewels were hidden there – but you could sit on them just fine. Our poor bums, sore from the subway tracks and the cement steps of the shelters, were more than happy to make contact with this new softness. Two bedrooms, one for the parents, one for Manfred. And finally, miraculously, wonder of wonders, a *toilet*! Dusty but clean. And, to top it off, a toilet flush that worked! It felt like a palace.

We argued over who would have the honour of christening the dream toilet. I won. All of a sudden, my gut began to express its suffering. I started farting so loudly that, under attack from such lethal gas, my rivals conceded defeat.

I locked myself in the cosy hideaway for a whole hour, despite Lukas and Manfred screaming and pounding on the door. Then there was another argument when I wanted to wipe my bum with the pages from some of the books I'd found on the collapsed shelves in the living room.

"Are you kidding?" shouted Lukas, blocking my way to

the toilet. "We're not still at the *Napola*, in case you hadn't noticed."

"They're my father's books," protested Manfred.

"Your father's books?" repeated Lukas, suddenly wary.

"Yes."

"What did your father do?"

"He worked at the Ministry of—"

"Wait a minute." Lukas cut him off, and went to get some of the books. "Shit! Shit! And more shit!" he cursed, as he inspected each one.

He made two piles. He chucked the first pile on the ground in the toilet and the second next to the stove in the living room.

"There you go, you can wipe your bum with them. They're Nazi books. Especially that one," he added, pointing to the book on top. "The rest of them will be fuel for our stove and keep us warm. A little bit of book burning will bring back happy memories, right?" he said with a nasty smile.

The book on the top of the pile was *Mein Kampf*.

I hesitated for a while. I couldn't use that to wipe myself. It was beyond me. I could still hear the voice of the *Heimführer*, who used to read us extracts in the dining hall. I was frightened the words would peel off the paper and sting me in the bum in retaliation. I sneaked the book to the bottom of the pile, hoping that perhaps we wouldn't get through the whole supply of paper.

After the fight about the toilet, then about the toilet paper, came the fight about the bedrooms. Claiming the advantage of age, Lukas nabbed the parents' room. Insisting on having his old room, Manfred suggested I share it with him. No, thank you. I decided that I could stick the two armchairs together to make a fine bed. It was OK to live together in an apartment, but sleeping in the same room as Manfred would remind me too much of the *Napola*.

Except that ... once it was dark, and the sirens started wailing, and the bombardments came unremittingly, and the floor trembled, and the ceiling cracked, Manfred and I, without a second thought, fled into Lukas's room. He didn't send us away. The three of us cuddled up together in the big bed. Holding hands. Tightly. But there was no way we were going to sleep, and we quickly worked out that we'd be safer in the cellar.

We stay in the apartment during the day, and at night we never leave the cellar. Unfortunately it's not a private cellar just for us, as we'd assumed by the absence of anyone else on the other floors. The neighbours are well and truly here; they live in the cellar all the time, and the lack of space is a real pain. Here we go again: sardines in a tin, a dormitory where everyone disturbs everyone else and no one sleeps.

Manfred is overjoyed because he's met up with a woman named Frau Betstein, who is a friend of his parents.

"My darling Manfred! Sweetheart, you're alive! What a miracle. How you've grown."

Grown? Wow, he must have been a total dwarf before coming to the Napola.

"Well, what do you know, your parents gave me a letter for you. Yes, yes, don't worry, they're fine. They went to the country while it was still possible. They were going to come and get you, so there must have been a hold-up. But there's no need to be anxious, I'll keep an eye on you now."

So Manfred ended up getting the letter he'd busted a gut looking for. Now he spends the whole time reading it and re-reading it, snuggled up with Frau Betstein, who, as the days pass – the nights, I should say – replaces his mother. She comforts him, looks after him, sorts out his clothes, shares her food rations with him. (The first night, idiot Manfred ate her food right under our noses, but the next day, back at the apartment, Lukas and I sorted him out. Now he knows that he has to hang on to whatever the old lady gives him and share it with us.)

There's quite a system set up in the cellar now. Everyone has sorted out their own spot, their living space. The most organized among them brought quilts, pillows, chairs. Like Manfred, people pass their time reading letters or looking at photos. Sometimes, when they have paper, they write. Letters? What's the point? There's no mail any more. And they talk, a lot. Apart from one old man, there are only women, so it's non-stop chatter.

They're all crazy in this underground crowd. Living down here rots your brain in the end. There is Frau Diesdorf, for example, who keeps a bathtowel on her head all the time. She's already ugly, but that turban thing stuck on her head like a beehive hairdo doesn't help.

"Frau Diesdorf, excuse me," asked a suitcase neighbour one day. ("Suitcase neighbour" because people use their luggage either as seats or to mark the dividing lines between their personal areas.) "Why do you keep that towel on your head? Just so you know that, if it's because of lice, it's completely useless, it doesn't prevent contamination and—"

"I do *not* have lice! I'm clean," spluttered the offended Frau Diesdorf. "Not like some. Let it be known that this towel is protecting me from explosions!"

So they had a fierce argument; who knows what it was about, they got so worked up.

Another woman, Frau Evingen, carries around her son's

artificial leg all the time. She claims it's her talisman. I don't even try to understand.

My suitcase neighbour is Herr Hauptman, an old bloke whose breath stinks. "If a bomb ever hits you, my boy, don't forget to lean forward."

"Why?"

"So your lungs don't explode."

I'm more likely to die asphyxiated by your bad breath than to get hit by a bomb.

I hate this cellar. But Lukas and Manfred are coping OK. I've already explained why that's the case for Manfred. For Lukas, it's because his suitcase neighbour is a girl the same age as him. Her name is Ute Oberham. They've got the hots for each other and never stop making eyes at one another. They're always taking advantage of the close quarters to touch each other's hands, knees, thighs; and then they go as red as beetroots, and look ridiculous. The girl's mother ended up cottoning on to their goings-on. She's a huge woman – I don't see why her fat hasn't disappeared at the same rate as the rations. One night, Frau Oberham swapped places with her daughter. Now Lukas is squashed between her spare tyres and the wall. Serves him right.

One woman is different from the others. She keeps herself apart as much as possible, given the lack of room. She doesn't speak – or only rarely. She is beautiful. I hardly ever see her standing up, but I can tell she's tall, blonde, and has beautiful blue eyes. (It's been a while since I've seen all the characteristics of the Nordic race embodied in one person.) Despite her threadbare clothes, she's elegant. She spends her time looking at a single photo. Sometimes a tear rolls down her cheek. It must be a photo of her husband, who is no doubt dead. Or it's her brother. It couldn't be her son; she looks too young to have a son at the front, unlike most of the other old hens here.

She often stares at me, tries to smile at me, but can't, and then there are more tears. I have no idea why she looks at me like that. It reminds me of the time when women were all over me because of my angel face. But that's finished now. I don't have an angel face any longer. I just have a dirty, pale, tired face. Sometimes I like the blonde woman gazing at me. It makes me feel all warm and fuzzy inside. But often it makes me uneasy. Luckily she doesn't persevere; she ends up returning to her photo.

When the old women try to talk to her, she politely avoids engaging with them, replying only yes or no. The others have finally understood that it's better to leave her in peace in her corner.

Back in the apartment, we try to get sorted. Manfred does the cleaning. Even though we tell him there's no point, since the dust comes straight back, he insists. Too bad, if he wants to play at being one of the *Trümmerjungen*, the "rubble kids". He also washes our clothes when the water isn't cut off. Lukas burned his *Napola* uniform in the stove. He was ecstatic that day, dancing around the fire, yelling, "Burn, filthy rubbish! Burn!"

He found a pair of trousers, a sweater and a shirt among the remaining clothes that belonged to Manfred's father. They're too big, but even if they fitted him I reckon he's less good-looking out of uniform. He's less good-looking now anyway. It must be adolescence. He's not as fine-featured: his nose and lips have flattened out, and his jaw has broadened. Since he can't shave any more, there are darkish patches of odd whiskers on his cheeks and upper lip. He's even got a few pimples on his forehead. I bet he'd be rejected if he had to go through the selection process again. Everyone in the cellar would be rejected, except the tall blonde woman.

There's no change of clothes for me. I don't fit into Manfred's clothes. But he's washed my uniform and darned the holes, so I'm almost presentable. It's just the lice that are driving me crazy.

Manfred is trying his hand at cooking and doing all right. He knows how to spice up rotten potatoes, preparing them in different ways, depending on what's around. He also makes some kind of semolina slop and a beetroot soup. When I see him with his little tea-towel tied around his waist like an apron, singing as he prepares our grub, I realize how hard it must have been for him at the *Napola*.

It's up to Lukas and me to scavenge for food. It's quite a process and we have to be strategic. First we have to listen to the neighbours at night in the cellar, to what they're whispering, so as not to be heard. Some of them know, for example, about such and such a deserted shop or warehouse. In which case, Lukas and I run off first thing in the morning, instead of going back up to the apartment. The deal is: first come, first served. If it's not too far away, we go by foot. Our training at the *Napola* means that we run faster than the Berliners. And we know how to fight: manners have gone out the window now; everyone fights to the death for food. When the shop is too far away, we catch the tram. Normally you need a special transport card, so most of the obedient Berliners don't take the tram unless they have a card. But we couldn't care less. As if a ticket controller is more dangerous than a mortar shell, a fine more deadly than a bomb!

If we haven't gleaned any tips from the neighbours, Lukas sets off early in the morning on the lookout for inside information. He listens, watches, spies. If someone is running, it means he's got a tip-off, so all Lukas has to do is follow him. That's how he heard that a Luftwaffe freight car had been abandoned with all sorts of food left inside. Lukas brought back tins of jam, coffee – the real stuff, not ersatz coffee – bottles of wine, even loaves of bread and chocolate. He looked like he'd just been in a boxing match, his face all swollen, but he was thrilled and pleased with himself. And rightly so.

What a feast we had that day. We had to make sure we didn't eat it all at once. We put some of the jam aside and I went out and swapped the wine for margarine and potatoes. I'm in charge of bartering.

In the evening, as soon as the air-raid siren goes off, we lock our precious things in a suitcase and head down to the cellar. Lukas sits on the case so no one steals it. But I still worry and keep an eye out. You never know, part of his flirting with Ute might involve him bribing her fat mother with chocolate.

I must say, sometimes I feel like giving something to the tall blonde woman. She's so thin. She obviously doesn't care about getting food, doesn't give a damn if she dies of hunger or of anything else.

One day Lukas played dress-ups. He put on one of Manfred's mother's dresses (a floral dress that hadn't been stolen). He scrunched up paper into balls to make fake breasts, used coal as eyeliner, and tied up his hair – he has long hair now, like us all. I thought he looked funny, but Manfred was not amused. He burst into tears and made

Lukas get changed straightaway. But he didn't have time because there was an air-raid warning and we had to rush to the cellar.

In the dark, old Hauptman put his hand on Lukas's bum, mistaking him for a new girl.

In between hunting for food and the long breaks to recover from the sleepless nights in the cellar, time passes strangely. We don't think about the future. Well…

On the Reichstrasse, and elsewhere in Berlin, it's chaos. Hundreds of cars are heading off to the west, but their path is often blocked by tarpaulin-covered carts filled with refugees, or else they're gunned down by Russian fighter bombers.

In the cellars, the rumour is growing: *The Russians are coming!*

32.

We had quite a disturbing time in the cellar last night. There were lots of bombs. The walls were shaking and above our heads the dim light from the kerosene lamp flickered under the crisscross of beams. Would it hold up if the building collapsed? Was it actually such a good idea to be buried alive? Or was it more dangerous to be trapped outside in the rubble?

No one slept a wink. All Lukas, Manfred and I wanted to do was get upstairs, jump in our beds and sleep. Sleep all day, hoping it would be a day – they hardly ever happen any more – when the air-raid siren didn't go off every hour. Too bad if we couldn't eat. We were too tired to go hunting for food. And, anyway, the less we ate, the less hungry we'd be.

But when we climb out of the cellar, there are people in the apartment. We can tell immediately from the smell in the air. Sweat. Gunpowder. As we creep quietly across the lobby, we bump into huge kitbags on the floor. One more step, and there in the living room is a soldier, lying on the armchairs which I usually make up as my bed. He's fast asleep, his arms dangling, his legs folded sideways, his chin sunk in the collar of his jacket.

Holding our breath, without a word, we turn and look towards the master bedroom. As there's no door we can see four soldiers lying close together on the bed. Then we look into Manfred's bedroom opposite, where two more soldiers are lying top-to-tail in the single bed.

"Ruskis?" whispers Manfred, terrified.

He's shaking like a leaf – I think I can hear his knees knocking.

We don't answer. We've lost our voices, our hearts are pounding, our legs are like jelly. I glance at Lukas. He's as white as a ghost, the blood drained from his face. But wasn't he looking forward to the arrival of the Ruskis? Now that they're here, don't tell me he's scared, too?

He raises his hand and signals us not to make a sound, not to move. No chance of that – we're petrified. He creeps on tiptoe into each room then comes back to us.

"Not Ruskis," he mouths, "Krauts!"

Relieved, I check out the rooms as well, Manfred right on my heels, like my shadow. They're definitely our soldiers: part of the last infantry units in retreat. Normally they travel through the streets of Berlin at night, only rarely do you see any during the day. They walk slowly, not marching in time, limping, dawdling, oblivious to the people gawking at them.

These ones are sleeping like logs. They look exhausted. They're filthy – their uniforms encrusted with mud – and thin, hollow-cheeked, unshaven. They've fallen asleep in weird positions, one guy's boots on top of another's helmet. Some are facedown, so they must have fallen on top of the bed just like that. I find them pathetic, ugly, pitiful – they already look like prisoners. They also look like they couldn't give a damn about having lost the war.

After staring at them for a bit, I turn to see Lukas, still in the lobby, armed with a submachine gun that he must have taken out of one of the kitbags. He points it at the soldier in the living room. I recognize that warlike glint in his eye. Here we go again: he's back to his obsession with taking out a German in uniform.

I run, not caring at all about the noise I make, or that I've dropped Manfred, who was clinging on to me. "Stop! You can't do that!"

"Oh, yeah? Just watch me!" shouts Lukas. "Get out of the way, or I'll shoot you!"

I jump on him and we roll on the floor. I try to grab the gun. He holds firm. That's when Manfred starts sobbing, and screaming, too. "Stop! I mean, stop! You're mad!"

It reminds me of our fight at Kalish. Except that here the fight stops short. Bang, bang, bang! The submachine gun has gone off, making three big holes in the living room wall. Lukas and I freeze.

"Are you hurt?" yells Manfred. "Are you dead?"

No, miraculously, we're neither hurt nor dead. And, even more miraculously, the soldier in the living room hasn't woken up. Nor have the others. None of them has moved.

Silence.

Aren't they going to react? It's impossible that they didn't hear our screams, the gunshots. Well, no, it's not: they're still asleep. You'd think they were dead.

The three of us suddenly get the giggles, and that doesn't wake the soldiers either. Then we stop whispering and start talking normally. Lukas wants to get rid of the men, which means killing them. I point out that we'll have to get rid of the bodies, and that won't be easy. He insists, and so do I. Things are getting heated and we'll be fighting tooth and nail again before you know it. The air-raid siren ends the discussion.

We have to clear out fast. The bombs will take care of the intruders.

Before we leave, I can't help performing one last test. I go up to the sleeping soldier in the living room, the highest-ranking one, with three stars and two stripes. I lean over and yell in his ear, "Look, *Hauptsturmführer!* Look at that boy there—" I point to Lukas – "He's a Jew! A Jew! The real McCoy!"

I feel better, liberated. All those years with that sentence stuck in my throat. Apart from that one time in the study hall when I made a pathetic attempt, I've never been able to utter it. Now that it's out I feel like I can breathe better.

Manfred pulls me out the door by the sleeve. "Stop saying rubbish."

"It's not rubbish. Lukas is Jewish, I swear! Why don't you ask him."

"Sure, sure, OK. He's Jewish, and I'm French. Come on, let's get going."

The soldiers stayed two days in our apartment and had disappeared by the morning of the third day.

People are panicking now. "The Russians are coming! The Russians are coming!" That's all we hear, everywhere, night and day. In the cellars and outside. There's no more radio or newspapers, but word of mouth is working at full speed. Relaying the truth.

The other night, Frau Oberham, the fat woman, went up to the blonde woman and peered over her shoulder at the photo she was holding in her hands, as usual. Frau Oberham shook her head, sighed loudly and said, "I know it's difficult, but you should burn that photo. If the Russians see you with it, they'll kill you."

The blonde woman didn't reply. She held the photo to her chest, as if the other woman had tried to grab it from her; and then she moved to another spot.

Now word of mouth has announced that the Red Army is on the outskirts of the city. Owners are turning up briefly at their apartments to destroy any incriminating evidence: portraits of Hitler, uniforms, party insignia, correspondence. They're raising white flags on balconies (to show the brigades, who are killing the occupants of houses with Nazi flags).

Lukas hangs a white flag on the balcony of our apartment. He orders me to take off my *Napola* uniform and burn it. When I complain that I don't have any other clothes, he leaves and returns an hour later with a pair of trousers and a sweater my size, both bloodstained.

He took them off a corpse in the street.

I put them on; I have no choice. Now I really look like a Skullface.

My uniform was still smouldering when the telephone rang.

We looked at each other, all three of us transfixed, more terrified by the ring than we had been by the air-raid siren, more shocked than by the presence of the soldiers the other day.

The telephone doesn't work, so how can it ring? Manfred and I had often played with it; there was no ringtone.

"Who could it be?" asked Lukas.

"How would I know?"

"Daddy! Mummy!" Manfred screams. Before we can stop him, he runs and picks up the receiver. "Hello… Yes… Who's speaking?" Trembling, he grows pale. The receiver stuck to his ear like a prosthesis, he stares at us, his eyes wide with fear. "*Nein! Nein!*" he screams. "Hello? Hello?"

Whoever it was has hung up on him. Manfred drops the receiver, which dangles from its cord like one of the "cowards" hanging from the lampposts in the street, and rushes over to me.

"So? Who was it?" asks Lukas.

"I think it might have been … a Ruski."

"Well, what did he say to you?"

"I don't know. I didn't understand, 'cause he was speaking Russian, only in German at the end."

"When he said *what*?" Lukas has had enough.

"He said, 'You SS?' I said no, but I don't think he believed me."

We all pause. Lukas looks at me. I look at Lukas. Manfred looks at us.

"We're getting out of here, for good," yells Lukas.

33.

The night of the Russians.

A sleepless night.

We've all taken up our positions in the cellar again, except the suitcases aren't there to mark out our separate spaces. Now we want to feel the physical presence of our neighbours, their warmth, breathing, trembling. The suitcases have been piled up in front of the door like a barricade. A useless barricade. It's merely psychological, but it makes us feel better all the same.

It's the 27th of April, 1945, and I keep thinking about turning nine a week ago. My birthday present arrived a week late: the Ruskis.

It's quiet tonight. *Too quiet*. Only a few bombs. The walls aren't shaking, but we are. No chatting, no gossip. Not a word. Everyone has their own idea of what will happen. Frau Diesdorf looks like she's flat out thinking under her bathtowel. Frau Evingen holds her artificial leg fiercely to her. Frau Betstein keeps patting Manfred's head over and over. The fat woman and Ute are clutching each other.

Although Herr Hauptman is seated, he's holding himself to attention, as upright as a mortar shell. Lukas won't stop looking at me, trying to give me an encouraging smile, but it's more like a grimace. It feels as if he's more worried about me than Ute. The blonde woman, as usual, won't take her eyes off her photo.

I think the scenario we're each imagining for ourselves is not that different: we're going to die, all of us. Except perhaps Lukas, since he's not German.

At 5 a.m. the roof suddenly starts to vibrate, waking us from the daze we've all slipped into. The sound of engines in the street above. They stop, probably parked along the footpath. A strong smell of petrol reaches us. Then silence again.

Frau Diesdorf cracks first. "I'm going to see what's going on!"

She stands up and removes the towel, which is a first. Some sort of coquettish gesture towards the new occupiers? Or is she planning on committing suicide by exposing her bare head to the bombs? She leaves, and fifteen minutes later we hear her charging down the staircase in a rush. She shuts the door behind her, pulls the bolt across to lock it, and hastily rebuilds the suitcase barricade.

"SO?" ask all the other women together.

"They're here! In the next cellar. I think all hell's broken loose."

"What do they look like?"

"No idea. I only saw two from the back. Big leather jackets, knee-high leather boots… The girl!" she says suddenly, pointing to Ute. "They mustn't see her! Hide her! Quickly!"

Action stations. The women pull out all the clothes they can from the suitcases and make a big pile against the end wall, where they hide the girl. Frau Oberham sits in front of the pile to form a screen and tells Lukas to sit next to her to double the cover.

And what about us? No need to hide the kids? Why only Ute?

Manfred stares at me, anxious, pleading, as if begging me to intervene and get the women to hide us, too.

Silence again. More waiting. An hour later – or two, or three, unless it was only a minute – footsteps echo on the stairs. Loud banging on the door. The lock doesn't last long, nor the heap of suitcases. The door gives way, swings open, and a beam of light from a torch scans the cellar, stopping on each of our faces. We blink, blinded, unable to focus, then each of us in turn, as the light moves on to our neighbour, stares at two boots, two knees, a torso – big, like Frau Diesdorf said – and finally a bearded face. Long, curly ginger hair. Red nose and cheeks, crimson. Black eyes. A falcon's stare.

"Ouri! Ouri!" yells the Ruski.

No doubt about it, he's a Ruski. He is so big that he has to bend down so he doesn't bump into the roof. He looks like an ogre. He's going to eat us all.

We look at each other: does anyone happen to speak Russian? Even one word, the one the Ruski keeps repeating, as he gets more and more annoyed by our passive silence. He stretches out his arm, rolls up the sleeve of his jacket and starts up his chant again, hitting his wrist, *"Ouri! Ouri!"*

There's nothing more effective than sign language. Now we get it. *Ouri* is a version of *Uhr*. "Watch." He wants our watches. Herr Hauptman and the women pull off their watches and throw them in the Ruski's pouch as he responds vigorously, *"Ya! Ya!"* He walks past Manfred and me without stopping, no doubt assuming that we are too young to be wearing watches. But he grabs Lukas, the left arm, then the right, pushing up his sleeves to make sure he's not hiding anything. Then, when he catches sight of the pile of clothes against the wall, he points his torch beam at it.

"Keine Uhr hier!" screams Lukas straightaway. *"Ouri, niet! Niet!"*

Hey, that's odd. Lukas spontaneously spoke in German... Isn't the Ruski supposed to be his friend, his ally? Wouldn't it be now or never, the moment to give up the language he's always hated? Why isn't Lukas declaring that he's Polish, or, better still, Jewish? Why isn't he taking advantage of it to get out of this hellhole? Is it because of Ute? Is he so in love with her?

The Ruski doesn't seem to grasp what Lukas has said. He's getting more insistent, garbling other Russian words, gesticulating again, pointing to his neck, his ears, his fingers. The women understand now: he wants jewels. One quickly removes her ring, another a bracelet, a necklace. After that, content with the loot in his pouch, he leaves.

Is that it? All he wanted were watches and jewels?

A sigh of relief passes through the cellar. We got off lightly. They didn't bump us off.

The tension recedes; there are a few smiles. In an attempt at lightheartedness, although her voice still sounds shaky, Frau Betstein announces that it's time for breakfast. She's got a loaf of bread in her suitcase that she'll share with everyone, and perhaps she'll make some hot tea.

But we rejoiced too soon. The Ruski comes back before Frau Betstein has had a chance to open her suitcase. This time there are two other soldiers with him and he's holding a revolver.

He points it at the blonde woman and gestures for her to stand up and climb the stairs. The woman obeys. She doesn't seem surprised. After climbing a few steps, she stops, despite the Ruski sticking the barrel of the gun in her backside. She turns towards me and stares one last time at me, before disappearing. What an odd look. It *landed* on me. Literally. Even though the blonde woman is no longer there, I can feel her looking at me. As if that look is never going to leave me. Suddenly I've got a pain in my stomach. And in my heart, too.

Then the two other soldiers take all the women out in the same way. That leaves Lukas, Manfred, Herr Hauptman, me and Ute, still hidden under the pile of clothes.

Next we hear screaming.

Tonight was the scariest of all. Afterwards, that was it. We soon worked out the Ruskis' three obsessions.

First of all, *"Ouri! Ouri!"* It's like they decided to pinch every single watch in town. Any watches. Even the worthless ones, the cheap junk with watch faces decorated with pictures. Some Ruskis have dozens of watches on each arm, timepieces filling their pockets. Apparently they send them home as presents; apparently they're a sign of wealth.

The second obsession is the question they ask every single man, systematically, whatever his age, "You SS?" It's better to reply in the negative or they shoot you. Without warning.

Finally, the third and most important obsession is women. Yes, the ones who really take the rap when the Russians arrive are women.

They get raped. Every single one of them.

Oh, for sure, the Ruskis prefer them young, but the word gets out fast and most of the young girls are hidden. Some, like Ute, under a pile of clothes, others in hiding spaces in attics – alcoves hollowed out of kitchen ceilings, places where suitcases are normally kept. Apparently maids slept there last century. A female doctor fitted out a room in a bomb shelter and stuck a huge sign on the door: "Warning! Contamination danger. Typhus patients." It's the most sought-after hideout in Berlin, mothers fight over it for their daughters.

If they can't flush out the young flesh, the Ruskis make do with whatever they can get. Even fifty-year-old women. Even the ugly ones. They don't give a shit. In fact they prefer the fat ones. As if the fat ones make them forget all the deprivation they've suffered. As if, as well as sex, they symbolize a full pantry. Frau Oberham, the fat woman in our cellar, has to put out more than the others.

Manfred and Lukas were shocked the first time they saw the women from our cellar come back in a hideous state, their eyes red from crying, their stockings down by their ankles, their clothes torn.

"What's wrong with them? What did they do to them?" Manfred called out in panic.

"I was hoping they wouldn't do that, not them too," Lukas shouted, shaking his head several times, like an old man.

"What? What did they do to them?" Manfred kept up, when no one answered him.

The woman who usually sat next to him had gone and hidden in a corner, still sobbing, and twisting around, trying to pull up her pants.

Manfred started to howl.

"Nothing! Nothing bad happened to them. I'll explain it later," I muttered, so he'd stop carrying on. "You're too little to understand."

Herr Hauptman just kept saying, "Be brave, ladies. Be

brave."

In the end, I'm the only one not to be shocked. Despite my youth, I'm very experienced when it comes to rape. I have quite precise memories of the rapes I witnessed in Poznan, when the German soldiers laid into the Polish girls.

Rape is the war against women. Now they're at the frontline.

Anyhow, rape is better than death. Women eventually resign themselves to this fact. They've got a saying: "It's better to have a Russian on top of you than an American standing over you."

And not all the Ruskis are brutal. Not all of them drag the women off at gunpoint. Sometimes they ask nicely, "Do you have a man?"

If the woman says no, well ... she has to follow the Ruski. If she replies yes, she has to say where her husband is. Given that most of the men haven't returned from the front, well ... she too has to follow the Ruski.

Everyone ends up resigned to the fact.

It's odd how we get used to things. Before the arrival of the Russians, we were terrified. We imagined them as monsters. Well, they're just men. (Perhaps, in the end, "men" and "monster" amount to the same thing?) Now the Ruskis are here, we just make do; bit by bit they're becoming part of the landscape. Among the ruins, the smashed and burnt-out buildings, the rubble, the ash and the smoke from fires, there are now their cars and horses. The buckets that the rubble women used to fill with debris have been turned into drinking troughs. Crates filled with hay and oats pile up on the footpaths. There are turds everywhere. The stench of animals infiltrates the apartments. All of a sudden, just plonked there, on the corner of a street, you'll come across a towering edifice of Russian anti-aircraft guns. When the Ruskis arrived, the April sun was as hot as the height of summer; now the east wind is gusting, as if the Russians have brought it with them in their kitbags. But when they set little fires on the footpath, using broken chairs and other debris, they let us join them at their bivouacs and we can warm our hands and feet. For the rest, the war continues in the west, artillery fire (the German response), the shrieking of air-raid sirens, and therefore the obligatory trips down into the cellar.

In our cellar, it's back to normal, especially in the mornings. It's the safest time of day, because the Ruskis have spent the night getting drunk and are now sleeping it off, snoring, scattered all over the place in deserted apartments. So it's safe for us to go outside. Ute can get out from under her pile of clothes and stretch her legs.

Manfred is no longer petrified when the women return from their Russian "*soirées*". I ended up explaining to him what they do upstairs with the soldiers, just so he'd leave me in peace.

"Right, this is what happens: they lie down, on a bed, a table, on the ground, wherever, and the Ruskis put their penises in the women's slits. Because they're German slits, designed for SS penises, it doesn't fit right, that's why the women scream and cry."

"That's disgusting!" Manfred shouted, his eyes wide.

"It's disgusting when slits and penises don't fit, yeah, but otherwise it's normal. That's how babies are made. That's how your parents made you, didn't you know?"

I moved away to cut short the discussion. Manfred's

ignorance was so annoying. To think that he was raised in a *Napola*! Good grief, what was he thinking during those Biology classes? They certainly drummed into us how vital it was for people of the same race to be having sex!

Our cellar has, however, changed a bit. One person is missing. The blonde woman. She hasn't come back since the first night with the Ruskis. It's odd that no one has remarked on her absence. It's like she never existed.

I bring it up with Lukas one day.

"Hmm, well, now that you mention it..." He looks embarrassed. He's never embarrassed when he talks to me. This is weird.

"Where is she? Do you know?"

He hesitates, lowers his eyes, looks at his hands and rubs them together one against the other, as if he wants to get some dirt off them. "They found her..."

"Her what?" One word at a time, he's so annoying.

"Her body. They found her body in the street. The Russians killed her. I'm sorry, Konrad. Really sorry," he adds, taking my hand.

Konrad. Am I dreaming or did he just call me by my first name instead of Skullface? He said he was *sorry*. He held my hand, an affectionate gesture from him... What's come over him? I don't get it.

"Did they kill her because she refused to be raped?" I ask. That wouldn't surprise me: she looked like she was brave, proud. Gentle but proud. A real German woman.

"No, I don't think they even tried to rape her. They killed her because of her photo. You remember that photo she carried around with her all the time? She should have destroyed it, like Frau Oberham told her. That's what did her in."

He pauses and seems more embarrassed than before, even though he has ended up spilling the beans. But he can see perfectly well that I haven't burst into tears. As if that's my style. Right, so the blonde woman is dead. It's sad, I agree. It's left an empty space in the cellar. I liked it when she stared at me. Not all the time, jut sometimes. But there are plenty of dead people – there've already been plenty and there'll be plenty more.

"So what was in the damn photo?"

That seems to be the right question, or rather the wrong one, from Lukas's point of view. Precisely the one he wanted to avoid.

"Come over here," he says, after another pause. He drags me aside, onto the bottom steps of the stairs. He puts his hand in his pocket and takes out the photo. Just when I'm about to grab it, he raises his arm and whisks it away. "I'll show it to you quickly, but then we have to burn it, OK? It's too dangerous for us to be seen with it; we could be killed, like the woman!" He lowers his arm, still hesitating.

"Come on, are you going to show it to me or not? Make up your mind, for God's sake."

He shows me.

In the photo, the blonde woman is posing with the Führer. The Führer himself! The Russians would definitely not have liked that. The woman looks younger, well dressed, happy. She's holding a baby in her arms. I wonder who she was? A famous actress? The Führer's wife? And was the baby the Führer's child? Impossible. We'd have known if the Führer had had a child. I notice the signature on the bottom right-hand of the photo: *Adolf Hitler.* An autographed photo! All the more reason to have got bumped off by the Ruskis.

"Well, she was brave," I say to Lukas, handing him back

the photo. "She must have really loved the Führer; not like the others, who couldn't care less what happens to him."

It's true. All we know is that Hitler is in his bunker, nothing else. And nobody cares anyway. When people refer to him now, they say "the other". We don't even have a clue how he coped with the arrival of the Ruskis in Berlin, the Russian flag flying from the Reichstag… So the blonde woman should be doubly praised for having stayed loyal to him in spite of everything.

"You know," Lukas continues, "I reckon it was not the Führer she loved so much, but rather her baby."

Perhaps. Yeah. Whatever. I'm getting bored; I can't see the point of this conversation.

Lukas hesitates again, then carefully turns the photo over. He points to the inscription on the back. *Konrad von Kebnersol. Steinhöring. June 1936.*

Konrad is crossed out and another name is written over it, in a different handwriting: *Max.*

I turn the photo over several times, quickly, while my brain attempts to make the necessary connections, to work out the link between the baby in the arms of the blonde woman and the inscription on the back.

The first name. *Konrad.* My name. The surname. Mine too. The date. My *Namensgebung.* My christening.

Which means that the baby is me. BBFH. Baptised By the Führer Himself.

As for the name *Max.* It echoes in my head as I mutter it several times. It sounds a bit like … like a musical note. It reminds me of something, but I don't know what.

"I'm pretty sure she was … your mother," murmurs Lukas, his voice quavering. "I'm … I'm so sorry for you."

I think for a minute. Am I sad?

No.

They can all go to hell! All mothers! The ones who raised children, like Lukas and Manfred, and the ones whose children were taken away from them.

Mothers are kaput!

That's war.

34.

What with all the rapes, everyone is having sex, all over Berlin. It's rampant. With the blessing of their mothers even, girls would rather give themselves to a young German, any one will do, than be raped by drunk Ruskis. Sometimes you come across entwined bodies on a staircase, behind a tree, a makeshift barricade, a pile of rubble. In the courtyards it's often difficult to tell the difference between the screams of a rape and those of consensual sex. It all sounds the same through broken windows.

And so one morning, at dawn, when Frau Oberham returns to the cellar after a night with the Ruskis, she unpacks Ute from her pile of clothes, takes her by the hand, motions for Lukas to follow her to the door, and asks him, "Right, how old are you, my boy?"

"Sixteen, Frau Oberham."

"Perfect! Ute is seventeen. You like her, she likes you, so go on, take her! She's yours."

With that, she slaps Ute's hand into Lukas's, spins him around and pushes him to the stairs.

"But, um … the thing is…" Lukas stammers, turning back.

Ute doesn't react at all. She seems oblivious; still half asleep and dazed by her uncomfortable night under the clothes, she's yawning her head off.

"Go on! Off you go! What are you waiting for? I don't have to draw you a diagram, do I?" shouts Frau Oberham, in a hurry to collapse under her bedspread and sleep.

Silence, while Lukas and Ute stare stonily at each other. Ute finally cottons on and blushes, gives a faint smile, pats her dishevelled hair with the flat of her hand, smooths her dress, then jiggles from one foot to the other while chewing on her lower lip. Still holding Lukas's hand, she shakes it from right to left, like children in round dancing. Lukas's cheeks are on fire. He tries to return Ute's smile, gives up, turns and glares at us all.

We're all staring at him. When he sees Manfred and me, we can't help giggling. (Having seen so many couples in the act, Manfred has loosened up a bit and understands exactly what Lukas and Ute are supposed to do right now.)

Lukas looks daggers at us and tries to pull himself together. "OK, all right!" he says, ready to take up the challenge. Gesturing for Ute to follow him, he climbs the stairs. Then comes straight back down. "We're not doing it here, in front of you all!"

It's decided that they'll do it in our apartment. So we head back there straightaway, for the first time since the arrival of the Ruskis. I say "we" because, despite Lukas's protestations, I have insisted on coming along so I can escape this damn cellar. I've been dreaming about getting back upstairs to my lovely toilet with its supply of toilet paper. And Manfred, still following me everywhere, comes along, too.

"Someone's got to keep a lookout, right?" I say. "If a Ruski turned up while you were at it, what would you do?"

Lukas has to concede in the face of my irrefutable argument.

Luckily, the apartment is empty, at least it is this morning. There is a lot of evidence that it has been occupied: horse shit on the parquet floor – the Ruskis always carry it around on the soles of their boots – rugs on the beds, which we never had, and dirty dishes in the kitchen. Everything is filthy, disgusting, including my toilet. There's no more paper. The pile of books is gone, only the covers are left. So *Mein Kampf* was used to wipe a Soviet arse.

Devastated, Manfred slips into cleaning mode and starts a full spring clean. Lukas nails together some wooden boards and improvizes a door to the parents' bedroom and locks himself in there with Ute.

I set myself up in the kitchen. I locate the leftovers: a can of meat that the Ruskis only ate half of, a piece of bacon, a few slices of stale bread, and some milk.

I eat.

When Manfred catches sight of me, he yields to hunger, drops his broom and joins me. The Ruskis are still asleep, so there are no bombs, no pounding of boots on the footpaths. It strikes me that, apart from the sound of our chewing, it's completely silent in the apartment, which is not normal.

"Go and see what they're up to. They had better get a move on, we don't have all day."

Manfred doesn't need to be told twice. He gets up to peer through one of the many holes in the planks that are serving as a door.

"They're not even naked," he says, disappointed, when he gets back to the kitchen.

"They don't have to be naked, you idiot! Lukas just has to drop his pants and take off Ute's."

"Well, I'm telling you, he hasn't taken off his pants and Ute still has her undies on. They're sitting on the bed, holding hands, gazing at each other, smiling. That's it!" pronounces Manfred, as he dips his slice of stale bread in some milk.

I sigh in frustration. At this rate, they'll never be finished before midday and it'll be touch and go whether we can clear out before the Ruskis wake up.

But a few minutes later, I'm proven wrong. Lukas must have gone on the offensive. There are whispers, faint at first, then more audible snatches of conversation. "No! Wait, not like that! Like this. Gently. Gently." It's Ute's voice. This is weird sex; whenever I've witnessed it, it has always been the man who leads the proceedings, not the woman. The war has obviously turned everything upside down.

"Yes, that's better! That's it, that's it! Keep going… Yes! Yes! Don't stop!"

There are no more whispers. Just the mattress springs squeaking, louder and louder, the floorboards creaking. Then the required "Oh, Ohh! Ah, Ah! … Ah! Ah! Ah!" Same old end to it.

So, although they had trouble getting going, at least they were quick about following through. At a rough guess – I don't have a watch to check, no German now has a watch – I'd say that intercourse between Lukas and Ute lasted five minutes at the most.

Once they finish their business, they join us in the kitchen. Lukas complains because Manfred and I have eaten almost everything, but Ute rummages around in the cupboards and finds more cans of meat, milk, tins of sauerkraut, porridge, oatmeal. A feast. We stuff ourselves.

* * *

The following days are identical: night-time in the cellar, daytime in the apartment. Repeat intercourse between Lukas and Ute, longer and longer, louder and louder. They're really getting a taste for it. Then a meal together. Since the apartment is the same every morning, we deduce that the Ruskis are not using it. So we take a risk and stay the night. Everything goes well. No one kicks us out, probably because our apartment has an advantage we weren't aware of: it's on the fifth floor. According to word of mouth, Ruskis don't like climbing stairs. Most of them are peasants and like contact with the earth, so they prefer to stay on the ground level. They feel lonely up high and, if they have to retreat, it takes longer.

Manfred has taken to his domestic activities with enthusiasm and made us a cosy nest. Ute should be helping, since she's a girl, but she has refused point-blank. Stuck-up bitch! Now that she doesn't have Frau Oberham on her back, and especially now that she's sleeping with Lukas, the little madam behaves like a princess. Anyway, it turns out that Frau Oberham was not her mother, but a teacher at the Nazi school she attended. When panic erupted, Ute fled with Frau Oberham, whom she is very glad to be rid of now.

On the first few nights, for safety's sake, she sleeps in the crawlspace above the kitchen, then Lukas has the bright idea of disguising her as a man, in an old suit he found in an abandoned case somewhere.

It's Manfred's job to cut her hair. So now she hangs round with us twenty-four seven, and they have sex night and day regardless.

OK, if Lukas doesn't care that the Ruskis think he's

a homo – if they ever make it to the fifth floor – that's his problem.

So now there are four of us to organize.

Lukas ransacks the houses where the Ruskis have spent the night and brings back their leftovers, which are often considerable.

Lukas has changed again. Eating better and screwing like a rabbit has made him into a man. He's handsome again. Manfred cut his hair – very short hair suits Lukas. It highlights his eyes and makes them seem bigger. His voice has lowered an octave. When he speaks, you can see that big ball go up and down at the base of his throat – the Adam's apple, it's called. From walking all over Berlin, climbing staircases in buildings, looking for food, the muscles he developed in the *Napola* are once again visible under his clothes, which makes them a bit tight now. Broad shoulders, narrow waist, thick legs, a real *Jungmann*, like he used to be. His personality has mellowed; he is more relaxed, less aggressive. Especially with me.

From time to time, when there's a glimmer of sunshine and fewer explosions in the street, we go outside. Just the two of us. We sit in the courtyard of the building and smoke a cigarette. One morning, just as we're about to light up, we see a woman with her skirt hoisted, doing her business right in the middle of the courtyard. After a moment of shock, staring at the woman going to the toilet in full view of everyone, we burst out laughing.

"So much for Nazi pride; it's long gone, isn't it, Max?"

Since the blonde woman's death, he's called me Max. I don't mind. It's better than Skullface. Anyway, it sounds good when he says it.

I glance at the crouching woman. She's dishevelled, dirty, barefoot. There are many women like her wandering around Berlin, barefoot and distraught. I think of the nurses at Steinhöring, the Brown Sisters at Poznan, the warden at the Kalish – all impeccable in their uniforms. I have to admit that the Nazi pride is well and truly gone.

I take the cigarette when Lukas offers it and indulge in this privileged moment, just the two of us, to ask him a question that has been at the back of my mind for a while. "Why don't you tell the Ruskis that you're Polish?"

Lukas takes the cigarette back, has a long drag on it and shrugs. "I've almost told them a few times, but ... I don't know ... it doesn't feel right. You know, when they invaded Poland with the Krauts, the Russians didn't treat us very well either."

That's true: the Ruskis were our allies at the beginning of the war. I'd completely forgotten about that.

"I'm wary. The Russians also have a long tradition of anti-Semitism," adds Lukas. "And anyway, I don't want them to send me back to Poland after the war. I've got no family there any more. I'd prefer to wait for the Americans. Things might change with them. Listen, Max," he says, suddenly animated, "as soon as the fighting is over, as soon as we can leave Berlin, we have to work out how we can go to the West and throw ourselves on the mercy of the Americans."

Still preoccupied, he takes drag after drag of the cigarette, without passing it to me.

"They've liberated the camps, did you know? Apparently there are a few survivors. Very few. I don't know if my mother is one of them. I'd better prepare myself for the worst..."

He stops to contemplate the swirls of smoke drifting off.

Because he's thinking about his mother, for a few minutes I'm afraid he'll flip out again, like he did at the *Napola*. But he continues calmly. "If they inform me that my mother is dead, then I'll be an orphan like you, Max. And we won't be the only ones. The country will be teeming with orphans of all sorts of nationalities. There's not enough room here for everyone. I'm sure the Americans will get us out of this shithole and send us somewhere else, far away, to their country, or… How would you like to go off to Canada, for example, or Australia?"

I try to think about it, but I don't have a clue where Canada is, let alone Australia. "I don't know. Germany is my country."

"Not any more, Max. Look at your country! What sort of a place is Germany now, hey?"

He gestures with his chin at the turd left by the woman on the courtyard stones. We can smell the foul odour from here. A bit further away, some soldiers are sitting on the edge of the footpath. They look exhausted, filthy, disgusting. Some have bloodied bandages on their heads, and withered or amputated limbs.

"What do you reckon will happen to you here? You'll end up in an orphanage, at best, or an adoptive family. Is that what you want?"

I shake my head. No adoption. Absolutely not. I haven't changed my mind on that issue.

"But … but if you found out your mother's alive, and if you manage to find her, wouldn't you go back to Poland?"

"No! We'd get out of here, off to Canada or Australia. And we'd take you with us. It's your turn now, buddy!" he adds, without letting me reply. "I had to live with the Nazis for years, so you'll get used to the Yids, right?"

I don't say anything, just return his smile. "Wouldn't Ute and Manfred come with us, too?" I ask after a pause.

"No, it's different for them. Their parents are here. They'll probably find them."

I'm trying to grasp the idea. "But what will we do in Canada or Australia?"

"I have no idea. We'll have to see!"

These precious moments are rare.

Even though I know Ute has a lot to do with Lukas's transformation (sex must have a calming effect, and reduce aggression, anger), I don't like her. Since she's barged into our lives, Lukas spends less time with me. Without her around, the two of us would probably have already left for the West. She's annoying the way she carries on like a princess. And just because Manfred and I are younger than her, she gives herself the right to order us around.

You know what we look like, sometimes? A family. A sweet little family with Daddy, Mummy and two kids. Manfred has got used to it; it makes him feel safe, and he likes to be mothered and told what to do. But I don't.

I hate families. I always have.

So one morning, while Lukas is out foraging for food, I say to Ute, as I bite into a piece of bread, which is miraculously covered in a good layer of margarine, "As soon as the war is over, Lukas and I are leaving for Canada. Just the two of us."

Ute rolls her eyes, then smiles complicitly at Manfred, as if to say: "Don't listen to him, he's talking rubbish!" and, without bothering to reply to me, she butters herself a slice of bread.

I decide to continue with my assault, this time with the heavy artillery. "Lukas is Jewish."

Now Manfred puts his oar in. "Don't listen to him, Ute. Konrad is forever cracking that joke. He's obsessed."

"Shut up, you! I didn't ask you to chime in! Lukas is Jewish," I repeat, staring down Ute, my blue eyes meeting her equally blue eyes.

To cheer him up, Ute pats Manfred's hair. He's got that hangdog expression because I've yelled at him.

"You've run out of things to make up, haven't you? You dirty little brat!" she says finally. "Well, for your information, it's impossible for Lukas to be Jewish. There's a secret something that proves you're lying," she simpers.

Thinking that is the end of it, she admires her nails – black with dirt, broken – with as much satisfaction as if she was just leaving the manicurist. Then she takes a big bite out of her bread.

"You want to discuss his uncircumcised penis? That's the little secret? I fell for that too in the beginning, but it doesn't prove anything. That doesn't prevent Lukas from being Jewish."

So I spill the beans and tell them the whole story: how we met at Kalish, his forced Germanization, what Lukas told me about his parents, our time in the infirmary, the death of his father and brother, his mother's deportation to Treblinka, then our time at the *Napola*, and the murders of the *Jungmänner*.

By the time I've finished my story, Ute and Manfred have dropped their pieces of bread on the table. I've made them lose their appetite. I'm quite happy eating calmly, savouring both the taste of the margarine on the bread and their bafflement.

"Gosh!" exclaims Manfred, the first to react. "I never believed you before … Lukas is Polish? A Jew? Impossible! He is…"

I can tell that, for once, he's remembering his Biology classes from the *Napola*. Perhaps he even recalls the drawing he did for me back then, of the pot-bellied Jew sitting on a globe of the world labelled *Money*. I finish his sentence for him.

"He is blond with blue eyes, I know. He's tall, slim and not short and stocky. He doesn't have either a big nose or fingers like claws, and yet, he's certainly Jewish."

Silence again. Not easy information to digest at breakfast.

"So you're not brothers then?" asks Manfred.

I shake my head and turn back to Ute, who still hasn't opened her mouth. At the Nazi school, she would have also heard a fair bit about Jews.

"Will you still have sex with him?"

She says nothing.

"What will you do with your baby?" I ask, just to ram my point home a bit more.

"What baby?"

"The one in your belly. The one you've made with Lukas."

"But ... I'm not pregnant!" she asserts, her voice rising.

A glimmer of panic crosses her eyes and she instinctively puts her hands over her belly, as if she were capable of detecting the presence of the baby.

"You could give it to the new leader of Germany, when we find out who that will be."

Yes, a new leader.

Because Hitler is dead.

He died yesterday. It was the 30th of April, 1945. We went back down to the cellar briefly so Ute could get her belongings. Frau Bestein's radio was working for once, broadcasting a funeral march by Wagner, while Dönitz's voice made the sad announcement. And then there was a power failure and the radio cut out.

Nobody reacted. Nobody cares. Including me.

"Hitler, finished. Goebbels, finished. Go Stalin!"

That's what the Ruskis are shouting in the street. (It turns out Goebbels committed suicide, too.)

Perhaps Ute will give her baby to Stalin?

35.

Unlike the bombing raids, which have slowed down, the cellar gossip is running at full capacity – it's a good way for us to learn how the Ruskis operate and how we need to behave with them. It's how we heard a very enlightening story that was doing the rounds, about a German woman living in Berlinstrasse.

One night two drunk Russians burst into her apartment. Despite her neighbours' warnings, she had refused to go down to the cellar. After kicking and smashing her door with their rifle butts, the Russians grabbed her, shoved her against a wall and ripped off her clothes, thrilled that, as luck would have it, they had a choice victim: she was pretty, young and well groomed. Just as they were about to rape her, they caught sight of a baby and a child, asleep in a little bed in the corner. They stopped in their tracks, helped the young woman to get dressed and apologized profusely.

"Your children?" asked one of them, named Andreï, in gibberish German.

He went over to the bed.

"Beautiful, such beautiful babies. Cute!" he added.

He took off his jacket and gently placed it over the children, who were without bedclothes. Then both soldiers crept out on tiptoes. The next day, Andreï returned with a warm blanket for the woman, as well as milk and chocolate. He came back several times with extra supplies. One day he showed the woman a photo of his children, whom he hadn't seen since 1941. (Russian soldiers don't get leave like ours do.) He burst into tears.

"The war is almost over, you must stay strong, you'll see your children again very soon," comforted the woman.

Andreï replied through the interpreter he'd brought with him, "I'm not crying about my children. I'm crying for all the children killed by the Germans." He stopped for a second to get his sobbing under control. "In my village, the German army knifed the children. Some grabbed them by the feet and smashed their skulls against a wall. I saw it with my own eyes. Several times."

An eye for an eye and a tooth for a tooth was Lukas's defence when he began his series of murders at the *Napola*. It would seem that the Russians apply that proverb when it comes to women, who were also raped by our soldiers, but not when it comes to children.

So, although we hide young girls in kitchen crawlspaces, under piles of clothes, or pretend they have typhoid fever, conversely, we put our children on show so the Russians feel pity for them.

In our little makeshift family that has emerged since Ute moved into the apartment, Manfred plays the role of the child. Although he's the same age as me, he's a head shorter, and puny; people think he's only six or seven. So he's the ideal candidate to turn up at the Russian mobile kitchens. And it never fails: feeling sorry for this pale, frightened little kid, the Russians often give him hot soup, chocolate, dried sausage – things that Lukas can't get among the leftovers in the apartments he searches at dawn.

Sometimes Manfred begs me to go with him. He carries on, whingeing that he's frightened, that the kitchens are a long way away, that he has to walk several city blocks. I refuse.

"Can't you make an effort, for once?" says that bimbo Ute, who does nothing all day, except for you know what.

"Come on, Max, be nice, off you go!" says Lukas.

When Lukas asks me, I go, but unwillingly. I hate the Ruskis putting me on their knees and curling my blond locks in their fingers. Even though I'm tall for my age and nothing about my tough manner arouses tenderness, somehow I often have more success with them than Manfred.

"Milyi! Milyi!" They say "cute" whenever they see me. They fall for my platinum hair and my bright, blue eyes every time. Just goes to show that my angel face always works a trick, even on the Ruskis.

That day, I'd got out of bed on the wrong side. I was in a foul mood. I refused to go with Manfred. No one could make me, not even Lukas. I'd give anything to turn back the clock. But there's no way; it's over and done with now.

So Manfred sets off as usual, his little basket on his arm. An hour later, he comes back, puts the full basket on the table, and something's different: inside is a whole, huge ham. A present from the Ruskis.

"Oh, Manfred! My darling! You are truly briilliaant!" squeals Ute in her horrible snobby accent.

"Bravo, well done!" says Lukas.

I don't say a word. I'm annoyed that idiot little Manfred has managed to do so well. Anyway, even if I wanted to, I don't have time to open my mouth, because – while ham in the basket is an unusual event – suddenly we hear footsteps on the stairs. Heavy, clumsy footsteps, tripping, missing one step, hurtling up two at a time, stopping, starting up again, but making it to the fifth floor. To our door. We never bother to barricade it with planks of wood, or to shove furniture up against it, so it gives way with the first kick. The outline of a man fills the doorframe. It's a Ruski. A Ruski swaying on legs as thick as tree trunks. A Ruski who reeks of alcohol. A Ruski who, unlike his comrades, isn't sleeping off his hang-over at this hour of the day, as he should be. Who knows what got into him to follow Manfred?

I feel bad. If I had gone with Manfred, I would have been more vigilant and this Ruski wouldn't have followed us. Or at least I would have been able to shake him off.

But now he's here.

Why did he follow Manfred? Wasn't he happy about handing over the whole ham? Has he come to get it back? No problem: we'll give him back his damn ham. Right now. And he can take the rest of the food too.

But the Ruski has no interest in the ham.

He's staring at Ute. She's wearing her man's suit trousers and shirt but not the jacket. As the shirt isn't buttoned to the top, you can see a bit of her cleavage. She hasn't wedged her hat on over her forehead; she's bare-headed. Instead of flattening her hair with water, she's let it go curly. And with an old tube of lipstick that she found on the ground one day, she's highlighted her lips.

She is going to get it in the neck. She'll cop it – rape.

To tell you the truth, I don't really care. But Lukas is horrified. He stands up. At least he tries to, but the Ruski aims his machine gun at him.

"SS?" he yells.

It's a legitimate question, I realize, as a wave of panic hits me. Lukas is blond. His eyes are the colour of steel. He's tall. He spent his adolescence in a *Napola* and he's got the bearing of a *Jungmann.* Since he's been sleeping with Ute, he looks like a man. So, yes, he could easily pass for an SS, a young one, one of those recruited late, at the last minute, or for a member of the *Volkssturm.* Those guys are always being killed by the Russians when they're found at the back of a cellar.

The Ruski has no interest in the ham, or in Ute. It's Lukas he's after.

"You SS?" he repeats, yelling even louder.

Terrified, Lukas only manages to shake his head in response. That's all he does, like an idiot, without saying a word. Why doesn't he reply? In his mother tongue, Polish? He's told me why he hasn't used it before, but he has to now. He *absolutely has to.*

"Niet! Niet! Ne SS! Polski! Yevreïskie! Yevreïskie!" I jabber a few words of Russian, screaming that no, he's not SS, but Polish, and Jewish, Jewish! Manfred and Ute, in the panic, join in too, screaming, *"Jude! Jude!"*

"Nix Juden! Juden kaput!" the Ruski retorts. *No more Jews! Death to all Jews!*

My mind is racing. I've heard of a few incidents in cellars when, in order to save their lives, Nazis have tried to pass as Jews. They are uncovered when they can't speak either Yiddish or Hebrew.

"Lukas, recite a prayer in Hebrew! You have to prove that you're Jewish!"

Lukas looks at me, aghast. He opens his mouth, but no sound comes out. I understand why he's gone blank right now. No doubt because of the shock. I don't know what else to do, so I charge, head down, straight at the Ruski, in the mad hope of grabbing his gun from him. Perhaps that will give Lukas time to react, to gather his wits. But the Ruski is faster than I am and, with one shove, knocks me to the ground, as easily as if he had cleared the ham off the table. Without taking his eyes off Lukas, he hurtles towards him, grabs him by the collar, yanks him to his feet, slams him against the wall and rummages in his pockets.

"You SS!" he pronounces, holding something up in the air.

I stand up shakily. There's blood running down my forehead, trickling into my eyes so I can't see what's in the Ruski's hand, the one that's not holding the gun.

But I could definitely tell that the "You SS" was no longer a question. It was a statement.

It was the 2nd of May, 1945. Berlin had surrendered, at 4 a.m. There was still fighting in the north and south of Germany, but there were no more shots in Berlin.

Except for one, a last shot that echoed in our apartment.

Even if Manfred, Ute and I had spoken fluent Russian, the Ruski would have pulled the trigger.

Even if Lukas had decided to reply in Polish, even if he'd remembered a Hebrew prayer, the Ruski would have pulled the trigger.

Because he was drunk.

Because that's war.

Because, in any case, no one *ever* wanted to believe that Lukas was Jewish.

And because, instead of burning it, he had kept in his

pocket the photo of the blonde woman and her baby (me) posing with the Führer.

Why? Why did Lukas keep that damn photo? What was he planning to do with it?

I wasn't sad when the blonde woman died. I wasn't sad when the Führer died.

But when Lukas died, yes, I was.

Now, only now, do I feel like an orphan. Damn it, dreadfully like an orphan.

36.

The hearse: a wooden cart. The shroud: an old raincoat Frau Oberham found in her suitcase. The cemetery: a patch of ground in the garden of an abandoned house.

That's how we're burying Lukas. Like the inhabitants of this house might have buried their dog, if their children had insisted.

We're allowed to do it. Everyone does it. In the ruined city, if the living desert their homes, the dead do the same thing: they don't head for the cemetery, but for the public parks or private gardens. That's when they're not rotting under the rubble.

Armed with spades we found in the street – sharp as knives, the Ruskis used them in man-to-man combat – we dig a hole. Not very deep. The black earth we excavate contrasts with the garden soil covered in white dust. You'd think it was snow, that we were in December, not May. The tree trunks, also white, are riddled with bullet holes, as if they were badly wounded in the fighting. Wounded but standing. Whereas Lukas, with a single bullet, has fallen.

Right now, I feel more anger than sadness. Why did

Lukas have to die? Instantly? Why wasn't he just wounded? Why didn't he stay upright, like the trees, instead of being laid out, inert, on the bare ground?

He didn't keep his promise. At the end of the war, we were *both* supposed to leave for Canada or Australia. He swore to me that day we smoked a cigarette in the courtyard. But now he's left *by himself*.

He's abandoned me.

Our little group makes a circle around the gaping hole. Herr Hauptman, the Betstein woman, Diesdorf and Evingen, Manfred, Ute and me. Now we have to put Lukas in the hole. Herr Hauptman takes the lead, grabs the body by the shoulders, while Frau Oberham grabs the feet.

I don't move. Unlike Ute and Manfred, who rush forward to give them a hand, I don't help. I've already done the digging. I dug hard, imagining that, each time I thrust the sharp spade into the earth, I was stabbing Lukas's murderer with a dagger. I dug hard because the physical exercise made me feel better, like at the *Napola*. Exercise banished my sadness for a moment.

I don't want to touch Lukas's corpse. This body, wrapped in a hurry, tied up with the belt of the raincoat, like a mummy; this body, already starting to go stiff, is no longer Lukas. There's a stain on the raincoat: the blood that ran out of his wound. The dark-brown halo makes it seem like there's a hole in his chest. It reminds me of the *Napola*, of the special target we threw our knives at – the cardboard Jew made for us by our teacher, which always ended up with a huge hole around the area of the heart.

I can't look at this body lying there. I want to keep the memory of Lukas: tall, proud, beautiful. Even if that's what killed him.

Frau Oberham gives a short eulogy. The deceased showed enormous courage. He sacrificed himself to save Ute. Then Herr Hauptman recites a prayer, also short. A Catholic prayer. (Ute, Manfred and I decided not to reveal that Lukas was Jewish. It would have been too complicated to explain. What would our cellar neighbours have thought? Would they have agreed to give us a hand with the burial if they'd known that Lukas was a Jew? Who knows?)

Lukas was killed as a German, and buried as one. Clearly destiny followed him right to the end. He probably would have preferred a Hebrew prayer, but what does it matter now? Nothing matters now. Will the worms feeding on his body notice the difference? Are they Nazi worms with orders to consume only Aryan carcasses, not Jewish ones? In any case, the Nazi worms have been defeated, they're *kaput*, too.

A series of shots disrupts the silence that follows the prayer. For a split second, we panic, confused. Has the ceasefire come to an end? So the war isn't over? When we look up, we realize it's fireworks the Russians have let off to celebrate the victory. Suddenly there's a festive air about the burial. And a need for speed: we have to get going. We pick up our spades, cover Lukas's body with dirt, and leave the garden.

The festivities will continue elsewhere, with a meal, a proper one, as is customary at funerals in normal times. Apparently – Frau Oberham heard it first – there's a rumour that the Russians are doing the rounds of houses, delivering food, portions of meat they want to share with the locals. They might even propose a toast to peace.

Like most of the Berliners, we can't resist the demands of our empty stomachs. We head off on tiptoe, still frightened of Russians getting out of hand, celebrating victory with a bit too much schnapps. But we're up for their invitation. Even me. I'm hungry. So I'm going to eat with Lukas's assassins.

That's peace for you.

Over the days that follow, news reaches us via Russian newspapers or from the Russians themselves: all the generals have been arrested en masse; Mussolini, also defeated, was killed by the Italians. There was fraternization between the Russians and the Americans when they ran into each other on the Elbe River.

Motorized vehicles are constantly coming and going; there are no more carts, no more horses, no more turds on the ground. The Ruskis are leaving. They've filled their trucks with pillows and eiderdowns to make the trip more comfortable. Russian military administrators will take their place.

Roneoed sheets are stuck up everywhere on the doors and walls of buildings, "Public Notice to all Germans", followed by the text of our capitulation.

The streets are teeming with never-ending banks of soldiers, sitting or lying on the edges of footpaths, exhausted after walking for days. There are plenty of others too, who were being hidden or cared for by women in shelters. They're all resurfacing now, at least the ones the Ruskis haven't already found. They're like rats sniffing out food. It's strange seeing Berlin populated by men again. Some of them are very active, running around, trying to appear energetic, searching apartments for weapons. What do they want with weapons now? To defend their women? Too late for that. Anyway, they won't find anything, apart from old, broken-down shotguns.

Little by little, the Berliners are returning to their homes. The women are cleaning and cooking. Not very much of the latter: the Russians are going to distribute more food rations to the general population, but it hasn't happened yet. In the meantime, the women are sewing. They're making flags out of scraps of material they scavenge here and there. With the black and white design of the swastika removed, the Nazi flags become Russian flags; they're the easiest to fashion, at least when it comes to colours. But they've also got to get going on the American, British and French flags. In courtyards everywhere, the sound of sewing machines has replaced that of gunfire.

It's still confusing, but the news on the radio seems to be saying that from now on the Russian border will extend to Holstein, that the English will get the Rhine and the Rhineland and America will have Bavaria. The French will get their slice of the pie, but we don't know which bit yet. Apparently the Allies have already landed at the airport in their thousands. All the little flags the women are turning out – soon to flutter at the windows – are for them.

Just like Germany, Berlin will soon be sliced up in four. Rumour has it that the southern neighbourhood will be for the Americans, the western for the British.

I have no idea what this division means. How will it work? What will happen to the people who live on the border zones? Will they have their heads in the north and their feet in the south?

I don't know where to go. I'm lost without Lukas. He was the one who made all the decisions after we left the *Napola*. He gave the orders. I wasn't happy about it, but now I really miss it. Since I was born, I've done nothing but obey orders, and now there's no one to tell me what to do.

North? South? East? West? How do I choose? Flip a coin? Lukas didn't take any of those directions. He went *down*, under the ground.

And now I remember, on that infamous morning when we were both smoking in the courtyard, he told me, "You have to seek out the Americans." Apparently the Americans are in the south.

So, that's my direction.

I walk and walk.

I left without saying goodbye to Manfred and Ute. While they waited for news of their parents, one went back to live with Frau Betstein, the other with Frau Oberham. No way I'm staying with them.

Sleep is all I want to do when I stop walking.

It's because I'm sad. Sadness is tiring. Much more than the tight schedule I was on at the Kalish. Much more than the physical exercises or the paramilitary training I underwent at the *Napola*. Much more than the running around that Lukas and I did over the last few months to find food.

I walk as far as I can. Sometimes I hitch a ride in a jeep or jump on a train – one of those crowded trains nicknamed the "Hamster Express" because hundreds of people are hanging off it. Afterwards I sleep, any old place. Outside, in the burnt-out shell of a tram or a tank. Or in an abandoned house I happen to come across.

I don't know how long I walk for. Days, weeks, months. Time has been abolished.

One evening, when I go inside an apartment, I realize it's not empty. The family it belongs to is still here. Except they're dead. Suicide by poison. (There's a lot of them in Berlin and the surrounding area. Group suicides by poison or hanging.)

The parents are in their best clothes. The father is wearing his *Oberführer* uniform, belted and buttoned all the way up. The mother has on a pretty silk dress and elegant black patent leather shoes. They're lying on their bed, in their bedroom, holding hands. In the children's bedroom, a boy about my age is lying in one bed. He's well dressed too: navy-blue Bermuda shorts, an olive-green shirt and tie. In the second bed, there's a little girl, younger than the boy. In her arms is a teddy bear. I continue my tour and discover a third bedroom, with an empty bed. Perhaps it belongs to an older brother who died at the front? My older brother died too. I've got something in common with the little girl and the little boy.

I'm an orphan now. I need a family to adopt me. This one will do fine. Not because it's a Nazi family, but because it's incapable of imposing any rules on me. And that's exactly what I need.

In the empty bed, there are real sheets, a clean, warm bedspread. I slip inside, shivering with pleasure, and fall into a deep sleep.

Without a single nightmare.

I don't even dream about Lukas. Nothing. An abyss, as if I was underground like him. *With* him.

When I wake up – I don't know if it's the next day or two days later – I tell myself to get moving. "Come on, get up! Keep walking! Find the Americans!" But the house is so peaceful. The children aren't up yet, or the parents. We must be allowed to sleep in. Sleeping in is so nice. How long is it since I've slept in? I go back to sleep, and I don't open my eyes again.

37.

There's a face leaning over me. A woman's face. Short brown hair, blue-grey eyes. Not young, but not old. She's wearing a white uniform: a skirt and shirt, with a sort of brown, quilted, sleeveless vest over the top. Some sort of bonnet, also white, is stuck on her head. She reminds me of a Brown Sister. Probably because of the brown and white of the uniform. With the slight difference that their horrible brown potato-sack dresses only had a ruff and short sleeves. On the contrary, this woman's uniform is more white than brown. And she's much less ugly than a Brown Sister. She's not grimacing and her smile isn't forced.

"Hey, hello! Welcome aboard!"

She's speaking English. I understood what she said. We had English classes at the *Napola*. In the beginning, only a few hours. But then she keeps going and I lose the thread. So she starts up in German, without batting an eyelid, as if she just has to press a button to switch languages. She's got a heavy accent, but her German is fluent.

"Are you hungry?"

Am I hungry? I can understand that question in any language. Of course I'm hungry! Just listen to the universal language of my growling stomach. I sit up and the woman feeds me soup. Slowly, spoonful by spoonful. She tells me that I can't have any solid food for the moment, that I couldn't digest it, because I've been undernourished for too long. The soup is good, hot but not scalding. It's made from real vegetables. I can list them precisely: carrots, turnips, leeks, zucchinis, green beans. American vegetables, I bet. Vegetables this tasty couldn't grow in soil that is so full of ash, like ours after the bombings. Does that mean I'm in America? Did I manage to travel that far?

Eating has got me thinking straight, and got my memory working again. I remember my long treks, the silent apartment, the dead family. The clean sheets I fell asleep in, for a long, long time ... until I heard noises in the silent house. Footsteps, voices. I'm pulled out of bed and laid on a stretcher. Swaying above me are shadows, people in uniform, soldiers. Not Ruskis, not Germans. I don't recognize the embroidered insignias on their sleeves and neckbands. Then there's a train trip, with other children. Lots of others.

The kidnapping from the house. The soldiers. A train jam-packed with children. And now this woman in a brown-and-white uniform ... I've been captured by the American version of the Brown Sisters. The Brown Sisters? Is that their code name? There are a few of them in the room now, all wearing the same outfit, all busy with children lying in bed like me. Some of the kids look like they're in a bad way. Worse than me.

"Poor little thing! When we found you, you were almost dead. It was a close call." The American Sister stops to wipe my mouth – I've been gulping the soup and it's trickling down my chin. "Your last name is Glaser, is that correct? What is your first name?"

Glaser? Where did she get that name? ... Oh, I get it! That was the name of the family in the apartment. The American Sister thinks the dead people were my parents and siblings. I shake my head vigorously to show her she's wrong. I feel OK – a bit limp and lifeless, but I'm not in pain; the only thing I don't understand is that I can't talk, it's as if my voice has been damaged. As if the pieces are at the bottom of my throat but I can't put them together right now.

The American Sister doesn't take offence at my silence. On the contrary, her smile broadens. She doesn't look mean like the Brown Sisters. A Brown Sister would have already slapped me for not replying to her questions. She gives me a few more spoonfuls of soup before trying again.

"My first name is Abigail, but people call me Abi; it's easier. Do you have a nickname?"

She's not mean, but she's sneaky. She's setting me a trap. If I tell her my nickname, I'll end up spilling the beans about my first name, and my last name – the real one. Not a word. I just eat.

"There's no reason at all for you to be frightened of saying the Glasers were your parents," she persists. "No one will hurt you. Even if your father was a Nazi officer, you have nothing to fear. Children won't be made to suffer for the sins of their parents."

She's speaking about "Denazification". I heard about it on my travels. The Állied occupation forces are arresting Nazis everywhere in Germany. They are checking the political activities of every German over eighteen.

Abi is mistaken about my silence. I'm not frightened to say that my parents were Nazis (and such Nazis!).

Nevertheless, they were not the Glasers.

"Me not Glaser. Me Konrad von Kebnersol. Two nicknames: Skullface or Max."

There we go, my voice is back in action. The words popped out without me thinking. And in English, what's more. Pidgin English. Now I'm speaking like the Polish kids did at Kalish. Which makes me think that, after being kidnapped by Brown Sisters, I must be in an American Kalish.

Shocked, Abi steps back. With the bowl of soup. I grab it out of her hands. I'm perfectly capable of feeding myself. She stares at me, a slight frown on her face; she looks like she's wondering if perhaps I'm not quite right in the head.

"Konrad von Kebnersol? That's your last name?"

I nod.

"And your nickname... What was it again?"

I repeat it.

"Odd, especially the first nickname. Why did they call you that?"

I don't reply. I'd have to explain that Lukas invented the nickname. I'd have to talk about Lukas. I don't want to. Lukas is dead. *Kaput*. Buried in Berlin. In a garden, like a dog.

"So, the Glasers are not your parents? But what were you doing in their house?"

To prove to Abi that I'm perfectly fine in the head, that I'm in fact very intelligent, I have to abandon Pidgin English in favour of German.

"If the Glasers had been my parents, they would have poisoned me, like the little boy and the little girl in the bedroom. I just went to their apartment by chance. To sleep."

"OK, Max, OK."

She's chosen to call me Max, not Konrad. Perhaps it sounds more American than Konrad?

"The reason I keep asking," she says, "is that we know where the older Glaser boy is. He's alive, and if he was your brother we could have reunited the two of you."

She pauses for a second, thinking I'm going to react, give myself away, jump for joy at the news of this big brother. Not a chance. My big brother is dead.

"Right, well, let's forget about the Glasers." She finally cuts off that avenue of discussion.

About time too.

She removes the soup bowl – that I'd conscientiously, greedily, licked clean – and places it on the bedside table. I want her to give me something else to eat. I'm still hungry.

"You are at the Kloster Indersdorf convent. My colleagues and I (she points to the other American Sisters in the room) are nurses and we work for an organization called the UNRRA, the United Nations Relief and Rehabilitation Administration. That means we look after all the orphans or unaccompanied children. We help them to find their families. Do you understand?"

Yes, I understand. But neither she nor her colleagues will be able to do anything for me. I don't have any family *at all*. I've never had any and that's something she'll never understand. I should explain it all to her, but I'm too tired. I shut my eyes without answering. That's an answer: *Leave me alone!*

She gets the message. "I'm going to let you rest now," says Abi, a note of disappointment in her voice. "I'll come and see you later."

She stands, moves away and – I half-open my eyes to check – leaves the room.

Unlike the kids around me, I don't want to sleep. I've already slept enough an the Glaser apartment and on the train.

It's too much like a dormitory here. I'm not used to dormitories any more. I can't stand them.

I try to decipher what Abi said. I'm in the Kloster Indersdorf convent, so I'm in Germany, in Bavaria, to be precise. That is the American sector. They look after orphans in this convent. Kalish was also a disused monastery. They looked after orphans at Kalish, too. "Look after orphans" was code for Germanization, before an adoptive family was found. Abi spoke to me in code language so as not to frighten me. She omitted to point out that they're going to Americanize me. They already use my American first name.

Abi seems kind, but in the end I wonder if she's not a bitch, too, like the Brown Sisters. I also wonder if Americanization is going to be as tough as Germanization was at Kalish.

I have absolutely no desire to be Americanized. I've got to get out of here. I glance over at the door. No wardens. I get out of bed.

Before escaping, I decide to have a look around. I'm in no hurry, and anyway, where would I go? At least there's food here – I should eat up before leaving.

I enter a room that is a dormitory, not a hospital ward. There are more children here – not sick, just shockingly thin. Like me. Some are sitting on beds, playing cards, talking. Others are by themselves, on chairs or lying down, staring at the ceiling, or else standing up, staring at the floor. They're all dressed in the same, grey clothes with white aprons that they must have been given here. I'm still wearing my own clothes, which makes me think I haven't been here long.

Still no wardens. Clearly the children have not received an order to stay silent. On the contrary, they're making a lot of noise. As I move through the room, I can hear lots of languages, and among them I recognize Polish, German, Russian and French, I think.

The next room is a huge dining hall, benches and tables lined up. As I pass, I nick a bar of chocolate and a carton of milk that I gulp down while hiding, crouched in a corner. It's so good, delicious. I'll come back here before I leave.

I go up to the next floor. On the landing there's a window through which I can see the courtyard of the convent. Two trucks are arriving; when the doors open, children get out.

"The country will be teeming with orphans," Lukas told me. He was right. He also told me I had to find the Americans. I'm not sure he was right about that.

I stop stock-still on the threshold of the next room, where children are lining up. One by one they stand in front of a soldier who takes their picture. The soldier is ... black.

I've never seen a black man in the flesh. Only in the films they showed us at the *Napola*, blacks fighting in the French army. They looked like they were in fancy dress, wearing filthy, oversized uniforms. We watched them doing target practice; they were terrible. The presenter said that, even though blacks didn't know how to use any sort of weapons, the French put them on the front line, to protect themselves. That was one of the reasons why we defeated France so quickly, he explained. Our famous *Blitzkrieg*.

Except that the war was not at all a lightning operation. *Six years. Not six months.*

Except that the French are now victorious. And the blacks, too.

Mesmerized, I stand watching the black soldier. He doesn't look like he's in fancy dress. He looks good in his uniform. He's tall and muscular, with a confident, feline bearing. When he smiles, you can see his big, straight, white teeth, and the way his smile is reflected in his eyes. He reminds me of Jesse Owens, the black athlete who won four gold medals at the 1936 Olympic Games. I wonder if he can run as fast as Jesse. If so, I'd better clear out before he sees me. No way I'd beat him in a race.

When I finally take my eyes off him, I notice three nurses busy in the room. The first is helping the children to follow the soldier's instructions and sit directly in front of the camera. "Raise your chin, don't lower your eyes, sit still during the flash." She adjusts their nametags, which hang around each of their necks on a piece of string. The second nurse is checking a register, and the third is writing in a notebook.

They're both black, too, like the photographer.

Something weird is happening in this room. Despite the wave of terror flooding through me, I try to think. Quick, quick! Because I'll have Jesse Owens on my heels once I get going.

This is the conclusion I come to: Abi lied to me. She omitted to tell me that before "looking after" orphans they made them endure a *selection process*. Just like at Kalish. And, judging by the ones in charge of the selecting, in order to get through, you have to be black. Or at least have dark skin and dark eyes.

I AM SCREWED.

"You managed to get out of bed?"

I almost jump out of my skin; Abi is right behind me.

"Are you OK? You don't feel dizzy?"

"Why are you taking photos of the children?" I ask, ignoring her question. "Is it a selection process? What do you do with the rejects? Knock them off? Send them to a concentration camp? Are you going to kill me?"

She looks at me in astonishment, as if she's thinking, "This poor kid is completely crazy."

But I am not at all crazy. In fact I have never been more sane. Abi has to understand that I am no ordinary child. You can't fool me!

"A selection process?" she says finally, articulating each syllable with a shocked expression. "What on earth are you on about? Listen, Max: children are not put through a selection process here. No one is killed here. And there are no more concentration camps."

She stops for a second to let her words sink in. But they don't sink in. I'm not convinced. Not yet.

"We're taking photos of the children so we can use them to help us find their parents," she adds. "Do you believe me?"

I don't answer, I'm lost. Either Abi is telling the truth or she's an excellent actress. I take another very hard look around the room. There are no measuring devices. No wardens. No soldiers hitting children. Just the tall black guy, laughing at every opportunity. And the children don't look frightened. I'm the only one who is a bundle of nerves, and that's not like me. I must pull myself together.

"Yes, I believe you."

It was only a murmur, but Abi heard.

"Good, that's great. Hey, since you're here, let's take your photo now. Hop in line, it won't take long."

"No."

"No?"

"NO."

Abi rolls her eyes and sighs, exasperated. I'm annoying

her. I don't give a damn. She annoys me with her obsessions. The Glasers before, and now the carry-on about the photo.

"Why don't you want us to take your photo? Don't you want to see your parents again?"

"My parents are both dead."

"Are you sure?"

"Yes. My mother was killed by a Russian and my father committed suicide."

"But perhaps you've got a brother or a…"

"My brother died, too. Killed by a Russian."

"Well, there must be an uncle or an aunt or a cousin who'd like to receive news about you."

I shake my head.

"OK, listen, the photo will still be useful for us, you never know. Wait in line and just do it, it won't take long."

As she walks off, I call out, "I've got a photo of my parents."

She comes back. "That's excellent! Show it to me."

I reach into my pocket for the photo of the blonde woman posing with the Führer. The photo that Lukas kept, the one that killed him. I got it back and I haven't let it out of my sight. It's the only souvenir I have of Lukas. I'm pretty sure he was intending to show it to the Americans. But I hesitate about giving it to Abi. I've got a feeling that she won't like it.

"So what are you waiting for? Show it to me," she insists, kneeling down next to me.

Well, it's her choice. I take the photo out of my pocket.

Abi reaches for it, looks at it and suddenly recoils, losing her balance. I put my hand out to stop her falling, but she flinches and pulls free, as if she can't bear the touch of my hand.

I knew she'd hate the photo. I should never have shown

it to her. I should have destroyed it. This damn photo will end up killing me, just like it killed Lukas.

But I'm going to stand up for myself. Abi is only a woman, after all. She doesn't even have a machine gun like the Russian who killed Lukas. And the war's over, right?

"You told me before that children shouldn't have to suffer for the sins of their parents."

That worked. She regains her composure; her eyes aren't flashing with anger any more. She tries to smile. It's a pathetic effort but she'll get there. "Come in here."

She drags me into an adjoining room, shuts the door behind me, sits at a little desk piled up with files, and gestures for me to sit on a chair opposite her. She places the photo on the desk, looks at it again – more calmly, not lingering on the Führer this time – and asks me, "Why do you say they're your parents?"

"Because it's true."

She doesn't seem happy with my answer.

"She –" I point to the blonde woman – "is the woman who had sex with an SS officer to produce me –" I point to the baby – "and give me as a present to him." I point to the Führer.

Abi stares at me. Then she rolls her eyes and drums her fingers on the desk, before opening her mouth to speak. But she stops, doesn't say whatever it is.

"Max," she starts again finally, as if it's an effort to stay calm. "You don't give babies away as presents. What are you trying to tell me? What does this photo mean? That your mother managed to meet Hitler one day? Then she told you that he was your father? It was no doubt just in a manner of speaking—"

I put my hand up to interrupt her. It's my turn to roll my

eyes and sigh. All right, I'll have to tell her my life story to make her understand. This is going to take a while. I don't know where to begin… At the beginning? I take the photo, turn it over and point at the inscription: *Steinhöring*.

"That's where I was born. Steinhöring. It's a children's home, near Munich."

There and then, before I can properly begin my story, Abi cuts me off. "Did you say Steinhöring?"

"Yes."

"Wait a minute!"

She rummages in the dossiers on the desk, pulls one out, opens it and removes a sheet of paper that she scans after putting on some glasses.

Those glasses make her look ugly, like a goggle-eyed fly.

"Our soldiers were in Steinhöring in April," she says, without really focusing on me. It's more like she's thinking out loud as she keeps reading. "They found three hundred babies there. *Three hundred!* Left by themselves in the bombed-out premises. The poor little things were in a terrible state. Our soldiers did not find a single document to identify them, nothing…"

I grab the piece of paper out of her hands. If only she'd stop jabbering on and let me speak.

"I know who those babies are. I know *how* they were produced. I know *who* produced them, *who* ordered them to be produced, *who* ran the selection process so that only the best were kept. I know where your soldiers can find more of them. I know everything. I was the first one of those babies."

Abi doesn't try to retrieve the piece of paper I took from her. She takes off her glasses. She doesn't look like a goggle-eyed fly any more, but her whole face is rigid with tension. I can tell that now she really is ready to listen to me. I take a big breath.

And off I go. *I was born on 20th of April, 1936. The birthday of our Führer…*

38.

By the time I finish my story it's dark in the little room.

Abi didn't think to turn on the desk lamp. She didn't move once, the whole time I spoke. She might as well have been a statue.

Only now does she decide to turn on the light. She moves slowly, wearily, as if the lamp is too far away, even though it's only a few centimetres from her. The view outside the window – a scrap of sky, of blue, has turned to grey, then black – fades, and now there is only the reflection of the interior of the room, in particular my face. I can see it as clearly as in a mirror.

It's been a long time since I've looked at myself in a mirror. I check to make sure I'm still as blond as I was. That my eyes are as blue as they were. Nothing has changed.

No, one thing has: I'm crying.

I'm crying for the first time. Does that mean I'm now like other children?

Lukas cried, too, that day at Kalish, when I told him my

story. The first part, before knowing him. That day, he said to me, "We both have to bear witness. Me, for what the Nazis are doing to the Poles and to the Jews; you, for what they have done to you."

I have kept my promise.

I didn't understand why Lukas cried when he heard my story. I didn't understand the meaning of the words "bear witness".

Now I do. I suppose that's normal. I've grown up. I'm nine and a half.

I guess, for a child, the years count two for one in times of war.

Author's Note

This novel was inspired by actual events:

The *Lebensborn* programme, initiated by Heinrich Himmler and put in place in Germany from 1933, and in the occupied countries during 1940–1941. It is estimated that approximately eight thousand children were born in *Lebensborn* homes in Germany, between eight and twelve thousand in Norway, several hundred in Austria, in Belgium and in France.

The kidnapping and Germanization of Polish children. (In addition to Ukrainian children, and those from the Baltic countries.) It is estimated that the number of children forcibly taken from their families was more than two hundred thousand.

The work of the UNRRA (the United Nations Relief and Rehabilitation Administration) which, along with other aid organizations for displaced persons, implemented ways for some of these children to be reunited with their families after the war.

My hero, Konrad, however, was not modelled on any living person. He is entirely my own invention. But Lukas does have a counterpart in historical reality. He is based on Salomon Perel. In 1941, Salomon was a Jewish teenager who, by some miracle, managed to pass himself off as an Aryan. He fought on the Eastern front in a German unit for a year, and then entered one of the elite schools for the Hitler Youth movement. Unlike Lukas, he survived.

A number of the characters – some are simply cited, others play a more important role in my story – are real historical figures:

Max Sollmann, the director of the *Lebensborn* programme.

Gregor Ebner, the SS chief of medicine, who not only ran several *Lebensborn* maternity hospitals, but also supervized the selection and Germanization of thousands of kidnapped children.

Johanna Sander, director of the Kalish home.

The *Braune Schwestern*, the "Brown Sisters", who orchestrated the kidnapping of children.

Herr Tesch, Frau Viermetz, Frau Müller (NSV, National Socialist People's Welfare), Karl Brandt (Hitler's personal doctor), his wife, Anni Rehborn.

In 1947–1948, Sollmann, Ebner and their accomplices stood trial at Nuremberg, but the Allied military tribunal did not uphold the "criminal nature" of the *Lebensborn* programme. They were released after the trial.

I would particularly like to pay homage to the remarkable book by Marc Hillel, *Au nom de la race* (*Of Pure Blood*), which provided me with indispensable material for the writing of my novel. Marc Hillel's book is, I believe, the only one to gather together all the information about the *Lebensborn* programme.

A Woman in Berlin, a memoir, was also a huge source of inspiration when I was writing about the experiences of my two heroes in the ruins of Berlin at the end of the war.

The following books also provided extremely valuable source material:

Napola, Les Écoles d'Élite du Troisième Reich, Herma Bouvier, Claude Geraud, L'Harmattan, 2009.

Berlin: The Downfall 1945, Antony Beevor, Viking Press, 2002.

Les Fiancées du Führer, Will Berthold, Presses de la Cité, 1961.

Europa, Europa, Sally Perel, Ramsay, 1990.

Children of Vienna, Robert Neumann, V. Gollanz, 1946.

The Erl-King, Michel Tournier, Collins, 1972.

I should also list the many internet sites I consulted, but I was unfortunately unable to make a record of them all.

Thank you to Zosia Orlicka for her translations from the Polish.

Lastly, a very warm thank you to Thierry Lefèvre. Several years ago, he suggested I write this novel and he has guided my work with his constant encouragement.

Amnesty International

Max shows how dictatorships and war breed fear and brutalise people. It is fiction, but it is inspired by an horrific truth. Indeed, it was the appalling revelations of the Nazi Third Reich and Holocaust that brought about the creation of the Universal Declaration of Human Rights (UDHR), signed in 1948, the first global document to agree terms for what we know to be right and just.

It's because of the UDHR that we now all have human rights, no matter who we are or where we live. They help us to live lives that are fair and truthful, free from abuse, fear and want and respectful of other people's rights. But human rights are still abused – often violently. Ethnic cleansing and violent conflict still happen. In 2015/16 there are nearly 60 million forcibly displaced people in the world.

Amnesty International is rooted in the UDHR. We are a movement of ordinary people from across the world standing up for humanity and human rights. Our purpose is to protect individuals wherever justice, fairness, freedom and truth are denied. We believe that people have the power to change the world.

If you're under 18 and interested in taking action on human rights, you can find out how to join our network of Amnesty youth groups at www.amnesty.org.uk/youth

If you are a teacher, take a look at Amnesty's many free resources for schools, including our 'Using Fiction to Teach About Human Rights' classroom notes on a range of novels with human rights themes, at www.amnesty.org.uk/education

Amnesty International UK, The Human Rights Action Centre
17–25 New Inn Yard, London EC2A 3EA 020 7033 1500
sct@amnesty.org.uk
www.amnesty.org.uk

THE EXTRA

Kathryn Lasky

A story of survival unlike any other

One ordinary afternoon, fifteen-year-old Lilo and her family are suddenly picked up by Hitler's police and imprisoned. Just when it seems certain that they will be sent to a labour camp, Lilo is chosen by filmmaker Leni Riefenstahl to work as a film extra. But Riefenstahl flaunts the power to assign prisoners to life or death.

Sarah Cohen-Scali is an award-winning French author and writes for both young adults and adults. *Max* was first published in France and has received international acclaim. In 2013, *Max* was awarded the prestigious Prix Sorcières.

"Succeeds brilliantly in the extraordinary feat of making us 'understand' the enemy. A moving novel, both tough and warm-hearted." *Prix Socières Jury*